ruthless Highlander ever learn to love?

If You Deceive

#1 *New York Times* Bestselling Author of *If You Dare* and *If You Desire*

KRESLEY COLE

$9.99 U.S.
$12.99 CAN.

ALSO FROM POCKET BOOKS AND POCKET STAR BOOKS

Be sure to read the first two books in Kresley Cole's MacCarrick Brothers trilogy

IF YOU DARE

Court's story

IF YOU DESIRE

Hugh's story

The Immortals After Dark series

Breathtaking paranormal romance by Kresley Cole

A HUNGER LIKE NO OTHER

"Rich mythology, a fresh approach, and excellent writing . . . superb." —Fresh Fiction

NO REST FOR THE WICKED

"Sizzling sex and high-stakes adventure." —*Romantic Times*

The Sutherland Brothers series

Sizzling historical romance by Kresley Cole

THE CAPTAIN OF ALL PLEASURES

THE PRICE OF PLEASURE

And don't miss Kresley's sensual story in the bestselling anthology

PLAYING EASY TO GET

ISBN 978-1-4165-0361-3

“I’ll see you safely clear of this place . . . for a kiss.”

The Highlander showed no alarm about what was happening outside. “A kiss now, or more later,” he continued.

“Oh, very well.” Maddy reached up to twine her fingers behind his neck. She tugged him down, briefly pressing her lips to the corners of his.

He stood fully once more. “Ah, *aingeal*, that was sweet, no doubt of it. But no’ quite what I had in mind.” He cupped his rough palm over her nape. “I’m demanding a deep, wet kiss. Until you’re panting.”

“Panting?” she murmured. “*Truly?*” How . . . titillating.

With his other hand, he cradled her face and brushed his thumb across her bottom lip. “It’ll be easier just tae show you. . . .”

Acclaim for Kresley Cole!

“One of romance’s fastest rising stars!”

—*Romantic Times*

“With a captivating brand of passion all her own, Kresley Cole is destined to be a star of this genre!”

—The Romance Readers Connection

“Kresley Cole writes like a master!”

—Romance Junkies

And praise for her novels . . .

IF YOU DARE

A *Romantic Times* Magazine Reviewers' Choice Award Winner

"Classic romantic adventure . . . *If You Dare* will leave you breathless!"

—*New York Times* bestselling author Julia Quinn

"Cole's voice is powerful and gripping, and *If You Dare* is her steamiest yet!"

—*New York Times* bestselling author Linda Lael Miller

"A tale that sizzles, generating heat that will scorch the reader."

—Reader to Reader

"A passionate, action-packed romance sure to satisfy every heart."

—Fresh Fiction

NO REST FOR THE WICKED

A *Romantic Times* Magazine Top Pick

"Sizzling sex and high-stakes adventure are what's on tap in mega-talented Cole's sensational new paranormal!"

—*Romantic Times*

"Kresley Cole writes another spine-tingling, adventurous, and passionate romance with her newest addition to *The Immortals After Dark* series."

—Romance Reviews Today

A HUNGER LIKE NO OTHER

A *USA Today* bestseller

"Unquestionably an awe-inspiring romance!"

—Reader to Reader Reviews

"With intense action, devilishly passionate sex, and fascinating characters, *A Hunger Like No Other* leads readers into an amazing and inventive alternate reality."

—*Romantic Times* (Top Pick)

"A unique romance—it truly stands on its own!"

—Sherrilyn Kenyon, *New York Times* bestselling author

"Not just another romantic read . . . it's a powerful experience!"

—The Best Reviews

THE PRICE OF PLEASURE

A *Romantic Times* Magazine Top Pick

"A splendid read! The sexual tension grips you from beginning to end."

—*New York Times* bestselling author Virginia Henley

"Sexy and original! Sensual island heat that is not to be missed."

—*New York Times* bestselling author Heather Graham

"Savor this marvelous, unforgettable, highly romantic novel."

—*Romantic Times*

THE CAPTAIN OF ALL PLEASURES

A *Romantic Times* Magazine Reviewers' Choice Award Winner

"An exciting, sensuous story that will thrill you at every turn of the page."

—Reader to Reader Reviews

"Electrifying. . . . Kresley Cole captures the danger and passion of the high seas."

—*New York Times* bestselling author Joan Johnston

"Fast-paced action, heady sexual tension, steamy passion. . . . Exhilarating energy emanates from the pages . . . very smart and sassy."

—*Romantic Times*

Books by Kresley Cole

The Captain of All Pleasures
The Price of Pleasure
A Hunger Like No Other
No Rest for the Wicked
If You Dare
If You Desire

Available from Pocket Books

If You Deceive

KRESLEY COLE

POCKET BOOKS
New York London Toronto Sydney

The sale of this book without its cover is unauthorized. If you purchased this book without a cover, you should be aware that it was reported to the publisher as "unsold and destroyed." Neither the author nor the publisher has received payment for the sale of this "stripped book."

POCKET BOOKS, a Division of Simon & Schuster, Inc.
1230 Avenue of the Americas, New York, NY 10020

If you purchased this book without a cover you should be aware that this book is stolen property. It was reported as "unsold and destroyed" to the publisher and neither the author nor the publisher has received any payment for this "stripped book."

This book is a work of fiction. Names, characters, places and incidents are products of the author's imagination or are used fictitiously. Any resemblance to actual events or locales or persons, living or dead, is entirely coincidental.

Copyright © 2007 by Kresley Cole

All rights reserved, including the right to reproduce this book or portions thereof in any form whatsoever.
For information address Pocket Books Subsidiary Rights Department, 1230 Avenue of the Americas, New York, NY 10020

This Pocket Books paperback edition June 2007

POCKET and colophon are registered trademarks of Simon & Schuster, Inc.

Illustration by Craig White

Manufactured in the United States of America

11

For information regarding special discounts for bulk purchases, please contact Simon & Schuster Special Sales at 1-800-456-6798 or business@simonandschuster.com.

ISBN 978-1-4165-0361-3

Dedicated to the readers . . .

For letting me share the MacCarricks with you.
Thank you and warmest wishes to you all.

Acknowledgments

Thank you to the wonderful staffs of the University of Florida research libraries. These guys know *everything* and helped me navigate all their many resources: obscure texts—filled with fascinating details to enrich fiction, Victorian diaries—with first person accounts of my era of interest, and mapping and imaging—for authentic historical settings. I greatly appreciate all your help.

The love of a good woman?
To save a wicked man like me?
Never . . . because there's no woman born
who's as good as I am bad.

—Ethan Ross MacCarrick,
Laird of Clan MacCarrick,
Eighth Earl of Kavanagh

I didn't steal it—I swear!
Oh, as if things never fall into your pocket!

—Madeleine Isobel Van Rowen,
sneak thief, opportunist

Prologue

Iveley Hall, Buxton, England
Spring 1846

Ethan MacCarrick thought the bored wife he was about to tup *might* be a bonny wench.

However, this was a best guess. At present, his vision was compromised by whisky, the great equalizer of women's charms. Even after the wind-whipped half-hour ride to her home, he was drunk; in fact, he seemed to be getting worse.

But the woman *behaved* as if she was pretty, he assured himself as he removed his jacket, tossing it toward a divan in her opulent bedroom and missing it. Even in his muddled state, he detected a superficial silliness about her that men would tolerate only if she was fair. Plus, she'd been confident when she'd propositioned him in the shadowy hall of the Buxton tavern, having had no doubt whatsoever that he would meet her tonight.

She had a French accent and was tall, he thought, though she was now reclined, and he'd only briefly stood next to her when they'd met. They'd been together just long enough for her to pass him an expensively perfumed note with directions to her home, to ask if he could be circumspect, and to murmur what she planned to do to him.

Ethan was a red-blooded male of twenty-three—her wicked plans for him had seemed just the thing.

As he crossed the spacious room to the whisky service, she rose to her knees on the bed. "Did you wait to leave fifteen minutes after my maid and I left?" She feared her husband might hear of this indiscretion when he returned from his trip.

Ethan served himself a drink. "Aye, I waited." He wouldn't have traveled with her, anyway. A rake's first rule of thumb? Always ride your own horse to a meeting with a woman you're about to bed, so you can leave when you like. Else they'll want to cling for the night.

Ethan *loathed* clinging women.

"Did anyone see you riding here?" she asked.

"No, no' a soul."

"Because I can't have my husband hearing about—"

"Enough!" She was already grating on his nerves, and he hadn't even used her yet. "You're no' the first married woman I've had," he answered honestly. "I've done this many a time before."

"Of course, I'm sure you have," she said hastily. When he finally made his way toward her, she murmured, "You're such a handsome young devil, Ethan. So tall. So strapping."

He drank, frowning into his glass at her use of his given name. He hadn't quite caught hers back at the tavern, when she'd been whispering in his ear, describing herself on her knees, sucking him deep. "*Young* devil? I dinna get the impression you were that much older than I am," he said as he reached the bed.

She laughed. "Just a bit." Her features were clearer now. She was pleasing enough. Maybe early thirties. "I'm old enough to know what I want, and when I saw you, I knew I had to have you." She took his drink from him and set it on the bedside table. "But I bet women throw themselves at you, don't they?"

"Everywhere I go," he said, not bothering to hide his arrogance. It was true. He was a young, rich laird, and women liked his looks. And it seemed the more drunken and cruel he became, the more they wanted him.

"So if it hadn't been me tonight, it could easily have been another woman from the tavern?"

"Easily," he replied. When he'd left, the raven-haired barmaid he'd been contemplating had cast him a hurt expression. So had her sister. He'd shrugged at them as if he hadn't cared. Because he hadn't. "One woman or two."

"Then why me?" the wife asked breathlessly, angling for a compliment he wouldn't give.

"I like married women better, find them more convenient." He never heard from them again. A married woman readily faded into the past, one among many in his memory—as she should. And if her husband was weak enough and stupid enough to get cuckolded, then he deserved it, and Ethan would oblige.

"So all I am is a convenience?" She gave a mock pout as she began unbuttoning his shirt with deft fingers.

"Aye, precisely."

His callous treatment seemed to be exciting her. "Say my name with your accent," she whispered.

"Doona know it."

She smiled. "It's Sylvie—"

"Doona need to," he interrupted sharply, making her gasp with desire.

He was used to women who liked a cold, domineering male in their beds, but he sensed she might want him to be worse than that. On his solitary ride over here, he'd had time to think about the situation, and his drunken mind said something wasn't right about her.

Her perfume cloyed, but not more than that of the woman he'd had last night. She was tall, voluptuous, and dark-haired—the type that normally attracted him. Yet as she licked his chest, brushing his shirt away from his body, he again found that something about her was off-putting.

People had long said that Ethan had no more feelings than an animal. Well, right now pure instinct was telling him not to take her. He frowned as her mouth eased down his chest to his navel, her destination unmistakable.

But could the message possibly be louder than the Scotch and the promise of a below job?

Aye, it is. He plucked her fingers from his trousers and stumbled back.

"What are you doing?"

"I'm leaving." Bending for his shirt, he lost his balance, but he swiftly righted himself. He knew he'd been drinking too much lately. He was the oldest brother and head of a family that suffered, and the responsibility of it, and the inability to change it, weighed more heavily on him than anyone would dare suppose.

But his drinking was helping nothing.

"Leaving?" she cried. "You can't be serious."

He gave her one curt nod.

"Then why did you come here? What did I do?"

"No' a thing." Where the hell had he dropped his jacket? "Just doona care to any longer."

"Tell me what you want, and I'll do it. *Anything,*" she added plaintively, making him shudder in disgust.

A clinger.

Turning from her, he said, "Doona want *anything* from you. No' anymore."

"You cannot do this!" She shot to her feet and stormed over to him. "Just pass me over like a woman you've bought." Her anger transformed the refined French inflection of her voice to a sharper, more common accent. Ethan had heard similar before—it was a lower-class accent. "Like some stray whore!"

"If the shoe fits . . ."

"No one treats me this way, not now. *No one!*" She darted in front of him. He turned from her once more, and she did it again, antagonizing him. Already his decision to leave was justified. "I'll have you horsewhipped for this!"

Finally he spotted his jacket. "Get the hell out of my way."

"I'll whip you myself!"

"Temper, temper, wench." He faced her with a sardonic expression. "Now I'm *really* no' going to fuck you."

She screeched, flying at him, nails raking down his face before he could shove her from him. He pressed his sleeve to his cheek and saw the crimson, stark against the white linen. "You goddamned bitch! You doona ken what you're provoking."

He headed for the door, but she beat on his back, screaming, "Do you know what I could have done to you?"

When Ethan whirled around, her face was streaming with tears, her eyes alight with fury. "Touch me again, and I'll break my rule about no' slapping crazed bitches who canna take no for an answer."

"Do it, then!" Had her expression flashed with excitement?

To scare her so she'd leave him be, he made as if to backhand her—

The door crashed open.

There stood a gray-haired, enraged man. *Must be the aging husband,* Ethan thought with a tired exhalation as he lowered his hand. *Pistols at dawn and another death on my hands.*

"He tried to force himself on me!" the wife shrieked, tears still streaming.

Ethan swung his gaze on her. "Are you mad, woman? You invited me here!"

More men filled the doorway, hardened ones—henchmen. A blond giant flanked the old husband, looking almost more enraged.

"Never!" she cried. "He must have followed me home from the inn tonight."

The husband narrowed his eyes on Ethan's face. Ethan swiped a hand over his cheek. "Oh, bloody hell," he said wearily. "She scratched me when I wanted to leave." Though Ethan was still drunk, even he recognized how ridiculous that sounded.

"Sylvie, are you injured?" *The husband's grasping for this like a lifeline.*

"You canna be serious. Can you no' see she's lying?" Ethan made a disgusted sound. "The witch asked me here, I vow it—"

"*No,*" she wailed loud enough to crack glass. "He tried to rape me, but I fought him. Do you see his face?"

Ethan gave her a look of pure fury, staring at her while telling the man, "Ask at the inn, ask anyone there. She invited me." But she had been circumspect. Would any of the patrons have seen them together in that hallway for the brief moments when she'd approached him?

The woman shook her head fiercely. "My maid was with me at the inn and when we came home. Ask Flora! Ask her!" Touching the back of her hand against her forehead, she sank to the edge of the bed. "*Oh, God,*" she whispered, "*I was so afraid.*"

Ethan gaped in amazement. *Christ, she's good—*

With a bellow, the old man charged for Ethan. Habit took over. Ethan threw a fist, breaking his nose—blood spurted.

"I'll see you in Newgate for this!" the husband roared, cupping his face.

It was important for Ethan to remember something. What was it? "Goddamn it, I did nothing to this woman . . . and she instigated it all."

"Get him!" the old man thickly commanded his men.

At that instant, the answer Ethan sought came to him, and he lunged for his jacket.

A blow crashed against the back of his skull. His face pounded the floor. Fists rained down again and again, kicks to the gut. . . . He fought the blackness for as long as he could; he had to explain, had to defend himself.

He dimly heard the bitch crying to her husband, worrying about the scandal if this were to go to trial . . . their reputations, their standing . . . other husbands with his power would take care of this themselves.

Ethan knew that in this isolated part of the country the lords were their own entities, laws unto themselves if they chose, always with henchmen willing to do black deeds. And they hated strangers, much less foreigners.

The note, his deliverance, was stowed in his jacket pocket just feet from him. He tried to speak but could only grunt in pain. An attempt to reach for it earned him a booted kick to the chest.

Forcing his eyes open, he saw that she was crying hysterically, seeming to believe her own lies. "With you and Brymer gone, I was an easy target."

The cuckold was soothing her, wrapping her in his coat. "I should never have left you—"

"Th-that fiend was in the house with me, with *Maddy*!" she added significantly. Whoever this Maddy was, the mere mention of her in this context made the old man swing his gaze on Ethan. Seeming dumb with rage, eyes glazed over with it, he assured her they'd take care of this on their own—no one would have to know. Ethan felt true fear rippling through him.

They'd make sure the Scottish bastard never raped another woman as long as he lived.

Castration. Cold sweat broke out over Ethan's body; they were going to take a knife to him.

The old man hesitated, then gave a nod. "Brymer, take him out back. See it done."

This Brymer was the giant with the killing look in his eyes. "It will be a pleasure." He hauled Ethan up, dealing a punishing blow to his jaw. Ethan tried to shake it off, but blackness consumed him. . . .

He woke to the bite of a rope cinched around his wrists. A bone-deep ache radiated from his shoulders up to his clenched fingers. He tried to open his eyes—only one swollen lid would crack enough for him to see—and found himself strung up to the rafter of some type of stable. A blood-soaked gag filled his mouth.

Ethan saw a tall, burly man sitting on the edge of a stool that was about to buckle under his great weight. His meaty leg bounced with nervous energy as he cast Ethan furtive, guilty glances. The man knew. He knew Ethan was being wronged. Of course, the wife would have done things like this before. Ethan yelled behind his gag and grappled against his bonds, frenzied to tell him about the note.

From behind him, he heard a door creak open. Brymer asked, "Is he awake yet, Tully?"

"Only just," Tully said, heaving his big frame to his feet. "I was thinking . . . m-maybe one of us should ride to the inn, and just ask a few questions."

"Van Rowen wants us to do a job on him," Brymer said. "So that's what we're going to do." Brymer was eager for it.

Van Rowen. Why did the name sound familiar? When Ethan got out of this, he would kill Van Rowen, ripping him apart with his bare hands. The man had no idea what he'd just brought down on himself and his entire family—

Ethan heard the unmistakable sound of a blade being unsheathed, and he fought to free his hands.

"But, Brymer, what would it hurt to ride—"

"I just returned from the inn. No one saw anything untoward." Brymer moved into Ethan's field of vision. "They just saw Mrs. Van Rowen eating a meal with Flora for about an hour before they left." He picked his teeth with the knifepoint. "Coachman swears he saw no one else and drove them home alone, as does Flora."

"But sometimes . . . it seems Mrs. Van Rowen might—"

"On the other hand," Brymer continued, ignoring Tully's words, "this one here's a *foreigner*, swilling spirits. The barmaid said he's a mean drunk and a Scottish brute."

That spiteful bitch . . . just because I passed her over . . .

"His die is cast, Tully. But as for you, you'll either follow your orders—or you'll take yourself off Van Rowen lands tonight."

No, no. Ethan could pay him a fortune *not* to do this.

Tully's shoulders slumped.

No, goddamn it, no!

"Hold his head," Brymer ordered.

Tully did as he was told, taking Ethan's head in his thick arms. Ethan fought against the grip, spitting curses behind the gag.

"Wh-what do you plan to do?"

"First off, I'm going to finish what Mrs. Van Rowen started," Brymer said with a nod at the marks on Ethan's face. "I bet the ladies fancy his looks. They won't ever again after tonight. Of course, that'll be the least of his worries."

When Ethan felt the cold blade against the heated skin on his right cheek, he twisted, using all his remaining strength to break free. Nothing.

The knife sliced cleanly; Ethan roared in pain.

"Hold him still!" Brymer snapped.

"I'm trying!" Tully clenched harder. "He's a big bastard!"

Brymer cut and cut until blood coated Ethan's neck. Soon Ethan was numb all over, barely conscious.

"What are you doing?" Tully asked.

"If you take the strip from the middle, it will never heal right when he gets sewn up."

The desperate need to fight was there, burning in him, but his leaden body wouldn't cooperate. When Brymer was at last done, Tully released Ethan, and his head lolled forward.

Brymer took him by the hair, yanking him up to smile at his handiwork. "Come look, Tully."

The man did. His eyes went wide, and he retched repeatedly before he lunged away, vomiting in the hay.

When Ethan saw the strip of skin lying in the dirt, blackness dotted his vision. He silently vowed, *I'm going to destroy you. You're all going to die as slowly as you've done this to me.* . . . Then his eyes slid closed.

He was roused by an anguished bellow sounding from the manor house. The bitch began screaming as well, a series of shrieks growing louder in succession.

A door slammed . . . someone ran toward them . . . seconds later a servant burst through the doorway of the stable, gasping, "*Stop! Let him free!*"

In a flash of clarity, Ethan comprehended what had happened. Another of the bitch's screams rent the quiet of the night, then sudden silence.

Ethan laughed behind his gag, crazed. Wetness leaked from his eyes.

Van Rowen had found the note.

One

London
Summer 1856

Ethan had long grown used to the sinking expressions people cast him when they realized it was he who darkened their doorsteps—but in the East End rookeries this tendency seemed even more pronounced.

Many saw Ethan and ran.

The sound of his boots booming across wet cobblestones was all Ethan heard as he chased a drunken cockney—one among many of his sources of information.

Lunging forward, Ethan clamped the cockney's shoulders, tossing him headfirst into the side of a tenement building. The man collapsed into a stunned heap.

Hauling him to his feet, Ethan drew his pistol, pressing the muzzle against the man's temple. "Where's Davis Grey?"

"I 'aven't seen 'im." He hissed in a breath between the copious gaps in his teeth. "I swear to ye, MacCarrick!"

Ethan casually cocked his gun. The drunk knew of his reputation, knew Ethan would just as easily shoot him as not back in this dark alley. "Then why did you run?"

"B-because ye scare the piss out o' me."

Understandable.

"I 'eard Grey was in Portugal, with an 'unger for opium. And that 'e might be returnin'. That's all. I swear it!"

After a hesitation, Ethan released him, deciding to believe him. The information meshed with his own, and this man likely wouldn't court Ethan's wrath by lying. "You know what to do if you see Grey. And you know what I'll do if you doona notify me."

The cockney muttered thanks for his mercy, then scurried off into the night.

For the last several hours, Ethan had combed the slums, using all his resources to track Davis Grey, a onetime compatriot and family friend—and now Ethan's target.

Though all his reports indicated that Grey wasn't in England, Ethan had wanted to make certain. Tonight he'd chased every lead he'd been able to think of in London. Tomorrow he would leave the city to hunt for Grey elsewhere.

As Ethan strode down the winding, narrow streets back to his mount, a surprisingly comely whore smiled and dropped her shawl, revealing her heavy breasts to him.

And he felt nothing.

When he passed under a flickering gaslight, he showed the woman the other side of his face. She turned away in disgust, yanking her shawl to her neck. It was because of women like her that he'd stopped seeking sex entirely.

At twenty-three, he'd still been in bandages when he'd fully comprehended he wouldn't be having any woman he didn't have to pay. He'd already vowed never to drink again after that night in Buxton. And for a young man suddenly deprived of drinking and women—two of his routine follies—a profession in the Network, one of the

Crown's clandestine organizations, had held definite appeal. Along with his brother Hugh, Ethan had signed on, but only after he'd delivered a subtle, but absolute, revenge against his enemies.

Whereas Hugh was an assassin in the Network, cleanly completing his assignments, Ethan would kill, spy, and extort to get a job done. Ethan was skilled at what he did, successful doing the jobs no one else wanted to do. His brothers called him a jack of all lethal trades.

Once he'd returned to his horse—a fine gelding with a strong and unwavering dislike for him—Ethan mounted up and decided to ride by the London town house of Edward Weyland, Ethan and Hugh's superior. More news might have come in. Besides, what else did he have to do?

When he arrived, he caught Quin Weyland just climbing into his saddle. "Is your uncle in?" Ethan asked. Quin also worked in the Network and was being groomed to eventually take over his uncle's role.

"No, he's out of town. But I saw Hugh just a few minutes ago."

"Just Hugh? No' Court?"

Quin absently shook his head.

Damn it, Hugh was supposed to be with Court, their younger brother, making sure he returned to London from the Continent.

In an irritated tone, Quin said, "I thought you told us Hugh was going to be able to handle this situation with Davis Grey."

"Aye, he will."

"You should have seen the look on his face when I apprised him of the threat."

"He should react that way," Ethan said impatiently. "Grey's a dangerous killer with an agenda." Grey had worked in the Network as an assassin—in fact, he'd trained Hugh.

"No, I meant when I told him it was *Jane* in danger." Jane Weyland, the fair daughter of Edward Weyland.

They'd heard word that Grey sought to kill Jane for revenge against Weyland because she was what Weyland treasured most in the world. To protect her, Weyland planned for Ethan to hunt and destroy Grey and for Hugh to act as Jane's bodyguard, trailing her.

Shouldn't be a problem. Where Jane went, Hugh yearned to follow.

Quin added, "Grey told me Hugh loved her."

Ethan quirked a brow. "We're talkin' to Grey now?"

"Years ago, before he turned."

Turned madman. Grey was known to wear a jovial expression, his demeanor complimentary and amenable, even while he was slitting his targets' throats.

"Well, is it true?" Quin asked.

"Hugh might have had an infatuation when they were younger," Ethan lied. Hugh was likely still in love with Jane to an unspeakable—an *embarrassing*—degree. "He hasn't even seen her in years." And had never told her how he felt.

"He rode off after her tonight quickly enough."

"Where's she gone at this hour?" Ethan asked.

"She sneaked out her window to meet my sisters and their young friend from out of town."

"To go where?"

"Haymarket Street," Quin finally answered. "I'm on my way there right now."

"Gin palaces and prostitutes." The rookeries were squalid, but Haymarket was seamy. "What's there to tempt them?"

Quin admitted, "The Hive."

"They dinna go there," Ethan bit out incredulously. The Hive, a warehouse converted into an unlicensed dance hall, was infamous for debauchery. "How do the women in your family even *find* these things?" Quin's two sisters and his six female first cousins comprised the Weyland Eight, as society called them. They were progressives, loving all things modern, and had dubbed themselves "sensation seekers."

Ethan called them "spoiled chits with too much coin and too much freedom."

Quin shook his head. "I wish I bloody knew."

"I canna believe they're voluntarily going into that place. You ken your sisters will no' come out in the same shape as they went in."

"Go to hell, Kavanagh—"

"Doona call me that," Ethan snapped. He hated being reminded of his title, of that life. "Why do you no' drag them home by their ears?"

"And be forced to give Jane a reason why she suddenly has none of the freedom she's accustomed to?"

"She does no' know she's in danger?"

Quin shook his head. "We are hoping you'll take out Grey early enough that Jane never has to know about any of us." He reined around when Ethan prodded his obstinate mount forward. "You're going?"

"Aye, I need to see my brother." *And make sure he's capable of the job at hand.* "What's the fare tonight at the Hive?"

Quin muttered, "An illegal courtesans' ball."

Ethan gave a humorless laugh. He could practically feel sorry for the unsuspecting "young friend from out of town." The lass was about to get an eye-opening lesson in depravity.

* * *

Regrettably, Ethan had seen the love-struck look on his brother's face before.

Though Hugh was an assassin—one of the most skilled and prolific in the world—his mind went blank when he was near Jane Weyland. He had difficulty speaking. His brow would bead with sweat like a green lad's.

Just minutes ago, Ethan had found him in this state in an alleyway that crossed Haymarket Street. Hugh had been so engrossed as he watched Jane stroll up Haymarket with her entourage that he hadn't even heard Ethan approach.

Hugh was never taken unaware; tonight a runaway dray cart could have slipped up on him.

The situation with Hugh and Jane was incomprehensible to a man like Ethan, who'd never felt even a casual regard for a woman. As Ethan often reminded his brothers, he himself remained immune to untidy entanglements like that.

But for some reason, Hugh wasn't shamed that a woman could make him so weak. And obviously, ten years of being away from her had done nothing to make his feelings ebb.

After Ethan had joined him in the alley, the two of them had begun exchanging terse words—as was customary—only this time they argued in lowered voices.

Hugh had always been disgusted that Ethan had *wanted*—and had offered—to kill Grey, who'd once been Hugh's friend; Ethan had always been disgusted that Hugh had fallen for Jane and opened himself up to such a glaring liability. Ethan's liability was his protectiveness of his brothers, but he'd been born into that one, and it couldn't be helped.

"I wager that right about now, you wish my offer to kill Grey had been accepted," Ethan told Hugh, his smugness conveyed even in hushed tones. "But no' to worry, little brother, it certainly has now. Weyland will do anything to protect his daughter." Ethan jerked his chin at Jane and her group as they passed the alley. He faced Hugh, then did a double take back to the group, only to stare.

The fourth woman in the group—a wee lass with shining blond hair—had caught his attention utterly.

The young friend from out of town . . .

She wore a deep blue gown and cape, tied at her pale neck like a choker, and a matching mask tilted up into points at the corners above her bright eyes. By the flickering glow of the gaslights, Ethan saw her dark pink lips curl intermittently into a mysterious grin, yet not when her friends were laughing. She seemed to be in her own little world.

Though she appeared lively and fresh, he sensed in her a world-weariness—the same that affected him so markedly.

He frowned to find that his heart had started to race—

Hugh had him shoved against a building wall, his forearm lodged against Ethan's neck, before he could tense.

What is this . . . ? Ethan rolled his eyes. "Rest easy. I'm no' ogling your precious Jane."

Hugh finally released him but appeared disbelieving. "Then what held your attention?" he demanded. "Claudia? The one in the red mask?" When Ethan gave no answer, Hugh said, "Belinda? The tall brunette?"

Ethan shook his head slowly, never taking his eyes from the blonde.

The unusual notice clearly stunned Hugh. "I doona know her, but she must be one of Jane's friends," he said in a wary tone. "And she looks no' more than twenty. Too young for you."

Ethan's age was thirty-three, and he felt every year of it, but she *was* young. So how could she possibly have that weariness about her? "If I'm as bad as you and Court and all of the clan believe," Ethan began, "then I'll find her that much more enticing for it, will I no'?" Ethan strove for a bored tone, but he suspected his bitterness came through. Truthfully, he wasn't as bad as they thought.

He was worse.

He had blood on his hands and a heart so cold that he was considered the evil brother of the three—and the other two were a gunman and a mercenary. Ethan was the sodding laird, and yet most in the clan feared him, wanting nothing to do with him—and that was before he'd been scarred.

Reminded of his appearance, he tried to turn away from the girl. If he approached her, a beauty like that would run in terror at the sight of his face. *Drop back in the shadows where you belong. Forget you ever saw her. . . .*

But then a loud masquerade-goer neared them, sporting a domino in the latest style, with a drop of cloth in the front. Ethan's lips slid into a smirk that tugged the tight skin of his face. *Perfect.*

In the blink of an eye, Ethan's hand shot out to snare the mask. The much smaller man opened his mouth to object, but Ethan gave him a killing look, and the man dashed away.

"Doona toy with her, Ethan," Hugh said.

"Afraid I'll ruin your chances with Jane?" Ethan asked as he donned the mask. "Hate to remind you, brother, but they were ruined before you even met her. And you've got a book to prove it."

"Your fate is just as grim as mine," Hugh said, "yet you're going after a woman."

"Ah, but I'm in no danger of falling in love with her"—Ethan turned to stride into the masquerade, tossing over his shoulder—"so it's no' likely my dallying will get her killed."

With a grated sound of frustration, Hugh followed him to the warehouse entrance, where they tendered admission to a bald man in a pig mask. Inside, the drunken crowd was thick; there had to be over a thousand people crammed in.

Oh, aye, the girl was about to get a lesson. All around them, obscene murals hung on the walls, and half-clad whores were openly fondling men.

Ethan couldn't see the group immediately in the crush, so he and Hugh strode to the second-story landing for a better view. They spotted the women in front of a small raised stage, scrutinizing an *exhibit*—which consisted of two women and a man, unclothed and covered in clay, posing as Greek statues.

In such an atmosphere of dissolution, the young chit looked . . . *bored.*

When Jane viewed the naked man with an appraising eye, Hugh's fists clenched. The blonde appraised him, too, but Ethan had no urge to hit anything. Ethan had known he was immune. . . .

The group moved on to a punch service tended by a half-clad courtesan, but the blonde turned back to the stage. With a sensual grin, she languidly blew the male model a kiss. Ethan frowned. *I doona like that.* Bloody hell. *Why do I no' like that?*

"I dinna think blondes were your type," Hugh said, beginning to sound alarmed.

Never looking away from the girl, Ethan said, "They're no'."

"Nor slim, short lasses."

"Tall and buxom for me," Ethan said absently. He watched her accept a glass of punch, delicately take a sniff of her drink, then partake heartily.

"Then what is it?"

"Doona know," Ethan answered in half truth. He knew why he was attracted to her—he could tell she was an extraordinary beauty, even with her mask—but he didn't understand the *degree* of his attraction.

He'd bedded women as lovely as she, so why did he feel an inexplicable sense of urgency to join her—to *get* her? Ethan knew he could find her again. She was friends with the Weylands. So why did he want her *at this moment?*

"Are you actually going to approach her?" Hugh asked.

"Bloody hell I am."

"I thought I was no' to reveal myself to Jane if I could help it. She'll recognize you."

"No' with this mask," Ethan said, then asked, "Why are you behaving as if my interest is so bloody consequential?"

"It's consequential because you've never pursued a woman in your entire life."

Ethan had never had to before that night in Buxton—and he hadn't bothered to after.

"No' even your fiancée," Hugh added.

No, Ethan's fiancée had been handed to him as though on a platter—and it had cost Sarah her life. He'd had no idea that by trying to salvage his life after what the Van Rowens had done to him he'd be destroying another's. . . .

Shaking off those memories, wanting to forget, Ethan strode for the stairs to go after the blonde lass, but Hugh shoved him back.

"What the hell is wrong with you?" Hugh demanded.

"Doona shove me again, brother, or I will put you down." Hugh was the only one who'd ever dared to challenge him like this. "Did you never think I just want to bed her?" Christ, he wanted to bed her, wanted her fiercely. *Finally!* his mind seemed to roar.

"Bed her?" Hugh got an uncomfortable look about him. "No, I dinna think that."

Ethan narrowed his eyes. So Hugh suspected or knew the truth about him. Ethan should have realized that the secret of his celibacy would have gotten out among the Network. The members gossiped worse than old matrons at the village well.

Ten years had passed since his face had been so horribly damaged. As he'd predicted, the only way he'd been able to bed women had been to pay them, and he'd done so for the first seven years. Yet there were only so many times a man could tolerate looking down at a woman he was using and seeing her thinly veiled revulsion—especially after he'd paid for her.

One unsatisfying encounter after another had taken their toll, and now his body couldn't seem to be bothered to desire, to ache, any longer. If he was attracted to a woman, it was tepid, like a shadow of what he used to feel. Though his manhood had been left intact that night, it might as well not have been. He hadn't had a woman beneath him in years.

And even more disquieting—he hadn't especially missed it.

Until now . . .

"She's a lady," Hugh insisted. "No' to be used by you."

"Then what is she doing here?" Ethan asked incredulously, waving his hand around the warehouse.

"The same thing Jane is—they're thrill seekers. Typical rich Londoners."

"In a place like this, even a lady is fair game."

"You doona know that she's no' an innocent." His expression severe, Hugh added, "Ethan, you're . . . you just canna be this bad."

Ethan raised his eyebrows.

"Damn it, if for no other reason, then you should leave the girl alone to concentrate on hunting Grey." Hugh ran his fingers through his hair. "If I canna count on you to take out Grey while I'm watching Jane—"

"Have you forgotten who you're addressing?" Ethan reached the end of his patience and snatched off his mask to stare his brother down. "I've wanted to put a bullet between Grey's eyes for years—a dozen times, I've had him in my rifle sights and my finger on the trigger—but I dinna because *you* thought the man could be redeemed."

Ethan had stalked Grey repeatedly, always keeping an eye on him. In fact, Ethan was the only one in the whole bloody Network who'd discovered Grey was killing on his own. "Now, when Jane's involved, you see reason. So how can you possibly think I would waste my opportunity to destroy someone I've craved killing?" When Hugh remained unconvinced, Ethan said, "I'm going to scratch this itch, then get to work." His tone and demeanor were bored.

He turned back, but the girl was gone, separated from her friends. He felt a flare of alarm. This was a dangerous place, and she was alone.

Or was she?

She could be meeting someone. She could even be married and already involved in an affair. He found himself striding down the stairs, donning his mask once more. He ignored Hugh's last call of warning, then plunged into the crowd.

Ethan was bent on finding her, which baffled him. He liked voluptuous brunettes, earthy women who gave as good as they got in bed. And Hugh was right—he didn't pursue women.

But if it took a delicate, angelic-looking blonde to provoke his body to this kind of reaction once more, then he'd be damned if he was letting the object of his lust out of his sight.

He promised himself he'd be inside her this very night.

Two

If Madeleine Van Rowen was ever going to lose her virginity outside of a collateralized, signed marriage contract, it'd be with the towering man she'd spied in the black domino. He'd just begun navigating his way through the crowds of the Hive, the gaudily extravagant dance hall in which she found herself tonight.

From her spot on a raised dais, decorated with swans and lusty satyrs, Maddy watched him over the rim of her second glass of punch. She was growing light-headed and suspected the drink was spiked with more than rum—the spirit du jour—but she didn't particularly care. She wouldn't mind getting foxed after the day she'd just endured.

Today she'd learned that she'd failed to secure the man she'd journeyed from Paris to London to marry. "*Madeleine, I'm just not the marrying type,*" he'd said. "*I'm sorry.*"

Preferring to drown her sorrows in private, she'd wandered off from her group of friends, the Weyland women: Maddy's childhood friend Claudia, her sister Belinda, and their cousin Jane. The three Londoner Weylands were always craving the next forbidden thrill, and the Hive was supposed to be . . . thrilling.

Jane Weyland, the de facto leader of their group, had told the younger Maddy not to wander off again. After all, gentlewomen needed to *stay together at all costs* when out in London at night. Maddy rolled her eyes even now.

Please, innocent girls, Maddy had wanted to say. Though this masquerade was packed to the rafters with not only prostitutes and their lecherous patrons but also thieves and swindlers, it still paled in comparison to her everyday life.

Her *secret* life.

Maddy told everyone she lived in the wealthy Parisian parish of St. Roch with her mother and stepfather, but she actually lived alone in a slum called La Marais—translated as the Swamp—and every night she drifted to sleep to the music of gunfire and brawls.

She was a sneak thief, a pickpocket who would steal a diamond as easily as an apple, and she wasn't above an occasional burgle. In fact, if Maddy hadn't considered the Weylands her friends, they'd do well to be wary of *her*.

After adjusting her sapphire cape behind her and then her blue glacé mask, Maddy relaxed on the dais bench, settling in to enjoy her view of the tall man. He stood well above most everyone in the room—six and a half feet in height, at least—and he had broad, muscular shoulders filling out his jacket.

The black domino he wore had a fluttering drop in the front, and though she could see his brow and lips and strong chin, the rest of his face was covered. He had thick, straight jet hair, and, she'd bet, dark, intense eyes.

He was clearly searching for someone, striding with aggression, his head turning this way and that, fighting the crush of what looked like thousands of people. When a gaggle of bare-breasted tarts blocked his path, angling for his attention, his brows drew together—with consternation or irritation, Maddy didn't know.

What she wouldn't give to bed a strapping man like that for her first time. After all, she was an aficionada of male beauty. Her friend Claudia would chuckle each time Maddy tilted her head and peered at a passing man on the street. Maddy grinned into her glass. Making men blush as she so obviously sized them up was one of the things she lived for.

But if today was any indication of her luck, her husband and first lover was to be the Comte Le Daex, an obscenely wealthy roué who was three times her age. He was so antiquated he still wore a wig, forgodsakes. She tried to look on the bright side—he wanted to wed her—and to ignore the fact that he'd handily survived all three of his previous young wives.

In a last bid to avoid marrying that man, Maddy had journeyed to London, calling on her childhood friendship with Claudia, specifically to snare her brother, Quinton Weyland. Unfortunately, Quin—with his curling hair, laughing green eyes, and robust finances—refused to marry.

It was time to face her three remaining choices.

First, she could continue on her own in La Marais as she had for years; second, she could reveal her litany of lies to the Weylands, confess her current pitiable situation, and beg them to make her their charity case; or third, Maddy could marry Le Daex.

The mere idea of admitting to Quin and Claudia everything she'd fabricated about her life made her flush with mortification. She could imagine Quin's laughing eyes narrowing with disgust. Maddy shook her head hard, resolving that she'd never tell them.

But to continue in La Marais, she faced a mountain of debt and a cold, uncertain winter. A *hungry* winter. Maddy loathed hunger.

So Le Daex it would be. How dismal. . . .

To distract her thoughts, she focused once more on the tall one as he made the perimeter of the building. His methodical and determined hunt, even the way he moved, fascinated her. He finally stopped, raking his fingers through his hair, turning in a circle in the crowd. She felt sad that he couldn't find the paramour he sought so urgently, and she drank to him, wishing him luck—

He raised his head to where she sat, and his gaze locked on her. At once, he turned that aggressive stride toward the swan-and-satyr dais.

Frowning in confusion—*she* was the only one seated here—Maddy lowered her glass. He must have mistaken her for someone else. She wondered if she should take advantage of his mistake and enjoy a few kisses with him. How delicious that would be. Just to squeeze those muscular shoulders while his lips brushed hers . . .

As he neared, his gaze held hers until she was captivated. Everything else dimmed. The drunken men were unseen; the high, false laughter of the courtesans below her was silenced.

He took the steps to her two at a time. When he stood before her, she stifled a gasp. She was eye level with his groin, and there was no disguising the fact that he was . . . aroused. She slowly tilted her head up.

He stared down at her, silently offering his big hand. His eyes *were* dark—and she'd never seen such intensity. She inhaled a shaky breath.

Le coup de foudre.

Bolt out of the blue. No, no. *No bolts for me!* Maddy was ever practical, never fanciful. She had no idea why that thought had arisen—because *le coup de foudre* had a second, more profound meaning.

The urge to take his hand was overwhelming. She clutched her glass in one hand and her skirts in the other. "I'm sorry, sir. I'm not who you seek, nor am I, er, one among these other women."

"I ken that." He took her elbow—gently, but firmly—and helped her to her feet. "If you were like these other women, I would no' be seeking you at all." He had a marked Scottish accent and a voice so deep and husky that it gave her shivers.

"But I don't know you," she said, sounding breathless.

"You will soon, lass," he answered, making her frown. But before she could say anything, he took her glass and set it away, then caught her hand to pull her from the dais into the crowd.

For Maddy, two flaws warred with each other for the title of What Would Prove to Be Maddy's Downfall: an overly developed sense of curiosity and a marked pride. She imagined the traits to be in a race, like two horses in the *mutuels* on which she occasionally gambled. Right now, curiosity took the lead, demanding that she hear what the Scot had to say—even when she realized he was taking her toward the rooms lining the back wall of the warehouse. She quirked a brow. The rooms where prostitutes more fully serviced their patrons.

He opened the first door they came upon. Inside the dimly lit area, a woman was on her knees before a young man, taking him with her mouth while he leaned down and pinched her swollen, rouged nipples.

"Out," the Scot ordered with quiet menace. "Now."

The woman obviously sensed a threat better than her

patron did, and she pushed the drunken man back to tug up her bodice and scurry to her feet.

The Scot swung a glance at Maddy as the pair lurched out, no doubt to gauge her reaction to what they'd just witnessed. She shrugged. One of her best friends and across-the-hall neighbor was a *popular girl*, and scenes like this took place constantly where she lived. Turn any corner and find a different vice on display.

At twenty-one years of age, Maddy had seen it all.

As soon as they were alone, he closed the door and retrieved a chair to wedge against it. Where was her alarm? Where was her well-developed sense of self-preservation in a place like this? The room was dominated by a massive bed—twelve feet square at least—draped in glaring scarlet silk; no one could hear her scream back here, and they would ignore it even if they could, thinking a prostitute was giving a good show.

Yet, for some reason, she sensed this man wouldn't hurt her, and she possessed unfailing and proven instincts with men—a priceless gift to have in La Marais.

In any case, if things played out badly, this wouldn't be the first time she'd kindly introduced her knee to a man's groin and her fist to his Adam's apple. He would be shocked at how dirty and fiercely this dainty mademoiselle could fight.

When he returned from securing the door, he stood before her, far too close to be polite. She had to crane her head up to face him. "As I told you before, sir, I'm not one of these women. I don't belong back here, nor should you be . . . collecting me as you did."

"And as I told you before, had you been a courtesan, I would no' have collected you at all. I know you're a lady.

What I doona know is why you're at this masquerade."

I'm trying to forget that soon I'll have to return to hell. . . .

She shook herself and answered, "I'm here with my friends. We're out for adventure." At least, the others were. She planned to pick pockets once the punch was flowing freely.

"And by 'adventure' you mean *affair*." His tone seemed to grow irritated. "A bored young wife looking for a bedmate?"

"Not at all. We're merely here to be scandalized so we'll have something to write in our little diaries." As if she could afford either the diary or the time to write.

"Is that why you allowed me to lead you back here? Because you thought I'd make good diary fodder?"

"I allowed you because it would have been fruitless to resist," she replied. "I've seen intent like yours before. Would anything have stopped you from taking me to one of these rooms?"

"No' a thing in the world," he said, catching her eyes.

"Precisely. So I decided that instead of being hauled over your shoulder and carried, I might as well follow you to a quiet spot so I could explain to you that I am not interested in this."

He stalked closer to her, forcing her back to a narrow table along the silk-papered wall. "My intent was no' only to get you alone, lass. And it has no' waned."

Three

Her demeanor was surprisingly composed, her brilliant blue eyes calmly measuring behind her mask, as if a six-and-a-half-foot-tall Highlander accosting her in a darkened room made for sex was commonplace.

Up close, Ethan could see that she was probably no more than twenty, but she was possessed of herself—and even more impossibly lovely than he'd believed when she'd passed him on the street outside.

"And what is your intent?" she asked. Her breaths might have shallowed at his undisguised attention, especially when his gaze dropped to flicker over her breasts. She was slim, too much so for his customary taste, but her small breasts were expertly displayed, her cleavage plump above her tight bodice. He wanted to rip off his mask and rub his face against that creamy flesh.

"My intent is to"—*have a woman beneath me for the first time in three years*—"kiss you."

"You'll have to get your *kisses*"—she stressed the word as if she doubted that was all he wanted—"from one of the hundreds of courtesans out there."

"Doona want them." When his gaze had met hers in the crowd and her pink lips had parted, Ethan had been stunned to find himself swiftly growing hard as stone. Now as he leaned his face in closer to her hair—a mass of white-blond curls, swept up to bare her neck—he smelled her light flowery scent and shot harder, his shaft straining hotly against his trousers. He savored the rare feeling, wanting to groan at the unexpected pleasure. "I followed you in here from the street."

"Why?" Her tone was straightforward, and he silently thanked her for not being coquettish.

"I saw you outside under a streetlight. I liked the way you smiled."

"And you just happened to have this with you?" She reached up, skimming her fingertips along the edge of his mask, but he caught her wrist, lowering it before releasing her.

"I liberated it from a passing patron when I saw you enter." The drop of his mask fluttered above his upper lip, and he'd quickly determined that no one could discern the extent of his scarred visage when courtesans had sought his attention in the crowd filling the Hive. When they'd hindered his progress, he'd been tempted to lift his mask to frighten them away.

"Truly?" Her lips slid into that mysterious half grin, and the need to see the rest of her face burned in him. "So the entire time I saw you searching the crowd, you were looking for *me*?" Her accent was unusual—English upper class mixed with a tinge of French.

"Aye, for you," he said. "You were watching me from your vantage?"

"Raptly," she said, again straightforward, again surprising him.

The idea of her noticing him gave him an odd sense of gratification. "You're no' from London, are you?" When she shook her head, he asked, "Why are you here?"

"Do you want the truth or an answer fit for a masquerade?"

"Truth."

"I've come to England to search for a rich husband," she said.

"No' unusual," he replied. "At least you have the ballocks to admit it."

"I have a proposal waiting in the wings at home," she said, then frowned. "Though I had hoped *not* to fall back on that one."

"How is your hunt going?"

"Not as well as I'd wished," she said. "A few discountable proposals."

"Discountable? Why?"

"Whenever I ask them to qualify themselves, they back off."

"Is that so?" he asked, and when she nodded solemnly, he felt a completely unfamiliar tug at his lips. "And how would a man qualify himself to you?"

"By giving me a token that would actually be dear to him, like an expensive ring or a pair of matched bays, or something along those lines."

"You've given this a lot of thought."

"I think of nothing else," she said so softly that he scarcely heard her. Then she added, "I did almost secure one. A truly good man." Her blond brows drew together as she clearly mused about him. "There might still be the slimmest hope with that one."

For the first time in his life and at the age of thirty-three, Ethan felt the unmistakable heat of jealousy.

What the bloody hell is wrong with me? "Then should you no' be working tonight on securing him?" he asked, his voice colder.

She blinked up at him. "Oh. Well, the man I mentioned went out for the evening. I'm his sister's houseguest, so I'm accompanying her tonight."

That generation of Weylands had only one male—*Quin*. Ethan ground his teeth. Quin had always been a favorite with the ladies.

She sighed. "*Ça ne fait rien.* It doesn't matter." Her voice was growing a bit slurred.

"No, it does no'." The hell she'd be *securing* Quin. Ethan would have to see her around London continually as their paths crossed—and if tonight was any indication, he'd have to continually cuckold Quin. "Forget him. He's no' here and I am."

She gazed up at him and tilted her head. "Take off your mask."

"That defeats the purpose of a masquerade, does it no'?" If he removed it, she would stop looking up at him with a growing curiosity glinting in her eyes, and instead, stare in horror. "I can enjoy you just as well with our masks on."

"And what makes you think I'd allow you to 'enjoy' me?" A flirtatious note had eased into her voice, so subtly he might have missed it. Not coquettish—but amused, intrigued.

She was playing, enjoying herself, but she had no idea what she toyed with. "I've a sense for these things." He brushed the backs of his fingers below the sapphire silk of her mask, down her cheek, and she allowed it. "Tonight you're aching for a man."

At that, she glanced away. "You might be right, Scot," she said casually, then faced him once more. Her voice a purr, she asked, "But are *you* the man I await . . . where I ache?"

He felt on the verge of grinning. Ach, he liked this excitement. This bandying. He liked that she flirted with him, even knowing she didn't plan to go further. Why hadn't a man like himself been attending masquerades every bloody week?

"I am that man." He took her by her tiny waist and lifted her onto the table along the wall.

"Scot, put me down!" she cried, but he could tell she was excited, well past intrigued now. "Why did you do that?"

"I want to be face-to-face with you when I kiss you for the first time."

Finally, his words drew a small gasp from her lips. "Are you always so arrogant?"

"Aye, always." He wedged his hips between her legs.

"You need to let me down," she said, even as she hesitantly ran her fingertip over his arm—as if she'd struggled not to but hadn't been able to help herself. "I've no time or use for handsome rakes with smooth words."

His lips did curl then, pulling on the tight skin of his face, forcing him to recall that he didn't smile—and that he was no longer handsome. "How do you know what I look like? This mask covers most of my face."

"You have a powerful body and a seductive smile. Gorgeous eyes," she said in a breathy voice that made his shaft throb. "You said you've a sense for certain things—well, I appreciate handsome men. An aficionada, if you will. There's a reason I spied you out tonight."

"Is that so?" When she nodded, he said, "Tell me your name."

"That defeats the purpose of a masquerade, does it not?" she answered, repeating his words. She placed her gloved hand on his chest and let it rest there, as if she couldn't decide if she should push him away or clutch his shirt and draw him to her. He caught her hand, rucking the glove up to bare her wrist, then placed a kiss on her satiny skin there.

She shivered, tugging her hand back until he released it. "Look at you, Scot. You're a practiced seducer, if I've ever seen one."

"Practiced?" For the last decade, his flirtations hadn't been practiced—they'd been nonexistent. And before that, he'd never needed to seduce.

Impulse had made him kiss her hand.

So where did the sodding impulse come from?

"Yes, practiced. That kiss to the wrist is a perfect communication. The brush of your lips demonstrates that you'd be gentle and sensual in bed. The firm hold on my hand as you placed it indicates that you'd be masterful at the same time."

Gentle? He thought back. Had he ever been *gentle*? Right now, he recognized he had no desire to be so with her. He wanted to grind his hips against her, rubbing his erection at the juncture of her thighs to proudly show her how fierce his reaction was.

"I've met a lot of your kind," she said. "Know that I'm invulnerable."

"I take that as a challenge, *aingeal*. I'm going to be inside you tonight, and I'll remind you of your words when I have your legs wrapped round my waist."

"Oh, Scot, that won't happen." She shook her head, and a few glossy curls tumbled free, bouncing over her shoulder.

"You're obviously no innocent." Which puzzled him, since he knew she was upper class. She must indeed be a jaded thrill seeker like Jane Weyland and her crowd. "Why no' spend a night with me?"

"You don't think I'm untouched? Why?"

"You looked like you could have yawned at the scene we found in here. No' many innocents would be unfazed by the sight of a prostitute giving a man a below job."

"Well, whether I am or not is incidental. The fact remains that I'm here to find a husband—not a lover. And I've no time for dalliances."

"Make time. If you're in London to find a husband, seems like you might no' be so disdainful to an unmarried man like myself." *He* didn't have time for this. Tomorrow he would leave town to hunt Grey, and for the first time, the call of a kill like that wasn't as strong as the call of a woman.

She laughed then, a seductively sultry laugh that made him yearn to kiss her. "You are so unreachable, you're not even a remote candidate."

He tensed. "Based on what little you know of me?"

All humor gone, she said, "I know enough to suspect that you would use me and never look back. And I'm not condemning, just stating a fact." Her guileless blue eyes were suddenly inscrutable. "I think we have a lot in common, you and I."

Four

"In common? Then you're achin' for us to tup, too."

Maddy grinned then. She simply couldn't help it. "And just like that, you disarm me." There was something about his rough—markedly rough—around-the-edges demeanor that appealed to her. Who was she fooling? *Everything* about him appealed to her, from his rumbling brogue to his muscular body to his peculiar fixation *on her.*

"I want to do more than disarm you."

Her smile faded. The Scot wasn't giving up, and she regretted leading him on. She was behaving foolishly, like a normal girl of twenty-one might, when she didn't have that luxury. Ever-practical Maddy felt herself closing down, the barbs sharpening, the walls going up. "My friends have probably begun to look for me by now. I need to get back to them."

His brows drew together. "You're truly . . . *leaving*?" He sounded baffled, as if he had no idea what to do with this.

"And you're truly not used to being turned down?"

"I'm no' used to being in a position to be."

"You never pursue women?" she said in a doubtful tone.

"Never."

"So I was the lucky first?" Normally she would roll her

eyes at comments like these and take them for what they were—verbal attempts to get into her skirts. But there was something about the way he said them, as if they were significant to him, as if they were not only truths but new and unwelcome ones.

And as if he blamed her for them.

"Aye." He exhaled. "You are the first."

"It's a shame that on your first sally you're going to fail."

His dark eyes narrowed. "And you call me arrogant? What makes you think you can dismiss me?"

"Because *you* are the one who sought *me* out."

"And I dinna do it in vain." He placed his hands against the wall on either side of her head, then leaned in as if to kiss her. "I'm taking you from here tonight."

Though she was dying to know what his lips felt like, she pushed against his chest, striving to ignore how rigid and big the muscles there were. "Not a chance of that, Scot. There's no chance in hell I'll leave with you . . ." She trailed off as he drew in closer. *He's going to kiss me right now!* Her breaths shallowed, and her eyelids nearly fluttered closed in pleasure at his clean scent and the heat emanating from his body.

She licked her bottom lip, and he noticed, giving her a wicked grin just as he was about to reach her. She couldn't stifle a soft whimper—

Whistles rent the air.

She froze. "Are those police whistles?" she whispered, her lips inches from his.

"Aye," he murmured. "I'd wager you'd like to leave with me now."

The entire building quaked as the crowd began to flee. She felt the vibrations through the table under her bottom, and the fog of desire cleared in a rush. *Self-preservation, Maddy!*

"Must go now!" Ducking out from under him, she hopped down, then dragged the chair from the door. Just as she was about to dash off, he grabbed her skirt and yanked. "Let me free!" she demanded over her shoulder.

"Can you no' hear the chaos outside? You doona stand a chance of getting past the police, but you'll likely be trampled."

She turned to him. "But my friends are out there!"

"They'll be safe. Two acquaintances of mine came here tonight and already had their sights on the women you were with. They'll see them home."

"But—"

"Both of those men are capable—and a thousand times more honorable than I am." He met her eyes. "Worry only for yourself, lass."

Nibbling her bottom lip, she said, "Earlier, I saw a back way out." Wary by nature and out of habit, she always traced an escape route from any building she entered. When she and the others had first arrived, Maddy had surveyed a back hall where she'd seen a couple donning jackets before entering it. They hadn't returned. "Could you help me get out?"

"I seem to recall that you'd never leave with me." He leaned back against the wall and drew a knee up, still holding her skirt. "'No' a chance in hell,' to be exact." He smirked, then immediately stopped, as if even a cold smile was unwelcome. She'd seen people do that when they had missing teeth, but his were white and straight and perfect. Perfect like everything else about him. Except for his arrogance.

"Then release me."

"I'll see you clear of this place . . . for the kiss I almost stole."

She had an insistent need to kiss him and, of course, her well-developed sense of preservation—these were not at cross-purposes, yet now was not the time. With a long-suffering sigh, she said, "If I *must*. But only after you get me to safety."

He showed no alarm about what was happening outside. "A kiss now, or more later. What would one kiss hurt?"

"What would it help?" she countered, but he remained unmoved. "Oh, fine." She crossed to him, then reached her hands up to his neck. Tugging him down, she briefly pressed her lips to the corner of his.

When he stood fully once more, he said, "Ah, *aingeal*, that was sweet, no doubt of it. But it was no' quite what I had in mind." He cupped his palm over her nape. "I'm demanding a deep kiss. Until you're panting."

"Panting?" she murmured, gazing up at him. "*Truly?*" How . . . titillating.

With his other hand, he cradled her face and brushed his thumb across her bottom lip. "It'll be easier just tae show you—"

More whistles shrilled. Screams grew louder outside.

"But they'll be back here soon—there's no time!"

He shrugged. "Then prepare yourself for more, later."

"Be specific, sir! What's more?"

He drew his head back as if he'd never expected her to agree. "I want to take you."

"Impossible."

"Then kiss you"—he grazed the backs of his fingers over the tips of her breasts—"here."

With a gasp at the surprise shock of pleasure, she jerked back, crossing her arms protectively over her chest.

"No, emphatically no." She wondered if he'd imagined pressing his lips against her there, and her face grew flushed. "Haven't you heard the old adage: At least *attempt* your own escape from the police before you allow a strange Scotsman to kiss your breasts?"

He either coughed or laughed into his fist, then frowned at her as if she were an unknown breed of animal. "You're a daft lass, do you ken that?"

"And you ask too much from this daft lass." When she opened the door to step out—and was almost trampled—he reeled her back in, slamming the door.

"A wee lady like you does no' stand a chance out there."

"I'm not *wee*." She was five foot three!

"Stubborn, too. But I canna let you run to your death."

I can always renege. "Very well, I agree to your terms. Now can you please get me to safety?"

"Too late. The terms have changed." When she held her tongue, he said, "You'll let me touch you where I wish, and you'll touch me as well."

"You're ruthless to take advantage of me this way!"

"You have no idea," he said in a deliberate tone, his eyes dark with warning. "What do you think will happen if you go to jail this eve? I'm the lesser of two evils—take advantage of that, for it is no' often the case."

If she were jailed, Quin would have to come bail her out. The humiliation! "Yes, yes! I agree," she said, planning to run from the Scot as soon as he freed her from this place.

"Good. Now doona let go of my hand." His hand was warm and swallowed hers when he took it, and they both glanced down. When he caught her gaze again, he said, "As I said—wee. But I'm thinkin' I like it."

She didn't have time to point out that *everything* was wee compared to him, because he opened the door. "Stay behind me," he commanded, having to raise his voice over the din of the crowd.

"Can you get to that hall?" She pointed out that back hall she'd seen, which was now pouring fleeing patrons.

"Aye, but there's no exit. That's why they're running *from* that direction."

"Just go that way! Please, I can find a way out of *anything*!"

He faced her, narrowing his eyes, but finally started forward into the chaos. He stiff-armed anyone who got in his way, and she easily trailed along in his wake. A less powerful man wouldn't have made any headway, much less defeated the flow to reach the hall, but he did. Then he barreled his big body through that crush as well, until he found an empty corridor.

"Yes!" she cried. "Go down there!"

He turned into it, and at the end, they came upon a door to the outside.

Bearing an oversize, ominous padlock.

He raised his brows at her, and she shrugged helplessly. She turned back, trying to determine another escape. They were trapped back here, perfectly snared—

A crash sounded behind her. She whirled around to find the Scot kicking forward, connecting the bottom of his boot to the door just beneath the lock. Splinters arced into the air. Another kick and the door flew open, making her gasp.

He was magnificent! And Maddy had seen her share of magnificent men. When she strode forward to exit, he grabbed her elbow. "No' yet, *aingeal*. Behind me, then."

She nodded breathlessly, staring up at him, not bothering to hide her admiration.

He glowered, pulling at his collar. "Stop lookin' at me like that."

"Like what?"

"Like I'm something I'm no'."

"I don't understand—"

Two policemen leapt in front of them, and the Scot tossed her out of the way. He elbowed one officer and punched the other, leaving the first stumbling to his backside with a busted nose and the other laid out cold.

When the Scot grabbed her hand and pulled her after him once more, she said, "You just hit policemen!"

He grated, "They got in my way."

Some of the gendarmes in her rotten neighborhood were honest, but most weren't. There'd been many a time she'd wanted to lay one flat. "But—"

"I told you I'd get you from here safely." He paused and turned to gaze down at her. "Doona think I'm no' prepared to move mountains for my reward."

Magnificent? No, *glorious*. She knew she was staring up at him like an idiot—dumbly, with her lips parted. Every girl dreamed of a rakish masked man to protect her from villains, or a highwayman to relieve her of her jewels and her virtue. Maddy was no different, and she had to wonder if she would, in fact, renege on their bargain.

Of course she would! She was wavering only because he'd planted those ideas in her head—of his kissing her breasts and her touching him. Add to that one of the most splendid demonstrations of male power she'd ever seen, and naturally she would falter a bit.

No one had ever fought for her before—never, no matter how badly she'd needed someone to.

Again, he seemed uncomfortable with what he saw in her expression. "Try to keep up, then," he said gruffly, then turned away, speeding them down back alleys, farther from the harsh whistles. Continually glancing back at her, he appeared surprised that she was keeping up, but she could run miles at a time.

When they finally slowed, he released her hand to hail a cab, freeing her to flee. Yet she found herself unable to leave him, as if she'd been moored to his side by an invisible force.

Why was she wavering? She needed to be escaping him, not sizing him up and wondering what his skin would feel like. . . .

Maddy loved to touch—cool silks made her shiver, velvets awed her fingertips, gloves plagued her—and he'd *invited* her to touch his body. Daily, she saw women stroke men, but she had never been able to imagine what hard, masculine flesh would feel like flexing beneath her hands. She loved beautiful men; she loved to touch.

He was offering her both to enjoy.

"You doona seem verra frightened," he commented over his shoulder.

"It takes more than this to set me on edge." Tonight was tame compared to her life in La Marais. She'd survived a multi-building fire there at eleven, and she'd lived through *two* cholera epidemics, a feat few in La Marais could claim; violence erupted in the streets daily.

Besides, she felt utterly safe with this Scot.

"Brave as well as bonny?" he murmured in that rumbling voice.

With that, Maddy knew her plan to renege had just gasped its last rattling breath.

Five

As soon as the carriage started off, the Scot yanked the curtains closed, reaching over Maddy to draw them shut on her side. Once he'd cast them into darkness, he peremptorily dragged her over the bench and onto his lap.

"Wait! What are you . . . ? You can't just . . ." When he flicked his tongue against her earlobe, pleasure rippled through her, quelling her need to put distance between them. She sighed, "Ohhh."

"I fulfilled my end of the bargain," he began, his words rough. "You'll fulfill yours now."

"Where do you think you're taking me?"

"To my home."

"Your *home*?" She shook herself. "As much as I'd like to be one of the many strange women to be entertained in your bachelor apartments—"

"Again, you'd be the first," he interrupted.

"Am I supposed to believe that?"

"Believe it or no'. It's the truth."

"What is it about me that has wrought such changes?"

He leaned back, seeming aggravated—at her or the situation? "I'd bloody like to know."

He wasn't feigning these things. Maybe he felt with her the same awareness, the same sense of familiarity, that she felt with him. Her attraction to him had been instantaneous and furious, so strong she felt as if she'd been plowed down by a locomotive.

Could he possibly be experiencing the same?

This was all madness anyway—she hadn't even seen his face. "Scot, if it's any consolation, I'm behaving completely out of character as well."

"Then what do you say we figure this out afterward?" He curled his fingers under her chin. "There's no reason for me no' to be kissin' you senseless right now."

Senseless? Part of her wanted him to render her senseless, to make her pant, while another part of her still couldn't believe any of this was happening. As he drew in, her eyelids eased closed. . . .

His lips were warm and firm as he grazed them against hers, and that mere coaxing contact made heat race through her. When she parted her lips for him, he slipped his tongue in to slowly stroke hers. Never had she experienced anything so blatantly erotic as how his tongue flicked and teased.

Never had she felt such an awareness that kissing like this was meant to be a prelude to sex.

She found herself lapping back—which doubled the sensations. He clutched her closer, groaning into the kiss, deepening it. She squeezed his shoulders, reveling in the power she felt in his muscles. She craved it, wanted his strength, wanted his arms around her.

Their tongues twined again and again, sending her to heights of need she'd never imagined. He must be feeling it, too—he adjusted her on his lap, groaning when his thick erection pressed fully against her bottom. She swore she felt the heat of it even through their clothes and couldn't help but imagine stroking it in her palm. In all her fantasies, she'd never dreamed of how *hot* it would be. She wriggled in his lap. . . .

He drew back, gazing down at her as though in shock, his lips parted, breaths ragged.

"I-I never much liked kissing before," she whispered, aware that she was, indeed, panting.

Brows drawn, he rasped, "Aye, me neither."

She whimpered, needing more. He cursed in answer. They both set in again.

He leaned her back against his unyielding arm so he could take her more thoroughly, slanting his lips over and over until she felt boneless and unguarded. *Senseless* . . . She moaned against his lips.

But he broke away again, appearing wary. "That was . . . that . . ." His eyes narrowed. "You keep kissing me like that, and this night will be over before it begins."

He was obviously so worldly and experienced, and yet she'd still pleased him. He continued to please her. She was excited, for some reason happier than she'd been in months. "Scot," she murmured, threading her fingers into his thick hair, "I'm glad I invited you on my escape."

"Already, I'm verra glad to be here."

It suddenly struck her as miserably unfair that her husband wouldn't be someone like this god who held her, who set her afire with every clever flick of his tongue.

But what if she could get *him* to marry her?

True, she still hadn't seen his face—and she didn't know his name. But to be fair, she could probably go out on a limb and guess that the Scot hadn't been widowed three times. And to be fair, she *had* seen the count's face.

Between this man's fierce kisses, her irresistible attraction to him—and a good deal of the decidedly potent punch—this struck her as a *brilliant* solution to her problem. "Scot, I don't suppose you're rich and looking for a wife?"

"One out of two. I'll never marry."

"*Never*, never? Or do you mean not until after a few years more of bachelorhood?"

"Never." He was emphatic, seeming irritated by the mere subject.

"Oh. Well, I really can't be going home with you," she said, just as the carriage rolled to a stop. He set her on the bench and opened his door—in front of an imposing redbrick mansion.

"Where are we?" she asked in confusion.

"In Grosvenor Square."

"*This* is your home?" she said, without looking away. It was grand and bigger even than Quin's! White columns proudly stood sentinel alongside wide marble steps. Pristine gardens were generously illuminated with hidden gaslights.

"Aye, my home."

She quirked an eyebrow. She could easily imagine herself as mistress of it.

When he reached for her hand, she said, "Wait! I can't just go in with you like this!" Though she was dying to see the inside.

"We had a deal."

"But not to go home with you!" They weren't that far from the Weylands'. What if someone saw her?

"This idea really bothers you?" When she nodded, he leaned out and commanded, "Drive," before shutting his door. The carriage rolled on once more. "Matters naught. I can take you in here as well as I can in a bed."

"Take me?" Her eyes went wide. "I thought the bargain was only to touch."

He pulled her into his lap again, his big hand resting on her hip with casual familiarity, as if they'd sat like this a hundred times. "Just trust me. I'll make it good for you. You'll have much diary fodder," he said with a hint of a grin.

"You can have me, Scot. Completely. By noon tomorrow. That will give me enough time to skim over your account books, and for you to get a special license. We can be wed before lunch."

He grasped her chin. "Understand, lass, that nothing on earth will move me to marry. *Nothing*."

When she realized he was just like Quin, her heart sank. "I understand." Unfortunately, she did and perfectly well—this was the second time today she'd heard that same sentiment, the second time she'd been turned down flat. Some men just weren't the marrying kind, no matter how much they *should* be.

Which meant girls like her picked through the leftovers of gouty old counts.

"Make sure that you do," he said, warning clear in his tone.

She absently nodded. At every turn tonight, she'd had her decision to marry Le Daex reinforced, but she shuddered to imagine the man heaving and grunting over her as he took her virginity. She, who adored beautiful men, wouldn't lose her virtue to one. Yes, it was unfair, and suddenly—or, after the liquor and the Scot's firm lips—it was intolerable.

She'd weathered misery after misery since her father had been shot, heaped on her as though by a cosmic jest. Like an animal caught in a snare, the more she struggled, the worse it seemed to get. She expected so little in return for her constant sacrifices, but this one aspect of her life—deciding who would introduce her to lovemaking—she could control. And her instincts were screaming that she could trust this mysterious stranger.

She nibbled her lip. Le Daex could be fooled to think she was untouched. Maddy's landlady and best friend in Paris had been a virgin at all three of her weddings. . . .

The Scot had told Maddy he'd be inside her tonight.

At that moment, she realized he was right.

"Very well."

"Verra well, what?"

"If you wanted more . . ." She could feel him instantly pulsing harder beneath her.

"You're . . . you want me tae take you," he rasped, but it sounded like a question.

"Yes. I want more than the terms of our bargain," she murmured. "I want you." *To show me this . . . to give me this night to secretly treasure.*

"What has changed your mind?"

She sighed. "My reasons are my own, Scot. Do you care anyway?"

He smirked, flashing white teeth. "No' in the least."

"So, um, in light of this, don't you think we should take off our masks?" she asked.

"It adds something, do you no' think?" He skimmed the backs of his fingers against her cheek under her mask.

She wasn't shy by any means, but this was her first real encounter, and she had concerns about the desirability of her sparse frame. In other words, her breasts were small. The mask would help conceal heated blushes, and it suited her fine. Especially since this would be just one night—a single night of mystery and need. And then of endings. "Yes, I suppose it does."

But he wasn't listening, appearing captivated as his fingers glided over the line of her jaw. "So delicate," he said absently, seeming not to realize he'd spoken aloud. Somehow she knew this wasn't a mere seduction. He was exploring her, his eyes dark with curiosity. "I've no' had a woman like you before."

"Like me?"

"So slight." He traced the shell of her ear, making her shiver. "I'm almost afraid to put my hands on you."

"Oh, don't say that."

"I said *almost*. Nothing could stop me from taking you tonight." He trailed his fingers down, running the pads over her collarbone. As he brushed lower, her breaths grew harried, her chest rising and falling madly under his touch. When he reached the edge of her tight bodice, he worked his fingers inside. Slowly delving, pressing deeper . . . deeper . . . until the tip of his forefinger met her throbbing nipple.

"Oh, my God," she moaned, clutching both of her hands on the back of his neck.

"Delicate . . . and sensitive." He languidly rolled her swollen nipple, rasping, "You like that."

Her eyes fluttered closed, and she nodded.

When he withdrew his hand she wanted to keen, but she was mollified to see that he'd begun an attempt on the laces of her bodice. The ties, however, were thin and difficult to manage even for her. After fumbling for several moments, he gave a growl of frustration and curled his big fingers inside the fabric.

When she realized he was about to yank, she opened her mouth to sputter her outrage—she'd gone into debt to afford this dress!—but then, he released her. With a frown of concentration, he endeavored it again.

Something in her softened toward him—even more. "Let me, Scot," she said, removing his hands with a tender kiss to each palm.

At different points in the evening, she'd noticed that he would hesitate, drawing back for the briefest moment as though to take time to think. He did that now. She'd begun to wonder if she was behaving incorrectly—this *was* her first affair—or if what was happening between them was just completely different from what he was used to. She suspected the latter.

Once she'd freed the laces at last, he pulled wide the edges of her gown. As he unhurriedly tugged down the gauzy cups of her corset to bare her, she swallowed. *It's dark. He can't really see me. . . .* When cool air caressed her breasts, she willed herself not to turn her face away or to cover herself with her hands.

He hissed something in a foreign language, possibly Gaelic.

"What did you say?" she asked nervously.

"I said I'm goin' tae kiss these all night." He ran the backs of his fingers over both of her nipples, his gaze flickering over her face, gauging her response. She sucked in a breath and felt the tips hardening even more, right before his eyes.

Then he cupped her with his hot, scratchy palms. "*You could no' be softer.*" He covered her small breasts completely, kneading until she grew sensuously warm and wet between her legs.

Exactly how had she been living without this?

When he removed his hands to shrug out of his jacket, she found herself arching forward for them. He made a grated sound that might have been a chuckle. "Greedy lass," he said, but she thought he was pleased. He returned his hands to her. "Then undo my shirt for me." He might have been making fun of her, but she didn't care. Her need urged her on.

As she struggled with his buttons, he leaned down to nuzzle her nipples, his hot breaths making them throb, but he didn't suckle her, only teased until she was squirming on his lap, writhing over his jutting erection.

He finally set upon her breasts with his hot mouth. "*Oh, my God,*" she whispered as he dragged his tongue over her stiffened nipple. When she vaguely perceived his hand under her skirts, his fingers ascending from her knee to her thigh, she said, "Scot, I . . . please go slow. I want you. Oh, God!" she cried as he closed his lips around her aching peak, sucking her hard. "B-but can't we go slower?"

He drew back. "Why?" he asked, seeming genuinely confused.

"I just think . . . maybe I would be more comfortable."

"I've been long without a woman," he said, his voice strained as he removed her from his lap to the bench. "I'll do it slowly for the rest of tonight." He wadded up his jacket and placed it behind her. "But for now, I need tae be inside you." Her other nipple received the same fierce attention as the first as he pressed her back.

"Oh, God . . . that feels nice." The way he touched her was proprietary, possessive—and a bit . . . *rough.* So why was she arching in delight? "But, Scot . . . you see . . ."

He leaned up then, meeting her eyes. "What is it?" His shirt gaped open, displaying his chiseled torso to her fascinated gaze, and she lost track of what she'd been about to say.

She could *touch* him. This was what she'd wondered about, *dreamed* about. She frantically yanked off her tormenting gloves to caress him. She sighed with delight when the muscles of his chest tensed and flexed to her touch so perfectly, as if she'd trained them over years.

She placed her palms flat and rubbed down over rigid indentations and swells, in a heaven of sensation, her fingertips tingling with delight at each new texture . . . his firm, smooth skin . . . the crisp hair in a trail just below his navel. She savored his reaction—his lids sliding shut, his jaw slackening.

Nearly dumbstruck with pleasure, she scarcely noticed that her skirts were suddenly rucked up to her waist.

Six

Ethan burned for this, finally to have a woman after so long. Though it had never been his way, he wanted her throughout the night, to take her again and again. To kiss every inch of her ravishing body.

Before sending her along.

"Oh, my word," she murmured, still seeming enthralled with his chest.

Her fingertips brushed him as though with reverence. He didn't understand this tenderness—it was foreign to him—yet he couldn't stop her.

"Your heart's thundering." She laid her hand over the center of his chest. "Are you nervous?"

"I'm no' *nervous*," he lied, his voice unaccountably gruff. It had been so long that he feared he'd shame himself with one thrust. And for the first time in his life he cared about what his partner would think. He wanted not only to pleasure her but also to impress her. He wanted to be the best she'd ever had.

"You said you've been long without a woman. A very long while?" she asked.

"Aye, a verra long while," he answered, shocked that he'd told her the truth.

"Well. I'm sure we can muddle through this together,"

she said, sounding calm, but she'd begun trembling. He wasn't the only one who was nervous.

Yet once his fingers skimmed up her smooth thighs to dip into the slit of her pantalettes, she relaxed. At his first touch between her legs, he shuddered with pleasure. "You're wet for me," he rasped, so damned excited by her. With one hand, he petted her breasts, and with the other, he ran his forefinger up and down her sex, taking her wetness to circle her little clitoris.

She cried out, arching her back. Soon she was undulating her hips with need, growing more wanton with each of his strokes. He wanted to taste her there, to delve his fingers inside her, but he knew he'd come immediately.

He absently recognized that two hours ago, he'd feared he was quit of this feeling, and now, with her . . .

Ethan was about to spill like an untried lad.

He had to take her before it became too late for him. When he removed his hands to hastily tug her pantalettes from her, she wriggled her chest to put her breast back under his palm.

My God, she's a hot little piece. He couldn't imagine what riding her would be like.

With her undergarments removed and her skirts bunched at her waist, she shivered and whimpered with abandon. One coaxing press against her inner thigh and her knees slid open, without teasing. He began to wonder if her ungoverned responses—so unpracticed and therefore unfamiliar to him—were *innocent* responses. He'd never been with a virgin and didn't intend to start tonight.

No, she kissed like a courtesan, accepting it when he took her mouth deeply, wetly. But just to be certain, he unfastened his trousers, releasing his sensitive shaft with a choked groan. "I want you tae stroke me." A virgin's touch would be hesitant, tentative.

She nodded and took him in her soft palm—his first contact in so long; he couldn't prevent himself from bucking into her grip.

With her brows drawn, she eased her other hand down to expertly heft and tug his sack. When she thumbed the wet slit of his penis in slow circles, his eyes rolled back in his head. All doubt dispelled, he grated, "That's enough. You're going to see a man spill his seed if you doona stop."

He nearly groaned when she nibbled her lip, clearly contemplating it. "Would that embarrass you?"

"No' at all. In fact, sometime tonight I'll have your eyes on me when I do."

"I think you must be awfully wicked."

"Aye, in bed, there's little I will no' do tae a woman or press her tae do to me."

She ran the back of a smooth nail down his shaft, which jerked up as if seeking her touch. "You're, um, very large."

"But you'll like it, I promise you." When he lowered his body into the cradle of her thighs, he buried his face against her neck. The scent of her hair and the feel of her breasts and nipples against his chest were making him crazed. Their kissing had nearly put him over the edge, and she'd worked him into a lather with her skillful fondling.

He was at that stage where he could scarcely feel anything but the ache in his ballocks, thinking of nothing but driving into flesh until he could relieve the pressure. "Just let me get this out of the way." He hadn't felt this frenzied in memory. "And I'll take you nice and slow later."

Her eyes were heavy-lidded but locked on his as he levered himself up above her, forcing her knees wider open with his own. He positioned his cock at her wet folds, running the tip up and down, his muscles straining as he fought not to shove into her.

Once she was writhing beneath him, he pressed his hips forward until just the swollen head was wedged inside her. The perfect, tight heat that greeted him nearly robbed him of his seed in that instant. "*It's so good, lass,*" he choked out.

He flexed his hips and thrust inside her fully, the wet glove of her body shocking him, scalding him—as if he'd never had a woman before her. The feel of her arching beneath him, her nipple budding even harder under his kneading palm . . . he'd never known such pleasure—*never.*

"Oh, God!" she cried. "This . . . this . . . it's too—"

He groaned, "I *know.*" Another exquisite thrust made him shudder violently over her. When he withdrew, her slick flesh squeezed his cock like a fist. He was already on the verge of coming. It had been so damned long. . . . Once more, he drove inside, needing to bury himself to the hilt. He ground against her, wanting in deeper—

She shoved her palms at his hips. "*N-no!*"

He shook his head hard and frowned down at her. "What is it? What did I do?"

"You have to stop!"

"*Stop?*" he bit out incredulously. "*Give this up?*" There was no way he could pull out of the most luscious little body he'd ever had—especially not after being celibate for three years. "You're too hot . . . too tight."

She was frantically trying to dislodge him. "P-please . . . you can't imagine . . . how badly this hurts." A sob broke from her.

He stilled instantly. "Are you . . . are you *crying*?"

When she didn't answer, just turned her face away, he gritted his teeth and muttered a vile oath. His mind in turmoil, he somehow began to withdraw. Inch by agonizing inch, he strained against the staggering pleasure as her sex seemed determined not to relinquish him.

He had to make his body understand that he wasn't to thrust back in and take the release he wanted so badly. That he was giving up this absolute pleasure—not to get it back.

Too late. As soon as he'd withdrawn he yelled out, uncontrollably beginning to spill against her. His hand shot down to stroke himself to complete release. His forehead rested on her chest, his mouth too close to her hard nipple to resist suckling her as he came. Over and over, he ejaculated across her thigh and against her sex, shuddering and groaning above her.

When he'd finally finished, he lay heavy atop her, catching his breath as he tried to sort out what had just happened. When he'd first entered her, all he'd perceived had been a nearly uncomfortable tightness and burning heat surrounding him, but now he recalled a hesitation, a pressure giving way.

She was—or she had been—a virgin.

Why would she do this? Why give this to *him*?

Even with the unplanned ending, taking her had still been amazing. He felt light-headed, nigh euphoric, like he'd figured being completely *satisfied* would feel. By God, he *was* satisfied—as if he'd done something he'd always been supposed to and had been rewarded beyond imagining. And the next time would only be better.

He raised himself on his elbows. "Ah, lass, why did you no' tell me." He ran his thumb over her cheek and felt wetness. "Ach, doona cry," he grated, brushing her hair from her forehead. "I dinna know."

Maddy blinked up through tears, watching as his eyes went from expressing heavy-lidded content to something like narrow-eyed suspicion.

At last, he sat up, and she scrambled away from him. The movement made her hiss in a breath at the fresh pain, and her tears began anew. As he fastened himself back into his trousers, she swatted her skirts down. She couldn't stop her shaking, knowing he'd kept going, ignoring her cries. She'd asked him to stop at least three times, and he'd just closed his eyes, acting as though he hadn't heard her, as though he'd gone mindless. If she hadn't shoved at his hips . . . she shuddered.

"Again, why did you no' tell me?"

She could feel his anger growing. Yes, she should have told him, had been about to, but she'd been distracted by his chest, overwhelmed by her first feel of a man's body. With trembling hands, she pulled her cape to cover her unlaced bodice, then collected her pantalettes and gloves. "I was going to—"

"Did you think to trap me?"

"Trap you? Wh-what are you talking a—"

"'My reasons are my own,' you told me," he interrupted. "Your reasons had something to do with seeing my home."

"No!"

"You picked the wrong man, *aingeal*," he sneered. "I could no' care less if you're ruined now."

Couldn't care less? Ruined?

"I will no' be manipulated and deceived, then reward you for it. *Nothing* could move me to marry you."

Openly crying now, she whispered, "Wasn't trying . . ."

"Damn it, then why did you capitulate so readily? I was having to work for you to allow a *kiss*, and then suddenly you're surrendering your virtue in the back of a cab? After telling me you're hunting for a rich husband?"

She wiped at her tears, embarrassed by them. "I decided to go through with this specifically because I recognized I am going to be forced to wed *someone else.*"

"What in the hell is that supposed to mean?"

"I told you I had a proposal. After meeting yet another eligible male who refused to wed, I concluded I would have to accept the offer of marriage I did receive. And before I went and married someone I don't desire, I wanted to discover what making love was like with someone I did want."

"Then it seems that I just enjoyed something that belonged to another man." He gave a bitter laugh. "So you planned to trick your unwitting fiancé into thinking you were still untouched? Cuckolding him even before the ceremony?"

"For the first time in memory, I made a decision to have what *I* desired."

"You *admit* to your scheming? I canna believe I thought you were different from every other deceitful female I've met."

"How dare you! I wasn't trying to deceive you. Is it so unbelievable that I simply *wanted* you?" Hurting, bewildered by what had just occurred, she whispered the truth, "Though how I ever desired you is a mystery now."

"But you did, and what's done is done now. You can never get it back, no matter how ill-considered the giving—or, God help you, the recipient—was." He untied his mask and tossed it to the floor, then sat motionless, only giving her one side of his face. In the shadow, she could see his profile was strong and bold. The beast who'd just taken her was, on the surface, a beautiful man. He didn't say a word to her and wouldn't face her, seeming to wrestle with a decision.

"Avail yourself of the carriage," he finally said in a dismissive tone, tossing cash on the bench between them.

At his words, she froze. This couldn't be happening. She'd guarded her virtue for years, defended it jealously, and then in a wild, reckless moment, she'd thrown it away on this animal, this oaf.

And received nothing but searing pain and humiliation in return.

Her vaunted instincts had served her ill.

He pounded his fist against the roof. When the carriage stopped, he turned to her slightly. "I'll be gone for a week or two. But afterward, I will return for you to decide what's to be done with you."

Her jaw slackened. "*What's to be done with me?*" How did he think to find her? She still wore her mask and hadn't revealed her name. And she would make sure she was long gone from London by the time he returned. The idea that she never had to see him again helped her temporarily stem her tears.

The count would've been a better lover than the Scot. He couldn't have been worse. She would run back to Le Daex eagerly—gratefully.

As if he read her mind, the Scot said, "And, *aingeal*, doona think of marrying anyone before then."

At that, he stepped out. Before he slammed the door, she could have sworn she heard him say, "*Or I'll make you a widow.*"

Seven

As Ethan rode for home, his mind was a knot of conflicting ideas. All of them involving the girl.

He'd realized that by the time he finished with Grey, she could be married to the fiancé she had "waiting in the wings."

When asking himself why in the hell he cared—he'd always preferred married women—he could posit no credible answer. At least, none better than the fact that he wanted her at his complete disposal. If she were wed, she would be Ethan's only *after* her husband had taken his due.

That was intolerable.

He reasoned that he felt possessive of her like this only because he had taken her virginity, claiming her as he had no other woman before. Tonight he had made her a woman, and on some primal level, he was proud that he had. Ethan didn't want another man enjoying her in between the times he did.

Yet there were only two ways he could have her exclusively—as his wife or his mistress. The former was impossible, and even that latter struck him as far too much of a commitment.

Let her fade into the past. . . . Now was not the time to have his mind on a woman.

If Ethan wasn't cold and focused in the days to follow, he'd get himself killed.

Before Grey's affliction had twisted him, the man had possessed untouchable instincts. Even addicted to opium, Grey had been able to escape the suicide mission Edward Weyland had dispatched him on six months earlier—and from what they knew, Grey was still strong enough to exact revenge for it.

Ethan had assured Quin that Hugh could handle the threat at hand. Yet tonight, Hugh had seen Jane for the first time in years, and Ethan had noted with frustration that none of his brother's feelings for her had faded whatsoever—even after so much time had passed.

This couldn't go on. Once more, he would be forced to act....

Ethan knew his faults and reveled in them—he was selfish, callous, and coarse, and he killed easily; his only redeeming quality was that he would die for his brothers and wanted them to have some measure of happiness.

But for some reason both Hugh and Court had always wanted—needed—more. They were never satisfied to continue with less than other men could rightfully expect. It maddened Ethan to know how miserable they both were.

Just as he'd done years ago, Ethan was going to have to remind Hugh of why he couldn't have Jane, though he didn't relish the task—it would only drive a wedge deeper between him and his brother. Just as he'd done before, Ethan would use the book that shadowed his family.

When he arrived back at his home, Ethan strode directly to the study to reach the *Leabhar nan Sùil-radharc*, the Book of Fates. Long ago, a clan seer had predicted the fortunes of ten generations of MacCarricks and inscribed them in the *Leabhar*. The lines within foretold events that had all come to pass.

The tome was centuries old but well preserved, its cover producing an unearthly gleam. The only marking it had ever accepted was blood, on the last page—the one written to his father. . . .

To the tenth Carrick:
Your lady fair shall bear you three dark sons.
Joy they bring you until they read this tome.
Words before their eyes cut your life's line young.
You die dread knowing cursed men they become,
shadowed to walk with death or walk alone.

Not to marry, know love, or bind, their fate;
Your line to die for never seed shall take.
Death and torment to those caught in their wake . . .

The last two lines were concealed, covered with indelible blood.

Both of Ethan's brothers believed the foretelling, abiding by the warning in it. They lived their lives by the book, and Ethan encouraged that. But Ethan's relationship with it was more . . . complicated.

He knew there was power within the tome—it was palpable and the book was indestructible. And there was much evidence to support the predictions: Neither he nor his brothers had fathered a babe, they all walked with death in their professions, and of the two times any of them had thought to marry, one fiancée had perished and another nearly had.

Just as foretold, their beloved father, Leith, had died the very morning after his sons had read the lines.

Coincidence could explain some. An undivulged or unknown childhood illness could explain why none of the three brothers had ever been petitioned for support of a child or marriage—though they'd actually hoped for it years ago. In fact, Court had once speculated that this was why Ethan bedded so many women. Hell, maybe Court had been right—maybe Ethan had been trying to get a bairn on any one of them.

And to explain the death of Ethan's fiancée the night before their wedding?

If one believed the rumors circling him, Ethan had cornered her on the roof of Carrickliffe, his family seat, and then pushed her to her death. . . .

Ethan didn't worship the book, taking it as his creed, because the three brothers were well and truly cursed on their own—so why bring the *Leabhar* into it? Ethan lived his life rationally, and a modicum of common sense said that, cursed or not, assassins and mercenaries and *worse* best not taint the innocent.

Then why in the hell was he even considering going for the lass tomorrow?

Did you ever think I just wanted you . . . ?

Ethan lay in bed for hours until dawn, scowling at the ceiling as he replayed every minute of the night. That same inexplicable sense of urgency to see her continued to claw at him.

Part of him wanted to shove her from his mind, even as another part of him had wanted to storm Quin's house last night and take her away. Again the need to *get* her, to possess her, surged within him. He didn't understand it. He hungered for her as he never had for any woman before.

He remembered his lack of response to the comely prostitute displaying her breasts. However, if he recalled the lass's soft, wee ones beneath his palms he shot hard as wood. Yes, he'd just had her and the pleasure was fresh, but his reaction to her still made him uneasy.

What if she was the only one who could provoke him to that kind of lust? Even with the abrupt ending, taking her had been . . . mind-boggling. Just touching her trembling body . . .

What if he never experienced that fierce need again without her?

There were other questions surrounding the mysterious chit that he wanted answered. If she was untouched, then why hadn't she been shocked at the sights in the masquerade? And how in the hell had she known how to fondle him with such skill?

Moreover, what could possibly have given her the impression that he'd be honorable enough to offer for her once she'd made her play?

And he wouldn't mind knowing why his shaft had been hard, miserably tight and throbbing, from the time he'd left her. He took it in his fist and stroked, but stopped directly, drawing his hand away with a hissed oath. Why should he spend in his hand—instead of inside her once more?

There was nothing to be done for it.

Ethan would make her his mistress.

With a resigned exhalation, he rose to wash and dress, determined to enter into some kind of arrangement with her this morning. As he set up to shave, he realized there were obstacles to this plan.

The first? If she truly hadn't been thinking to trap him, then she would be outraged by his accusation and *disinclined* to accept him.

The second? He'd hurt her last night. Ethan recalled her responses, her exquisite body writhing beneath his, first in pleasure—but then in . . . agony.

Now that the haze of the night had faded, he comprehended that the pain he'd given her would have been substantial. She had asked him to go slowly, yet he hadn't taken the time to ready her. He'd been frenzied for release, stupid with lust. He'd taken her hard, rutting over her, when she'd been so delicate and fragile.

Damn it, he hadn't meant to hurt her, to make her . . . cry.

Women's tears did not affect him—this was simply a fact, a part of the coldheartedness others had seen in him since he was a teen. So why had seeing hers troubled him so much?

There'd been a brief moment when he might've promised her *anything* to get her to stop.

With practiced care, he grazed his razor past the jagged end of his scar. Another obstacle? Quin might actually care for the little witch. Or Ethan's superior, Edward Weyland, might step in. The girl's parents were probably shabby-genteel, land-rich and cash-poor but still influential, if they were friends of the Weylands. Though none of them could force Ethan to wed her, they could bloody well irritate him on this subject.

Yet everyone had a price—she'd been hunting a rich husband for a reason—and Ethan had already ruined her.

Perhaps there were debts weighing on her family, or maybe she had sisters who needed dowries. Ethan was prepared to pay a fortune to make her his mistress, to slake himself on her for a time, and get past her. All he wanted was to put her up in a house close by, somewhere convenient to his needs, and in return, he could make her family's problems go away.

He drew the razor across his face again, then stared into the mirror, regarding the greatest obstacle to his plan.

If I see the girl again, there will be no mask. For the first time in years, he studied his reflection. His scar was deep, stretching taut over the length of his right cheekbone, then twisting down the front of his cheek. Stitches had left uniform depressions at the edges. Every inch of the mark whitened starkly with any expression.

Brymer had done his job well.

That night, once Van Rowen had realized his mistake, he'd hurried to the stable and had grown sick at what Brymer had already done to Ethan. Dazed, Van Rowen had offered restitution or an exact reprisal to himself.

But Ethan had had bigger plans for him and his wife—and for Brymer. When freed, Ethan had just gritted his teeth against the pain and blindly lurched to his horse. Sheer will had gotten him off Van Rowen lands before he'd blacked out in a ditch for two days.

Just months later, before Ethan had been able to finalize his revenge, Van Rowen had provoked a drunken duel. He'd turned without drawing, dying in what was known as a "gentleman's suicide."

As for Sylvie, Ethan had rendered her penniless, leaving her to rot in a slum.

For some reason, Ethan had spared Tully. But his confrontation had left the man so shaken, Tully had promptly disappeared from the area and likely still lived in fear.

And Brymer? Ethan had gutted him—his scarred visage the last sight the bastard had seen on this earth. . . .

Before he'd been cut, Ethan would have been a fitting match for the girl. Now she would probably laugh at his appearance. Hadn't she professed herself—what had she called it?—an *aficionada of male beauty?*

Ethan tried to smile, but he found it uncomfortable, the sight repulsive, even to himself. Hating the Van Rowens anew, he threw down the straight razor, sending it clattering into the basin.

Eight

An hour later, after having run into Hugh—and engaging in yet another brotherly row—Ethan made his way to Quin's. This morning, Ethan was more acutely aware of how people on the street stared at him. In return, he gave them his most menacing glower.

When he reached Quin's home, he found himself anxious. Hell, the girl would likely spurn him for his behavior last night anyway. He supposed it didn't matter as long as he got this settled with her, for good or ill.

Quin scowled when Ethan strode uninvited and unannounced into his study. "Excellent, another MacCarrick to deal with. Already this morning, I've had to haul your brother away from a fight with another man over Jane."

"I saw Hugh just a short while ago—he dinna tell me there was a fight." *So much for loving her secretly from afar, Hugh.*

"In reality, I wouldn't so much call it a *fight*—that would imply two contenders," Quin amended. "Needless to say, after witnessing Hugh in a rage like that, Jane's reluctant to be near him, much less to go into hiding with him."

Going into hiding. And that had been the subject of the brothers' dispute. Hugh had actually agreed to take Jane out of the city—just the two of them. *Disaster awaits. . . .*

"What are you doing here?" Quin asked. "I thought you were going after Grey."

"I combed his haunts last night. I doona believe he's made London from the Continent yet."

"Then what do you want?"

"To talk to the lass staying with your sisters."

"Madeleine? Is this about Grey? How could she know anything?"

Madeleine. Ethan liked the name. But then he frowned as some memory tugged at his consciousness. "This is no' about Grey. It's . . . personal."

"What in the hell could you have to say to her? How do you even know her?"

"I met her last night, at the masquerade."

"I wondered what had spooked her!" Quin rose and paced to the window. "I should have known only one man in London could terrorize the poor girl like that."

"Terrorize? Oh, aye, such a sweet, innocent girl. Did you know she's been trying to trap you into marriage?"

Quin turned back. "I might have suspected something when she told me she'd dreamed of being my wife since she was a girl and then asked me if I would ever consider marrying her. So devious—how does she sleep nights?"

Dreamed of marrying Quin. Ethan ground his teeth, suddenly needing to pummel Quin's unscarred face.

"Here's the thing, MacCarrick. I did consider it. She's secretive, occasionally dishonest, and inordinately concerned with money, but she's also kind and winsome and intelligent. Any man would be proud to call her his wife."

"Then why did you no' keep her?"

"You *know* why." Quin's role in the Network required him to seduce women, often traveling the world to do it.

"Besides, she has a proposal in hand," Quin said as he returned to his desk. "She's going to accept him directly."

The hell she was. "Who?"

"You don't expect me to tell you that?"

"You know I can have that information in a day." Ethan's job wasn't only to deal the blows that no one else wanted to deal. He also brokered information.

"Why are you so bloody interested in her? She's a lady and a virgin, not your usual fare of jaded whore."

"Do you *want* me to hit you?"

"Just stay the hell away from her, MacCarrick. I don't know what dire thing happened at the masquerade—she refused to talk about it even to Claudia—but when I saw her this morning, she looked as if she'd cried all night."

Cried *all night*? Had it been *that* bad? "Aye, Quin, something dire happened. She made a play to get me to marry her. One that failed."

"A play to wed *you*?" Quin gave a harsh laugh. "You've some nerve. The girl is utterly lovely. Yes, that's clearly what she wanted, as evidenced by the fact that she fled London this morning."

Ethan froze. "What did you say?"

"She's gone, couldn't get out of here fast enough."

Goddamn it! Ethan would have to kill Grey before he could go after her. "Tell me the chit's name and how to find her." He stalked around the desk, and Quin shot to his feet.

"Throw her to the wolf? I don't know why you've suddenly taken an interest in a well-bred girl, much less someone who's a friend of my sister's, but you won't get the information from me."

"She does no' get much say in the matter, no' after I relieved her of her virtue last night."

Quin's eyes widened, and he lunged at Ethan, throwing a punch. Ethan caught his fist, crushing it with his hand. "Doona fuck with me, Quin. My patience wears thin."

Quin gritted his teeth in pain. "Ethan, I know you're not a man concerned with morals. But I didn't think you'd despoil an innocent more than a decade younger than you are." When Ethan released Quin, he sank to his chair, shaking feeling back into his hand. "My God, she's ruined. I know you will never do the honorable thing, and her betrothed won't want her now. I must go offer for her at once."

"Stay away from her," Ethan grated. "She's *mine*." When Quin still looked to argue, Ethan made things simple. "Marry her, and I'll kill you."

"You don't even know who she is!" Quin snapped. "And you won't marry her yourself."

"No, I will no'."

"Then why are you here? What had you planned to do with her?"

"After I've taken care of Grey, I'll bloody figure it out then. I'm going off to save your cousin's life, so you ken why there's a time element here." Ethan couldn't care less about Jane, other than the fact that his brother was in love with her to an unspeakable degree and would be devastated if she died. "The sooner I get my mind on killing, the better for everyone. So tell me the girl's name. Then we'll talk about her betrothed."

Quin got an analytical air about him, studying Ethan for a long moment. Then he flashed an expression of realization. "Little Madeleine got under your skin, didn't she? She has that way about her. I knew to be on guard, but you . . . you were probably blindsided." He nodded, giving Ethan a smug grin. "I'm going to give you her information because Grey must be stopped at all costs—and unfortunately, you are the best hope we have. But I'm also assisting you because in this kind of arena, you're no match for her. She'll have you not knowing up from down."

Ethan gave a humorless laugh. "That so?"

Quin met his eyes. "Ethan, I could almost feel sorry for you."

"Just tell me her bloody name."

"Very well. Her name is Madeleine Van Rowen."

Nine

Sharp pops of gunfire, screams, and the sound of breaking glass.

Maddy sighed as she finally reached La Marais. *Ah, home sweet home. . . .*

Though the distance across the Channel from Dover to Calais was only twenty miles, the crossing usually proved grueling. Her return had been no exception. For the better part of a day, the small steamer—a floating tub awash in vomit and choking coal smoke—had labored against treacherous currents and boiling gales.

Then, in the third-class train car from Calais to Paris, miners and garishly dressed confidence men had leered at her—and very nearly fleeced her. For some reason, every time she rode in a train she dropped off, asleep in seconds if she didn't battle it.

Even knowing her fellow travelers would steal from her, she'd begun her familiar cycle of blinking her lids, then jerking awake, as though one of those mesmerists from *le théâtre* whispered in her ear, luring her down. Luckily, she'd escaped unscathed, but as usual, she was in a torpor for hours after the train, groggy and lethargic.

And after she'd completed those arduous travels, she was rewarded with . . . La Marais.

Her cab rolled to a jerky stop in front of her ancient tenement building. Centuries ago, this area had been the playground of kings, and her building, with its slate roof and high Gothic style, had probably been a lord's mansion in the sixteen hundreds. Yet it had since been sectioned off into cheap boarding rooms, and like the entire area, it had been ravaged by time and marked by decay.

As soon as she stepped from the cab, Maddy heard the unmistakable, heavily accented English of her two nemeses, the sisters Odette and Berthé Crenate.

"Miss High-and-Mighty Madeleine's returned," Odette called from their stoop across the street, fluffing her titian-dyed hair. "And in a cab, too. No omnibus for her."

When the driver lugged Maddy's trunk from the rear boot, Berthé added, "Careful, driver, she'll try to get you to take her trunk up—and she's *au sixième*."

Maddy swung a glare at the sisters. They loved to ridicule her sixth-floor home. In Paris, the highest floors were reserved for the poorest—her building only went to six.

"*Au sixième?*" the man asked with raised eyebrows and an outstretched palm. After Maddy paid him, he drove off without a backward glance.

Fantastic. Somehow she had to get the trunk up one hundred and two stairs. In an unlit stairwell.

"*La gamine* has her work cut out for her," Odette added, snickering.

Maddy stilled, balling her hands into fists. *Gamine* meant "imp" or "urchin," but it also meant "street child." She loathed it when they called her that.

Just as she was about to wade into the fray, Maddy heard from behind her, "Berthé, Odette, *fermez vos bouches*." Maddy turned to find her friend Corrine emerging from the dark building, descending the front steps. Corrine, a fellow expatriate Englishwoman, was like a mother to her. Years before, when Maddy had had nowhere else to go, Corrine had taken her in.

Grabbing one end of the trunk, Corrine raised her eyebrows and waved Maddy on to pick up the other. With a sigh, Maddy did, and together they wound around the harmless drunks snoozing on the stoop. Inside, they entered the tunnel-like stairwell. Maddy had climbed the rickety steps to her room in the pitch blackness so often that she didn't even have to use the rope that acted as a banister.

Once they reached her landing and dropped the trunk, Blue-Eyed Beatrix swung open her apartment door directly across from Maddy's. Whenever Bea heard the board at the stair-head groan, she hurried out, hoping either Maddy or Corrine was leaving the building and would fetch her goods from outside—any of the three Cs she lived on: coffee, croissants, and cigarettes—so she wouldn't have to make the journey down the stairs more than twice a day.

Bea was a prostitute, known in La Marais as Bea the Whore. Maddy found the name offensive; moreover, it really was useless in a definitive sense, considering that most of the females here—like Berthé and Odette—were prostitutes as well.

Maddy had begun to call her Blue-Eyed Bea because of her pretty eyes, but this had proved eerily prophetic. Maurice, the man Bea had fallen in love with, had a nasty habit of giving her black eyes—or "blue eyes" as the people in La Marais called them. She had one right now.

"How did you fare, Maddée?" Bea asked breathlessly. "Was the trip a success?"

Maddy was bedraggled, exhausted—and back here. A good wager said *no*. Bea was a bit simple sometimes. "I failed. I told you both he was out of my league." She removed the key ribbon she usually wore around her neck and unlocked the door to her colorful apartment. Scuffing directly to the bed, she fell forward on it. "It was a debacle, all the way around," she muttered against her threadbare cover.

Corrine sat beside her and patted her shoulder. "Let's have some tea, then," she said. "And you can tell us all about it."

Talk about her disastrous trip? What could it hurt? Maddy couldn't feel worse. "Very well. *Faisons du thé*. Lots of tea."

While the water boiled and her friends began unpacking all the dazzling gowns she'd soon have to sell, Maddy drew back her scarlet baize curtains to open the casement windows to her balcony.

She was secretly proud of her home, pleased with what she'd been able to do to it with such limited resources. To conceal the crumbling plaster, she'd pasted a collage of bright playbills and opera posters on the wall. The entire room was awash with sumptuous fabrics, thanks to a friend at *le théâtre* who alerted Maddy whenever a company discarded props and materials. Maddy always got there before the ragpickers.

On her diminuitive balcony, ivy flourished in tin cans and petunias still bloomed. Chat Noir, a fickle rooftop cat owned by no one, was patronizing her balcony to laze in the sun, and a late summer breeze blew, fluttering her wooden wind chimes. Maddy wasn't *au sixième* solely because she was poor. The sour smell permeating the street didn't reach this high, and from her vantage, she could see all the way up to Montmartre over a sea of roofs and a forest of clay chimneys.

When she turned back to the room, the sun caught Bea's face. "Maurice or a client?" Maddy asked, pointing at Bea's puffy eye.

Bea sighed. "Maurice. He gets so angry." Her tone forlorn, she said, "If only I didn't anger him so much."

Corrine and Maddy made disgusted noises, and Maddy bent down to toss pumps at her. There was no convincing Bea that she deserved more, no matter how hard they tried. Though she was lovely and kind, Bea wouldn't believe that anything better than Maurice awaited her.

La Marais had a way of doing that to its inhabitants. Their unofficial motto was *de mal en pire*—"from bad to worse." Their reasoning was that one's situation, no matter how unbearable, could always deteriorate. Especially if one dared aspire to more.

"Best to accept one's lot," they said. To which Maddy inwardly answered, "Fortune favors the bold."

But it hadn't this time for Maddy. . . .

When the tea was ready, they adjourned to her balcony, sitting on milk crates and drinking from mismatched cups. Chat Noir deigned to allow Maddy to pick him up and settle him in her lap. She couldn't help but grin at how hot his fur was as she petted him.

"I thought he was cross with you," Bea said, with a nod at the big tomcat.

"He was. Forsook me for weeks." All she'd done was explain to him that he didn't want *her* for his keeper. He could do better—perhaps even find someone who could afford to feed him more than apple cores.

She stretched her legs out to her iron railing, musing

over how much she'd missed this—the easy camaraderie the three of them shared.

Maddy did enjoy being around Claudia and the Weyland women, but she had so little in common with them now. Bea, Corrine, and Maddy were of a kind—each with her secret sorrows and tragic past.

Like Maddy, Bea had come to La Marais young. Her mother had been married to a poor soldier, and she'd followed his regiment around the world with Bea in tow. To this day, Bea always woke at dawn, and the sound of drums still depressed her spirits. Her own and her mother's food and safety had depended on keeping that soldier alive. They'd managed to until Bea was twelve; then they'd lost everything.

At sixteen, Corrine, an educated English parson's daughter, had married a fancy French tailor traveling through her hometown. "I'm a tailor. I own a shop," he'd said, which—more literally translated—had actually meant, "I live four floors above a shop, I stitch sailcloth for a living, and I spend every centime I earn on gin."

Corrine had had two more husbands since then, each raising the bar for indifference and laziness. She might have tolerated the former but couldn't stand the latter—her work ethic was remarkable. Though she only received rent for *au sixième* and a small pension, she considered the building her personal charge and slaved herself to the bone to fight the decay. Yet she waged a losing battle. Her broom, washrag, and near ceaseless labor were no match against time and neglect.

"Are you awake enough yet, Maddée?" Bea asked. "Won't you tell us what happened with your Englishman?"

Maddy was only halfway through her cup, so she opted for a brief summary. "I went to London, I flirted and cajoled, but he simply didn't want to marry—much less marry me. As I suspected," she added a bit pointedly, since they'd browbeaten her to go. Maddy had known better—but not because of the law of *de mal en pire*, she hastily assured herself. No, simple reasoning said that if Quin was rich and cultured, and she was uneducated and lived in a gutter, then there was no future between them. "He told me just two nights ago that he wasn't the marrying kind."

"I hate it when they say that," Bea murmured, and Corrine raised her cup in agreement.

Though Maddy had thought the memory of the Scot would be too fresh, too raw, she found herself saying, "But there was another man. . . ."

"And?" Corrine prompted.

"He was a tall, strapping Highlander whom I met at a masquerade ball. We had this . . . this *je ne sais quoi*, a connection—a strong one, I believed." Since that night, she'd thought about him at every hour, no matter how hard she tried to put that man from her mind. "And I don't even know his name."

"*Le coup de foudre*," Bea said, nodding enthusiastically.

"Love at first sight?" Maddy gave a humorless laugh. "I thought so. I'd *known* so after strong punch and his sinful kisses."

Bea's eyes lit up. "Oh, Maddée, you finally took a lover, *non*?"

Maddy sighed, then explained everything that had happened, before finishing, ". . . and after that, he tossed money at me like I was a pesky problem to be resolved and abandoned me in the cab."

"It won't be painful like that again," Bea assured her. "The first time is always the worst, and if he was *très viril* . . ."

Maddy knew that had to be true, but she still feared what her next experience might be like—though she could say with certainty it wouldn't be with anyone *très viril.* "On my trip back here, I decided if I'm never with another man again, it will be too soon." Affecting indifference, Maddy briefly raised her face to the sun, courting freckles on her nose, but she didn't care. "He turned out to be an ass, anyway. I wouldn't want him if he begged me to marry him."

"What about your instincts?" Corrine asked. "Surely you were warned away if he was so terrible?"

"My instincts told me he was . . . good." She didn't miss that Bea and Corrine shared a look. Corrine never rented a room to a male unless Maddy gave approval.

"Why didn't you tell your London friends of your plight?" Corrine asked.

"I thought about it. I imagined revealing all over tea and scones. I would begin with the setup: 'Well, the thing of it is . . . after Papa died, my mother and I didn't move to Paris because she'd missed her birthplace—we fled creditors in the middle of the night. After a year in a slum, she did marry a rich man, named Guillaume, and for a while we lived in the wealthy part of Paris—what you believe is my current address and my present situation. But it's not now! I pay the maid there to save my mail for me and tell visitors I'm away.'

"Then would come the denouement: 'Sylvie died years ago, and my miserly *oncle* Guillaume tossed me out on my ear. Actually, I live in a slum teeming with danger and filth. I'm really an orphan, and not in the exciting sense of an heiress orphan but in the penniless pitiful sense. Because I couldn't *steal* enough to pay for the dresses and paste jewels necessary for my plot to ensnare Quin, I borrowed money from a lender who will happily break my arms over a late payment.'"

Corrine pursed her lips and sniffed, "Well, when you put it that way . . ."

Bea added, "Oh, Maddée, *c'est déplorable*!"

As if bored by Maddy's dramatics, Chat Noir deserted her with a yawn. He leapt to the railing, sidling along, drawing Maddy's gaze down to the street. Two burly men had just arrived at the building. "Are those Toumard's men?" she asked without looking back. "Who else besides me would be foolish enough to get involved with Toumard?"

She'd borrowed heavily—for more than she could make in a year with sporadic work selling cigarettes, serving in the cafés, betting *mutuels*, or picking pockets. When she turned back, she saw that their expressions were pensive. "What is it?" Maddy asked. "Tell me. My day can't possibly get worse."

"Come, then, let's go in so they can't spot us," Corrine said. They grabbed their milk crates and hurried inside. "Maddy love, those henchmen came round yesterday, too. They were searching for you, demanding to be let into the building. We're keeping it locked at all times."

"And I will only see regulars!" Bea added with an earnest nod.

"They were here already?" Maddy pinched her forehead. "I'm not even late."

"They said Toumard raised his rates. The interest is escalating each week."

Maddy sank onto her bed again. "But why?"

"You know how gossip spreads around here," Corrine said. "You went into debt to buy a new wardrobe, and then you left town. Everyone figured a cull was happening. Berthé or Odette probably told him, and he could be betting on your success."

But even after delivering the news, Corrine was still

wringing her lye-eaten hands. Beatrix had begun studying her chipped cup.

"What else?" Maddy forced a smile. "I can take it." She could find a way to weather bad news. Somehow she always did.

Corrine hesitantly said, "Toumard might have another agenda. He might not be keen on getting paid back at all."

Maddy swallowed. She'd heard that was how Berthé and Odette had gotten started in their present line of work. They were barmaids who'd owed money. Instead of getting their arms broken, they'd gone into a more lucrative trade—facilitated and overseen by Toumard.

Corrine set her cup aside. "If we can't come up with the money . . ."

Bea's eyes started watering. "Maddée will have to flee for her life."

"No, Bea, no," she rushed to assure her. "*Maddée's* not fleeing anywhere. I have all this under control. I'm going to marry the count."

Le Daex was her mother's only legacy to her, the alliance having been arranged by her years ago. Maddy was supposed to have wed him when she'd turned *fourteen*—but her mother had died just before then, Maddy had balked, and that's when Guillaume had kicked her out.

"But you told me you sense Le Daex is a bad man," Corrine said. "And there are those rumors. . . ."

Maddy stifled a shiver. "No, no. I will outwit Le Daex, outlive him, and inherit." She'd heard his last three wives had entertained similar aspirations before dying under mysterious circumstances. "Then we'll all be rich, and we'll leave La Marais for good. Everything will be fine. You'll see."

Ten

Maddy lived in a ruthless world.

Growing up in La Marais, she'd made observations—she'd learned her environment. And she'd quickly comprehended that here, for most, civility and ethics had been stripped away, until nothing remained but the pursuit of elemental needs—food, shelter, intercourse—and the overwhelming drive to avoid death and pain.

The latter had compelled her to don her last gown, trudge down one hundred and two steps, and begin making her way to Le Daex's. She couldn't afford the omnibus fare to the count's, so she walked. She didn't need to be walking—she was losing weight already, after just a week back—and she'd had to take in her clothes, including this last fine gown she owned.

Each day in La Marais, Maddy made countless decisions, and the stakes were high. At every turn, her choices could lead her to reward—or fate would ruthlessly check her.

Each night before she went to sleep, she catalogued her actions for the day, analyzing them for weaknesses or exposures. She would ask herself, *Did I do anything today to leave myself vulnerable . . . ?*

Marrying a man like Le Daex would be one of her most critical moves, yet she would do it to avoid Toumard's punishments—or plans. She'd sold her other gowns and paste jewels, but she hadn't been able to keep up with the man's demands for money. His lackeys hounded her more and more.

Out on the street, Maddy passed the usual prostitutes in the usual alleyways, perched on their knees servicing clients. The pained expressions on the men's faces had always fascinated her. The young ones, usually dressed in regimental uniforms, pleaded with the tarts not to stop. The older ones commanded them not to. Maddy had always wondered what could be so pleasurable that they feared its incompletion so much.

The Scot had certainly made sure he'd completed his, by his own hand. She stumbled, nearly catching the hem of her dress.

With him, she'd had a taste of passion and had begun to understand more about the scenes she witnessed routinely. At night, when she was alone in her bed, she recalled the pleasure he'd given her—before the pain. Even after he'd hurt her so terribly, she thought of him—more than of Quin, whom she'd failed to snare.

As the neighborhood grew higher in elevation and therefore more expensive, she passed the boulangerie shop that was the bane of her existence. As was her custom, she stopped to stare through the window.

The warmed shelves were piled with glazed treats, begging her to come liberate them. Inside, behind the counter, were the downtrodden ice creams jailed in a patented ice cream freezer. Alas, she'd never figured out how to pocket goods that melted or flaked apart with the merest touch.

Leering at the food was only an appetizer of anguish for her. Maddy's true torment was watching the young bourgeoisie wives sitting inside. Her hungry gaze drifted to a group of them now.

They were her age and happy, gossiping and glancing over fashion plates, leaving food untouched. Some had gurgling babies in perambulators with silver teething rings, and all of them probably had respectable husbands at home—men they could adore and be adored by in return, men who would protect them and their children.

Maddy envied them so bitterly that her eyes watered and her stomach churned with it.

I would give anything to be one among those women. Anything.

She coveted everything they had. She wanted a happy, well-fed baby of her own whom she could love and care for, much better than her own self-serving mother had cared for her. Maddy wanted to wear a watch pinned to her bodice to check if it was time to meet her husband back at their warm, secure home. She wanted to read fashion magazines—not to *dream* about a new wardrobe but to *plan* one.

Maddy admittedly sought a rich husband, but not for the reasons everyone supposed. Precious jewels and baubles were welcome, but incidental. She yearned for the safety and security money would bring to her—and to the family she imagined of having.

She'd turned her matrimonial focus to the very rich because those men were in less danger of losing everything, as her own father had. Her papa had been dearer to her than anyone, always striving to make up for her mother's lack of affection, but the fact remained that he'd left his daughter defenseless in a world that seemed to lie in wait, ready to punish any misstep she might make. . . .

The old boulangerie shopkeeper eyed Maddy through the window. Though she was dressed in her costly gown, he recognized her and glared. He put on a grandfatherly face to paying customers, but he was hateful to her, chasing her away with a broom on more than one occasion. She gave him a lewd gesture, turning on her heel and continuing on her way.

A single woman in La Marais dreaming about a stable home life with a passel of children and a decent husband to safeguard them all was beyond ridiculous. She might as well yearn for a tree that bloomed gold.

But even worse, Maddy still believed in . . . love.

Even after her parents' ill-fated May-December union, and even after seeing the twisted relationships in the garret, Maddy still longed for a man to love her.

In a ruthless world, dreams like hers were liabilities. . . .

In lieu of them, she'd take Le Daex and the luxury of not having her arms broken.

Ethan peered down at the informant whose throat he clenched, regarding him pitilessly. He released his grip enough for the man to gasp a breath, and then he squeezed harder. "Still saying that's all you know about Grey?"

The bug-eyed man nodded as best as he could, and Ethan finally released him, leaving him in a collapsed heap in an alleyway.

He strode back inside the Lake District tavern from which he'd plucked that man earlier. But this time he took a seat at a back table, sinking into the shadows to contemplate all he'd learned in the last week.

In his inexhaustible hunt, Ethan had ridden hundreds

of miles and had thrashed so many informants that his knuckles stung. He'd discovered that Grey might indeed be afflicted with a hunger for opium, but he was far from being out of his mind—Grey had secretly reached England, surprising them all.

Yet then the man had made the critical mistake of viciously knifing a woman in the Network. Grey's preferred weapon was his blade, and the brutality of the killing had alerted Ethan to his whereabouts. . . .

Grey was already on Hugh's trail.

Ethan had to be faster than Grey, better. He'd always managed to be in the past, though they'd been closely matched adversaries, each with his own talents.

Grey relied on technique; Ethan on brute strength. Grey spoke four languages with flawless native fluency and was eerily brilliant with strategic matters, but there was a reason he'd become so lethal with a blade—with a gun, he couldn't hit the broad side of a barn.

Ethan would take his humble street smarts and his aim any day.

Weyland considered Grey the most talented natural killer he'd ever encountered; Ethan was deemed the most doggedly brutal and relentless in pursuit. . . .

Ethan knew he was closing in on the man now, but he hadn't been able to force Grey into the open. So he'd decided to anticipate Grey's moves.

Hugh had taken Jane to Ethan's remote lake house just a few miles north of this tavern, to stay for a few days before traveling to Scotland. Grey would likely have uncovered information about the residence by now and would pursue her there, but the place was most readily accessible from the ferry that ran from this very tavern. Otherwise, it would take days to go north and circle back south to get to the estate. This tavern was the portal, and Ethan would act as sentinel here, waiting for Grey to come to him.

The trap had been baited; Ethan *felt* he was close.

As if there wasn't enough pressure to kill Grey, Edward Weyland had demanded that Hugh and Jane enter into a hasty marriage of convenience before they'd departed together. Hugh hadn't reacted particularly well to denying himself Jane ten years ago. Now, after being near her constantly, bloody married to her . . . Hugh was going to lose his mind.

After the lake house, Hugh planned to go to the Highlands to hide out at their brother Courtland's ramshackle estate. If Ethan couldn't catch or kill Grey, then he at least wanted to buy time for Hugh to escape with Jane. Hugh would travel by horse into the Scottish forests. He was an expert rifleman and hunter, the wilderness his element. . . .

Ethan's thoughts were interrupted when he spied Arthur MacReedy and his barely bewhiskered son entering the tavern. *Of all the people.*

Ethan recalled then that the MacReedy family had a hunting lodge in the Lake District and spent the fall at leisure in this area. Ethan knew a lot of things about the MacReedys—he'd been a day away from marrying Arthur's daughter, Sarah.

Meeting up with them now was a timely reminder of when Ethan had ignored the curse and sought to have a normal life, to take a bride, and try to father an heir.

To get past what had been done to him.

His planned marriage to her had in no way been a love match—he and Sarah had never met until the days leading up to the ceremony—but the union had made sense.

Sarah had been a renowned beauty, and Ethan had been a wealthy young laird. Everything was supposed to have been settled—until the night before their wedding, when she'd stood at a high turret of his family's ancient hold. She'd gazed at his face, at his newly healed scar, alternately with pity and disgust.

He reached out his hand and rasped, "You doona have to marry me, Sarah. . . ."

"Kavanagh," MacReedy the elder said, nodding at him once, respectfully—as he should.

In return, Ethan cast the man the menacing expression he deserved. MacReedy and his son walked on.

When the barmaid finally sauntered over to Ethan's table, she averted her eyes, no doubt thinking that with eye contact, he would proposition her. After all, a man with a face like his would have to be paying for it.

He was sick of the furtive looks or horrified glances women always cast him. What he wouldn't give for a woman to look him full in the face and address the fact that he was scarred, maybe even say, "How did you receive such an injury?" He would never reveal the truth, of course, but he wanted to experience what it would be like simply to have the subject on the table for once.

Without facing him, the barmaid asked him what he wanted to drink or eat. He declined curtly, though he was tempted to snap, "As if I'd have you. Just five nights ago, I took a woman who would shame you."

And there his thoughts turned to Madeleine yet again—Madeleine *Van Rowen.* Ethan had barely hidden his amazement when Quin had revealed the girl's identity, though the connection wasn't improbable. The Weylands had a family seat near Iveley Hall, the former Van Rowen manor—which Ethan had seized at Van Rowen's death. It made sense that upper-class families like theirs in the same county would associate.

Yet Ethan could scarcely believe he'd slept with the girl, the *Maddy* referred to on that night—the one mention that had turned the tide of Ethan's fate, putting Van Rowen in a fury.

Learning Madeleine's identity had made Ethan reevaluate the entire night of the masquerade. The morning after, he'd practically convinced himself that she'd been innocent of any deceit. He'd only recognized how truly devious she'd been, how arrogant, when he'd discovered that she was the child of two of the most vile people he had ever imagined.

Ethan had always heard that those in desperate situations behaved in unpredictable ways. This had not been so for the Van Rowens. They had been so easily manipulated that Ethan's revenge hadn't satisfied whatsoever.

Van Rowen had already been in financial straits. He'd leveraged all his lands and investments to pay for his much younger wife's jewels and silks, frantic to keep her happy.

Working insidiously, Ethan had bought up the man's loans, forcing himself to act slowly, though he'd burned to make them pay. He had never let them know he'd been the catalyst for their ruin, and they'd never suspected a young Scot could destroy a powerful English landholder.

So many accused Ethan of being unfeeling. In truth, he felt too strongly—always had—and Ethan's hatred for the Van Rowens had boiled over into every aspect of his life. He'd tried to let the revenge go when he'd won—when Van Rowen and Brymer had been killed, and Sylvie left penniless.

Ethan had thought his work had dulled some of the rage, but his encounter with Madeleine made him realize the same fury still simmered.

Now he knew why her accent was tinged with French. The final report he'd received on Sylvie and her daughter several years ago had had them living in a Parisian slum called La Marais.

Some digging had uncovered that Sylvie had actually hailed from that place, and Ethan had been gratified to learn that she'd fled back there. She deserved to root about a slum, and any spawn of hers and Van Rowen's could keep her evil, deceitful arse company in misery, as far as Ethan had been concerned.

Instead, the widowed Sylvie had married a rich Parisian; Quin's current address for Madeleine was in the well-heeled parish of St. Roch. If Sylvie lived there now and could clothe her daughter in such an affluent way, teaching her airs, then obviously she hadn't been punished enough.

The woman had brazenly dispatched her daughter to England to secure Quin while enjoying a backup proposal from the aging Count Le Daex, a man so rich that his wealth outstripped even Ethan's. The thought of Sylvie benefiting from a match like that sickened Ethan.

Worse was the idea of Le Daex enjoying young Madeleine. Ethan's hands clenched.

He exhaled a breath and forced himself to relax. Before he'd left, Ethan had thought it imperative that Le Daex discover what his fiancée had been doing behind his back in London on a particularly wild night.

Insidious dealings—Ethan excelled at them, and he happened to have many contacts in Paris.

There'd be no rich count for the grasping Van Rowens.

And yet, despite knowing what blood ran through Madeleine's veins, Ethan's desire for her refused to wane. If anything, it grew worse each day. Filled with conflicting thoughts, he was uncertain what his next move should be.

Damn it, he needed to focus—he could decide what to do about her later. He rose from the table, stepping out a side door into the night air.

When two passing boys froze at the sight of his face, he scowled, making them run.

Madeleine would react the same way.

Movement from the corner of his eye drew his gaze up—

Davis Grey stood on a balcony across the street, his gaunt face creased into a smile, his brows raised, no doubt dumbfounded by Ethan's uncommon carelessness. The man's pistol was already drawn and cocked.

What the hell have I done . . . ? Rage consumed Ethan as he snatched his own pistol and fired.

Too late. Pain exploded in Ethan's chest, the bullet driving home.

Eleven

"*I'm doomed*," Maddy whispered to herself as she wandered La Marais in the dark in a silk ball gown.

Oh, what was she thinking? She was always doomed in varying degrees. Why had she ever thought she would get a concession from fate? One bloody bit of luck?

"I'm *more* doomed than usual," she amended. Toumard's pair lay in wait in the alley beside her building, forcing her to roam the streets until they gave up. She was in debt, with no prospects to pay them, and the one thing she'd possessed of value—her virtue—had been wasted with a laughable return.

And now she would pay for that wild, reckless night.

Because the count had heard from a contact in London, who'd heard from another, that his prospective bride had been free with herself, running with a fast crowd in London. The hypocrite! He'd demanded an examination to determine if she was still a virgin or possibly carrying another man's babe, as if these were the medieval times the ancient count had likely grown up in.

Maddy hadn't even known that people actually did that anymore. She'd been tempted to huff and whine, "But I was wearing my chastity belt!" Instead, she'd blankly refused his demand—trying to sound outraged, instead of baffled at the timing—and he'd withdrawn his proposal.

Refused by the count. He might as well have slapped her.

Worse, she'd allowed it to happen. She'd managed men for years and knew dozens of ways she could have finessed the situation, ways to wriggle and finagle to get what she wanted. She could cry at the drop of a hat and could have acted overwrought at his capriciousness. If that tactic hadn't worked, she could have adopted a seductive demeanor, or simply made sure she was examined by a bribable physician. And yet . . .

She *hadn't*.

Did I do anything today to leave myself vulnerable?

A bit.

As though she'd been outside her own body, she'd heard the words spilling from her lips: "I never wanted to marry you anyway! And your wig smells fusty."

She'd burned her ships. Why? She was never so foolish—except with the Scot.

Maddy should never have gone to England. Returning to her native land after such a long exile had made her miss it even more. She had been arrogant and rash there, and apparently she hadn't left those traits behind.

"Oh, please, just *one* crumb of fortune!" she whispered urgently to the sky. As if in answering jest, she spied thunderclouds swelling, obscuring the stars. Where would she go if it rained? Not all drunks on stoops were as passive as her building's collection. They could be ferociously territorial.

The air was thick and damp, presaging the storm. Maddy hated storms. Every tragedy in her life had been accompanied by thunderclaps and pounding rain.

The morning her father's second had come to report his death in a duel, lightning had punctuated the man's words.

The day of her father's funeral, rain had spilled in torrents. When Maddy and her mother had returned from burying him, they'd been turned away, their home of Iveley Hall having been seized by creditors while they'd been gone.

Though one ring or brooch could have kept them for years, it was considered in poor taste to wear jewelry to a funeral, so they'd fled with nothing more than the clothes on their backs. As they'd ridden away, Maddy had looked back at the manor through the rain-streaked window of the coach and known she would never find a way to return home. . . .

The fire that had nearly taken her life when she was eleven had raged, whipped to a frenzy by the fierce winds of a storm, yet barely dampened by the scattered bouts of rain. Maddy had been trapped inside the small apartment she and her mother shared several floors up. She'd been convinced she would die even before a burning beam had fallen on her and fractured her arm.

When she'd finally battled her way through the flames to reach the window, Maddy had blinked against the smoke, gaping in incomprehension down at the street.

Her mother—obviously one of the first ones out—stood outside.

In that moment of flames and terror, Maddy had thought, *I'm as good as alone.*

To this day, she had nightmares filled with fire that always ended in that gut-wrenching recognition. . . .

Maddy jerked, startled, when the sky opened up. As the rain poured, she ran beneath the closest cover, a chestnut tree.

And laughed until she wept when the leaves began to fall on her in clumps.

* * *

Clawing the cobblestones in pain, Ethan lay in a pool of his own blood funneling from his upper chest. He cracked open his eyes, realizing he'd released his hold on his pistol when he'd fallen. As he listened for Grey's approach, he heard people filing out from the front of the tavern.

Gritting his teeth, Ethan swept his hand to the side until he brushed his gun. Stretching his arm, his very fingers, he glanced his fingertips off the handle, spinning it—

Too late. He looked up to find that Grey had a bead on him, gun raised. As Grey approached Ethan, his demeanor was as pleasant as ever. With his free hand, Grey poked his finger through a still-smoking hole in his shirt and jacket, and grinned. Ethan's bullet had only hit a deceptive billow in the man's bagging clothes.

"And people said you were better than I?" Grey said.

I was for ten years. . . . Ethan tasted blood in his mouth and knew he was about to die, even if Grey didn't plug another bullet into him. "Hugh will destroy you," Ethan said, choking out the words.

Grey shrugged. "So everyone keeps assuring me. And yet, I'd always believed it would be you."

The tavern's nearby side door creaked open, and noise and dim light spilled out into the alley. Grey glanced up, then faced Ethan once more, furtively stowing his pistol. "That's a kill shot, old friend, and we both know it." He cast Ethan his disconcertingly sympathetic smile. "You had to have been thinking about a woman earlier with an expression like that." He turned to lope away, saying over his shoulder, "I hope she was worth it."

Ethan rolled to his side for his gun, biting back an agonized yell, but Grey had already disappeared.

Though Ethan couldn't see who'd exited the tavern out the side door, he could hear them.

Grimacing to the clouded night sky above, Ethan listened as the MacReedys sodding *debated* whether to help him or not: *"I'll no' get dragged into trouble."*; *"We do owe him."*; *"He's turned into a blackguard."*; *"Think he might've deserved the shot?"*

"Warn my brother," Ethan grated to them, blood spilling from his mouth, but they ignored him. His body was beginning to shudder with cold. "*Listen to me. . . .*" They didn't.

He had failed Hugh utterly. Never had Ethan been so careless, walking into the street without even a cursory scan of the vantages surrounding him. He was dying, and he had only two thoughts—getting a warning to his brother . . . and the fact that he'd never get to see that damned little witch again.

Ethan perceived hands under his arms, and braced for the pain as they lifted him, but he still blacked out. . . .

He had no idea how long he'd been unconscious, but when he came to, he was in a bed, with a shaky-handed surgeon removing the bullet while others held Ethan down. He roared with agony as the man plucked metal and charred cloth from the wound then splashed whisky into it.

Before he began stitching, the doctor tossed back half the bottle down his own throat. "I did what I could," he said when he finished.

"Will he live?" the MacReedy whelp asked.

In and out of consciousness, Ethan caught the doctor's parting words: "Let's put it this way. If he recovers from a wound like that and the fever to follow . . . I'll quit drinking."

Twelve

"I'm beginning to wonder if anyone has even noticed the blackguard's missing," MacReedy the elder said. "It's possible no one's coming for him."

"Aye," the whelp replied in a distracted tone.

"Bugger off, you weak-kneed old bastard," Ethan growled, ready to claw at the gaudily papered walls after five weeks of being trapped in the MacReedys' lodge. "You think I canna hear you?"

He could. Every day as he lay bedridden, slowly recuperating, Ethan could hear the sounds of their leisure—the fan of cards shuffled, or the taps as MacReedy emptied his pipe or their dominoes connected.

Tap . . . tap . . . tap . . . all bloody day long, until Ethan thought he'd go mad.

Why has no one come for me? He felt like an unwanted dog tied to a tree, then forgotten.

"Go to hell, MacCarrick!" the whelp replied.

"Where do you bloody think I am?" Clenching his fists in the blanket, he surveyed "his" room. Most closets boasted more space. "You're brave now, but by God, when I'm on my feet again, I'm going to make you eat your goddamned teeth."

A few moments later, MacReedy the elder stepped into

Ethan's small room, eyes grave. "Son, I'm no' going to talk to you about that language again." The first time had been after Mrs. MacReedy's ill-fated attempt to read psalms to Ethan—he had *declined* in language so foul he'd thought he'd heard something burst in her brain before she'd skittered from the room and fainted. "Debt or no', I'll be tossing you out," MacReedy said calmly before stepping out once more.

The debt. Always back to the debt with this family. They knew they owed Ethan because he had delivered the completely unbelievable lie that Sarah had slipped instead of jumped, ensuring that she would have no suicide stigma and would receive a Catholic burial. Ethan had also ensured that he would be shadowed for more than a decade by rumors of his pushing her to her death.

MacReedy knew Ethan hadn't lied to protect Sarah's memory for her family; in fact, Ethan blamed them for forcing her into the marriage. And he'd been sure to let them know it every time he encountered them, which fortunately hadn't been often.

Yet now Ethan was trapped in their home.

When he'd awakened from two weeks of delirium, he'd immediately tried to rise, frantic to leave this place and find out what his careless actions had wrought. Was his brother safe? Had Grey gotten him, too?

Ethan had promptly ripped open his wound and blacked out. The consequent stitch repair by the shaky physician had earned Ethan *another* week's worth of fever and guaranteed he'd been even weaker than he had been the first time he'd come to.

Every bloody time he tried to rise and leave this place, he ripped open stitches and passed out. With his height and the size of the cramped room, he invariably knocked his head in the fall, making his total time trapped in bed at over a month and counting.

He'd been forced to *ask* MacReedy to find out if Hugh and Jane had left for Scotland. Ethan had also had to pay the whelp to wire London to report his situation.

MacReedy the elder had learned that Hugh had indeed left the lake house the very night Ethan had been shot. At least there'd been one good thing about Ethan catching that bullet—Grey's waiting to kill Ethan had allowed Hugh to begin his journey north into the Highlands, putting Hugh firmly in his element.

Ethan was confident that his brother was safe for the time being. The problem was that Hugh would be holed up on Court's estate in utter seclusion with the woman he wanted more than anything on this earth—now his temporary wife. At worst, the curse was real, and Hugh would be risking her death and torment. At best, Hugh was still secretly an assassin, massive and stony and awkward around people, such an unfitting match for the celebrated beauty, who loved to socialize.

Not to mention that Hugh took his orders to kill from Jane's own father. . . .

But in the condition Ethan was in, there was nothing he could do to help his brother. The inaction ate at him. He burned with urgency. With nothing to do but think, he stewed, alternately dwelling on his failure and on Madeleine.

Though Ethan had ruined her chances with Le Daex, Ethan couldn't say that she wouldn't find another after so many weeks had passed. She was tempting, and if she was provided with a large enough dowry, a man could be moved to overlook her lack of virtue.

Ethan had shown mercy to Grey and look what had happened. He would not make the same mistake twice by allowing Sylvie to go unscathed.

When he was finished with Grey, Ethan would lure Madeleine away from Sylvie back to one of his more obscure estates, with an offer of security in a mutually beneficial arrangement. Or, if she proved stubborn, he was not above promising marriage, with no intention of going through with it.

He wondered if her parents had warned her about a scarred, black-haired Scot, but he doubted it. Sylvie lacked the imagination to make the connection. Van Rowen had been eaten with shame and guilt over the incident and likely wouldn't have spoken of it before his death six months later.

In any case, it wouldn't matter if the girl had been warned. Ethan would have her one way or another. He'd been disfigured—the exquisite daughter offered up would appease him. Once she was in his possession, he'd use her until he tired of her.

Then he would throw her out, thoroughly ruined, on her pert little arse, saving countless foolish noblemen from Sylvie's clutches.

Madeleine had told him that his kind used and gave nothing back.

Miss Van Rowen had seen nothing.

Thirteen

For the love of Christ, let it be someone come for me, Ethan thought the next day when he heard a carriage on the drive.

He closed his eyes in relief when he heard Hugh's voice in the front parlor. Though Hugh was usually so silent, Ethan distinctly heard him attempt to make conversation with the MacReedys. He wasn't polished with it, but he seemed to take his fumbles with a light heart.

When Hugh entered, Ethan noticed his brother looked hale and . . . *happy*?

"Ethan, it's good to see you!" he exclaimed as Ethan made a painstaking attempt to sit up in bed. "Grey told me he'd killed you."

Ethan quirked a brow. "So we're talking to Grey now?"

"No, of course no." He grinned. "Those were his last words."

"You . . . killed him." Grey was dead at last? "How?"

After all this time—it wouldn't be *Ethan* who destroyed Grey.

"Well, *I* dinna kill him precisely." Hugh pulled at his collar. "More like Jane and I did it together. It's a long story. I'll tell you on the way back. If you're ready to go home now?"

"What do you think? It's about bloody time someone came for me. I sent a wire weeks ago."

"There was no wire from you. I've searched everywhere—even had runners combing the countryside. That's how we located you here."

"*No wire?*" he bellowed, then heard the whelp take off, slamming out of the house. That was why he'd been stuck? Because the whelp had pocketed the telegraph fee? "I'm going to kill that puny bastard."

"Do it another time. I have to get back to London. Do you need help getting dressed?" When Ethan reluctantly nodded, Hugh helped him to the edge of the bed. "Let me see the damage." He gave a whistle at the sight of Ethan's wound. "That was close. Another inch—"

"And I would no' have been trapped here for five weeks."

"A bullet wound, though? Exactly how slowly were you moving for Grey to be able to hit you?" Hugh asked, and Ethan's fists clenched. "The skin's healing nicely. A couple of weeks more for the stitches—if you're careful with them." Frowning, Hugh said, "Why are you still so weak?"

"Because the food here tastes like sawdust," Ethan said. He'd probably lost a stone of weight.

"That might be, but you're still going to have to thank them for it."

"The hell I will."

Hugh lowered his voice. "If you doona, I will no' tell you how Grey died. And I might just leave your arse here. . . ."

Twenty minutes later, Hugh and his coach driver were heaving Ethan up into his carriage. "That was no' so bad, now, was it?" Hugh grated with a last shove.

Ethan gritted his teeth, collapsing back onto the squabs. "Sod off, Hugh." His wound was singing, his head was spinning, and yet even after being blackmailed into muttering gratitude to that family, excitement drummed in him. Because Ethan had realized that Grey's death meant his duty was done. Ethan was free to go to Paris as soon as he got his strength back.

Suddenly he felt ravenous.

"Now, tell me how the hell Grey died," Ethan said once the coach began to roll along.

Hugh peered out the window as he answered, "Well, Jane plugged him with some arrows, and I . . . tripped him."

Ethan grew still. "Grey died by *tripping*?" This was too humiliating.

"It was worse than it sounds," Hugh said quickly, facing him again. "Gruesome. A trial, truly. So how did Grey get the drop on you?"

"I was careless, and I paid for it." He shrugged, wanting away from that subject. "What else has happened in the last five weeks? Have you gotten your marriage annulled yet?"

"No, I dinna."

Ethan exhaled. "You told me Grey died weeks ago, and you still have no' done this?"

"I'm . . . staying married. Jane is mine now."

"But the curse," Ethan said, scowling at this absurdity. "Your past—"

"She knows about my past, about her father, about everything. Grey was sure to reveal all to her. And of the curse . . . it's no' as we thought, brother. Court's gotten married to Annalía, and, well, he's to be a da."

"No. That's no' possible." Ethan grew light-headed. *Never seed shall take. . . .*

Hugh shook his head. "It's true. Annalía's big with his child. I saw her myself."

"The babe's no' his."

"That's what everyone thought you'd say. Annalía's a good lass, but for your benefit, I'll tell you that Court was her first and only, and that it was just the two of them together for weeks."

Ethan had met Annalía and knew she wouldn't possibly lie about the parentage of her babe—or take another lover besides Court. But still, to have this sole development refute what they'd believed for so long? "So how do you explain why Court's never gotten a bairn on any girl before? And then he does it so quickly with her?"

"Everyone who knows about the book and what's happened agrees that the last two lines of the foretelling must say something about each son finding the woman meant for him."

This was exactly what Ethan had feared—his brothers getting their hopes up, to be crushed. And yet Ethan couldn't argue the reasoning. Many a time, he'd used the book in just such a way as this. "You believe that?"

"I do, Ethan, and I hope you will, too."

"So you feel certain that I can marry and have bairns?" Ethan was unaccountably restless after hearing this news, even as he felt removed from the entire conversation, as if he were watching it instead of participating in it.

"Aye, if you find the right lass. And then you can get back to the life you're meant to lead."

"I am—"

"No, you're no," Hugh interrupted. "You're the Earl of Kavanagh. You've got responsibilities and lands and people. You've got a title to pass down."

"Maybe I'm more satisfied in my current occupation."

"It's no' the life Da wanted for you—no' killing and being shot. And no' being alone nearly every damned day and night of your life," Hugh snapped.

"Just because you and Court have suddenly settled down does no' mean I have the same needs. I like the hunt. I like the danger."

"For how long, Ethan? You're no' getting any spryer. You bloody got tagged by *Grey*."

Ah, that was low, and they both knew it. Ethan narrowed his eyes. "So you think you can just walk away from your job without looking back?"

"Aye, because now I have something to look forward to."

"Have you ever thought that you should no' be staying with Jane for reasons other than the curse, and other than your past?" Ethan demanded. "This all goes back to common bloody sense—something I'm discovering my brothers dearly lack, especially in their choices of brides." He flashed an expression of realization. "Jane's with bairn, is she no'? Apparently, it's quite easy for MacCarricks to propagate these days. That's why you are staying with her? And that's why she had to accept you."

"No, she is no' pregnant. We're waiting." At Ethan's look, Hugh hurriedly said, "*No'* as in abstinence."

"Waiting," Ethan said with a slow nod. "So my mercenary brother has gone off and married an excruciatingly rich heiress and gotten a babe on her, and my other brother is practicing contraception like a radical. Let me guess, her idea?"

"*Our* idea. And I have thought over my marriage, Ethan.

For weeks, I agonized over keeping Jane or no'. Every time I tell someone I married Jane Weyland, they laugh, thinking I'm jesting." Hugh frowned, muttering, "That's grown wearying quickly."

"It *is* laughable," Ethan said, never one to palliate his words. "She's a famed beauty and wit, with an enormous extended family. You canna stand to be around groups of people and rarely talk to most."

"Aye, I know. But she is happy being my wife—turns out she's wanted to marry me since she was a girl." Hugh sounded so bloody proud. Ethan had to admit he'd never have suspected that from Jane. "And I'm making an effort for her."

"A man canna change his nature," Ethan said.

"No, no' often," Hugh replied. "But I believe when men like us do, the change is profound."

"What's that supposed to mean?"

"Take Court. He was almost as selfish as you are, but now he's different."

Ethan didn't bother denying he was selfish, but he said, "Aye, take Court. Another example of a ridiculous match. Annalía's an heiress—Court does no' have two guineas to his name. And he's a bloody mercenary while she could no' be more genteel. How's he to support her? Leave her at home with a new bairn while he marches off to wage war for money?"

"He's retired."

Ethan gave a humorless laugh. "They'll starve. And they'll do it at his run-down manor in the middle of the Highlands—unless he lives off her." He scowled deeply. "The hell that will be happening. I'll settle money on him before he becomes the first MacCarrick to live off his wife."

"No, when he was on his last campaign, I reinvested for him what he had managed to save," Hugh said. "Court actually has a steady income now. And when Jane and I were hiding out at his property—waiting for *you* to kill Grey—we needed something to do, so we renovated the manor house. Put it this way—I saw work as the only thing I could do to keep my hands from Jane. Trust me, Court's home is a bloody showplace now. And Annalía loves it there."

"And how long will that last? How long can it? You two baffle me. I thought my brothers had more sense than this."

"If what I enjoy now is due to senselessness, then I doona want sense." Hugh sank back, appearing to have given up on convincing Ethan. "You will no' understand, you canna, until you feel it, too. It's like trying to impress upon a virgin what sex is like."

And with one word, Ethan's mind was back on Madeleine. He'd been doing so well. At least ten minutes had passed since the last time.

Wait . . . Ethan narrowed his eyes. "I hate it when people make asinine arguments like that. That's like our mother telling us that we could no' comprehend—or forgive—her behavior toward us after Da died, until we'd been in love." When she'd said that, Ethan had replied, *"Bullshite. I doona have to jump off a bloody bridge to understand the landing will prove disagreeable."*

Ethan could never forgive her for her actions. There was no excuse for the woman to have blamed her sons for Leith's death, no excuse for reacting so irrationally. She'd screamed, tearing at her hair, uttering things that could never be taken back. . . .

Hugh said, "No, Ethan, she was right."

"Of course you agree—now that you've been inducted

into the cult of marriage. I canna decide if I'm amused or disgusted by all this."

Hugh stared out the window, and his tone turned grave. "If I . . . if I lost Jane, I could no' predict my actions, but I know I would no' be verra concerned with watching what I said."

"I've decided. Disgusted."

"Have you never thought about marrying?"

"No, never. I thought we were no' *supposed* to, and to say my personality isn't favorable to it is an understatement." Ethan sounded so sure, but now, for the first time in his life, doubts on the subject had begun to creep into his thoughts. Both of his brothers were wed and sounded happy, and apparently, the curse wasn't as they'd believed.

Ethan had heard that a man's life flashed before him just before he died. Ethan had been on the verge, and nothing had flashed before him—but then, he'd had few meaningful moments in his adulthood. He'd never had friendships like Court had with his band of mercenaries. Ethan had never felt the selfless love for one woman that his brother Hugh had for years.

That night in the alley, Ethan had believed he was going to die—and he'd realized how pointless his life had been. And for some reason, at such a critical time, he'd thought of that lass. . . .

After a quarter of an hour of silence passed between them, Hugh said, "What are you going to do when we arrive in the city?"

"Ready for a trip to Paris." Unfortunately, he'd need to spend a few days in London before setting off. He'd eat and regain his strength, healing more as he arranged the logistics of his plan.

"What's in Paris?"

"Madeleine Van Rowen."

"*Still* thinking about her?" Hugh raised his brows. "This is interesting."

Ethan shrugged. "Doona read anything into it."

"This is no' still about revenge, is it?"

"And if it is . . . ?" He wanted to finally finish his retribution, to make Sylvie suffer as she was supposed to have. The fact that he would get to enjoy Madeleine in the process was insignificant to his main goal.

Yet even as he assured himself of that, another part of his mind whispered, *You're seizing on this revenge as an excuse to go after her.*

"Because she canna be made to pay for what her parents did." In a low tone, Hugh added, "What if she's the one?"

Ethan jerked, startled. "What? You must be jesting."

"Have you ever thought about another woman as much as you do her?"

Ethan had never, since he'd been old enough to notice females, had one fascinate or frustrate him so badly. "*If* I was convinced of your beliefs on the subject of the curse—which I'm no' saying I am—the fact would no' matter. There could be no union more doomed. It's ridiculous even to contemplate."

"Would you really go despoil an innocent girl to exact more of your revenge?" Hugh looked as if he was praying for Ethan to say the right thing—for Ethan *not* to be the bastard he feared him.

But he was. "No." Ethan paused, letting Hugh relax before adding, "I *already* despoiled her. I took her virtue that night of the masquerade."

"You would no'." Hugh appeared aghast. "You have to marry her."

"The hell I will."

"She's my wife's friend. I will step in, Ethan."

Ethan gave him a menacing sneer. "You think to stop me from enjoying her? *Nothing* will stop me, least of all you."

Hugh studied his face, then he raised his brows. "I see. Well, the picture's becoming clearer."

"What's that supposed to mean?"

"Look at the facts: Madeleine's the first woman you've been with in God knows how long, and you canna stop thinking about her. After all the years you've wanted to kill Grey, now you never will be able to, and something like that would normally consume you. The fact that Grey bested you should rankle as nothing else, much less the fact that *Jane* shot him when you could no'. In the past, you would have made an attempt to thrash that MacReedy whelp even if you had to crawl to do it, but you canna be bothered about anything because all you want to do is get back to *her*."

Refusing to be baited, Ethan said, "I want to enjoy her for a few weeks. Nothing more."

"I wish you all the luck in the world with that, brother," Hugh said, then Ethan thought he heard him mutter, "*Welcome to the cult.*"

Fourteen

This was where Madeleine Van Rowen lived?

Ethan gazed up at the six-story building before him. The dilapidated structure had obviously once been a mansion but now looked as if it would collapse if he put a shoulder to it and leaned. Most surprising, it was in the middle of La Marais, one of the worst slums in Paris.

Madeleine was believed to live on the top floor—usually taken by only the poorest, since continually carrying water and food up the stairs was grueling.

He climbed the front steps to the stoop, then wound around drunken men fixed there in varying stages of unconsciousness. But the door was locked. He'd have to wait her out, or wait for another tenant to open the door. Descending the steps once more, he dropped back to the closest corner. He leaned against a wall and drew his knee up, surveying the world she inhabited.

Men strutted by with machetes or guns visibly secured in their belts. Prostitutes actively solicited—then took their work into every alley. Children ran naked and grubby in the streets.

It reminded him of the rookeries in London, except this was more harrying, more chaotic. If Madeleine truly lived here, then every day she passed this madness, was *part* of it.

He tried to picture her here among these street people, elegant and fragile in her blue gown, and he couldn't whatsoever. Nor could he believe that Madeleine had chosen to live in this place over the luxury of St. Roch. He could too easily imagine Sylvie hearing the rumors about Madeleine in London and punishing her daughter for failing to secure either Quin or the count. So why hadn't Ethan found Madeleine clawing at the door in St. Roch begging for entrance . . . ?

Just this morning, Ethan had arrived in Paris, a full ten days after leaving the MacReedys'. Once he'd checked into a hotel, he'd begun his search for her in St. Roch, at the address Quin had given him.

Ethan hadn't wanted Sylvie to see him, so he'd asked around the neighborhood, to uncover if Madeleine was even in town, or possibly where her favorite haunts were.

No one had any idea who he was talking about until he'd described Madeleine.

A gardener thought she came by the house a couple of times a month. A groomsman had caught an omnibus with her a week ago. She hadn't gotten off at the last stop before the slums. He'd remembered wondering why a woman like her had continued on.

Ethan had recalled that Sylvie's former address had been in La Marais—and he'd discovered that, for some reason, it was Madeleine's *present* address.

Her trail had been easy to pick up here. It seemed everyone in La Marais knew "Maddy *Anglaise*" or "Maddy *la Gamine*," and they obviously liked her, because they were closemouthed with information concerning her.

A group of older women sitting on a stoop had ignored him, smoking their pipes and chatting—until he'd flashed the diamond ring he'd brought with him in case Madeleine proved . . . averse. When he revealed his plans to wed her, the women couldn't seem to direct him to this building swiftly enough, and they only asked that Ethan remember their names so that Maddy would "*passez le gras,*" or "pass the fat"—give a kickback to the ones who'd assisted in securing her good fortune.

As Ethan waited, he mused that Madeleine might actually be persuaded to come with him. Even after she saw his face. Surely she'd be desperate to leave this place any way she could.

Madeleine Van Rowen beholden to me. He liked that idea—

Ethan tensed when he spotted the door to her building opening. A tall, gray-haired woman with a bucket emerged from the dark interior. She strode around the drunken men fixed on the stoop, seeming not to notice them, then made for a pump not a block away.

The door was easing closed behind her. Fearing Madeleine might have warned others about a tall Scot, he dashed for the entry, then slipped through the doorway. Inside, he made for the pitch-black stairwell, forced to use the rope banister as he climbed blindly. The steps were unsound, the corridor so tight he had to sidle up.

What if she was indeed upstairs? He could see her in mere seconds. . . .

As he alighted on the sixth-floor landing a board groaned beneath him, and a blowsy woman shot out of her room—a whore, by the look of her heavily painted cheeks and lips. A glance behind her confirmed Ethan's guess. In a haze of cigarette smoke, a man lay tied to her bed and blindfolded, turning his head dumbly at different sounds.

Ten minutes in this neighborhood—not to mention in Madeleine's home—had certainly answered Ethan's question about how the lass had learned to fondle him so well. She must see men serviced hourly.

"I'm looking for Madeleine Van Rowen," he told the woman.

"And who are you?" she asked, blinking.

Good, she spoke English. Ethan could speak French but preferred not to, outside of penalty of death.

"Are you the man from London?"

Had Madeleine spoken of him? If so, he couldn't imagine what she'd said. Still, he took a chance. "Aye."

"Which one? The first one or the second?" At his nonplussed look, she said, "The Englishman or the Scot?"

Madeleine must have been talking about Quin. Still thinking about that bastard. "The . . . Scot."

She shut the door behind her, ignoring the man's protests, then clasped her hands, her mien delighted. "Maddée told Corrine and me all about you! The masquerade, *n'est-ce pas*?" She wagged her finger at him. "You were *très mauvais* to our Maddée. But here you've come for her at last!"

Madeleine told her friends all about me? He couldn't imagine what she'd said, or what, in particular, they had deemed *très mauvais*.

She leaned in and said in a conspiratorial tone, "You're just in time, too, with the debts coming due." *What debts?* "I'm *Bea*." Bea was simple, he realized. Kind, but simple. "I'm one of Maddée's good friends."

"Aye, Bea." He feigned a look of recognition. "I've heard much about you."

She patted her hair, pleased. Then she frowned and pointed directly at his face. "Maddée didn't say you were battle-scarred. From the Crimean War, yes?"

"No, no' exactly—" He broke off because she'd already shrugged and turned to another apartment door.

"Maddée's not here just now—out working." She dug in her blouse for a ribbon around her neck with keys strung together. "But I'll let you into her room to wait."

"Perhaps you could direct me to her place of employment?"

"Who can keep up with her? The bridge or the corner. Different taverns and cafés. Who knows?"

He felt his face tighten. "And what exactly does she do?" In the nearly seven weeks since he'd been with her, she'd become destitute. Who knew if she'd succumbed to her neighbor's profession?

At his expression, Bea cried, "Oh, no, Maddée serves drinks or occasionally sells cigarettes." She proudly added, "*Turkish* ones." Then in a chiding tone, she said, "Our Maddée's a good girl. Not *popular* in that way at all."

"Of course," he said smoothly, relieved. "I just doona like that she has to work."

Bea's eyes lit up. "*Exactement!*" she exclaimed, bustling to open the door. "So, here is her room." She smiled widely as she showed him in.

Ethan drew his head back, stunned by the interior.

"Amazing, *n'est-ce pas*?" Bea was right to be proud. Though Madeleine's apartment was basically part of an attic room—the ceiling was slanted until he could barely stand up straight even at the apex, and beams crisscrossed overhead—Madeleine had made it into a fantastical space.

The top floor of an old mansion like this would have been used for servants' quarters or possibly a schoolroom, and there were remnants of the mansion's former glory—elaborate gilt and wainscoting decorated the long, narrow space. Above the wainscoting along the more damaged wall, she'd pasted colorful posters.

Two large windows dominated her bedroom area and were framed by red drapes and fronted by a small balcony outside. Glancing out, he found that she had an unimpeded view of Montmartre. On her balcony, plants grew in profusion and wooden wind chimes clanked.

"Maddée loves to sit out there."

He nodded, then said, "Do you no' need to get back to your . . . friend?"

"He is not going anywhere," she said, stating the obvious with an insouciant wave. "Well, go on, open up."

Ethan unlatched one of the windows, swinging it wide. An unseasonably warm breeze blew, and the chimes began tolling, the curtains fluttering. A black cat leapt inside from the balcony, pawed at Ethan's trousers, then wound around his legs. "Her pet?"

"*Non*, she cannot feed Chat Noir. He doesn't often take to people like this. This is a good sign."

Ethan shrugged. Considering how people universally disliked him, the fact that some animals took to him always surprised him. Indeed, beasties seemed to either love him or hate him.

Turning his attention back to Madeleine's home, he crossed to the second of the two windows. When he found a bucket hanging beside it, he realized Madeleine *didn't* haul water and supplies up those rickety stairs. She pulled them up, and easily too—with two pulleys working in tandem to lighten the load. *Clever girl.*

Past the second window, a velvet curtain cordoned off a ridiculously small wooden tub—but then, she didn't have to fold six and a half feet of body inside it. Atop a simple plank bed was a bedspread, intricately sewn together of rich-looking materials, yet wearing thin.

He'd suspected that perhaps Sylvie had thrown Madeleine out after they'd lost the count. But Ethan felt a sense of permanence here—this was Madeleine's home and had been for some time.

Though pleasing now in the warm afternoon sun, her apartment would prove a hell to heat in the winter. The roof undoubtedly leaked, and many of the panes in the windows were cracked or missing, replaced with thin cloth. Artistic flare wouldn't keep her warm in the coming months.

Another thing he noticed—though she had a stove and kettle, there wasn't a scrap of food but for a single shining apple.

An unfamiliar, heavy feeling constricted his chest. No wonder she'd had that air of weariness about her, one of the tantalizing things that had first drawn him to her. And no wonder she'd been hunting for a rich husband. But why would she endure this destitution for so long when she had a wealthy parent and even wealthier friends?

"Why doesn't she live with her mother?"

Bea blinked again. "She did not tell you?"

"Tell me what?"

From the stairwell, a woman called up, "Bea! Is that you?"

"*Oui*!" she yelled near Ethan's ear. "*C'est moi!*"

"The drunks said a man slipped in—is he one of your regulars?"

"*Non*! I saw no one." To him, Bea whispered, "I have to go now! Corrine would be very upset to know you are here." She sighed. "But then, she does not understand *l'amour* as I do."

In a low tone, Ethan said, "When will Maddy return?"

"I could not say. Best make yourself comfortable. Knock across the hall if you need anything." With that, she left him.

Alone, but for the cat weaving around him, Ethan searched through Madeleine's meager belongings. She had a few dresses, all of them frayed, yet bold in color and design, with a modern look to them. He didn't find clothing fitting for London, but she'd probably already sold that wardrobe. Had she given up the blue gown she'd worn that night with him?

In her chest of drawers—which only boasted two of the four possible drawers—her wee underthings were meticulously folded and overly mended.

He uncovered a stash of contraband in a hollow under a loosened windowsill. Inside, a silk handkerchief enfolded two silver engraved money clips, which she would no doubt have melted down after a waiting period. Also inside was a betting book, and her personal tally had more pluses than minuses. Stacked neatly by the book were coupons for coal and fruits—purchased this last June.

Fascinating. She was a thief, a gambler, and someone who bought discounted coupons in the summer for goods that grew dear in the winter.

After he replaced her belongings, he spied a milk crate beside her bed. Atop it lay fashion periodicals—*Le Moniteur de la Mode* and *Les Modes Parisiennes*—and a book, *The Bohemians of the Latin Quarter: Scenes de la Vie de Bohème.* He frowned, recalling that he'd heard of that book. It contained sketches of "Bohemians," poor artists, as they went about procuring food, drink, and sex. Did Madeleine consider herself one of those artistic garret types? She definitely had talent to have transformed this place.

He exhaled, sinking down on her small bed, with the purring cat quick to follow. Ethan knew he was alone but still glanced around before petting it.

Admitting that his revenge plot had glaring holes, he wondered if Sylvie would even *care* if he took her daughter away out of wedlock. The idea of removing Madeleine from the woman's use no longer seemed to apply. The girl was already very distinctly removed.

Perhaps he should merely walk away.

He picked up Madeleine's pillow and brought it close, wanting her scent. His eyes slid closed in pleasure. No, there'd be no leaving until he had her beneath him again.

Besides, he liked solving mysteries, and if Madeleine's life wasn't a mystery . . .

Decided, he stood and began pacing as if he was . . . nervous. A man of his experience, cynicism, and bitter derision was anxious about seeing the chit again.

Because now she would see his face.

He crossed to stand before the partially cracked mirror hanging above her chest of drawers. Every time she looked into this glass, beauty stared back at her. Regarding his own brutish reflection, he gave a harsh laugh. Beauty and the beast.

But this beast has money, he reminded himself, *something she obviously lacks.*

Dusk was coming soon, so he climbed out onto the balcony, hoping to catch sight of her before the sun went down. He noticed that two neckless bruisers, obviously henchmen, had begun casing the front of the building. Bea had mentioned something about debts. Were the men here for Madeleine?

Ethan rotated his shoulder, testing the stitches in his chest. If he had to fight the two, he might not tear his wound too badly—

The stair head groaned. His entire body tensed with anticipation. He lunged for the door and yanked it open. He found himself staring at Bea, who'd yanked open her own. They frowned at each other across the hall.

The woman he'd seen earlier with the bucket stood at the stair head, only now she carried a broom. Though gray-haired, she had a wholly unlined face, making her age difficult to approximate. "And who might you be in Maddy's room?" she demanded. "Who let you in?"

Out of sight of the woman, Bea was shaking her head frantically, waving her arms.

"I've come for Madeleine. I'm waiting for her here—unless you know where she is."

"You're the Scot! The one who hurt my Maddy!" She changed her grip on the broom, raising it above her. "I'll be damned before I tell you. We're going to get rid of you before she comes back. She has enough on her plate without you!"

Bea finally stepped forward. "Corrine, maybe we should wait. Maddée said he's the one she truly liked. Truly—"

"Shut your mouth, Bea!"

She liked me? Ethan thought, then castigated himself. As if he gave a damn.

But Bea persevered, saying out of the corner of her mouth, "Maddée said that the Scot was the one she—"

"That was before this one threw money at her, treating her like a whore." She glared at Ethan, then turned back to Bea to say, "No offense."

"*Non?*" Bea blinked at Corrine as if she didn't comprehend the offense.

Was that how Madeleine had viewed the money he'd tossed to the bench? He'd thought he'd simply been paying for the cab. "I wish to make amends to her," Ethan said. "And to explain a few misunderstandings."

Corrine studied him from head to toe. With one shrewd look she'd probably nailed his net worth within five hundred pounds. Strangely, his scar received only a passing glance.

"I just want to talk to her," Ethan said, sensing she was wavering, "If you'll tell me where she is." For good measure, he added, "And I liked her, too."

"See!" Bea cried.

At length, Corrine lowered her broom, setting it against the wall. "Unless you've come to offer for Maddy, you don't have any business here."

"That's precisely what I intend to do," he said.

She exhaled a relieved breath. Over Bea's excited clapping, Corrine said, "In that case . . . Maddy told me she was going to try to get work in the Silken Purse, in Montmartre."

He nodded. "Excellent. I'll go there directly."

"That's up the hill," Bea chirped, smiling encouragement. "Look for her waiting in line in the back." Then her face fell, and she turned to Corrine. "The Silken Purse? Corrine, are you sure?" When Corrine nodded, Bea spoke in French so rapidly that he couldn't keep up. All he could catch was "she said that he said," "then her cousin heard," "he told them," and finally, "Berthé."

Corrine paled.

"What?" Ethan demanded. "What exactly did all that mean?"

"It means you have to hurry. Maddy's about to get attacked."

Fifteen

Any question as to if he'd be so fiercely attracted to Madeleine again was answered the moment he spotted her outside the tavern.

At a nearby corner, he rested his shoulder against a wall and watched her waiting in line. In the light of the dying sun, he could see she was more breathtaking than he'd figured. When she'd worn her mask, he'd been able to see her bright blue eyes, full lips, and determined chin, but the rest of her delicate features had been hidden. He now saw her nose was slim and pert. Her cheekbones were high and aristocratic.

Stunning.

Yet even with her seemingly guileless blue eyes, she didn't look innocent. Far from it. Her blouse was opened wide to reveal cleavage he hadn't recalled she had. She wore a black ribbon choker around her pale neck, and though part of her hair was braided atop her head like a gold crown, the rest curled long and loose down her back.

Her cheeks were rouged, and her skirts were strangely cut—they didn't flare out at the waist as usual but were tight around her hips and backside.

Madeleine looked older and a bit . . . *wanton,* as if she was ready to be tupped, and he responded with a swift heat that shouldn't even have surprised him anymore.

Her gaze was darting over the other women in line as she examined the situation. She reminded him of a fox, crafty and wary as she calculated her next move.

When an aproned barkeep opened the back door, all stood at attention. The man spoke in French, saying something about taking only two more girls for the night—anyone else seen on the premises would be arrested for loitering.

Immediately they jockeyed for position. Madeleine didn't stand a chance against the bigger women—the ones glaring at her and crossing their thick arms over their chests in warning. If she challenged them, she *would* get attacked.

Obviously realizing that fact, she backed from the fray, pausing only to squire to safety a young girl wearing a cigarette tray.

The wee girl looked like she was about to cry over not getting in. Madeleine furtively chucked her under the chin, then held up a gold coin, pinched in her fingers. "I'll bet a hundred francs against any of you," Madeleine began in a carrying voice, "that I'll be one of the two in tonight."

Like vultures surrounding carrion, they circled Madeleine and the girl, tensed to pounce. Ethan pushed up from the wall, striding forward to intervene; Madeleine turned her head to meet some of their stares, taking her eyes from the money. Surely she would know better—

The brawniest one lunged for the coin, slapping Madeleine's hand. The coin went flying into the air, pattering on the bricks ten feet away. The group dove for it, pulling hair and slapping. Madeleine slipped inside, dragging the wide-eyed cigarette girl behind her.

From the pile of women, one exclaimed in French, "It's a stage coin!"

The rest began a chorus about killing *la gamine.*

Ethan grinned from the shadows. *La gamine*—the name fit. She did have an impish air about her. He hurried to the front entrance of the tavern, suddenly finding it imperative to see what the chit would do next.

The other barmaids were visibly shocked that Maddy and the cigarette girl, aptly named Cigarette, had made the cut. Maddy had helped the girl because Cigarette reminded her of herself at that age—hungry, desperate, praying for a break.

Wait. That was Maddy now—

Oh, deuce it! Berthé was here, sneering at her from behind the counter. Sometimes Berthé and Odette worked the taverns, but only to solicit new customers. Berthé's presence boded ill.

Maddy hadn't been in the Silken Purse in years, but she'd never been this impassioned to save her arms before. That group of women outside would be waiting for her later, ready to make her pay. Maddy prayed she'd be able to do so *in coin.*

The interior hadn't changed since the last time she'd seen it. There was an entrance hall and then two large rooms—the main area where food and drink were served and the darker back room, where popular girls like Berthé served drinks while arranging to sell more.

Gaslights dotted the tavern's walls, their cut sconces stained yellow from tobacco smoke. Behind the bar, the wall was lined with vast mirrors, the glass etched with the brand names of ales or gin.

Some older men were already drunk and singing songs from the revolution, but other than their small gathering and a few lone drinkers, the place was empty. She'd heard the bell on the front door ring a few moments ago, but she'd been watching out for Berthé and hadn't seen who'd entered.

Naturally, the one time she'd contrived to get into the usually packed tavern it would be slow. Leaning her elbow on the bar, her chin in her palm, she regarded herself in the back mirror. Even with rouge along her cheeks and a dash of face paint to cover the smudges under her eyes, she appeared tired.

Suddenly she frowned, rubbing her hand over the back of her neck. She had the eerie feeling that she was being watched. Her gaze darted in the mirror, but she didn't see anyone in the main room watching her. The back room was shadowed, and she saw the outline of a man, but she couldn't distinguish features or even determine if he was turned toward her. She was curious but knew better than to go back there.

Assuring herself it was nothing—just overwrought nerves—she turned back, resting her head on her hand again. *One little break*, she thought again. *A single crumb of luck.*

When she did get her break, she wouldn't hesitate to take it, as so many in La Marais would. She had to believe that someday she'd leave this place. She, Corrine, and Bea always used to dream about sailing away somewhere, maybe even to America. Maddy would open a dress shop in a city like Boston, and Corrine would sew Maddy's designs. The first time they'd hit on this idea, Bea's face had fallen. "But what will I do?"

"Model, of course," Maddy had said as Corrine nodded

earnestly. "We can't very well open a dress shop without a model."

Bea's blue eyes had lit up. "I am so good at standing still! Oh, Maddée, you won't believe how still I can be!"

Maddy grinned at the memory even now. . . .

As if Maddy's prayers had been answered, a big party of English tourists filed in. Berthé got them, but then a group of rich University of Paris students entered. *Mine, all mine*, Maddy thought as she donned her brightest smile and swooped in on them.

Soon, the place was packed with businessmen, lower bourgeoisie shopkeepers, and *les Bohèmes*. She steered clear of the latter—especially the ones with cheap clay pipes and wear on the elbows of their coats.

She was earning a small windfall in gratuities, doing better than she ever had, and she'd even managed to eat two lemons and at least half a dozen cherries off the bar service. As she prowled to make it a solid dozen, the barkeep noticed and rapped a cane over her fingers—hard.

Biting the inside of her cheek, she shook her hand out, and again had the sense that she was being watched.

Luckily, she could still hold a tray. And over the next two hours, she served countless tankards of ale, bowls of punch, and opaque bottles of absinthe. Berthé was jostling her whenever they met at the bar, but Maddy could still balance a full tray—she was light on her feet, even for all that her boots were two sizes too small.

Yet at every turn, she felt pinpricks of awareness over the back of her neck.

When Cigarette sold out, Maddy felt generous with her windfall and gave her fifteen sous to pay off anybody who might want to beat her up. The girl deftly swung her hanging tray aside to hug Maddy, then skipped away, her braids flopping.

Just as Maddy turned back, one of the university students took a firm hold of her waist and yanked her into his lap. She studied the smoky ceiling as she listened to his comparisons of her to Leda and various nymphs and to all his hopes and dreams for his and Maddy's future. His musings grew tedious, so she *accidentally* knocked his drink off the table onto his feet. She vowed to replace the drink at once—putting the charge on his bill, of course.

A group of four middle-aged men were more direct in their propositioning. When Maddy caught their eye, they waved her over, and one asked how much it would cost for her to sleep with all of them. One hundred francs? She smiled tightly, choking back a retort. When the man got up to four hundred francs—what she could only imagine earning in a really bountiful year—she still firmly shook her head. To mollify them, she directed them to one of the more likable girls in the back, asking them to remind her to *passez le gras* back to Maddy.

Surprisingly, the men were still nice to her and even ordered a bowl of punch. That was one of the most expensive orders in the Silken Purse. She dashed away to get it.

On her return, she rushed to serve the sizable bowl, grinning at her fortune. . . .

Ethan had decided to examine what a typical night in Madeleine's life was like, garnering insights into her present situation—such as why she was forced to work so hard instead of eating chocolates on a divan in St. Roch. With each minute passing, he grew more uneasy.

Though this was just another tavern and he was here to observe as he had night after night in his job, he had to struggle to retain his customary detachment. He found himself engrossed with Madeleine's behavior—the skill with which she eluded groping hands, her generosity with the young cigarette girl, the way she made the men laugh with her sly sense of humor.

He could tell every time she received a proposition—she seemed to stifle a haughty air, biting back angry words. He'd counted at least a dozen, meaning he'd wanted to kill at least a dozen admirers.

If Ethan was to be an objective observer, then why had he decided to come back later and punish the barkeep for striking her with a cane? And why, when a young man had planted Madeleine in his lap, had Ethan come very near to wiping the floor with the man's face?

In the end, Ethan had learned much about her tonight—and everything he saw, he grudgingly *admired.*

Even now, the chit worked tirelessly, carrying that punch bowl with a proud expression—

Suddenly, Ethan saw another girl's foot sweep out, hooking Madeleine's ankles, tripping her forward. Before he could react, Madeleine and the full crystal bowl crashed to the ground.

The tavern grew silent except for some men snickering. Ethan wanted to thrash every single one of them.

She tried to get up, but her foot slipped in the liquid. She hit her little fist on the floor, her expression a mix of exhaustion and resolve. Just as he rose to help her, she scrambled up. Brushing off her skirt, she swallowed and closed her eyes, as if praying the crystal bowl wasn't truly broken. When she opened them once more, her eyes were dazed and glinting.

The barkeep roared Gallic curses and opened his palm, stabbing it with his other forefinger. Chin up, she dug into her skirt pocket as she scuffed to the bar. As she paid the coins out, she clutched each one, unwilling to part with them. Once she'd surrendered at least what she'd made this night, the barkeep pointed to the door. Patrons booed, but the man was unmoved.

Shoulders back, she trudged to the entrance, but she had to know the women from earlier would be waiting. Ethan quickly followed. In the entrance hall, a loud party was entering, and in the commotion, she smoothly filched an umbrella from the stand as she exited.

Ethan slipped out behind her and silently trailed her down the crowded stairs. Sure enough, Madeleine's enemies awaited her. With false bravado, she hit the umbrella into her cupped palm and asked, "Who wants to be first?"

He stood directly behind her, casting the women his most murderous expression over Madeleine's head.

The closest one's eyes went wide, and she backed away. The others followed, until they'd all scattered.

"That's right!" Madeleine called after them. "Remember my name!"

Suddenly she froze. After a hesitation, she began to turn toward him.

Ethan's heart thundered. After waiting weeks, he was finally going to see her again. He wiped his sleeve over his damp brow.

She needs me more than I need her, he reminded himself, then asked, "Friends of yours?"

Sixteen

Maddy didn't shriek or startle, just gripped the umbrella like a cricket bat as she turned.

She gasped in recognition. "The Scot!" It couldn't be him, yet those eyes, that accent, and his towering height told her it could be no other. She surveyed his face, shocked to find that the man she'd thought was so perfect was horribly scarred.

He stood motionless, as if steeling himself for her reaction. She didn't think he even breathed while she stared at the jagged mark.

"Well, I see now why you wouldn't take off your mask." She tilted her head. "You had to cover up the ten-inch-long scar twisting across your face."

His eyes narrowed. "*Aingeal*, there is only one thing on my body that's ten inches long, and if you'll recall, the scar is no' it."

"The scar *is* that long." She gave him a smirk as she said, "Regarding the other, well, I hardly even remember." As if she'd ever forget that searing pain. "How long have you been spying on me?"

"I was no' spying on you. I was making sure you dinna get waylaid by bloodthirsty French barmaids. Now, I think it's time I told you my name. I'm Ethan MacCarrick, and I've—"

"Why?" She tossed aside the umbrella, then skipped down the steps, starting down the street.

When he caught up to her, he was frowning. "Why what?"

"Why do you think it's time I learned your name? Why would you think I care to? I don't, so *bonne nuit*." Maddy hadn't thought this day could possibly get worse. She quickened her pace to get home before something else happened. She would rid herself of these torturing boots, crawl under the covers, not to wake for days—and forget she'd ever seen the Scot.

"You doona even want to know why I'm here?"

As ever, she was curious. *How did he find me? How much does he know about me?* But after his cruelty the last time she'd seen him, and after the day she'd had . . .

She couldn't think of much more than the money she'd lost on the punch bowl and how badly her feet hurt and how she craved the oblivion of sleep. "No." She paused, tapping her chin. "Not unless you've come to return my virginity, which, regrettably, I misplaced in a cab in London." She raised her brows in question. "Don't have it with you? No? Then . . . good-bye." She reveled in his expression before she hurried on. Priceless. That bastard had actually imagined that she'd be happy to see him.

"Are you going home?" he called from behind her. "Say hello to the henchmen on your way in." When she slowed, he added, "How much do you owe?"

At that, she snapped over her shoulder, "Why would this be any business of yours?"

He caught up with her once more, striding beside her. "Because I might offer to help."

"And why would you do that? Out of the goodness of your black heart?"

"No. I admit I want something from you. If you'll just listen to my proposition—"

"*MacCarrick*, is it?" At his nod, she said, "I think I can predict what your *proposition* might be, and I'm emphatically not interested!"

"Maybe, maybe no'. Share a meal with me, and we'll discuss it."

"I'm not stupid. You want to go to bed with me again. Which will never happen. I couldn't have been persuaded to even *before* I saw your face. Now? I won't even waste my time talking about it. There's nothing you could offer that would affect that."

She could almost hear him grinding his teeth to a pulp. "I believe you're in need of a lot of things I could offer."

"What's that supposed to mean?"

"Winter's coming and you're living in a wet, drafty hovel."

She nearly stumbled. "You were inside *my* apartment?"

"Aye, Bea let me in. We talked for a bit."

"So she's the one who told you where you could find me? Why would she do that? Did you threaten her?" she demanded. "Were you cruel to her because she's . . . because she's popular?"

"No, she helped me because she said you *liked* me," he answered, raising his eyebrows.

Bea had revealed that? How embarrassing! Maddy sounded like a simpering girl at her first cotillion.

"Corrine told me how to find you at this tavern."

Corrine, too? "I can't imagine why they helped you—my last word on the subject of you was that you were an ass."

"Corrine entreated me no' to let you get hurt by some woman named Berthé."

She slanted a glance at him. "How did you find my apartment in the first place?"

"Quin Weyland gave me an address in St. Roch, and I followed your trail to La Marais."

"You're friends with Quin?"

"I'm a family friend of the Weylands. Even related to them in a way—my brother recently married Jane Weyland."

"That makes no sense. The last I heard, Jane was supposed to marry some rich English earl."

"Believe me, I doona see it either."

"So you knew who I was the night of the masquerade?"

"No, only that you were an acquaintance of theirs as well. Listen, Madeleine, with the rate you've lost weight since I last saw you, the apple I found in your garret is likely the only dinner you're returning to, and the men outside your building are no' the type to show mercy."

She could deny none of it.

"All I'm asking you to do is share a dinner with me and hear me out." When she was still shaking her head, he snapped, "Do you really need to mull over the choice of a warm meal with me or facing those men?"

If Toumard's men were there, she'd be forced to wander the streets again. Yet still she said, "Yes, MacCarrick. Yes, I do. You were hateful that night, and the only thing that got me through it was telling myself I never had to see you again. 'Decide what's to be done with you,' you said. How galling. I want nothing from you—not then, and not now! I've taken care of myself since I was fourteen." She was almost home, to her bed, to oblivion.

"Aye, and a capable job you're doing. With the poverty, hunger, and debts. Seems you might have stuck around

Quin's till I came back if this was what you were returning to." He waved a hand at the street.

Homeless men gathered around fires in clay pots, casting long shadows over the buildings. Gunfire popped in the background. Somewhere in the dark a fistfight broke out.

"Quin told me you were intelligent and practical. Surely you've the sense to at least hear me out."

"Quin talked to you about me?" she asked, slowing.

"Aye, and he knows I've come to Paris to see you. He would no' like to learn that you live in a place like this."

She would die if Quin knew! She twined her fingers. But would her pride force her to go along with the Scot? At that moment, she feared pride had just taken a generous lead over curiosity toward her downfall. She finally stopped. "I don't want him to know."

"Then come along," he said in a stern tone that must usually send people scurrying to do his bidding—because he looked perplexed when she only raised her brows at him. "Come with me, and I'll get you a room at my hotel, and you'll enjoy a nice hot meal."

"Now it's to your *hotel*? Do you think I'm a fool? Besides, I thought you preferred intercourse in moving conveyances."

He made a sound of frustration, then dug a small jewelry case from his pocket, presenting it to her. "Have dinner with me, listen to my proposition, and I'll give you this. No strings attached."

Her hand shot out for the case so swiftly that he had to blink. She whirled around, opening it. A diamond ring! "You don't mind if I examine this more closely?" she asked over her shoulder.

He quirked a brow, waving her forward. "No' at all."

She needed a streetlight. Of course, the sole one in La Marais had been torn down, its iron sold for scrap. But she could feel the stone's weight and knew it couldn't be paste. *A diamond, a real one.* This would pay off Toumard and keep her for *years*. "One dinner earns me this?"

"Aye, you can keep the ring, regardless of your decision."

"Would you vow you won't try anything unseemly with me?"

"Unseemly? Aye, I can vow that."

She could tell the ring wouldn't fit her thin fingers, so she pulled her key ribbon from her skirt pocket. After untying the red ribbon and threading the ring along it next to her apartment key, she stowed it back into her deep pocket.

When she faced him again, he appeared to barely check a smug smirk, no doubt thinking she'd just agreed. "It's obvious you always get what you want," she said. "Maybe it'd be good for you to be turned down flat by a girl from the slum."

At that, he obviously reached his limit. He took a step forward, looking as though he planned to toss her over his shoulder.

"Ah-ah"—she wagged her finger at him—"I wouldn't do that. You won't catch me, not in my neighborhood."

He seemed to grind his teeth again, then clearly lit on an idea.

From his jacket, he pulled an apple—it was *her* precious apple, abducted from her home.

"No!" she cried, forced to watch as he took a big bite, chewing with exaggerated relish.

"So I take it we have an engagement for dinner," he said between bites.

Seventeen

When Ethan tossed the core away, she looked as though she would cry, and for some reason he almost felt guilty. He gentled his tone. "Come with me, Madeleine. I promise your apple will be a worthy sacrifice."

Even now, dressed as she was, she seemed so out of place in La Marais. She was tired, but her hair shone in the street fires, and her eyes were bright, not like the sunken eyes of the denizens all around them. She appeared so fragile, yet she had no reaction to the shots fired at regular intervals not more than a couple of blocks away in any direction.

"I still have to go home to let my friends know I didn't get hurt," she said. "They'll be worried."

"So you plan to wade into a dangerous area in order to inform your friends that you're safe? That's ridiculous."

"It's not *dangerous*," she scoffed.

The mere idea of her down here at night was insufferable. "Do you no' hear the guns going off?"

She gave him a look that said he was daft. "Well, it's not as though they're aimed at *me*. If you're afraid, then stay here until I return."

Little witch. "I'm no' *afraid*—"

"Then you won't mind waiting here. You can't tell me

Corrine and Bea were worried and then expect me to ignore their worry."

At another time, he might have been impressed with her loyalty and concern for her friends. Now, it only irritated him. "If you think I'm letting you go down there alone, you're mad."

She put her hand on her hip. "And what will you do about it?"

He lunged forward, seizing her elbow, and began dragging her back up the hill.

"MacCarrick, I *live* here. I only want five minutes." She cursed him in French. "You can't order me about, Scot!" Her hard little boots connected with his shins.

He grated, "Damn it, Madeleine, we'll send them a message from the hotel."

"No one will deliver a message to La Marais after sunset!"

"They will if I pay them enough." He considered throwing her over his shoulder, but he risked opening his stitches. When she still resisted, he said, "We'll send them food as well, then. Would that sway you?"

She eased her scuffling. "How *much* food?"

"I doona bloody care. As much as you like."

She got a gleam in her eye that he thought he'd soon be growing familiar with. "I will hold you to—"

A woman cried out from just behind him. Ethan shoved Madeleine back as he twisted around. In a murky alley, a prostitute was pressed up against a wall, studying her nails and feigning moans as one man took her from behind. Another man awaited his turn.

When Ethan turned to Madeleine, she shrugged at the sight of people having intercourse just feet from the two of them, with the same indifference she'd demonstrated the first night he'd met her.

He couldn't imagine all the things her young eyes had witnessed.

Stitches be damned. "I doona want you here," he said simply, about to sling her over his shoulder, but the waiting man strode forward from the shadows and addressed them in a strange tongue. *Argot*, Ethan thought, the French cant of criminals. The man pointed to Madeleine with raised eyebrows.

She gave a bitter laugh and muttered, "He wants to know if you've finished with me."

A haze fell over Ethan's vision. He dimly heard her answering retort, speaking argot herself. The bastard thought Madeleine was a whore, thought to use her in a filthy alley. . . .

Ethan yanked her behind him as he pulled his gun. The man took one look at Ethan's expression and drew his own pistol. Too late. Ethan had already drawn, cocked, and aimed.

Madeleine glanced out from behind his back, then touched his shoulder. "Don't, MacCarrick." Her voice was urgent. "*Allons-y*. Let's go. I'm ready to go with you now."

"Why should I no' kill him?"

"Because his gang will come after me and my friends. You didn't want me here, and now I want to go with you. Please, Scot. . . ."

At length, he backed them away, keeping his gun raised and the man in sight until they'd turned the corner. He finally stowed his gun, wincing in pain. His wound had started to throb.

"Do you always carry a pistol?" At his brusque nod, she said, "Why?"

So when a criminal mistakes my woman for a whore, I can kill him. He shook himself, trying to throw off the surge of protectiveness that welled within him. *His* woman? She was a means to an end.

She tilted her head at him. "I don't understand why you were afraid of gunfire when you *have* a gun—and obviously know how to use it. In any case, I wouldn't have let anything happen to you." She frowned. "Well, probably not. Unless it inconvenienced me to step in or I had something better—"

"I was *no'* bloody afraid," he grated again. *I suspect I'm going to throttle her before all this is done.* "Damn it, just come along. . . ."

When they arrived at his hotel, the brasserie downstairs was still open, but Ethan didn't want to take her in there. He didn't care if people stared at his face—he was used to it—but he didn't want her analyzing him, discerning his reaction.

"We'll eat in my room," he said, clasping her hand and leading her to the stairs.

Instead of protesting vehemently, she gazed up at his scar. "It really bothers you, doesn't it?" No furtive glances for her.

He narrowed his eyes. "Wouldn't it you?"

She shrugged, and they ascended in silence to his floor. Inside his room, she whistled and turned in a circle. "Pricey. Nothing but the best, then?"

He rang for a waiter. "Why no'?" he said, carefully shrugging from his jacket.

She'd just returned from surveying the balcony's view when a liveried waiter arrived to take a bill of fare. The man handed the single menu to him to order, but Ethan waved him to Madeleine.

She accepted it with a regal inclination of her head, sitting at the room's polished dining table. "Do you speak French?" she asked Ethan as she skimmed the offerings.

"Nary a word," he lied. "Only Gaelic and English."

"Lobster," she immediately told the man in French, casting Ethan a furtive glance. He gave her a blank look in return. She amended her order to six lobster entrees with accompaniments—soups, cheeses, pastries, fruits, salad.

"And if you box up half of the order and have the porter deliver it to an address in La Marais, my . . . husband will add a forty percent gratuity."

"La Marais?" the waiter said, choking on the words.

She sighed. "Seventy percent."

While Madeleine scribbled the address on the bill of fare, Ethan told the waiter, "Bring up champagne while we wait." To Madeleine, he said, "Feel free to choose the vintage, lass."

In French, she ordered, "Whatever's most dear."

With a bow, the man departed. When he returned directly with the champagne, poured, then left once more, Madeleine seemed content to drink and explore the room.

Ethan sank back into a plush armchair, content to watch her opening drawers, investigating closets, even rooting through his bag. *Sionnach*, he thought. She again reminded him of a fox, so wary, so sly.

She touched all the fabrics in the room, brushing her fingertips lovingly over the counterpane, even over his trousers in the closet press, seeming unaware of what she was doing. He, however, was quite aware and wanted her to run her fingers over those trousers like that when he was in them. She effortlessly made him randy as hell.

When she ambled into the bathroom, he leaned forward to keep her in view. She eyed the plunge tub, which was big enough to swim in. "Unlimited running water?" she asked, coveting it with her eyes.

"Aye. You're welcome to it."

He thought he heard her mutter, "You mean, you'll let me *avail myself*."

By the time the food arrived a short while later, she was visibly tipsy, which wasn't surprising considering how thin she was. The sizable table proved too small for all the fare, so she had the server spread out the plates on the room's thick Brussels rug for a picnic.

Once the man left, she sat on the floor, with the dishes all around her. Ethan shrugged and eased down with her, careful with his injury.

"Casual as ever," she remarked.

"What's that supposed to mean?" he asked, reaching for a lobster dish, but she changed her grip on her fork to a dagger hold.

He raised his palms in surrender, his gaze flickering over her small frame as he said, "You obviously need it more than I do."

She couldn't seem to decide if that had been a cutting comment or a statement of fact. He couldn't either. "Tell me what you meant," he said.

"You acted so familiar with me that night in the carriage."

"Aye, it happens when two people have intercourse."

She glared at that. "No, you acted as if we'd been together for years—just a night among many between us."

Sometimes it felt that way. . . .

"Here. I'll let you have this to eat," she said, solemnly handing him a *garnish*. Then she took her first forkful, rolling her eyes with pleasure.

Though he would have thought she'd inhale her food, she savored each bite as if it would be her last. She had a sensual, tactile way of eating that was . . . stirring. When she ate juicy strawberries and clotted cream, he ran his hand over his mouth. When she licked the cream from her fingers, he uncomfortably shifted the way he sat. Any male could easily imagine her actions in a different light. Finally, he could take no more.

"Enough," he said as he levered himself to his feet. "You're going to make yourself sick." He clasped her hand to help her up.

She reluctantly let him. "But I haven't eaten more than a regular meal."

"Which is still much more than you're accustomed to right now."

When he led her, grumbling, to a seat at the empty dining table, she stared over her shoulder at the food. He again experienced that tightness in his chest, the same he'd felt when she'd been about to cry over her apple.

"Lass, there's more where that came from. You doona have to behave like it's your last meal."

She laughed without humor. "Spoken like a man who's never missed one."

Eighteen

The Scot hadn't even raised a brow when tray after tray of food had arrived—fruit, pastries, lobster, salads, and a trio of desserts. Surveying all the dishes she'd just enjoyed, she realized he'd been right—the apple had been such a worthy sacrifice.

Yet Maddy had been suspicious when he'd wanted to dine *in his room* and had almost fled with the ring. Then she'd concluded that he didn't want to be in the restaurant because of his face, which was understandable, considering how extensive the scar was. She couldn't believe he'd hidden his true appearance from her that first night—willfully hidden it, even as he'd taken her.

He brought her glass of champagne to her seat at the table. Though she was already light-headed, he'd drunk nothing. She'd noticed before that he seemed to favor one side, and now he sat gingerly on the bed as though he was in pain.

"You told me you've lived alone since you were fourteen," he said. "I'm curious to know how you pay for rent and food."

"You mean, if tonight's performance was any indication." She'd lost more than she'd made—until the Scot had given her a *diamond*! Unfortunately, it would be difficult to sell promptly for its true value. And she needed money immediately. But then, she'd already snared a gold watch from his bag and some silverware from the dinner settings.

He wisely said nothing to her comment. She wasn't keen on answering his questions, but she figured she'd have to until she could either eat more or pocket more of the silver. "Sometimes I deal cards and sell cigarettes at a café near Montmartre." She shrugged as she drank. "If not that, then I run a shell game at fairs or bet the *mutuels* on the side."

"I saw the book by your bed. Doona tell me you consider yourself a Bohemian."

"Not at all. The book is recent and set in a neighboring quarter. I was merely picking up tips on getting things for free. I have no sympathy for them, even the ones who are poorer than I am." She absently murmured, "Do you know how hard you would have to work to be poorer than me?" Shaking her head, she said, "Many of them purposely leave their wealthy families to come starve in La Marais."

"Quin told me your mother and stepfather live in St. Roch. Did you no' do the same by leaving?"

"My reason for leaving St. Roch had nothing to do with *pretension*. And it's a matter I don't wish to discuss."

"What kind of woman lets her daughter live in the slum?"

Maddy set her glass down and rose, turning toward the door.

He lunged for her wrist, moving swiftly for such a big man. "Just wait," he said, gritting his teeth as though in pain.

She glared at his hand. "I've told you I don't want to talk about it."

"I will no' bring it up again." He released her and she swished back to her chair, resuming her drinking. "But I wonder that you're so inclined to leave when you've no' even heard why I'm here."

"Yes, your 'proposition.' I'm quite certain I know what it is. You as much as told me so that night."

"Aye, I'd thought about setting you up as my mistress. And it seems you might have waited in London until I returned, if this life was what you faced."

"I didn't want to be your mistress. That would mean I would have to repeat the actions of that night." She shuddered. "I think I might rather die. The only way I'd ever endure that again is in marriage—"

"Then it appears I'll be marrying you," he grated.

She gave him a look of pure disgust. "I have had a day like no other, MacCarrick. I really don't need to sit here and listen to this."

"What if I told you I came here specifically for you? To collect you and take you to Scotland to wed?"

"I'm in no mood for your jesting." She stared at his impassive face with dawning horror. "Oh, Lord, you're . . . *serious. Marriage* is what you've decided needs to be done with me?" In a panicked tone, she said, "I only mentioned marriage because I was certain you'd violently balk again!"

He glowered at that, then seemed not to know how to proceed, running his hand over the back of his neck.

"You actually thought I'd welcome your proposal?" she sputtered in disbelief. The arrogance! "You looked at my 'hovel' and thought I'd weep with joy and consider you my savior. Should I fall to my knees?"

"I think no,' else all that silver stowed in your skirt pocket will clink about like chimes."

She quirked an eyebrow. She didn't get detected often, and she'd been careful tonight. He was good. "I don't know what you're talking about."

To his credit, he didn't press that subject, instead returning to the proposal. "It would make sense that you might be pleased to receive *any* offer of marriage."

"You told me you would *never* be moved to marry." She made her tone woeful. "Oh, if only I'd listened! Then I wouldn't have tried to trap you seconds later."

"Things have changed. Recently I was injured, and it brought my life into focus. I have a title, and I've realized I need an heir, so I must marry."

"What's your title?"

"I'm an earl in Scotland. The Earl of Kavanagh."

"Planning to make me a *countess*?" she breathed with wide eyes. "How novel! I've *never* heard that one in Montmartre."

"It's true."

"And why would you choose me?"

"None of my options seemed enticing, and then I thought of you. After I asked around and learned much about you, I determined we would suit. You're known to have a steady, practical personality, and to be intelligent."

"You could make a much more advantageous match."

"You underestimate your charms."

"No, I don't. I know I'm pretty and intelligent, but I have no connections—and no dowry. In case you haven't gathered, I'm abysmally poor."

"I have no need of connections and have more money than either of us could possibly spend in a lifetime. I can choose my bride based only on if I find her *pretty* and *intelligent*."

She quirked an eyebrow at that. "Why do you think *I* would actually have *you*?"

"You told me at the masquerade that you wanted to marry a man with money. I have money. You told me you wanted an expensive ring, and I've given you one worth a small fortune. You'll be a countess and have more wealth and homes at your disposal than you've dreamed of."

Homes and wealth? Countess? Was this odd Scot genuine? Hadn't she just begged for one break? One pause in the endless series of heartaches?

And then this MacCarrick just happened to show up at her door, proposing?

No! Gifts don't fall from heaven like this! Not for me. Something is off!

"All you have to do is leave Paris with me. I'll wed you in Scotland."

"Why not marry here in *la ville lumière*?" In a dry tone, she said, "You're clearly such a romantic, and this *is* Paris . . ."

"Because I'm the laird of my clan, and I'm expected to marry at the MacCarrick seat with a grand wedding for all the clan to enjoy. And marrying in front of witnesses from my county in Scotland will help ensure my children inherit without challenge." When she remained unconvinced, he quietly said, "Money, protection, a life of ease are all within your grasp. Marriage to me is that repulsive a proposition?" He absently dashed the back of his hand over his scar.

"Yes, and before you begin thinking it's because of your face"—he dropped his hand, seeming surprised he'd been touching it—"I'll ask you to hark back to your behavior that night. You ruined what could have been, *should* have been, wonderful. I thought I had a firm grasp of what cruelty was, but you educated me further."

"It was no' that bad—"

"Yes, I've heard some women enjoy overeager Highlanders pawing at them, nearly ripping their clothes off, then delivering excruciating pain. For some reason, I just couldn't understand the appeal." She shrugged. "I'll bet it eats at you, knowing that I found you to be a horrible lover."

The black look he gave her was rewarding. "Given the chance to do things over, I'd have done them differently."

"Is that supposed to be an apology?"

"I doona believe in apologies. Instead, I'm offering you a future, which is more valuable."

"That night, you kept going even though I was hurt."

"I dinna know—"

"You mean to tell me that an experienced man of the world couldn't tell when a woman beneath him is in pain and on the verge of sobbing?"

Did he stifle a wince? "You had a mask on. I could no' see your tears. And I swear to you, I stopped as soon as I realized."

"Right. And then you . . . you finished what you'd started, adding to the humiliation."

"I dinna intend to humiliate you. That was . . . involuntary."

She frowned. "Involuntary? What does . . . ?" She trailed off, feeling herself flush at the notion of him overcome with lust. "Oh. Well, the fact remains that even when you realized, you almost didn't stop."

"But I did. And one day you'll understand just how goddamned difficult that was." He looked to the right of her and said absently, "It's hard for you to imagine because you were feeling pain, but I was no'." His brows drew together as if remembering the encounter right then—an idea that made her shiver. "I was feeling more pleasure than I had in years."

"Then why *did* you stop?"

"I dinna want to hurt you." He turned back to meet her eyes. "I suppose that means I'm no' yet thoroughly beyond redemption."

"Redemption? I hope you didn't come here expecting *me* to redeem you, MacCarrick, because if so, you've chosen the wrong girl."

"No, I came here expecting you to marry me." Raking his heated gaze over her, he said, "And I think I got her right."

Nineteen

Ethan was confounded by how much she *wasn't* jumping at this opportunity.

"So how rich are you? As rich as Quin?"

"No. Quite a deal more than Quin."

Instead of being pleased by this, her face turned cold. "You're rich, titled, and not too terribly old. You could have anyone you wanted. Yet you chose a dowryless girl you don't know?"

Too terribly old? "I've already explained this."

"And I don't accept your explanation. Something is wrong with you or your situation, and you're hiding it. You chose me, a foreign girl, so I wouldn't have heard about unsavory predilections or tales of gin-swilling or shaky finances—"

"I doona drink liquor. My finances are solid." He wondered why he sounded so fierce about this, when he had no intention of marrying her. "And the only unsavory predilection I have is that I plan to use you well, until we're both spent, every single night."

Her face screwed up into an expression of distaste. "Would you really want me, knowing that the only reason I'd accept a man like you is because I'd rather forgo hunger pangs and torture by henchmen?"

"Does no' matter why. Just that you do."

"It doesn't feel right to me. I know how aristocratic lords are—there's *always* something wrong, always some secret." Though he wouldn't have thought it possible, he realized she was more cynical than he was.

In a deliberate tone, he asked, "Are the reasons why I have no' made a match no' obvious?"

"Because of your foot-long scar?" She rolled her eyes.

"Damn it, witch, it's no' that long," he said between gritted teeth.

"Maybe it's not if you measure end to end, but if you trace every turn, it is."

How badly he'd wanted a woman to acknowledge the scar, to get the awkwardness out of the way. And here this chit was looking him in the eyes, facing him fully, discussing it—but not in any manner he'd ever imagined. "You're daft."

With a huff of irritation, she crossed to his spot on the bed. She lifted a knee to the edge, tilting her head as she studied his face. She smelled of strawberries and sweet woman, and his cock shot harder. He was struggling not to clutch her waist and roll her to the bed—

She . . . *touched* his scar.

Biting her lip, concentrating, she traced her finger along it.

A beautiful woman was touching his face—*analyzing* it. The mark was disgusting—why wasn't she repelled?

When she apparently couldn't get the length she'd claimed, she *tugged* on his face. He willed himself not to snatch her hand away, anxious to see what she would do next. *What will she say? What will she call me . . . ?*

At last, she simply seemed to grow bored with it. "Well,

perhaps I was wrong," she conceded. "But the scar *is* big—very big. How did you get it? Did it hurt?"

"Of course, it bloody hurt," he snapped, reminded as ever that she was the daughter of the one who'd dealt him that blow.

She drew back from him, the intimacy lost. Then assuming a haughty expression, she clucked her tongue. "Running with scissors, Scot?"

"One day, I'll tell you all about it," he lied.

She huffed back to her spot on the floor and mouthed, "*Big*" to him before plucking up another strawberry.

"Well, thank you for dinner and the ring," Maddy said half an hour later as she rose to leave. "Both proved agreeable."

"Madeleine, the watch you've pocketed belonged to my father's father. You canna have that one, but I'd be glad to get you another."

She jutted her chin up, digging for it and tossing it on the bed.

"And you managed to get that candle holder you were eyeing into your pocket, too?"

Deuce it, how had he seen her?

"Commendable, *sionnach*."

"What does that word mean?"

"It means 'fox.' That's what you remind me of."

"Do you know what you remind me of? A wolf in sheep's clothing. Tonight you've been more civil, but it's obvious to me that it's a strain on you. It's not your nature."

"Aye, that might be true," he said, surprising her with his honesty. "I'm no' polite, nor am I one for wooing and compliments. I say what's on my mind whether a lady's in the room or no', but—"

"But if I look past the tarnished surface," she interrupted in a saccharine tone, clasping her hands to her chest, "there's a good man beneath? Just waiting for the right woman to turn him around? Tell that to Blue-Eyed Bea. She believes it again and again. I do not." She put her hand on the doorknob.

"No, I was no' going to say I'm a good man. I canna make that claim. And I doona believe a man can change his nature. But I was going to point out that I'm likely the best you're going to get. I will no' ever strike you, you will never want for anything, and you will never have to back down to anyone again. There's a reason you have no' asked the Weylands for help. You're prideful. Why no' go back to England as their equal?"

"On the surface, this seems logical." So why did she feel like she was about to pocket a scarf and a hidden gendarme was watching her every move? She suddenly narrowed her eyes, suspicion flaring. "You've never asked me about my proposal, the one I told you I had waiting in the wings."

"It was obvious to me that you had no' and would no' accept him if you were still living in poverty, and the last thing I wanted to do was remind you of another candidate."

"No, I was ready to accept him, but *he* refused *me*. After waiting for so long, he was suspicious of my virtue."

MacCarrick's brows drew together. "Do you think I could possibly have something to do with that? Of course, I wrote him of my conquest." When she remained unconvinced, he said, "Which begs the question: Why did you keep him waiting?"

"I had a bad feeling."

Instead of scoffing, he nodded and said, "Do you have a bad feeling now?"

"I don't know." She couldn't tell. She was exhausted, bewildered, and probably drunk. She didn't think she should believe him, but if she trusted her instincts . . . "I just need some time to think about all this." *Am I doing something to leave myself vulnerable?* "It's a big step."

He ran his hand over his face. "Then at least stay here. What happens if you get caught by those henchmen? They'll take you straight to their boss."

"I *never* get caught." That wasn't true. She had been caught several times, but no one had ever made it to the police station with her in tow.

When she opened the door, he quickly rose, and his hand shot to her elbow. "Going out into the night again? That is out of the question." He seemed alarmed at the idea of her escaping him. "Damn it, Madeleine, would it be so terrible to have a man take care of you? To protect you?"

Protect? She swallowed, the image of the ladies in the boulangerie flashing in her mind. Had the dream ever been this close . . . ?

"I'm no' leaving Paris without you, lass." Softening his tone, he said, "You're going to be mine—I doona know what I have to do to effect that, but it must be so."

Maddy knew men. They could feign love and affection easily, yet jealousy, when absent, was hard to conjure. She'd noted the look of rage on MacCarrick's face when the man had asked if he was done with her. She'd seen how swiftly he'd pulled his gun.

He was possessive already. *So why am I so afraid of this?* She could establish parameters to protect herself, limit her vulnerabilities.

De mal en pire. From bad to worse. Was she afraid to take this chance because she didn't trust him—or because La Marais had already beaten her?

Never. *Fortune favors the bold.*

And that's when she knew she was going to go along with this. "I will consider your proposal."

He exhaled and schooled his features, but she'd seen he was relieved—very much so.

"But I have some conditions. . . ."

Twenty

"*The hell we're no' having sex till we're married!*"

"I'm in earnest, Scot. I won't make the same mistake twice."

He'd just been fighting an overpowering sense of relief that she was staying when she'd thrown these ridiculous conditions in his face. "I will no' question you about your past, and, aye, I'll be faithful to you. Fine, I agree to those conditions. As for your wanting to start a family right away—then, aye, God willing," he baldly lied. "I'll certainly do my part to contribute. But the fourth condition is unacceptable. I've a man's needs, and they will no' simply disappear during our engagement—"

She strode for the door. Why had he ever assumed this would be easy?

"Those are my terms," she said without looking back. "I think I'm being very generous."

"So am I. The ring you're walking away with will keep you in apples for many a year."

She turned to him. "I don't even *like* you."

"Yet I have it on good authority that you did once."

Her lips thinned, and he wagered she was silently vowing to kill her friends. "Worse, you don't even like me."

He didn't bother denying it. He was feeling a lot of

things about her, but *a liking for her* was not one of them. "You're negotiating with me as if you have a leg to stand on. Where does a girl like you get the ballocks to risk losing a man with money and power who's willing to marry her? You've been ruined, remember? Most wealthy men would only accept a virgin. Since I relieved you of yours, this is your good fortune that I'm still interested."

"I know that I'm not negotiating from a position of power—but I don't trust you. I *fiercely* don't trust you."

"Do you want this condition for leverage or because you fear me getting a bairn on you before marriage?"

"Both," she readily admitted.

Seeing that she would hold firm on this for now, he said, "Fine. I'll agree that we'll wait—if you vow to slake me in other ways, whenever I want it." When she frowned at him, he said, "I doona care how I'm satisfied—just that I am."

"You're only saying that because you think you can seduce me to do more."

That was precisely what he'd planned. He didn't like how she continued to anticipate his moves.

"It won't happen because I have no interest in you that way," she added.

"You'll learn to want me again."

"You're amazing! If your behavior didn't kill any spark of desire for you, then your true appearance did."

He narrowed his eyes, stalking toward her. When he'd backed her against the wall, he reached his hand out to cup her nape. "You canna deny you enjoyed my kiss," he said as he slowly drew her into his chest.

Her breaths shallowed. "B-because I believed you were different then."

"Do you ever think about what happened in the carriage before I took you?"

When her cheeks grew flushed, he had his answer.

"I do," he admitted. "I think about it. Constantly." He knew he needed to use a measured seduction to get what he wanted. Though it took will, he moved his hand from gripping her neck to cradling her face. "And I remember that you liked the way I kissed you and stroked you."

She gazed at his lips, with her brows drawn as if she was thinking of it just then.

He leaned down and murmured at her ear, "You were so close to coming for me."

She gasped, shivering against him.

Nuzzling her neck down past her choker, he said, "Why do you think you will no' enjoy it again?" Their ragged breaths were the only sounds in the room. "I'm going to kiss you now, and if you doona respond, then I'll leave and never bother you again. If you do . . . then you're mine."

"I'm not going to agree to that . . ." She swallowed. "Agree to your ridiculous"—he drew in closer—"little test." Her hands were balled against his chest. "Silly, really . . ."

He slowly slanted his mouth over hers, but she tensed, pushing against him. He didn't release her, just continued to tease her lips with his tongue. After long moments, her fists relaxed, and she rested her palms against him.

At last, her lips parted for him, letting him taste her as he'd wanted to for weeks. She brushed her hands up from his chest, twining her fingers at his neck, pressing her body against him so sweetly.

When he deepened the contact, she gave a whimper, then began kissing him back, filling him with a sense of triumph. Maybe she didn't find him repulsive. Why would she feign this? Her lapping tongue made his blood race, made him want to reach down and cup her arse to grind her against him. He'd been prepared to seduce, to cajole, to pleasure her. But he hadn't been prepared to lose himself from a mere kiss—again.

She tugged on his neck, rubbing against his front, and he groaned. How could she render him so crazed so swiftly? He was already nearing the edge of his control, fighting the nearly irresistible urge to toss her to the bed and mindlessly cover her.

With a will he hadn't known he possessed, he forced himself to release her. After struggling to collect his thoughts and to catch his breath, he rasped, "It does no' have to be bad, Madeleine. I'll teach you to trust me again, and we can bring each other pleasure."

She looked stunned, guarded, almost worse than before, so he tried to make his tone light. "Though I think after a couple of days, you'll find it easier just to lie back and receive me."

"Why? Is it difficult to please you? It didn't seem that much so in the carriage."

He clenched his jaw and forced himself to even his tone. "No' necessarily. It's just that you'll be doing it three or four times a day."

"With a man of your advanced years?"

Advanced years? By God, I am *going to throttle her.* "Let's just say that I've got a lot to make up for. And it begins tonight."

"I haven't agreed, MacCarrick."

"You will. But before you do, I reserve the right to try to seduce you completely."

After a long hesitation, she said, "I'll agree, *if* you'll get me my own room tonight. As for the other, I guarantee *nothing*."

"Why would I get you a room? As of this minute, we're engaged." Ach, that sounded unnatural.

"I just want to soak in that tub and think about everything. My head's spinning." She swayed on her feet. "Please, if you knew the day I've had . . ."

"How can I be certain you will no' run off in the night? You did before."

"If I promise not to?"

"I will give you some time to bathe, but from now on, we share a room."

She exhaled, then reluctantly nodded.

"I'll return in half an hour," he said before leaving. As he made his way downstairs to the street, he took in the chill air, trying to shake off her effect on him.

Damn it, he could go a night without touching her—a small sacrifice for the larger plan. He didn't know how well he'd acquit himself anyway. He hadn't slept more than a few hours at a time since he'd decided to journey to Paris for her, and weakness from his injury lingered.

He frowned. How would they sleep tonight? He understood why he'd had to insist they share a room, but it had been strange to do so since he'd never stayed the night with a woman in his entire life. He'd shuddered at the prospect of waking to most of them and had resented even the *idea* of the intrusion into his life.

After sex, when they'd sighed, reaching for him with their clinging arms, he'd bolted every time. Throwing on his clothes as he hastened out into rain, snow, or whatever element—he'd just made sure he escaped. *Clingers, every bloody one of them.*

Women had a lamentable and ridiculous tendency to conflate sex and affection, not understanding that these were two distinct scenarios—and that he only had interest in the former. Ethan thought they ought not go together at all. . . .

A laughing older couple, clearly married, passed him on their way into the hotel. He studied them, supposing some people had success with matrimony. Ethan's own parents had been deeply in love. But then, their union had ended in tragedy. Would his brothers fare better—

Did Madeleine really just agree to marry me?

If he took away the charade, the fact remained that she'd accepted *his* proposal—after seeing his face.

He scowled. The only way a man who looked like him could land a beauty like her was because she was starving and in danger and she believed he could protect her. The only reason he was so repulsive was because of what her parents had done to him.

In his mind, she was his. He was *owed* her. Owed the use of her soft body. In fact, it was his due to touch her anytime he pleased. Hadn't he told her she'd satisfy him whenever he desired it?

So why had he left now? Anger simmering, he stomped back up the stairs to stake his claim.

Twenty-one

As Maddy sat in the vast plunge tub, rinsing complimentary lavender shampoo from her hair, she mused that she might—just maybe—have gotten back on her feet.

Just with that ring, currently threaded on her length of ribbon and glinting at her from the nearby bureau, she could dig her way out of debt.

And if the Scot genuinely wanted to marry her, she'd be rich! A countess even.

She leaned back in the hot water—so high it practically hit her shoulders—allowing herself to relax as the steam rose all around her. She definitely could get used to this.

Maddy frowned. But then she'd have to allow him to make love to her. If only he could do that part as well as he kissed. Nevertheless, she could endure much to receive all this. And at least she'd come to believe that he hadn't meant to hurt her that night. He'd flinched every time she brought it up.

She opened her eyes—

He was just there, watching her!

Shooting to her feet, she dove for a bath towel. She yanked it over her shoulders like a blanket, but she feared that with his eagle eyes, he'd seen her arm. How had she not heard him come in? "You said you'd give me half an hour!"

"And you said you'd satisfy me whenever I wanted it. I want it now." He removed his jacket. "Drop the towel."

"I-I never agreed to be naked!"

"You want me to marry you without ever seeing your body in the light?"

"Most do!"

In a flash, his hand shot out, stripping her of the towel. When she grappled for it, he whirled her around, and with his grip both gentle and firm, he pinned her wrists together behind her. He was maneuvering her as if he was searching for her scar, but the sight of her breasts seemed to stop him.

His voice roughened. "I only got to see these in shadow before." He made some growling sound, and his big palm covered one. She froze at the shock of heat. He hissed in a breath.

Would he still want her after seeing her body completely? She wouldn't want him anyway! Why couldn't she have bigger breasts? She squeezed her eyes closed, mortified.

Softly kneading her flesh, he grated, "No bigger than a teacup."

Maddy wanted to *die.*

"You might be *intelligent*, but you're no' *pretty*," he sneered.

Die immediately.

He dropped his hand to palm her bottom, and low masculine sounds broke from his chest. "You're bloody *beautiful.*" He sounded infuriated by that fact.

She peeked open her eyes and found his muscles tensed. His erection was huge, straining against his trousers.

Beautiful? After he's seen me naked in the light?

His hand began rubbing all over her, along her hips, over her belly and breasts, as if he didn't know where to touch her next—as if he was overwhelmed by a bounty. His brows drawn, his breaths haggard, he said, "*So fair* . . ."

Though he was clothed and scrutinizing her, Maddy's pleasure heightened with each stroke. *He thinks I'm beautiful.* The idea was so pleasing . . . her eyelids fluttered closed. The more he touched her, the more she wanted just to lie back and let him explore her like this. *What is happening to me?*

When he swept a hand over the curls between her thighs and rasped, "The color of your light hair," she shivered, having to stifle a moan.

"Aye, just let me look at you, lass," he bit out once she relaxed in his hold.

When he released her hands, she took a breath, as though gathering courage. He could tell she had the urge to cover herself—she blushed and glanced sharply away—but she didn't.

He'd taken her virginity, enjoyed her, touched her, and had never comprehended—or savored—exactly how lovely her body was.

The room's lamp cast light over her pale, smooth shoulders. Her long hair cascaded in wet curls, brushing over her hardened nipples. His gaze followed the rivulets of water sluicing down from her breasts to her belly and lower, and he hungered to follow that trail with his tongue and lips.

He heard a low rumbling sound and was surprised to find it came from within him.

She was slim, but somehow shapely, utterly womanly. Her hips flared from her tiny waist, giving her an hour-glass shape. Her arse could not be more pert and lush. And the two dimples above it . . . ? Ethan stifled a groan. He wanted to press his thumbs over them as he held her in place and thrust against her.

But her sensuous little breasts riveted him. . . . They were small yet high and plump, and her nipples were so sensitive, budding with the lightest touch. Though he remembered he'd always preferred heavy, full breasts, after cupping hers in his palm, he couldn't quite recall why.

She was perfect—but for one thing. His attention turned to her scar, the one she hadn't wanted him to see. He took her elbow and tugged her closer to the steam-fogged lamp, raising her arm. The mark covered about a third of the bottom of her forearm and looked like a typical burn scar, with white twisting lines contained within borders of red.

"You broke it, too?"

Her eyes widened before she made her face blank.

"When?"

She shrugged as best as she could with her arm seized. "I don't know. It happened a long time ago."

"You raised your arm against something that was burning. And it broke the bone."

Now her lips parted. "How could you . . . why would you say that?"

"I know scars." His lips curled in a bitter smile. "Where were you in a fire?"

She hesitated just a heartbeat, then said in a blithe tone, "At a manor we lived in. When I was younger. One of the servants was drunk and careless with his pipe."

"In other words, your garret caught fire from a drunken tenant."

She shuddered, then whispered, "I wasn't always poor, MacCarrick. I did live in a mansion, and there were servants and parties and friends."

"Aye, I know that." *I'm the one who took it all away.* "Or you'd hardly be friends with the Weylands."

"W-will you please let me go?"

His chest felt heavy and uncomfortable again, goading him until he released her.

She sank down into the water, her back to him, streams of her hair curling down. Her shoulders curved in miserably. Her ribs were visible, not terribly bad, but enough to show she'd missed meals.

Goddamn it. This was not the time to be developing a conscience. He cast about for something, anything, then recalled how much she'd insulted him this evening. "You've a lot of nerve to comment on *my* scar."

She sucked in a breath.

He knew why he might be moved to say something like that at a time like this, but he wasn't too far gone toward absolute cruelty to understand why he *mightn't* have said it.

"Stand up and come here," he demanded. "I want to touch you more."

"No! It's bad enough baring my body to you, but to be ridiculed—"

"Ridiculed?" he asked, incredulous. "There's no' anything to ridicule!"

"The th-thing you said about my scar. And about my . . . my breasts being small."

"You did repeatedly insult me tonight, and it's no' as if I need you to remind me what I look like."

She peeked over her shoulder, her cheeks even more flushed. *Does she feel guilty for her insults?*

"As for your breasts, if you could no' tell by the raging cockstand I had while touching them, or when I outright told you I find you beautiful, I'll say it plain: I look at your wee body and reasoned thought leaves my brain. So if you want to see a man lose his mind, you'll come to me and let me touch you more." When she still didn't rise from the water, he said, "If you doona want my hands on you again, then come touch me."

She nibbled her lip at that. A promising enough answer for him. He promptly began to strip down, pulling his shirt over his head.

"Uh, wait! I don't want to do that either. . . ." She trailed off, brows drawn as she stared at the stitches in his chest. "What happened to you?"

"Doona worry. It'll soon scar, and you'll have more to belittle about me."

Ignoring his comment, she said, "You've lost weight, too. Is this the injury you spoke of?"

"Aye."

"What happened?" When he didn't answer, she quirked an eyebrow. "Scot, you really must stop running with scissors."

"You are such a daft lass." As he sat on a cushioned stool, removing his boots, he found himself telling her, "I was shot."

Curiosity lit her eyes. She leaned against the side of the tub, resting her chin on her hands. "*Shot?*" She flashed him an expression of realization. "No *wonder* you were afraid of the sounds of gunfire."

"I was no' bloody afraid—"

"So, who would shoot you?"

He shrugged. "A bad man."

"I can see you've had other serious injuries. So what do you do that's so dangerous? Are you some kind of renegade? Or insurgent? I know—you're a soldier of fortune!"

Ethan had never been secretive about what he did, only for whom he did it. "Maybe I'm a bit of each."

She opened her mouth to say more, but when he stepped out of his trousers, she turned away. He used the opportunity to join her in the water. She gasped, darting for the side to flee, but he caught her by the shoulders. Relaxing against the back of the tub, he dragged her to him, groaning when her breasts slid over his torso.

Gentle, he reminded himself as his hand rubbed down her back to cup her arse. He could still very well frighten her away, and after seeing her completely naked in the light, he did *not* want to frighten her away.

When she pushed against him, he curled his hand around her nape, tugging her back.

"MacCarrick, no." She grabbed the sides of the tub to hold herself apart from him. "I'm not . . . I don't want this."

"Why no'?" he asked, skimming his forefinger between her breasts.

She shivered, but answered, "B-because I'm exhausted and overwhelmed. I just need to *think* about all this."

Her arms were shaking with effort as she resisted, making her breasts quiver lusciously. Her nipples were hard and taunting him. He wanted to suck them for hours. He wanted her to touch him—

The image of her pounding her fist on the floor of that tavern flashed in his mind. Reminded of the weary resolve he'd seen, he studied her face. He could see faint smudges beneath her eyes. The day she'd had would throw anyone.

Her hands were slipping along. . . .

"Though you tempt me sorely, I'll let you go so you can rest tonight," he said, disbelieving what he was hearing himself say. "For a kiss."

She flashed him an expression of disappointment and in a deadened tone said, "Fine. Get it over with."

He moved his hands to cradle her face, making her frown. He stroked her cheeks with his thumbs as he kissed her forehead, the tip of her nose, then her mouth with a mere brushing of his lips against hers.

When he released her, it took her a moment to blink open her eyes.

"The first rule of a successful cull," she murmured, "give a little, then take it all."

"Am I to get away with nothing, Madeleine?" he asked, amused for some reason. As he stifled a smile, her gaze dipped to his lips. She looked like she might kiss *him*. But then she abruptly twisted from his hold to rise from the water.

When she stepped out and turned for a towel, he was surprised to see his hand reach out to swat her adorable arse. She swiftly covered herself, casting him a startled glance over her shoulder. But whatever she saw in his expression made her give him a baffled half grin.

Then she sauntered out of the room, collecting her ring, actually seeming more relaxed.

As he finished washing, he wondered how he could be so bloody jovial when his shaft throbbed miserably. He told himself it was only because she'd accepted the plan. He'd won the first battle.

It is no' because she's accepted me, agreed to marry me. . . .

After drying off, he returned to the room with a towel wrapped around his waist. He found her dressed in one of his shirts with the sleeves rolled up. It hung off her shoulders and down to her knees. Around her neck, she wore the ring on that long, red ribbon.

She'd also borrowed a pair of his thick gray socks. They swallowed her feet, bunching down around her ankles. She nibbled her lip, rubbing one wee foot over the other, and again his chest felt tight. "I hope you don't mind."

"No, no' at all." *Can she possibly be more fetching . . . ?*

"How are we to, um, sleep?" she asked.

He stiffened, his mood souring. "Doona care." *Just as long as it's not with me.*

She padded to the linen closet for a blanket and pillow as though she'd read his mind. "Oh, well, you see, I don't really sleep well with anyone in the bed with me."

Ethan drew his head back. "So *you* doona want to share a bed with *me*?" After all those women in his past who'd yearned to sleep with him, this chit looked as if the prospect was appalling.

"That's part of the reason that I wanted my own room," she said. "But I'll happily settle on the divan—"

Swooping her up, he ignored her sputtering protests and dumped her in the bed. He'd make her sleep with him—just to punish her for being contrary. If she hadn't weighed less than a feather, his wound would've been singing, but he didn't care. "You'll be in this bed with me tonight." After throwing off his towel, he joined her.

"I don't want to sleep with you!" She rose to her knees, haphazardly marching on them to the edge. "This, MacCarrick, is my fifth condition."

He caught her makeshift nightgown in his fist, reeling

her back. At her mutinous look, he took her in his arms once more to shove her under the covers.

When she shimmied to the side of the bed, tugging against his hold, he said, "Stay, and I'll buy you new clothes tomorrow." He needed to anyway. There was no way they'd go about in public with her dressed shabbily compared to him. Already people were going to wonder what a woman like her was doing with him. Money would be the natural conclusion, but he'd be damned if he handed others that answer.

She froze, shoulders tensed. "But not . . . not *every* night, MacCarrick?"

She sounded so horrified at the proposition of sharing a bed that he said, "Every . . . single . . . sodding one."

"I want this sacrifice remembered," she muttered, hitting her pillow before lying down on the far edge of the bed.

Sacrifice? Good, she wouldn't prove to be a clinger. He was pleased. Of course.

But an hour later, once she'd fallen asleep, he remained awake, watching her. He found two things interesting about how she slept: silently, and curled up with her knees pulled tight to her chest—the position people took when receiving blows they couldn't defend against.

Ethan understood that her harsh life had made her guarded, but now he wondered specifically what had happened to her once she'd left England. He hadn't known she'd been in a fire, and by the look of the scar, she'd been young when she'd received the injury. She was obviously resilient, even as she appeared so delicate and vulnerable to him.

Surrendering to the urge, he lightly grasped a handful

of the blonde glossy curls drying over her pillow. As he rubbed his thumb over the silky texture, he began to ponder what the mysterious appeal was of holding another in sleep.

Some men genuinely seemed to like it. He remembered Hugh coming home from a day spent with Jane when they'd been younger. He'd had that moonstruck look about him, even more pronounced than usual after meetings with Jane. Ethan had thought he'd finally tupped her, but Hugh had been disgusted with Ethan at the idea. "No, I *held* her. While she slept," Hugh had said, then he'd exhaled with pleasure. "For over an *hour*."

Now, Ethan eased out his hand to feel the enticing warmth of Madeleine's body. Willing her not to wake, he edged closer to her, stretching out behind her, only wanting to test this out for a minute. But she woke and tensed. Well, if the dam was breached . . . He ran his hand under her side and tucked her against him.

He waited for her to relax. Minutes passed, and still she was stiff. He could be contrary, too, and he forced her to remain in this position. He even dragged her tighter to him, which put her pert bottom in his lap and his face against her neck, sending him awash in the scent of her hair. Not surprisingly, he shot hard against her. He looped his other arm under hers and around her chest so that he completely enfolded her.

He ached to be inside her, so why was he feeling that perplexing sense of satisfaction again? As if he was where he was supposed to be?

He'd been exhausted for days, and soon her warmth lulled him. The last thought he had was that if the little witch would relax a bloody bit, sharing a bed might not be the burden he'd thought it.

Twenty-two

Men just aren't built like this anymore, Maddy thought with a sigh. Like gladiators, like warriors.

Tilting her head this way and that, she studied him sleeping in the muted morning sun. He lay on his back with an arm raised over his head, the cover precariously positioned low at his waist, displaying his broad chest and muscular torso. She flushed when she saw that his morning erection elevated the heavy cover.

Maddy had awakened without hunger in a warm, soft bed after a full night's rest uninterrupted by nightmares. And apparently, now that the critical needs of food, safety, and shelter had been met, her body had an entirely different need to contend with.

She was aroused, and his clean, masculine scent and the warmth emanating from his body were making it worse. She had to struggle not to run her fingers over his skin as she recalled the scenes from the night before—how her breasts had rubbed against his unyielding chest in the tub, or later when his hard body had wrapped around hers. Though she didn't want to sleep that way each night, she'd felt surprisingly safe with him. His erection had pressed against her bottom, but he'd kept his promise, never making an advance.

She'd never thought she would enjoy intercourse again, but now she was beginning to believe she could tolerate sex with him—and if he could do it as splendidly as he kissed her, she might even enjoy it once she grew accustomed to his size.

Of course, this didn't mean she planned to let him take her before their wedding. She had to hold firm on that—she knew too many women who'd been promised marriage only to return to La Marais big with child and utterly destitute.

Yet after they'd wed . . . what would a second attempt be like? She might not be looking forward to it, but she was definitely curious.

In fact, everything about him made her curious. For instance, why was he so skilled with a pistol? And who'd shot him so recently? She'd noted at least one other scar that looked like a bullet wound and would bet there were more on his back. What did he do that was so fraught with danger?

Who'd cut his face so terribly, leaving that bone-deep scar?

Already she had a good idea of how intensely it troubled him. But the truth was that even an aficionada like herself could see past it. Indeed, MacCarrick's face was still captivating to her, his features pleasing and even. He had a strong, straight nose, firm lips, and a square jaw shadowed with the night's growth of beard.

The good was so exceedingly good with this man, that it far outweighed the bad.

Maybe in the gentrified Grosvenor world he knew, people were flawless, but that was no longer Maddy's world. She was so used to seeing Crimean soldiers returned from war with parts of their regimental uniforms empty and pinned up that MacCarrick's scar was mild in comparison.

In the hierarchy of characteristics she needed in a potential mate, unmarred skin was not a contender compared to virility, strength, and wealth—all of which this Scot had in spades.

She mentally catalogued his good points: He was rich and seemed generous with his money. He was a sinfully skilled kisser and possessor of the most gorgeous, sculpted body she'd ever beheld. He was fierce—this Scot was no gentle giant—which suited Maddy fine.

The bad points: He was selfish, stubborn, rough, aggressive, and untrustworthy.

Would Ethan MacCarrick be difficult to manage? Absolutely. She had no doubt that she was going to have to draw on every man-managing skill she'd ever learned—and then call on every ounce of patience she could muster.

But she could do it to say good-bye to debts and her hardscrabble existence, and *bonjour* to a new life with a mysterious Scot who'd made her blood burn with both passion and fury.

Finally surrendering to the urge, she trailed the pads of her fingers down the underside of his raised arm, watching, enthralled, as the muscles lining the side of his torso briefly flexed. She gently brushed the skin around his wound, feeling unaccountably saddened that someone had sought to hurt him—or kill him. Why did the idea of him in pain bother her so much? At heart he was still a stranger.

She shook her head, deciding then that she wasn't going to lie to herself anymore. Something about him had attracted her from the very first—attracted her as no man had before. She'd been overwhelmingly drawn to him before she'd seen his face and scar—*she still was after.* And last night, his unpracticed, awkward smile as he'd cuffed her bottom had shown her a different side to this Scot, softening her anger toward him. . . .

After making an unhurried exploration of his chest, her finger meandered down the rigid length of his stomach. Reaching the trail of crisp hair below his navel, she lazily stroked it with her nails.

When he slid his knee up, and his shaft pulsed beneath the cover, she gasped and glanced up, finding his eyes on her. She'd never seen any so compelling—so fierce, the irises jet black with flecks of amber.

Though he was studying her face, she didn't bother trying to disguise the desire she was feeling. His brows drew together, as if he didn't know how to respond.

She grazed the backs of her fingers over his scar, and his expression changed, his demeanor growing surly. "Why do you sleep curled in a ball?" he asked, his voice even more rumbling in the morning. At her blank look, he said, "Sometime in the night, I got you to fall asleep against me, but then when I woke, you were curled up on the other side of the bed." His tone was strangely accusatory.

"I don't know. I guess it's warmer in that position. Paris can get so cold in the winter."

"It could no' be warmer than when you were against me."

"I . . . you're right. I just feel crowded with another in the bed." She barely stifled a shudder. She all too clearly remembered those horrible nights in the infirmary after the fire, sharing a bed with other indigent girls, who unremittingly bumped into her ruined arm all through the night. That pain was as fresh in her memory as it had been when she was eleven. "You don't feel claustrophobic?"

He gave her that look that she'd begun to think he reserved solely for her—a mix of irritation, scowl, and a threatening glower. "It's no' like you take up much room, then, is it?"

Patience, Maddy. Changing the subject, she asked, "So, are we leaving for Scotland today?"

"We're scheduled to leave tomorrow night, but we can push that back if we canna get a week's worth of clothing for you."

"You're really taking me shopping?"

"I said I would, did I no'?"

"Well, if you do everything you say you will, then that means I'm going to be married, and not hungry, and living with you in Scotland." Today she would start a new life with this mysterious man beside her—and for once, she was delighted with her luck. "How are we going to get there?"

"A train from here to Le Havre, then by sea."

"Ah, *la porte océane.* How long will it take?"

"By steamer, it's no more than four days to the southwest coast of Scotland."

"A steamer! I've never been on one, except for the Channel tubs."

"The *Blue Riband* will be lavish, Miss Van Rowen. You'll have much silver to steal." His tone might have been cutting, but she was too excited by their plans and couldn't hold back a grin. He frowned at her lips, then continued, "I've a lesser estate on the coast across the sea from Ireland. We'll spend a night or two there before continuing north by rail to my family's seat of Carrickliffe."

"What's Carrickliffe like? Do you think I'll like it there? Is your clan nice? Will they like me? When I'm not tired and hungry, I'm usually very likable."

"It's a fine estate in the Highlands, with a castle, and, aye, any bride would like it. My clan is verra serious, verra solemn. I doona think they would know what to do with you."

"In other words, they won't like me."

"Does no' matter, since I'm rarely there. And besides, they doona like me either."

She nodded without argument.

"What? You can easily see this?"

"Well, yes," she answered. "You're not very serious or solemn, so I expect that they don't know what to do with you either."

He looked at her as if she'd sprouted two heads. "I *am* serious and solemn."

"No, you're not. At the masquerade, you made me laugh. You had a devilish sense of humor that I enjoyed."

"I think I would know myself," he said more gruffly.

"I won't argue with you, Scot. Though now I do have to wonder exactly why they don't like you."

"Let's have this discussion when you've been around me for a few days. It might become more apparent."

She quirked a brow, deciding not to pursue that subject—yet. "What about your family?" she asked instead. "Do you have a big family? I've always wanted a big one. I wish I had siblings. I know you have one brother . . ." She trailed off. "You said he married Jane—that will make her my sister-in-law, too!"

"Aye, it would. And I have another brother who's also

recently married. My mother is still living, but I have no contact with her."

"Oh. Are you close to your brothers?"

"I'd do anything for them, but I doona believe we're close," he said, revealing the tiniest hint of regret in his voice. For a man who seemed to cloak his emotions at every opportunity, his tone was telling. "Enough questions. We've much to do to prepare for the trip."

She nodded. "Before we leave, I need to pack up some things—"

"You doona need to pack anything. I told you I'd buy you new. Besides, the spoils would no' be worth the effort."

Her lips thinned. If he was going to continue ridiculing her poverty, then she was glad she hadn't told him she could overlook his scar. She'd give up knowledge of that chink in his armor as soon as she deemed it unnecessary to possess.

"In any case, MacCarrick, I'd like to give some things to my friends and say good-bye to them."

"We'll see, if there's time."

It nettled her how dogmatic and domineering he was with her, but Maddy would pick her battles. If she was patient, with time she could manage him—she just needed to bite her tongue until she uncovered his weaknesses. Besides, she wouldn't fight him on this—not until she'd determined he absolutely wouldn't permit her to see her friends. "You know, since it appears that we're actually going through with this, I think you should tell me how you got your scar." When she touched it again, he looked as if he'd just stopped himself from flinching.

He hesitated before he said, "I was in a knife fight."

Her eyes widened. "Did you kill someone? Was it broken up? Did you win?"

"I dinna win at first"—he cast her a disquieting smile—"but I did in the end."

"Get my wife anything she could possibly need," Ethan told the modiste at one of the most exclusive dressmaker's in Paris. "Her trunks were lost, so we'll be starting anew. And we'll need garments to take with us today—a week's worth of dresses."

When he and Madeleine had first entered the shop, a few of the girls working inside had turned their noses up at Madeleine's scuffed boots and worn clothes. She'd donned an indifferent expression, but he could tell she was embarrassed, and for some reason, the idea of that made his hackles rise. *How dare they?*

Ethan stressed to the modiste, "I want you and your employees to understand that *nothing* is too good, or too costly, for her. Her wardrobe—and their attitude—should reflect that."

The woman nodded enthusiastically, and a sharp clap of her hands sent shopgirls rushing to set up garments and fabrics in a back dressing room.

Madeleine grabbed his arm and tried to steer him aside. "No, MacCarrick," she urgently whispered, "An entire wardrobe? Not in a place like this—that will cost a fortune! There are bargain shops on Rue de la Paix."

He raised his eyebrows. "I thought you said we have a lot in common. In your situation, I would take me for all I'm worth."

"I'm not in this for the short cull. Your continued healthy finances are very important to me."

"So that you will no' harp on this, I'll tell you what I make a year—just on rents."

When he told her, she actually swayed as her jaw slackened. "You're not lying? Not jesting?" He shook his head. "Oh. In that case, I'll spend with impunity."

"Fine. Now, doona be uncomfortable with the girls for staring at your shabby clothes," he told her in a patronizing tone. "These women matter no' at all."

She quirked an eyebrow. "And you shouldn't be uncomfortable either. Even if they likely think your scar is"—she paused, then enunciated—"*big*."

When he made comments about her poverty, she ridiculed his scar. He was coming to see it as a game they played. "Have your fun, then. But now you'll have one less dress to call your own."

"Then that's one less dress you can almost rip off me."

He frowned down at her. "Do you have an answer for everything?"

"Yes. But I specialize in questions," she said, wandering off to survey scarves.

Ach, she baffled him. He was beginning to think she was a little *too* clever. If he wasn't careful, this game could come back to bite him on the arse.

When he'd awakened this morning, he'd sensed her leaning over him and had feigned sleep, until she'd begun to touch him so sensually and tenderly. He'd opened his eyes to find her staring down at him.

Damn if she hadn't been aroused, her pupils dilated, breaths shallow. He'd savored it. He couldn't remember the last time he'd known for a fact that a woman truly desired him.

In the past, the few women who'd seemed to be aroused by his scar had invariably liked more pain in their bed play than pleasure. Ethan was all for a hard, teeth-clattering tup—preferred it, in fact—but he had no interest in flaying a woman's skin.

Madeleine was beautiful, and if *she'd* deemed him attractive, then perhaps he wasn't as bad off as he'd thought. Perhaps he'd been overly critical of his face, his demeanor affecting his appeal with women.

He knew that soon he'd wear Madeleine down, and once she'd succumbed to him fully and he'd tired of her, he'd explore this with other women, voluptuous women with bouncing breasts who liked hard sex. . . .

Even as he thought it, his eyes were drawn to Madeleine. He could admit she had surprised him—in fact, she continued to with her unusual behavior. He watched her caressing the silks and began to grow hard yet again. For a man who'd feared himself quit of this feeling, he was astonished at how easily she aroused him.

Ethan narrowed his eyes. Madeleine had seemed to be obsessed with touching, and now he discovered it was a clever ruse to cover her thefts. She was skilled, extraordinarily so, and if he hadn't been trained to descry minute details, he never would have noticed what she was doing.

He strode over to her. "Put it back," he commanded under his breath.

She gave him an innocent look, with guileless blue eyes. "What are you talking a—"

He squeezed her elbow, silencing her, and she finally unthreaded the silk scarf from her blouse sleeve.

"Madeleine, the little thieveries must end."

She cocked a brow. "So sure they're *little*?"

"Christ, I wonder if you're no' worse than I am." He didn't mind people suffering if they wronged him first. Actually, he relished it. But he had no feud with this store owner, and she might not be able to easily suffer these losses.

"You steal, gamble, and speak the cant of the streets. If I'm to be our moral guide, we're both hellbound, lass."

She gazed up at him, lips curling. "But at least we'd be together."

He knew she was teasing, but she still disarmed him, and his anger began evaporating. . . .

When the modiste invited Madeleine to sit down with her and peruse fashion books, Ethan was provided coffee and a newspaper in English. He tried to read, but he grew distracted by Madeleine's voice, though she spoke softly, in a lilting French. Her questions and comments surprised him—as did her confidence when speaking with the older modiste.

"But what if you did this fabric and the ruche like this? With some bombazine?" she asked. "And why must that one be symmetrical? If this is hunter green sateen and atilt, it will look vanguard but elegant at the same time."

The woman stammered some answer.

"No, no, madam, this should be a stiff collar, upturned high on the neck and open here. And if the petticoat is visible, then we must make sure it's fabulous—I know, a white tulle over rich glacé silk!"

When they finished and Madeleine went off to choose reticules and gloves, the modiste approached Ethan. Her expression was overwhelmed, probably resembling the one he'd been sporting quite a bit of late.

"Your wife's taste is . . ." She trailed off, and Ethan thought she would say *unusual* or *interesting*.

". . . amazing. She has untouchable instincts with fabrics and color."

"Aye, naturally," he said, as if he were well aware of this. "Just make sure you leave room to let out her gowns. . . ." He trailed off when Madeleine stared past him to the store's front window, her eyes going wide.

He swung his head around, expecting to see the henchmen outside. Instead, he caught sight of a well-dressed man with a more garishly clad woman strolling by and slowing, no doubt intending to enter the shop.

Madeleine was staring at the man only. Ethan sensed something cold about him, something dangerous—which might explain why the blood had rushed from Madeleine's face.

Twenty-three

Maddy darted behind a bolt of cloth, unrolling it to hide behind, struggling to calm her breaths. She'd felt MacCarrick's eyes on her and knew he must be puzzled, but Toumard was just outside! And looked as if he might enter at any time.

As was customary, Maddy had noted a back door when they'd first arrived and was easing toward it when MacCarrick told the modiste, "We'll have the shop to ourselves this morning."

"But, *monsieur*—"

"Close up. I'll spend more in a couple of hours than you'll make this week. *If* we have leisure and privacy in buying it."

Maddy peeked from behind her cloth, trying to see him as these women did. His bearing screamed wealth—that was obvious. His clothes were unadorned but finely made and unmistakably expensive. Yes, he appeared rich, but he also appeared powerful—and, with the scar, menacing.

Maddy wasn't all that surprised when the shop owner crossed to the door and bolted it, turning her sign to *Fermé.*

"The shades," MacCarrick said. "Otherwise patrons will knock."

With her lips thinned, she said, "Yes, *monsieur*," and motioned for an assistant to draw the curtains.

Nearly clutching her chest in relief, Maddy gave him a shaky, grateful smile. He was expressionless for a moment, his eyes flickering over her lips and eyes; then he cast her a scowl as he strode over.

"Why are we avoiding that man outside?"

He seemed to be analyzing her, and she found herself having difficulty lying to him—a handicap she hadn't encountered for years. "Just someone I'd rather not see."

"Have you stolen from him?"

"No, never! I've never done anything to him. It's just . . . I owe him a bit of money."

"He's the one who sent the thugs after you?" When she nodded, he said, "What would you borrow from him for?"

"Dresses. I needed dresses to go to London."

"How much do you owe?" He looked to be patting his pockets for his money—to pay off Toumard? When she hesitated, he said, "You will no' indulge me with an answer, Madeleine?"

"I don't even know," she admitted. "He changed the interest to an escalating rate. I can't keep up with it."

"You were late to pay him, then?"

"No, not before he changed the terms of the deal."

MacCarrick narrowed his eyes. "Is that so? You dinna find that strange?"

"I did. But it's not as if I could go complain to anyone."

"You can now, lass," he said, curling his fingers under her chin. "We'll take care of this matter before we leave. I will no' have you fretting over this."

Just like in London, he was acting heroic and protective. Just like in London, she found herself gazing up at him in that way that made him glower.

When the modiste delicately coughed to get their attention, he gruffly said, "Go on, then."

The woman led Maddy back to the dressing room. The space was large, with a silver tea service and a wine rack inside, made to cater to a woman's mother and sisters and friends, consulting on a new wardrobe or ball gowns for the latest season. Maddy felt a jab of disappointment at the thought that she would be alone.

She'd just undressed to her shift when MacCarrick strolled in. He sank back on a divan, relaxing his towering frame with a kind of lethal grace. He didn't appear discomfited in the least. "She can dress in front of me," he said, his tone bored as he opened his newspaper. "It's nothing I have no' seen before."

The shopkeepers shrugged, no doubt having seen this again and again.

Had this been anywhere but Paris, Maddy might have protested, but he'd just saved her from facing her despicable creditor. How could she deny MacCarrick anything?

The near encounter only reinforced her intention to stay with the Scot. She could put up with much never to see Toumard again—oh, and to be fantastically rich—even trying on clothes in front of MacCarrick.

But every time they pulled a gown above her head, her shift rode up, exposing her bottom to him—and her front as well in the four-way mirror. Just as embarrassing, she'd caught him frowning at her scar, and he even seemed to notice when others peered at it.

Over the next hour, she tried on day dresses and evening dresses, skirts and blouses, cloaks and gloves. A milliner was brought in to see to her hats and bonnets, and a shoemaker provided pair after pair of colored satin slippers and boots of a buttery soft kid leather.

She already had enough clothing for several days, but after MacCarrick and the modiste spoke outside, additional dresses were unexpectedly available to Maddy—appropriated from someone else's tailored wardrobe.

At first glance, these garments were hideous, but then she realized that, hidden under the weight of tasteless trimmings, the dresses were cut well, with a modern flair even, and made of expertly styled fabrics. As usual, some rich Parisians had gone overboard with the embellishments—but then, they'd probably wanted to demonstrate their wealth at every turn.

To make the gowns her own, Maddy simply directed the seamstresses to take them in and discard the abundant tassels, tufts of silk flowers, and fur pom-poms.

Once she'd selected everything but undergarments with nary a comment from MacCarrick, they stripped her down to her stockings and garters to try on lingerie.

She was as mortified as a provincial when she felt his eyes on her. She willed herself not to raise her hands for cover, sighing in relief each time they slid a nightgown over her.

MacCarrick was holding up a paper, but she knew he wasn't reading. He kept turning it aside until he set it down completely and leaned forward on the edge of the divan. His lids grew heavy, but his eyes were alert and flickering over her. She reminded herself that she could endure this scrutiny and more for all that MacCarrick was doing for her. Even being displayed in lingerie to his fancy.

Though he'd had no interest in the dresses, he voiced his opinions on the lingerie forcefully. "In the red one. I want to see her in the red," he demanded, his voice growing husky.

Maddy swallowed, stepping into a crimson gown with two lace-trimmed slits at the sides that climbed all the way to her hips. Even with these women in the room, she began to respond to his attention, her breasts feeling heavier every time he shifted uncomfortably in his seat. As the lace cups caressed her nipples, she pictured how his muscles had flexed under her fingers this morning. When she recalled how he'd explored her the night before . . .

She had to bite the inside of her cheek to keep from sighing out loud.

Ethan had never thought he'd enjoy shopping for a woman as much as this.

He was buying her far more than was necessary, but he was deriving too much pleasure from the process to stop himself. As he watched Madeleine dress and undress, into and out of wicked silks, he abandoned the pretense of reading the paper and used it only to conceal his raging erection.

Earlier, Madeleine had been nervously darting glances at him in the mirror. Now she held his gaze, her lips parting. Her nipples had hardened and her breaths were shallow.

Christ, she . . . wanted him. She'd seen every inch of him, and she'd bloody touched his scar, and yet she wanted him. Was *pleading* for him.

He nearly shuddered with pleasure. Her desire was the most powerful aphrodisiac he could imagine.

"Out," he abruptly ordered the women.

"Monsieur?"

"Take a midday break from the shop. Now." The look on his face silenced them, and they darted from the dressing room.

When the door shut behind them, Madeleine swallowed but said nothing.

"You know what I want, and you know better than to question me," he said as he neared her, removing his jacket. "I like that."

"I won't question you, even though I wonder if you'll appease your lust whenever you feel like it."

"Aye, with you I will. And it's no' only *my* lust that I plan to appease." He ran a hand into one of the high slits, then slipped his finger between her legs. When he felt her sex, a harsh sound broke from his chest. She was wet for him, slick and lush. "Seems you might need *appeasement* more than I do."

At that she shoved her legs closed, twisting out of his grasp.

"Doona close your legs to me," he growled.

"Then stop trying to embarrass me!"

"I was only stating fact."

Through gritted teeth, she said, "Make an effort not to."

"As your husband, I'll no' be denied, Madeleine."

"You're not my husband yet."

"If I were, would you let me take you in this room?"

"Yes, if that was what you desired." She'd surprised him, but she clearly meant it.

"I will be soon, so what's the difference? I want to be inside you. Now."

She shook her head firmly. "Not until we're wed."

"Then perhaps I should no' be buying you a new wardrobe as befits a wife, if I'm no' yet a husband?"

She stiffened, crossing her arms in front of her chest. "I'm not a whore. Buy me the clothes or not, but don't expect sex in return. And don't confuse my desire for you—and for self-preservation—with desperation."

"And do you desire me?"

She put her chin up. "Yes. But I can still walk away."

"Ah, *aingeal*, it's too late for that. . . ."

Twenty-four

MacCarrick stalked around her, as if deciding what he wanted to touch or do first.

"You already know you need me for more than just money or clothes, do you no'?" He seemed angry with her, but she couldn't understand what she'd done to make him so. Finally he stopped in front of her, leaning in to press his mouth to her neck. As he brushed the straps from her shoulders, his rough palms made a delicious contrast to the silk. "Answer me."

"Yes," Maddy admitted. The garment whispered to the floor, leaving her in nothing but stockings and garters.

He nodded slowly. "Good lass," he said, then bent his dark head over her pale breasts. She watched in the mirror, glorying in the way this man seemed to crave kissing her there. His hands were huge, the palms callused, yet the manner in which he worked them over her body was adoring.

Her thoughts grew dim when he took her nipple into his mouth, his tongue circling it. After suckling both tips until they were hard, swollen points, he stood fully and walked behind her. Cupping her leg behind her knee, he lifted her foot onto the low stool, spreading her legs in front of the mirror.

When she glanced away, he said, "Stay like this. I want to see you." Then he coaxed her to face the mirror as his jet eyes flickered over the reflection—possessively lingering on her breasts and between her thighs. Most wouldn't find his visage beautiful, but at that instant, he was the most irresistible man she'd ever beheld.

Just when she was about to beg him to put his hands on her, he cupped her between her legs. Though she'd wanted his touch, she still jerked in shock.

"Relax, I just want to pet you here," he said as he spread her legs more. "Look at my finger stroking you," he rumbled at her ear. "You doona want me to stop?"

"No . . ."

"Then tell me you desire me again."

"I do . . . you know I do."

With a triumphant gleam in his eyes, he pressed her up against the mirror, delving his finger inside her wetness from behind. Her damp nipples met the cool glass and she moaned, lost.

Her sheath hugged his finger, shockingly tight as Ethan lazily thrust it inside her. With his other hand, he wrapped her hair around his fist, tugging her head back so he could watch her reactions in the mirror. How had he ever thought her experienced? Her responses were ungoverned, bare. She was so passionate—and his possession to do with as he would.

She wore nothing but his ring on that ribbon dangling between her breasts, and her garters and stockings. The red silk of her garters stood out against the pale skin of her thighs.

"So lovely," he heard himself say. Her skin was sleek and soft, her nipples dark pink, like the bow of her lips.

She hissed in a breath when he tried to fit a second finger into her, and her hand shot behind her to his wrist, her arm straight to push him away.

"Shh, I'll stop." He withdrew it. Again that heavy feeling arose when he was reminded of how badly he'd hurt her that night—he hadn't prepared her. He vowed to himself that when he did decide to take her, he would frig her for a damned hour till she begged him for it. "Here, put your arms back around my neck." She hesitated. "Just trust me."

Once she tentatively grasped his neck, he began to tease her nipples, lightly pinching the tips. When she moaned, he ran one hand from her breast to her flat belly then to her sex, but she tensed. "Trust me. Let me make you come. . . ."

She gasped at his words but allowed his touch. With one hand, he spread the flesh around her clitoris wide and smoothed the pad of his other forefinger side to side over her swollen little bud. "Do you like that?"

"Oh, my God, yes," she said, panting. Soon she was trembling, her hands gripping his neck tightly. Keeping her open, rubbing her clitoris over and over, he watched as she grew wetter, her flesh glistening. When she began to undulate her hips to his fingers, he thought he'd spill in his trousers.

With her brows drawn, clearly aching for her climax, she met his eyes in the mirror. "*Ethan*," she whispered, saying his name for the first time.

And it sounded like a benediction.

In a flash, he understood that she hungered for this passion and pleasure, but that wasn't all she was longing for at that moment. There was yearning in her eyes, so raw and furious he was staggered by it. Then her lids slid shut, which was good, because he was shaken.

"Let yourself go," he grated at her ear, barely recognizing his own strained voice. "Come for me, Madeleine."

When she did with a strangled cry, he knew she was his.

He leered at her reflection as her back arched, her breasts quivering. He felt a savage thrill as she rolled against his finger, tensing and shivering to his touch. "That's it," he murmured. "You like that."

He slowed his strokes as the tension began to leave her body. Though he had a fierce need to come, he decided he'd further demonstrate to her that he was no horrible lover. He dipped his finger into her wetness, spreading it all around. Without warning, he sped up the rhythm once more.

"*What . . . ?*" she cried, lowering her arms, trying to wriggle away from him, but he looped an arm around her waist to hold her firm. "Oh, God. It's too much!"

But he was merciless, rubbing her, kissing and licking her neck, until she'd stopped struggling. When he sucked her earlobe, she began meeting his fingers again. "Do you find me a horrible lover now?"

"N-no—"

"Tell me when you're goin' tae come again."

"Now, *now*," she said, the word breaking on a moan. As she climaxed, he slipped the forefinger of his free hand into her sheath, thrusting it fast. "Oh, yes, Ethan! Feels . . . so . . . *good*," she cried.

His head fell back, and he groaned to the ceiling, feeling her sex squeezing his finger so tightly, in a rush of wet heat.

Even after she'd finished, and though he was about to explode, he took his time, delving inside her as she sagged against him. He wanted to accustom her to the feeling, to trust him to touch her this way.

Her response was so rewarding that part of him said to let this be only about her, to act as though he could give without taking. But when his cock ached like this he didn't feel very giving.

Unfastening the front of his trousers, he pulled himself free with a hissed breath. Then taking her hips, he pressed his shaft against her arse, his thumbs covering those dimples above her bottom. He groaned as he thrust over her plump curves, settling between them to grind against her. His cock head was so slick he daubed wetness against her lower back. He could readily come like this, but he wanted her hands on him. He choked out the words, "I need you tae ease me." He slid his cock against her hip. "Touch it."

She inhaled, trying to catch her breath, then nodded. Reaching down, she brushed the pad of her finger softly on the crown, making unhurried circles around the slit, but he grasped her wrist and put her palm to his shaft. "No teasing. No' yet." He met her eyes in the mirror. "I'm starving for this, *aingeal*."

"How should I . . . what do you want me to do?"

"Stroke me as you did that night in the carriage."

When she wrapped her soft palm at the base and drew her fist up, a wave of pleasure and elation swept through him. How in the hell had he lived without this for so long?

"Tighter," he commanded, and she gripped him harder. "That's it." He thumbed her nipples to urge her on. "Good, Madeleine . . . ," he grated. "It's so damned good."

He squeezed her against him, covering her breasts with his hands, groans and coarse oaths breaking from his chest. "Faster." She did, pumping her fist on him as he bucked into it. "*Clever girl*," he rasped against her damp neck, "*you're making me come*."

At the last second, he placed his hand over hers, pressing down. Yelling out, he ejaculated, pumping hot seed directly against her wicked garter, over and over.

When he was finally spent, he shuddered and stayed her hand, astonished by the pleasure he'd just experienced, unable to remember its equal, but for the night he'd taken her.

He still held her against him and wanted to stay like that as they caught their breath, yet he expected her to disentangle herself. Instead, her head fell back against him, and he had the leisure of watching her breasts rise and fall with her panting, her flesh perfectly flushed.

She caught his gaze in the mirror. Between breaths she whispered, "If you give me a chance, I'll be a good wife to you, Scot. Just please, don't hurt me again."

"I will no'," he said, holding her tighter, and for the briefest moment, he might have meant it.

Twenty-five

Madeleine stood on her toes and pressed a kiss to his cheek, touching his scar with her lips—not even seeming to mind.

Having never experienced this kind of gentle affection from a woman, he had no idea how to proceed with it. She seemed delighted by what had happened, humming as she strolled to the *salle de bain* to freshen up and change into one of the previously tailored dresses.

When she returned, clad in her smart new clothes, with her shining hair braided atop her head, he found himself saying, "We'll go to the garret now. If you want to take something to your friends, we can put a couple of bottles of champagne on the tab."

"Really? For Bea and Corrine?"

"Aye." And that one gesture earned him an expression from her that could only be described as *adoring*—the way she'd regarded him that night in London. He pulled at his collar.

The overjoyed modiste had used her break to tally their bill, saving him time when paying. He thought Madeleine was going to faint when she sneaked a glance at the total. But he would have spent twenty times that if he'd known how he was to be rewarded.

As the girls wrapped the bottles of champagne and fitted them into a narrow carrying basket, Ethan told the modiste that he'd wire directions for shipping the rest of Madeleine's clothing once they finished tailoring them. Whatever was completed today, they should send to his hotel.

When he and Madeleine exited the shop and he offered her his arm, she took it without hesitation. On the street, passersby gave them openly quizzical glances. He knew they wondered what she was doing with him, which reminded him that he used to be handsome. Before, he would have been a fitting match for her. Instead, he was a man who had to spend money on a woman to get her attention.

Ethan was feeling something for her, some kind of appreciation for what had just happened between them, but that only disgusted him. He was like a starving wolf that had been fed a scrap and was happy to get it—a thirty-three-year-old man grateful to have his cock stroked. He ground his teeth, seething. He was never supposed to have ended up this way.

And her parents were to blame for everything.

Things used to be black and white. He was a man not bound by any fixed moral code; she was the daughter of two people who'd wronged him.

How could there possibly be any hesitation or second thoughts about what he was planning?

There wouldn't be. All he cared about was getting her beneath him enough times to work her from his system.

"Thank you for today," she said, smiling up at him. Was she pleased with him because he'd spent a fortune on her or because she'd enjoyed what had happened between them? Why did he even care?

"You're welcome," he said, for probably the first time in his life.

When they arrived by cab in La Marais and he helped her down, the streets were harried and chaotic once more. Madeline stood out here like a diamond in dust.

"Oh, look, there's Berthé!" she whispered. "The one who tripped me last night. Make sure she sees us."

He hid a frown. Did Madeleine want to be seen *with him*? Or did she only want to show off her new finery? Just when he'd decided on the latter, he felt a distinctly proprietary patting on his arse.

"*Madeleine*," he growled in warning, and she yanked her hand up.

"Sorry," she murmured. "I just couldn't resist."

Why was he oddly . . . flattered?

At her building, he followed Madeleine inside and to the stairwell. "Hold onto the rope," she said, taking the bottles and hastening ahead of him as though she could see in the dark.

As soon as the stair head groaned, Bea's door swung open, but it was Corrine who rushed out to meet them. "Toumard's men came by again," she said. "You have to get out of here, Maddy! They roughed up Bea—"

"What?" Madeleine cried. "Bea?"

Corrine nodded. "She wouldn't tell them where you'd gone, and then she had to go and spit in one's face. She'll be all right, but she's lying down now, resting."

The news of this threat made that feeling of protectiveness for Madeleine surge in him again. "Go check on Bea," Ethan told her. "Corrine will tell me what happened."

Once Madeleine hurried to Bea's room and softly closed the door behind her, Corrine said, "I see that look in your eyes. You really are going to take care of Maddy from now on."

He hesitated before giving her a quick nod. "Madeleine accepted my proposal."

Corrine sighed in relief.

"But I need to know some things about her past, and the lass is tight-lipped." When Corrine nodded ruefully, he asked, "How did she burn her arm?"

"Oh, that was in the fire of forty-seven. Her building went up like a wick, and she was trapped upstairs. She very nearly lost her arm and came close to losing her life."

If she had been eleven or twelve, she'd just been forced away from her home to move to a foreign city. Her father had just died. . . .

"That's one of the reasons Maddy's so terrified of Toumard—his men love to break arms," she continued. "Maddy's been like a cat sidling round a boiling pot of porridge these last few weeks. Fit to break your heart."

The idea of her being afraid, day after day . . .

Toumard was as good as dead.

"Why does Madeleine no' live with her mother?"

Corrine lowered her voice. "Well, she doesn't like people to know this, but her mother's . . . dead."

"You canna be serious," he snapped. She nodded, and suddenly all Ethan could hear was his heart pounding in his ears. "Dead . . ."

All the time I've wasted hating, wanting to hurt someone—someone who didn't even exist any longer. . . .

Corrine's hands twined. "Maddy's been an orphan for years. Her mother died when Maddy was fourteen."

He pinched the bridge of his nose. "An *orphan*."

Ethan had thought he'd been hell-bound before. Now there was no doubt. He gave a bitter laugh. This must be a jest.

He'd deflowered a penniless waif. An orphan.

"She had friends in England," Ethan said. "When her mother died, she could have petitioned them for help, and they would gladly have given it."

"She'd been here for some time already. Living in La Marais makes you feel a bit . . . worthless, especially in the young. She was ashamed. The only reason she went after that man in England was because Bea and I wouldn't let it rest. We eventually got her to promise to try before she married Le Daex."

"Le Daex, the count?" he demanded. "Her mother didn't arrange that?"

"Yes, years ago. But after she died, Maddy ran away before the wedding. We only recently revived that cull with La Daex. But all it did was get Maddy in debt."

And put an unprotected young woman under Toumard's notice.

Ethan supposed he'd hoped Madeleine had been close to Sylvie, that they were two of a kind. Instead, Sylvie was dead, and Madeleine had suffered destitution for years by Ethan's hand, bearing the brunt of a revenge meant for another. She'd suffered alone.

And Ethan had planned to hurt her worse.

How could it be worse for her? He remembered the look on her face as she'd picked herself up in that tavern. How many times had she had to do just that over the last ten years here . . . ?

Just walk away.

This information, taken with the way Madeleine had said his name like a bloody benediction—with that undisguised longing . . . *Even I'm no' cruel enough to do anything more to her.*

He briefly closed his eyes as he finally admitted the truth to himself. He had come here because he *wanted* Madeleine. The revenge aspect only allowed him to justify the idea of a man like him using a young innocent like her.

If you are no' bent on punishing her, then what right do you have to her?

None. None whatsoever.

He couldn't take her away to hurt her, and he sure as hell couldn't keep her. He'd fix her problem with the lender, then get out of her life. Hell, he could even send some money later.

Abandon her here? After he'd convinced her that he was taking her with him?

What choice did he have? If he took her away, would he find himself saddled with her? He had a profession, a solitary one, and he wanted to get back to it. *Damn it, I doona want to get stuck with her.*

Help her, then leave her. Of course. "Tell me how to find Toumard."

Twenty-six

"Shouldn't you be resting?" Maddy asked when Bea rose from the bed and dressed.

"Maddée, if I rested every time I had a blue eye," she said in a deliberate tone as though explaining to a child, "I would do little else, *n'est-ce pas*? Now, let's sit on your balcony and you can tell me everything that happened last night."

When Bea opened her door, MacCarrick and Corrine appeared to have just finished their conversation. His stony gaze flickered over Bea's eye, and his jaw clenched. To Maddy, he said, "I'll return soon."

"Are you going to see Toumard?" At his short nod, she said, "Can I come with you?"

"Absolutely no'. Stay here, enjoy a going-away drink together."

"Very well," she finally said, confused by his mood change. He seemed to have trouble looking her in the eyes just before he left them to wait in Maddy's apartment.

The three had just agreed to sell the pricey bottles when the door opened once more. MacCarrick had returned.

To open the champagne.

"Some things are meant to be enjoyed in the moment, are they no'?" he said, with another fuming glance at Bea's face. To Maddy, he added, "So that you doona go out to sell it by the glass . . ." He filled her new reticule with cash.

Her jaw dropped at the wad of money. "This is four hundred francs! Do you want me to go buy a piano? Or a cabriolet?"

"*Un bateau*!" Bea cried with a clap. "A boat!"

Maddy leaned into her, play-shoving her with her shoulder. MacCarrick didn't come close to smiling.

"Well, let's pour it up!" Corrine said, taking out chipped porcelain mugs from under Maddy's stove. When she offered a cup to MacCarrick, he waved his share away. "Doona drink."

"*Plus pour nous*," Bea said, her tone delighted. *More for us*. Even after her run-in with the henchmen, Bea was likely deeming this one of the best days of her life.

"I'll be back," MacCarrick said to Maddy with a curt nod.

"Please be careful, Scot."

When the door shut behind MacCarrick once more and they heard him stomping down the stairs, Bea fanned herself and whispered, "I'm in love. Maddée, do you know he sent us lobsters last night? I'm not jesting." She added with a sigh, "*Pretty lobsters* . . . "

Maddy grinned. MacCarrick was turning out to be such a . . . surprise, giving her a new day, a new beginning. She hurried to the balcony to watch him striding away. *So tall, strapping, confident.* Just as he had been the first time she'd spotted him—when he'd been hunting *for her*.

"I think you might have a diamond in the rough there," Corrine said behind her.

Maddy was beginning to think so, as well. In London, he'd been the first person ever to fight for her—and now he was marching out to do battle again.

"*Très viril*," Bea added, joining them.

There was that, too. She blushed to recall the way he'd pleasured her so perfectly in the shop—*twice*. She believed that her nights spent tossing in her sheets, yearning and lonely, were ended.

"Now, Maddy girl," Corrine began with a sniffle, "we've got to drink two bottles of champagne and get you packed by the time your fiancé comes back."

Maddy nodded, then set about divvying between her two friends the new cash windfall, her stash of coupons, and her contraband. After she'd packed the few things that were dear to her, they sat outside drinking and awaiting his return.

She was stunned to realize this could be the last time the three ever sat here like this. "If he's legitimate, I'll send more money as soon as I can." In fact, she'd be sending *for them*, but she didn't want to get their hopes up before she knew if she could trust him implicitly.

"And if he's not legitimate?" Bea asked.

Maddy hesitated. "Corrine, can you hold my room for a couple of months, just in case?"

"Naturally," Corrine said, then added, "but I do hope this works out with him. Just remember, Maddy, with a man that strong-willed, you'll get more with honey than with vinegar."

She sipped her champagne. "And if I run out of honey . . . ?"

What would be worse for her? Ethan thought on the way back from killing Toumard. *Mixed up with a man like myself or left behind?*

At heart, Ethan was a selfish bastard. If he took her

away, eventually this superficial noble streak would fade. *A man canna change his nature.*

Get away from her . . . just bloody think *about this for a while. Doona do anything drastic.*

But the idea of leaving her behind felt so wrong that it pained him physically.

If Maddy didn't get out of this slum, then at best, she'd become like Corrine—working to the bone, old before her time. Or she could become like Bea—or worse. Then Madeleine would have some man lifting her skirts in a reeking alley while his friend waited.

Ethan's fists clenched even now. If Toumard had had his way, that would have been her within mere weeks.

Ethan had already known he'd have to kill Toumard. When the man had coldly informed him what he'd been planning to do to Madeleine—*sample* her before putting her to work—Ethan had burned to. He would have shot him in cold blood if Toumard hadn't drawn on him.

Breaking the arms of the henchmen . . . ? Well, that had merely been sport.

If Ethan left Madeleine, there were a thousand more like Toumard eager to prey on a girl like her, and she now had no marriage prospects. Except for bloody Quin. Ethan would have to remember that. As soon as Quin learned that Ethan had left her alone, he'd come charging down to Paris to save her. Perhaps Ethan should let him.

The thought of them together clawed at him.

Damn it, do nothing drastic. . . . Ethan was a man who liked to have a plan. Now that his initial one was absolutely extinguished, he cast about for what to do next. The facts: The most desirable woman he'd ever beheld desired him back. He'd contributed to her painful past and could ease her troubles now. He'd vowed that he wouldn't rest until he'd had her again, and when he made decisions, he bloody stuck by them. He would take her away, seduce her, then settle money on her. He'd be getting her out of this place—in the end, she'd be thankful.

Yet when he arrived back at her building, he was still uncertain. Then he found her hurrying from the entrance, her face lit with a relieved smile. Having grown accustomed to expressions of disappointment or fear whenever he arrived somewhere, he looked over his shoulder before catching himself.

When they reached each other, she appeared to check him over to make sure he wasn't hurt. Shortly after, Bea and Corrine emerged to see them off, handing Maddy her small bag.

"Write to us," Corrine told Madeleine as she wiped away a tear.

"Of course." Hugging them both, Madeleine sniffled. "Take care of each other."

Bea gave a watery nod, and another round of lingering good-byes ensued before he could steer Madeleine away. As he led her to the top of the hill, she waved over her shoulder until her friends were out of sight.

While they waited for a cab, Ethan said, "Madeleine, I need to speak with you." It seemed everyone on every stoop watched them. "I've thought of some things."

"I see." She didn't appear surprised. Had she expected him to disappoint her?

Why? She sodding *liked* him. Even his brothers—who Ethan knew would die for him—didn't seem to *like* him. He made Court wary, and he continually disappointed Hugh.

How would Hugh feel, knowing his older brother had

taken the virtue of a defenseless girl? Then abandoned her in Paris?

Hugh's parting words in London echoed in Ethan's head. "*What if she's the one?*" he'd asked again. "*The irony would be that you've somehow found her, you actually get to keep her, and yet you intend to hurt her beyond forgiving.*"

But Ethan *already* had hurt her, well before he'd ever met her. And the longer she was with him, the more likely it was that he'd hurt her again. It was simply his nature; he had no talent at pleasing others.

Perhaps Madeleine needed to better understand what he was truly like.

"What do you want to tell me?" Maddy asked, trying to hide her disappointment. She'd known this situation was too good to be true, and now MacCarrick looked as though he was plagued with second thoughts. When he began to speak, only to fall silent, she asked, "Did you pay off Toumard?"

"You owe him nothing," he replied in a cryptic tone.

She frowned. "Did you . . . kill him?"

"Aye, I plugged a bullet into his skull." His eyes flickered over her face for her reaction.

She sighed. *A fierce protector returning from battle.* When she nodded up at him, he seemed confounded that she wasn't running away.

"Damn it, lass, why do you keep looking at me like that? I doona care for it. And I just informed you that I bloody killed a man this morning."

Maybe MacCarrick wasn't having second thoughts—maybe he was merely feeling guilt for what he'd done. "I hope you don't feel bad about that. La Marais is a better place without Toumard in it. But we do need to get you out of the city. Do you think we can stay aboard the steamer before it departs tomorrow?"

He froze, then jerked his head back. "I will never figure you out. I ken that now. Because you're *crazed*."

She waved his comment away. "Did you offer to pay him?" she asked.

He said nothing.

"So you offered to pay him, and he refused. He never wanted money from me. He planned to put me to work like Berthé, didn't he?"

MacCarrick's eyes bored into hers, raw fury burning in their dark depths. His voice was seething when he said, "*Aye, after he'd bedded you himself.*"

"I see." She felt a wave of revulsion. "Well, he didn't leave you much choice. If he refused your money and I left town, he'd just terrorize Bea and Corrine. What did you do to his men?"

"I broke their goddamned arms." Whatever he saw in her expression made him snap, "No' again! Stop lookin' at me that way—I've told you I doona like it."

"Yes, very well. But, again, we really have to get you out of here, and quickly." When a cab passed them, she gave an urgent whistle, but was roundly ignored. She muttered a curse; then suddenly her eyes went wide. "Oh, MacCarrick, what about your injury? You didn't pull the stitches open, did you?"

He opened his mouth to say something, then closed it, raking his fingers through his hair. "You're no' . . . you're just no' right in the head if this does no' bother you. You're ignoring warning flags about me because you want out of this hellhole so badly."

"As many times as I've seen death here, Toumard doesn't warrant even a passing thought."

"Toumard's far from the first man I've killed."

"I thought as much. I suspect you're involved in some kind of dangerous, secret occupation."

"Aye, and I would no' give it up—even when married."

Maddy studied his face. "This isn't about you feeling guilty, is it? You really are trying to get rid of me."

He said nothing. *Deuce it, no!*

She had the ring and the money and clothes. Toumard was taken care of. She had a future again. Why couldn't she just brush this off as a good cull while it lasted?

Because she wanted *him*. She wanted more of his unpracticed smiles. She wanted more of what he'd given her just this morning—unimaginable pleasure.

"You are." *Deny it . . . deny it!* He remained silent. "Then just a suggestion. Do something truly horrible to scare me away. Do something a lot worse than killing a thug—known for maiming young women—in order to protect me and my friends. Now, I'm a big girl," she said with false bravado. "I can take it if you've changed your mind," she lied, planning to cry for days if he threw her over. "And obviously I've done something—"

"No, you have no'," he said quickly, forcefully.

"Then why did you pursue me so strongly last night, and now you can hardly look me in the eyes? Nothing has changed except that you got to know me better." She couldn't help it; her eyes began to water.

He ran his palm over the back of his neck. "Damn it, lass, every bloody thing I've learned about you I've liked. Maybe I've recognized that you could do better than me."

"What do you mean?"

As though the words were pulled from him, he grated, "When I left, Quin thought you might be . . . in a compromised situation."

"What do you mean by a 'compromised situation'?"

"He suspected things with you were no' as he'd thought them." MacCarrick's voice broke lower when he said, "Quin intended . . . to come marry you if I dinna."

Her lips parted. Was this what caused MacCarrick's hesitation? Did he think Quin was a better man than he was? Quin *was* a good man, and she would've been proud to have him, but she'd never felt as drawn to Quin, whom she'd known all her life, as she did to this rough Highlander she barely knew.

"He was the one you wanted, so you could—"

"I don't want Quin," she interrupted in a quiet tone, meeting his gaze. "I want you."

He looked bewildered—as if she'd just struck him—and had to cough into his fist before he could speak. "Did you no' hear me? You can marry the man you sought."

"The one I sought before I met *you*." A cab finally rolled to a stop before them. "I've told you what I want, Scot. Now make a decision about me. But when you do, it must be final."

He opened the door, then paused, clutching the handle as though in a death grip.

She drew a breath before she said, "You can't leave, then come back for me in a month, and you can't throw me over in a few weeks—"

With a frustrated sound, he grabbed her by the waist. Tossing her inside, he growled, "*Then get your arse into the cab.*"

Twenty-seven

Ethan stared at the ceiling of the train car, reeling from the magnitude of what he'd done.

The chit seemed determined to stick to him like glue. Because she *liked* him. He'd admitted to murder, and she'd given him that adoring expression again.

Sometimes being with her reminded him of going hunting with Hugh. His brother was a master rifleman, so fast to aim and shoot that even Ethan, no slouch, found himself doing a double take, frowning. That's what he felt like with her. Always doing a double take. Always perplexed with her.

Ach, if he wasn't careful, he could get used to those looks she gave him.

And when she'd met him eye to eye and told him she'd chosen him over Quin? The excitement he'd felt from winning her was indescribable. . . .

"I have to warn you," she said, then, "Trains have a tendency to make me very"—she yawned—"sleepy."

Within five minutes of their departure, her body slumped and her forehead hit his shoulder, but she jerked awake.

She did this several times until he said, "Just fall asleep. I will no' let anything happen to you."

She nodded. "Maybe I could just lie there . . ." She stared hungrily at his chest as if she was fantasizing sleeping against it.

"I thought you dinna like sleeping with another."

"Only in bed."

"Why?" Before he'd thought better of it, he'd patted his chest, coaxing her to lie there. When she curled up against him, his arm decided to slide around her. "Why only in bed?"

"When I broke my arm, I had to go to l'Hotel Dieu. A hospital for indigents. And they packed four girls into a cot." Her voice was getting softer. "Every night, these fevered girls would thrash about, hitting my arm again and again. If the floor hadn't been freezing and covered with filth, I would have slept there." When she fell silent, he jostled her a bit until she continued, "I had to wait there for days after I'd been cleared to leave."

"Had your mother already died, then?"

She sighed. "Corrine told you."

"Aye. Doona blame her—I can be persuasive, as you know. Now, answer the question."

"No, she hadn't."

"Why were you stuck there?"

"My mother just . . . forgot me for a little while. When she was getting us a new place to live."

Ethan briefly closed his eyes. Yes, he'd hoped she'd had much in common with Sylvie. Instead, she had more in common with Ethan. They'd both been hurt by the woman.

"Why didn't you tell me your mother died?"

"*Orphan* sounds so . . . pitiful. And I didn't want Claudia and Quin to know anything about how terrible it is—

was—in La Marais. I didn't know if I could trust you not to tell your friends."

"How did Sylvie die?"

Madeleine drew back. "Did you know her?" she asked with a frown.

Lying easily, he said, "Never met her."

"You called her by her first name."

"Quin told me your parents' names and Corrine called her that today." He put his whole hand on the side of her head and pressed her back to him.

"Oh. Well, she died of cholera when I was fourteen."

That disease was a grueling way to die, and in his job, he'd seen it firsthand more than once. The victim's body evacuated all liquids, then pain and spasms wracked the muscles, blood thickening in every vein. And all the while the victim was sentient—very aware of dying.

He felt a ruthless satisfaction to know that was how Sylvie had met her end, but then his brows drew together. "You were no' . . . you were no' *with* her when she died?"

"Yes. But she passed away very quickly. Within a day."

Yet *another* horror she'd witnessed. "You dinna get it from her?" Cholera was highly contagious if one didn't know how to prevent its spread.

She tensed. "I'm stronger than I appear, Ethan."

"Of course, lass." She was one of the strongest women he'd ever encountered—even if she looked like a defenseless waif. She was brave and resourceful as well.

He could stare at her for hours.

He'd taken her with him. And, God help them both, he was glad he'd done it.

* * *

Maddy woke alone in a luxurious stateroom. A circle of bright sunlight beamed in through a port window, telling her it was late morning. She remembered passing out in the train last night and supposed the last few weeks of worry had caught up with her. Ethan must have carried her aboard and put her to bed.

Rising to examine the room, she ran her fingers over the rosewood furnishings, wrought with ormolu and gilt, then over the rich counterpane.

The bed and the bathtub were as large as the hotel's. In fact, everything in this room was big—as if the designer had been dared that he couldn't possibly have such large fixtures and furnishings on a ship. Apparently Ethan never did anything second-best.

Eager to go find him and to explore the ship, she quickly washed then dressed in a cobalt blue walking gown of stiff fitted silk. She'd just finished unpacking the broad-brimmed hat with the matching cobalt ribbon when he returned.

"Good. You're awake."

"Good morning, Scot," Maddy said, giving him a bright smile.

He frowned at her. "You look well rested."

"I should be. I think I slept eighteen hours." She waved a hand around the room. "I could get used to this. You weren't jesting when you said the ship would be luxurious."

He took a seat at the mounted desk and motioned her to sit on the bed. "Now that we're here, there are some things I want to speak to you about. Some rules."

"Certainly." She sat with her hands in her lap.

"First of all, there's to be *no stealing*. And we're to act as husband and wife, which means you will no' be flirting with any of the men as you did in the tavern," he said with a glower. "And doona bloody steal anything. You ken?"

She blinked at him. "I'm getting the feeling that you don't want me to . . . *steal*?" Growing serious, she said, "I didn't *enjoy* taking things that didn't belong to me. I only did it out of necessity. Take away the necessity, and I won't steal. It's as simple as that."

"What about the flirting?"

"Jealous, Scot?"

"No' likely. If you blatantly trifle with other men, people will wonder about our marriage."

"Are those the only rules? Should be simple enough. How long should I say we've been married?"

"A week. This is our honeymoon."

"Would you like me to fawn over you when we go about in public?"

"No' at all. In fact, I will no' want you underfoot. There's no reason for us to be constantly together." At her surprised expression, he said, "Understand, Madeleine, I've been a bachelor for many a year and a loner besides. It will irritate me if you're always around."

Though his words hurt her feelings, she nonchalantly tapped her temple. "Be overfoot."

"There's more than one hundred and fifty other passengers aboard. I'm sure if you make an effort, you can befriend one of the other wives on board."

"I'm not a wife."

"They don't know that. So you should be able to entertain yourself during the days—all day."

"I shall endeavor to make friends and stay busy—and out of your way."

"But I'll expect you back in the cabin when the sun goes down."

"Very well. You've made my instructions clear." She rose, kissed him on the cheek, then collected her reticule.

"So you're going?"

"Of course," she said, her tone sunny. "Have a wonderful day, Ethan."

The baffled look on his face before she walked out was priceless. Had he expected her to fight for the right to be near him? She couldn't force him to want to spend more time with her. That just had to come.

Besides, Maddy well understood what it was like to be saddled with someone she'd rather not be around. Her own mother had had a cloying personality, and her neediness had always made Maddy crazed. Maddy would be deuced if she'd behave the same way. *Distant, aloof.* That's what she would be like.

Out on deck, Maddy discovered that the *Blue Riband* was one of the finest ships she'd ever seen. It was a sleek steamer with full sail rigging—and no paddle wheels above the waterline. She'd have to ask Ethan about that. If she hadn't seen the two smokestacks, she would have sworn they were on a sailboat.

Though they weren't to get under way until the high tide tonight, the ship already appeared full. Couples strolled a marked promenade; game tables were set up on board, with special holders for the playing cards so they wouldn't blow away. Nannies chased children across decks that gleamed in the bright sun.

The activity helped distract her from her wounded feelings, and now that she had the luxury of a day at leisure, she would enjoy it. She would lie on a chaise and have someone fetch her tea while she reveled in the fact that her boots didn't hurt her. *The life!*

The wind blew up, whipping the stiff fabric of her dress, and the crisp sound pleased her. After a quick scan of the decks, Maddy determined that her dress was finer than any she could see on the other women.

A group of seated young wives took her measure—they reminded Maddy of the boulangerie women, but these were richer. Maddy subtly raised her chin, but only so she could incline her head to them when she passed, as if she were royalty.

They all had jewelry—pearl earrings, chokers, and diamond brooches. Maddy's ears and neck felt bare. But it didn't matter, because she could brazen out the situation, fabricate reasons why she had none.

L'audace fait les reines. Audacity makes queens.

By the time the ship made port, she'd have convinced the "other" young wives that she yearned to wear all her many, many jewels, but she was a helpless slave to fashion—and this year Paris fashion dictated wearing no jewelry—except, *naturellement*, when dining at court.

Twenty-eight

"Madeleine, damn it," Ethan yelled, "I said to wake up!"

Maddy shot up in bed, sucking in a ragged breath. Her cheeks were wet, and the sheets were twisted. She stared dumbly into the darkness, tears continuing to fall.

He lit a lantern, then hastened back to the bed with his brows drawn. He awkwardly patted her shoulder, then removed his hand. "Uh, there, now. You should . . . you need tae stop cryin'. Directly." He looked as if he was bewildered by her tears. "Why did you have a nightmare? Is it because you're away from your home?"

"No, I often have them," she answered in a whisper. This was so mortifying. They'd had such a nice night once they'd met back at the cabin—dinner, then kissing, then touching. But now . . .

Maddy hadn't wanted him to see her nightmares, not yet at least.

She remembered an issue of *Godey's Lady's Book* she'd read. An entire article had addressed how prospective grooms were attracted to radiant, carefree women. "*Brides from happy families make happy families!*" *Godey's* had declared.

Ethan had just witnessed an example of how carefree she *wasn't*.

"Do you want to tell me what you dreamed?" he asked.

Even if she wanted to, she didn't think she was ready to tell him the details of her nightmares—or of her troubling fear that she might somehow turn out to be a bad mother, like her own. When she shook her head in answer, he appeared relieved. To his credit, he still offered, "Uh, maybe tomorrow, then?"

"Maybe," she sniffled, then pointed at the lantern. "C-can we leave that lit?" When he frowned at her, she quickly added, "Unless they charge for oil?"

"We'll make it like daylight in here, if you care to."

"I've always wondered—why would you ever be in the dark if you can afford not to be?" Dashing the last of her tears away, she asked, "Do you ever have nightmares, Ethan?"

"I used to. But no longer."

"Truly?" she asked, surprised he admitted to them. "How did you get rid of them?"

"I took care of what was bothering me." At her questioning look, he said, "I doona let wrongs go unanswered. Someone had given me pain"—his expression grew so harsh it made her chilled—"and then I gave it back."

Making an effort *not* to cheat, Maddy acted as dealer for a game of *vingt-et-un* among her new coterie of young matrons. Already she'd collected a group of them who thought her royally rich and her style fabulously avant-garde—so much so that they refrained from wearing jewelry because she did.

Ethan had seemed astonished that she'd made not merely *one* friend but a baker's dozen of them. Her new acquaintances helped keep her busy each day while she stayed away from him.

So he could read agricultural journals in the stuffy club room.

After a mere four days of being engaged to him, Maddy now found herself *missing* him. But ever since she'd had that nightmare, he'd been even more standoffish. Hour after hour, Maddy had played cards and dice and listened as the women talked of their husbands and children, so she could stay away until sundown.

Of all the coterie, Maddy liked Owena Dekindeeren best. She was a no-nonsense young Welshwoman, who'd married a Belgian businessman. Though only twenty, Owena already had two children.

Lost in thought, Maddy almost didn't hear her say, "We can't all be so lucky as Madeleine with her attentive husband."

Maddy slowed her shuffling and frowned. "What do you mean?"

"At first I thought your husband was monitoring your gambling, like my Neville does with me," Owena said. "But I vow, I think your husband simply likes to look at you."

"Oh, yes," Maddy began in a scoffing tone, "he's so attentive he comes by once a day."

Another woman said, "No, no. He only approaches you once a day, but we often see him lingering nearby."

"His expression is so dark"—Owena grinned—"and . . . *hungry*." The women tittered, fluttering their ostrich-feather fans, scandalized.

But why would Ethan come by and not speak to me? Maddy wondered, absently shuffling. *Why has he been so distant—?*

Realization hit her. Cards flew among the coterie. *Ethan is already falling for me!*

Maddy mumbled apologies as she hastily scooped cards from the table and from one woman's bucket hat. Yes, falling in love with her. And that was precisely why he'd been so cold!

"Shall I deal, Madeleine?" Owena asked, amused. "You look distracted."

"Oh, yes, please," Maddy said, her thoughts racing. . . .

Although Maddy's own mother hadn't loved her, Quin hadn't fallen for her, and even Ethan seemed not to like her very much at times, Maddy boldly believed she was a lovable person.

People generally liked her, and she'd always made friends easily. And if she turned on the charm? She was nigh unstoppable. MacCarrick didn't stand a chance, she reasoned, and the poor man probably sensed his heart's impending surrender—which would explain his increasing coolness.

Naturally he would put up a brusque front as a defense! For a bachelor of his advanced years, yielding to marriage was one thing, but yielding one's heart was quite another.

And he'd already betrayed hints of his growing affection. Late into each night they touched and kissed and talked of nothing serious, learning each other's bodies. He taught her how he liked to be caressed and wanted her to reveal what she desired from him.

He'd nuzzle her neck and her breasts so gently, kissing her lips tenderly. He'd compliment her, pleasure her, and then gruffly insist she sleep against him as he held her close.

Whenever they were alone in their cabin, he would walk around naked and unabashed—what male wouldn't, with a physique like that?—and she would lie on her front, chin on her hands, gazing at him in wonder. As she studied his unclothed body moving, she couldn't help recalling some of the scenes she'd witnessed in La Marais. Applying the general ideas to him, her curiosity grew each minute.

Every morning, she'd joined him at the basin to explore him as he struggled to concentrate on shaving. She'd run her fingers over his backside, then to his torso and lower, which always earned her a trip to the bed.

Her attraction to him was getting worse. Every encounter between them made her want two more, and her affection for him wasn't far behind. Especially since he'd begun once again to demonstrate that sense of humor she'd enjoyed. Her heart melted each time he grated teasing words to her with a self-conscious grin.

At breakfast today, he'd looked out from behind his paper and said, "Have you been cheating when you gamble on board?"

"As if I need to. Winning against the passengers is as challenging as hunting cows."

"Doona scoff, young lass," he'd said, making his brogue low and rumbling. "Cows can be wily beasts."

She'd batted her eyelashes as she asked, "Ethan, would you lay down your life to protect me if a cow had me cornered?"

"Aye"—he'd resumed reading—"I'd smite the bovine down."

Maddy had laughed until he'd folded the paper down, with his brows drawn and his lips curling into that unpracticed grin.

She sighed happily. MacCarrick *would* resist her, of course. *Ah, but in the end, it will do him no good.*

She decided, then and there, in the middle of a hand of blackjack, that she was going to make the Highlander fall in love with her.

The problem with telling Madeleine not to be underfoot was that she'd listened.

Ethan had expected her to make a friend or maybe two—not to gather up a gaggle of women to follow her around and emulate everything she did. They'd even stopped donning jewelry because she wore none.

Though Madeleine had proved to be charming and sociable, Ethan was still surprised at the sheer ease with which she'd made friends. Having never quite managed the feat himself, he'd always believed it difficult.

She played cards and gossiped with them all day, having no trouble staying away from him.

And this meant that if he wanted to see her, he had to pursue her all over the ship. He'd strived to stay away, passing most of the days in the ship's club room. Since the majority of male passengers were gentlemen of leisure and landowners, the reading journals available on board consisted mainly of agricultural periodicals.

Ethan was out of study with the subject. He could man a howitzer and shoot a target between the eyes from half a mile away, and he knew the comprehensive geopolitical conditions of every country in Europe and Asia, but the newest farming techniques for loamy soil proved foreign to him.

He'd decided that since he was traveling to Carillon, one of his working estates, he could examine the operations while he was there. So he'd dived into the journals, intending to learn—and to keep his mind from Madeleine.

But staying away proved challenging, knowing what awaited him. On the few occasions he'd approached her, her face would light up, making it all the more pleasurable to see her. No one in memory had smiled upon seeing him, and he always had to stifle the urge to look behind him.

Today, the longest he'd made it was an hour before he'd found his feet eating the distance to wherever she was. Even merely watching her from afar was agreeable to him.

So he spent the days in a state that he could swear was close to bloody pining, counting down the hours until night when he could have her all to himself.

He, Ethan MacCarrick, craved a woman's attention.

And he felt himself lowering his guard around her. He'd actually caught himself wondering what she would think about Carrickliffe, and about his brothers and their wives—and, ach, that sounded odd.

Madeleine was already friends with Jane. This situation could get tricky if Ethan hurt the girl terribly.

What had Quin predicted? That Ethan wouldn't know up from down anymore? *Bully for you, Quin, you've got me pegged.* His lips curled. *But she chose me over you, you sod.*

Things used to be cut-and-dried for Ethan. He used to be detached from others, but now he wasn't so sure. At least with her. Even as he looked hard for things to dislike about her, at every turn he was burdened with additional examples of how well she fit with him.

Each night he and Madeleine indulged their lusts. He'd experienced more pleasure at her hands than he had in a decade before. He *could* get used to that—if he wasn't careful.

Toward dawn, they continued their nightly battles in bed wherein he attempted to get her to sleep against him instead of balled up in that way that made his chest feel uncomfortable.

If someone had told him a week ago that he'd be fighting to make a woman cling to him in sleep, he'd have laughed.

If he could just have her fully one more time, he thought he could beat this constant need. So every time he touched her, he would take more. He kept his fingers inside her longer, wanting her to crave the sensation of being filled, to train her body to hunger for his. If the situation had been reversed, this would have been the way to make him want more. Conditioning.

He knew he was playing for more now, though he didn't understand precisely what he wanted from her.

Yet she remained unfaltering. He was beginning to believe she truly wouldn't sleep with him outside of marriage. If so, once they landed he would only be able to put her off for a few weeks before she demanded matrimony. Or she'd leave.

Now neither of those scenarios was acceptable.

A plan began to form. Other women had enjoyed his coarse treatment. Cold and domineering had served him well in the past, getting him into the skirts of more women than he could count—it could work with her as well.

Twenty-nine

That night after they'd eaten, shared a bath, and were both naked in bed, Ethan proved Maddy's theory again and again.

Though he plied her with champagne, he was brusque and distant with her—which amused her because she viewed this as the desperate, last-ditch defense of a rattled bachelor.

She could handle his moodiness. It wasn't difficult because the idea of sharing a life with him appealed to her more and more, especially after a day like today—she'd left food on her plate and had enjoyed tea without hauling water up to her window; tonight, after their light, teasing touches in the bath, the promise of complete pleasure lingered between them.

"Ethan, I've noticed you're cross with me tonight for some reason," she asked innocently. "Have I done something to offend you?" *Besides threatening the wall around your heart.*

"I want to take you," he said curtly. "You're supposed to be mine, and I've already claimed you. Tonight I mean to be inside you again."

"Honestly, Scot, your moods confuse me so. I can

hardly keep up with them. Maybe it's the champagne and I'm overly sensitive, but your treatment of me is very erratic—"

He pressed her shoulders to the mattress, levering his massive body over hers. But she wasn't afraid in the least. "Just lie back, wench."

She snickered. "Did you call me *wench*? Well, you certainly dated yourself there, didn't you? Sometimes I forget how old you are. What's your age, anyway? Thirty-seven? Thirty-eight?"

"I'm thirty-*three*." Looking completely at a loss, he released her. "Am I . . . do you think me *too* old for you?"

"Not at all, Ethan," she answered honestly.

"Then admit it, you will no' sleep with me because of my scar. I'd never had any trouble seducing before I received it—"

She laughed then, clutching her stomach, rolling on the bed. "You're fishing for a compliment!"

"Are you mad? Stop bloody laughing!"

After several tries, she finally did. "I'm sorry, I just didn't imagine you would be so vain."

"I was no' fishing for a compliment."

"Then how would you explain your comment, when you know very well why I won't sleep with you, and you know it has *nothing* to do with your appearance? And so, to appease your hungry vanity—"

"Damn you, witch, I am no'—"

"—I will tell you that I find you utterly attractive, handsome, and virile."

His words seemed to die in his throat. His brows drew together as if he'd been confounded.

"I was going to tell you that morning in Paris," Maddy said, "but you kept ridiculing my poverty, and I didn't want to relinquish the one chink I'd uncovered in your armor."

He looked away when he asked, "And the scar?"

"I'm sorry you were hurt, in whatever mysterious fight you were in." She brushed her fingertips along it. This time he accepted the touch, his eyes briefly sliding shut. "But the mark highlights the fact that you're a strong man, who's been honed by a hard life."

He scrubbed his hand over the back of his neck. "I doona understand you."

"This is all a test, isn't it? You want to see how deep my affection for you goes or to determine if I'll be able to put up with your surliness and tolerate you in marriage."

"Aye, if that's what you believe. And only one thing can prove it—and that's for you to let me have you now."

"Scot, that's not fair."

"Do you no' want to convince me?"

She nibbled her lip, wondering how he would react if she attempted something she'd seen again and again and had always been curious about. He certainly didn't seem the type to chastise her for being overbold.

"I wonder if"—she pressed a kiss to his chest—"there might be something else I could do to prove my affection." Another kiss lower. His entire body tensed, and his thick erection pulsed. "Something I've been imagining."

"You canna be talkin' about," he shook his head hard, "about *that*—" He hissed in a breath when she nuzzled the trail of hair below his navel, letting him feel her hot breaths. His hands shot out to cradle her face, and he rasped, "*Ah, you beautiful lass, you are. . . .*" He shuddered, drawing his knees up around her. "You've been . . . you've been thinking about this?"

"Uh-huh," she murmured, kissing the rigid indentations of his stomach. "When I watch you shave."

"You canna tease me with this." His brows were drawn as if he were in pain. "You doona know how badly I want it."

"I've always been curious to try this." She slowly rubbed her cheek along his shaft, making his knees fall wide open.

"Pull your hair aside. I want tae see you takin' me."

Once she'd pulled her hair over one shoulder, she leaned down again, letting him feel her breaths against the slick crown before she flicked her tongue over the slit.

His eyes rolled back in his head.

His reaction emboldened her. He needed this, truly ached for something she could gladly give him. When she circled her tongue around the smooth head, closing her eyes in bliss, she discovered that she ached for it, too. Enthralled with this new delight, she teased and played, wanting to do this all night.

"Ah, God, that's it," he grated. "Now take it in your mouth. . . ."

She hesitated, then ignored his command, beginning to feel a kind of power with the act. Again and again, she lapped at the moisture on the crown until he was arching his back, seeming in anguish.

"I have no' had this in a verra long time," he said, choking out the words. "Play later." He grasped her head in his shaking hands, easing her down.

But she drew back. "I want to savor my first time."

"Indulge—me," he growled.

"What if I said no?" She pursed her lips and blew against him, making him shudder and buck his hips. "Looks like I hold all the cards—"

Like a shot, he grabbed her by the waist, tossing her to her back. As she sputtered and cried out, he pulled her around, positioning her so he could repay her in kind. He appeared menacing over her as he clutched her wrists under her back, pinning her so she couldn't move.

"Looks like wee lasses should no' play with men like me." When he took his time settling between her legs, she gasped helplessly, knowing she'd never been more aroused. "Especially no' in bed."

Ethan sidled his shoulders under her knees until her legs rested over his back.

Then he merely grazed his lips up her satiny inner thighs, making her pant, her breasts rising and falling fast. He lazily placed wet licks against her belly, slowly descending from her navel.

"Spread your legs." She did, opening her sex to him, and his cock pulsed, wanting to be buried inside it.

Though he'd only planned to tease her as she had him, when he saw how visibly luscious she was, he couldn't stop himself from pressing his opened mouth directly to her core. He slid his tongue out to taste her for the first time and found her so deliciously slick.

Instantly, he groaned, his fingers biting into her soft thighs. She cried out at once, undulating against his mouth. As he delved harder with his tongue, flicking her clitoris, her heels dug into his back in total abandon.

Then he somehow made himself draw back.

She raised her head and opened her eyes, brows knitted in confusion. "*M-more,*" she panted. When she looked at him so hungrily, he nearly wasn't able to deny her.

"Now do you ken how I felt?"

"*Yes, yes.*" She tried to free her hands, writhing with her legs spread, until he didn't know how much longer he could keep his mouth from her. "Ethan, I-I won't tease you. I promise."

"Good, Maddy." He forced her legs wider to take her more deeply, to get more of the exquisite taste he'd only sampled.

"*Oh, my God,*" she moaned, making his breaths come rough. He'd begun grinding against the bed.

He spread her flesh, took her clitoris with his tongue and lips, then slowly suckled her. "*Yes,*" she cried, arching her back, rocking her hips to his mouth. "*Ah, Ethan . . .*"

As she began to climax, she moaned his name again and again, making him certain he was dreaming—no man could know this much pleasure. When he'd suckled her spent, her legs trembled around his shoulders and neck.

He released her, moving up to take her place, but she clutched his chest, rubbing her face against his neck. She whispered in his ear, "*I love the things you do to me,*" making his chest swell with pride and his erection pulse unbearably beneath her.

Then she kissed down his body, her hair trailing down his heated, sensitive skin. He yelled out when her hot little mouth closed over him. Wet, sucking, hungry . . .

He growled, "*That's my good lass. Nice and deep.*" Disbelieving, lost, he struggled not to clench her head to hold her while he thrust. She was taking him greedily, moaning around his shaft. It was as if he were an outsider looking in as she had a love affair with his cock—she adored him with her tongue, consuming him with licks and tender kisses.

The experience was mind-boggling. She worked his flesh lovingly, yet wantonly, mystifying him. But when she was about to bring him to come in her mouth, and he felt himself on the verge of losing control completely, he gave a defeated groan and pulled her away.

"Ethan?" she asked, her tone dazed when he drew her up to his chest. "Am I doing it wrong?"

"No, no. I just doona want tae do anythin' . . . tae make you shy with this." Feeling wicked, his cock about to explode, he looped an arm around her neck and kissed her.

As he teased her with her taste, he began to handle his shaft. "A particular favorite," he said against her lips, "want you tae love it as I do." He stroked harder, his other hand palming her arse. He broke away to ask, "*Do you want tae watch me?*"

Wide-eyed, she nodded, and he eased his grip around her neck so she could look down at his fist pumping furiously.

Her eyes on him only aroused him more. When he came, the force of his release was violent. He yelled out, and his back arched sharply, seed spurting up across his torso as she gaped.

Once he'd at last finished, they lay catching their breaths. Feeling overpoweringly satisfied, he held her for long moments, petting her hair. Damn, if she hadn't *enjoyed* giving him a below job—yet another example of how well she fit with him.

He finally made himself rise and clean off, but when he returned, she cried, "Oh, Ethan! Your injury is bleeding!"

He glanced down at his chest and shrugged.

"Come here, please." She eased up on her knees and beckoned him. "Let me check you." When he returned to the bed, she sidled close to examine him. "You didn't pull the stitches open, thank God. But it's bleeding more than I thought it would."

As she rose to collect a wet towel, he tilted his head to stare, riveted by her pert arse. "I dinna take you for the nurturing sort," he said absently.

Towel in hand, she said, "I will be with a man like you."

"Like me?"

She climbed back into the bed with him. "Yes, Scot, you're the dark horse I'm betting on." She lovingly brushed his hair from his forehead, catching his gaze. "You get all my extra sugar and apples."

"What about servicing mares? I've one I want to be led to."

"And I'm sure she wants to be covered by a virile stallion, but she needs to secure greener pastures for her future first."

Even to himself, his tone sounded fascinated as he murmured, "Daft, cheeky lass."

She slid him that grin; he stared dumbly. All at once he understood why a man might go a little crazy over a woman.

Thirty

A sea squall had whipped up late in the night, and the ship was pitching.

"Tell me how you came to be in La Marais," Ethan said, as if to take her mind off the storm. He was leaning up against the headboard, with her lying on his torso.

"What did Quin tell you?" Maddy asked, drawing back so she could see his face.

"That your father died in a duel and creditors seized your home. Your mother was French and took you back to Paris."

She shrugged. "That's about it, really."

"No, it's no'. I want to know everything."

"So you can have more ammunition to be mean to me?" she asked.

"No. I'm curious about you."

"I'll tell you, but first you have to reveal something about yourself that I didn't know."

He frowned. "Like what?"

"Something about your past. A deep, dark secret."

He seemed to be giving this a lot of thought, taking his time before answering, "I used to think I was cursed."

Her eyes widened. "Truly?"

"Aye. There's a book that's been handed down in my family for centuries—it contains foretellings that have all come true. They have for my brothers and myself as well."

She eyed him suspiciously. "Are you jesting with me? Because I would never take you for superstitious."

"O' course I'm superstitious—I'm bloody *Scottish*."

"In any event, this doesn't sound like a deep, dark secret to me. I think it's adorable that someone as strong and powerful as you, with so much control over your destiny, has irrational beliefs."

"Adorable?" he spat. "And I suppose you doona have any irrational beliefs?"

"I do. Very much so. But then, I don't have a lot of control over my own destiny."

They both fell silent.

She quickly reached up to touch his shoulder. "Ethan, I didn't mean that I felt forced to come with you. I chose to. And I'm glad I did."

His demeanor grew guarded. "I've told you what I will, now it's your turn."

"It's not a pretty tale," she said. "And I don't want to hurt your opinion of me."

"What do you mean?"

"*Brides from happy families make happy families.* That was in *Godey's*, which is an irrefutable source."

"It will no' hurt my opinion. Now tell me."

"Do you want the long story or the cursory one?" she asked.

"Tell me everything."

She took a deep breath and began, "Well, contrary to what everyone thinks, my life didn't fall apart on the day of my father's death. It was on a night six months before that."

A night of secrets and fury that she had never been able to understand.

"It was all so dreamlike, Ethan." Lightning crackled just outside the ship, and she shivered. "I went to sleep safe and secure, and I woke into a different life, a foreign world filled with strangers. It's hard to explain."

He rubbed her arm with his big scratchy palm. "Try."

"I've struggled for years to put together what occurred that night." Her brows drew together as memories assailed her. "The first thing I noticed when I woke was how jumpy the servants were. They peered at me as if to gauge what I knew of the night before. Finally, I learned that two of our family's most trusted servants had been fired—my father's right-hand man and my mother's maid and confidante." She trailed off, studying his expression. "Are you going to ridicule everything I'm about to tell you?"

"No' going to ridicule anythin'."

She exhaled, then admitted, "I think my father . . . found my mother in bed with another man."

"Why would you think that?" he asked in a measured tone.

"Because it became apparent that my normally passive father had . . . struck my mother over the night." Maddy could well remember her mother's glaring blackened eye, and how her father hadn't been able to bear looking at his once beloved wife.

"That does no' mean—"

"He'd come home early from a business trip that very night. And honestly, knowing my mother, I would be shocked if she hadn't committed adultery regularly during their marriage. She was a weak, selfish woman, and my father was a good deal older than she was."

"I see." Ethan was tense, his body stiff as a plank. She studied him, wondering if he was disgusted—or dreading what she might say next.

"At one point that day, my father absently patted my head and said, '*Maddy girl, Papa's made some mistakes.*' Then he wandered off aimlessly. He was never the same. It was like I'd never known either of them."

"After that night, what happened?"

She noticed Ethan's jaw was clenching and said, "I don't know if I should be telling you this."

"I need to hear it, Madeleine."

"But it doesn't—" She broke off under his hard stare and murmured, "Very well."

Ethan knew the events—had orchestrated them—and now, in a low haunted tone, she supplied the aftermath.

"Half a year after that night, my father died, and the creditors descended upon us. My mother and I came home from my father's funeral and were turned away from Iveley Hall—that's the name of my childhood home—in a violent storm. I was so frightened. Especially since my mother was completely unprepared to care for me. I remember asking her once, 'Are we going to find a place to live soon?' Instead of answering, 'Of course. We'll have a spot of luck any day now,' my mother snapped, 'I only know what you know, Madeleine. So what do you think? Tell me.'"

A place to live . . .

As Madeleine recounted the harrowing trials of an eleven-year-old girl forced away from everything she had ever known, Ethan felt tears on his chest. He learned how painful it had been to be turned away from her home, from all the possessions that a young girl would believe she couldn't live without—her dolls, her dresses, her beloved pets . . .

. . . how terrifying and sordid La Marais had been when she'd first seen it.

And he'd learned that Madeleine knew nearly enough to put everything together. She was keenly perceptive, and obviously had been an observant child. Already she suspected another man had been in her home.

How long would it be before she uncovered enough to determine it was Ethan?

When she'd finally fallen asleep, curled up and clutching her ring on the ribbon, he stared down at her, unable to stop himself from petting her soft hair.

After tonight, he understood far more about the depth of her courage and indomitable spirit. Those traits in her made the failings in Ethan's own character all the more obvious.

That recognition was painful and unwanted.

Most people assumed bad men didn't try to better themselves because they couldn't be bothered to make the effort or because they didn't know how to make the right choices. Few supposed it had nothing to do with the future and everything to do with the past. Recalling black deeds with a different perspective was hellish.

Ten years ago—when he'd been older than she was right now—he'd pitied himself, swilling liquor, behaving cruelly, and he'd been punished. Madeleine had done nothing but show strength of character and a will that humbled him, yet she'd been punished, too, for her parents' mistakes.

Punished by Ethan. He often imagined how he might begin to explain that to her:

"I was drunk one night and decided to tup, well, Sylvie, your mother. She cried rape to your father—a weak-willed cuckold who was easily swayed and kept henchmen on hand to do foul tasks. Brymer cut off half my face, so later I gutted him. After I bankrupted your father, no doubt pushing him closer to his suicide, I seized your home and assets, turning you and your mother out into the streets."

If she hadn't run screaming by then, he could finish, "Then Sylvie took you, at the tender age of eleven, to hell, and I knew about it. I let it happen when I could have spared you. And if all that wasn't bad enough, I ruined your engagement with the count and came to Paris specifically to deceive and use you."

What if she's the one . . . ? Hugh had asked. Ethan gave a bitter laugh.

What Hugh didn't understand was that her being "the one" or not was incidental. The curse being false or not had no bearing. Ethan could never have Madeleine because the damage had already been done, and ultimately she would hate him.

Whatever he was experiencing with her would end. *Common bloody sense. . . .*

Just as before, Ethan's die had already been cast.

Thirty-one

"This is a *lesser residence*?" Making a credible attempt at keeping her jaw from dropping, Maddy gazed out the coach window at the oceanfront mansion they neared.

"Aye. It's called Carillon, named after the series of bells in the village," MacCarrick said as they rolled along the long gravel drive. "And yes, it's less grand and more obscure than my other estates."

She swallowed and nodded. "Of course."

The stately manor house was built in large ashlar blocks, like castles usually were, but these were dark cream-colored and smooth. Along the drive, they passed terraced gardens, walled gardens, wild gardens. Grass pathways and crystal-clear streams wended through the property.

"It's very beautiful," she said absently, but *beautiful* couldn't adequately describe this place. When she saw a peacock strutting across a green lawn, she realized Carillon was like a fairy tale. "That's a . . . peacock."

"My grandmother was eccentric, and she brought them here. They're nearly wild now."

"Is that a *palm* tree?"

"Aye. The water that travels the Irish Sea is warm, making it temperate here. It rarely snows or freezes."

This place was to be partly hers? "I don't think I've ever seen such a splendid home."

"The steward's let it fall into a sad state of neglect."

"How can you tell?"

"At this time of year there should be hay rolls and autumn crops planted over the back fields we passed earlier. There were neither. I see the paint is chipping on the trim of the manor and the stables, and the fences need mending throughout. The fountains are no' running—since I'd wired the staff of my coming arrival, that means they're likely broken. I doona keep estates in this condition—*ever*."

"I don't think it looks that bad," she said, trying to lighten his mood.

He gazed out the window. "You would no'."

"What's that supposed to mean?"

"Would anything no' seem palatial next to La Marais?"

Though she'd been thinking the same thing, she was growing tired of his jabs. Since they'd made port, he'd grown cold again—worse than he'd ever been. *Honey, not vinegar,* she reminded herself.

Yet she was on the last of her stores. "And here I thought we'd go a day without you reminding me where you plucked me from."

"I was only making a point," he said, but their row was delayed when the coach rolled to a stop in front of the manor. "Speak of the devil," Ethan grated when they found a middle-aged man and woman awaiting them. "Silas the steward."

When MacCarrick helped Maddy down, he ignored the man and said, "Madeleine, this is Sorcha, Carillon's housekeeper. Sorcha, this is my wife, Lady Kavanagh."

Maddy understood why he had to introduce her like that, but the lies sat ill with her. Sorcha smiled shyly and curtsied.

"Show Lady Kavanagh up to our rooms and see that she has everything she needs." To Maddy, he said, "You'll join me for dinner."

Sorcha curtsied again, then turned for the front door, with Maddy following. Inside was a marble tiled foyer, which opened up into a high-ceilinged room. Graceful wooden stairs curved in a horseshoe, with both sides carpeted.

After following Sorcha up the steps to the wide first-floor landing, Maddy briefly peered over the railing to see Ethan downstairs. He strode across the room in another direction, boots booming, a visibly terrified Silas trailing in his wake.

When she glanced back up, Sorcha had opened a heavy door to the master suite and was bustling inside. Joining her there, Maddy found that both bedrooms of the suite were ornately paneled, with Maddy's room lightly painted and Ethan's stained much darker. Plush carpeting ran throughout, and the ceilings were soaring.

Standing in the rooms' connecting doorway, she glanced from her graceful pencil-post bed to his immense bed, which looked as big as a normal room. How would Ethan want them to sleep here, now that they didn't have to share a stateroom?

"It's very fine," Maddy told Sorcha. The manor was, but the interior was also a bit staid. Some of the rooms they'd passed had seemed . . . grim, even. Making this place more comfortable and less rigidly orderly would be a rewarding task.

When she realized that she could soon make these changes as mistress, she decided to ask Ethan if they could come back and redecorate when things settled down.

"It's fine, aye," Sorcha said shyly, "but wait till ye see the view." She drew wide the curtains to reveal tall bay windows and a glass door that seemed to take up the entire wall.

Opening the door, Sorcha beckoned for her to step outside. Maddy walked out onto a marble balcony—and lost her breath.

The sea . . . was directly there. Cerulean blue water glittered in the sun, stretching out for miles.

The house was situated on a cliff, tucked back from the rocky headlands and a sprawling beach. Down below was a marble terrace fronted by a balustrade that matched the balcony's. From every point of this side of the manor one could overlook the beach and the Irish Sea.

"My Lord," Maddy whispered. If she'd been infatuated with Carillon from seeing its gardens and hills, the sea side enamored her.

Yet her excitement was tempered with a growing sense of uneasiness. The idea of her being mistress to an estate like this seemed . . . fantastical.

Fortune favors the bold, she reminded herself. *Yes, but this is ridiculous.*

"So, did you find out why Silas was remiss in his duties?" Madeleine asked after an uncomfortable, reserved dinner with Ethan. He'd brusquely adjourned to his study, without inviting her, but she'd followed him anyway.

"Aye. Strong drink. All day long," he said, taking a seat behind an imposing, mahogany desk. "The estate's been neglected sorely. Which makes me fear how my other properties are faring under myriad stewardships."

He looked so concerned that she sidled behind him to

knead his shoulders. "Surely you'll be able to find a suitable replacement. It seems Carillon would be a feather in any steward's cap."

"I suppose."

"You can run an advertisement in the paper and have inquiries forwarded."

"What do you mean?" He tensed beneath her fingers. "We're staying here until this is resolved."

She forced herself to ask in an even tone, "So how long do you predict we'll be delayed here?"

"I have to find a replacement, then acquaint him with the operations."

She drew her hands away, then crossed to the other side of his desk. "How long?"

"A week. Maybe two."

Maddy's heart sank. "I can't stay here with you unmarried that long."

He waved her concerns away. "I've already told everyone we're wed."

"You could marry me in the village Sorcha told me about earlier, and then we could stay here for as long as you needed."

"My God, is that all you care about? My tenants have endured three harsh winters because of Silas, and now they have no hay or vegetable stores for this winter."

"I don't understand. What did he do?"

"It's what he dinna do. If a field flooded, he dinna have it drained. He neglected to order seeds at the correct intervals throughout the year. There are a dozen other examples of dereliction."

"But why wouldn't anyone write to you, to alert—?"

"They canna bloody read and write! And it's no' their

responsibility. It's *mine*." He pinched the bridge of his nose, exhaling wearily. "Madeleine, I'm going to be gone most days salvaging this situation. I hope you can entertain yourself."

"Of course," she said, exhaling with disappointment. "I'm used to not seeing you until the night." She rose to leave, but at the doorway, she turned back. "I'll stay here ten days on the outside, Scot."

"What's that supposed to be? A threat?"

"No, just a statement of intent. Maybe I am selfish, but I need this security."

He narrowed his eyes. "You doona trust me."

She nodded, clearly surprising him. "You're right. I don't, not yet."

"So what does a man like me have to do to earn your trust?"

"Honestly, I don't know. I guess it just has to grow over time."

"You mean in ten days?" he said. "That's all the time Miss Van Rowen has allotted me."

The ship had seemed a different world.

Now Ethan was on his property, introducing Madeleine as his wife, to his own people. And the lie didn't bother him nearly so much as how easily the words slipped from his tongue.

Ethan's steward problems were very real, but at the same time, he was using the situation for his own ends. He could in fact advertise and have inquiries forwarded. And of course, he could simply marry Madeleine here.

He'd always abided by his decisions, stuck to his plans.

Now, he began to feel like he was losing control—the reins slipping from his grasp.

He'd made a decision to keep several various estates because they'd been in the family for generations and because when run correctly, they paid for themselves or even produced a profit. He'd thought he'd hired the best land agents in his absence.

Instead, his tenants here had suffered, and he was becoming increasingly uneasy about the state of his other properties. When he went back to the Network, he wouldn't have time to check on each of them and right any wrongs.

Slip.

He'd made a decision to appease his anger on the only child of the Van Rowens. Now he wanted her more and more each day. Another slip.

Ethan was brutal, selfish. He knew this, had no wish to change. Yet now he'd caught himself wanting to put Madeleine's needs over his own. Slip.

He'd always held something of himself back in bed; her kisses could make him lose his mind. . . .

I think I want her . . . for my own. Damn it, if a man consigned a woman to hell for ten years, he'd best not envision a cheery domestic future with her.

Ethan had always felt things too strongly. And if he allowed himself to feel something more for her, then lost her, he didn't think he'd ever be right again.

He found himself eyeing the whisky service. *Another slip to come?*

Thirty-two

"No, no, Ethan," Maddy muttered to herself, kicking a stone as she explored Carillon. "I can show myself around." For the last three days, she'd done just that.

On her first foray, she'd discovered an orangery, with walls of glazed glass and a glass dome roof. When she'd been about to exclaim with delight—*citrus*, there for the grabbing—she realized it was no longer in use and had only a couple of scraggly orange trees within. A great furnace with pipes leading under the floor had probably once supplied heating and steam, but now looked broken.

Another day, she'd come across a stair to a widow's walk high above the house, where wives had gazed out at the sea, spying for their husbands' return. She wondered if any woman before her had climbed this spot to gaze out—in the other direction. . . .

Maddy endeavored to stay away each day, going for long strolls. But there was no coterie here. Sorcha was kind but content to keep her distance from the mistress of the house. Maddy was terribly lonely, missing Bea and Corrine so much that she ached.

If she ever did see Ethan during the days, his manner with her was brisk and unapproachable. But when he came to her in the nights . . . his body told a completely different story.

He'd nuzzle her neck and rumble how much she pleased him as they touched each other. If she kissed or stroked him in a way he liked, he made sure she knew it, lavishing praise. These idylls were so perfect and fulfilling that she'd actually begun to crave making love to him, often imagining what he would feel like inside her once more. Denying him that final step was becoming increasingly difficult with each encounter, even as he inexplicably pressed for it less and less.

After they were spent, he would cradle her face and kiss her so tenderly that she thought she might cry. Each night, he trapped her in his arms, making her sleep against him, but she was growing used to his strong, warm presence.

At night, she was adored, protected. In the days, she felt utterly alone.

The difference in his demeanor was enough to make her crazed. Was he so anxious about the property that he was behaving differently with her? With her determination to stay away, there was no way he could accuse her of being irritatingly "underfoot."

Maddy knew there were aspects about her that would be unattractive to a potential husband—much less to a rich, powerful peer. She was dowryless, uneducated, and, well, a former criminal. Ethan had known all that and had still pressed for her hand.

But perhaps revealing the wretched details of her family's past had tipped the balance out of her favor. . . .

From his study window, Ethan watched Madeleine endeavor to tame a peacock with bread crumbs. When it fanned its tail feathers and chased her, she laughed all the way across the lawn.

Ethan wanted to be down there with her.

After just a week here, he was beginning to understand that it didn't matter if they weren't together. She was still in his thoughts constantly. He wasn't eating. His sleep was restless. Each day grew closer to inevitable pain, and he resented it.

He was never supposed to have wanted her like this.

With her bright smile and laughter, she was everything a soulless bastard like him would crave as a dying man does life—a feeling he well knew.

There was something more with her, fundamentally more. A connection, a yearning fulfilled, he didn't bloody know. He couldn't even explain it to himself. Sometimes, he felt like she was already a part of him—had always been.

The stronger his feelings became, the more he realized he would be destroyed when he and Madeleine parted. *What if I just keep her?* he asked himself again and again.

Sometimes he wondered what it would be like if he quit the Network and assumed the life that had always awaited in the background.

Take a wife, oversee his properties, look after his tenants. He'd discovered something deeply appealing about working so closely with his lands. Indeed, it seemed to call to him.

Yet the last time he'd had these thoughts had resulted in tragedy.

When he'd planned to marry Sarah MacReedy, it had been out of a sense of obligation to the title. Now Ethan found he might *need* that life—if Madeleine was part of the bargain.

But if he kept her, Ethan would just end up hurting her worse than he already had. It was inevitable. She would discover his involvement in her past and his present deceit, and it would devastate her.

To partially exonerate himself, would he tell Maddy her parents hadn't been as she'd believed? Would he tell her that her father, whom she spoke of so lovingly, had been a pathetic cuckold, and her mother hadn't been merely spoiled and selfish, as Madeleine seemed to believe, but out-and-out evil?

Did Madeleine need to know that her parents were responsible for a twenty-three-year-old man being strung up in their stables and tortured?

There could be no union more doomed than his and Madeleine's. If he did have children with her, they would be *Van Rowen's* grandchildren—*Sylvie's* grandchildren; Ethan had bloody made sure Madeleine *starved*.

Doomed . . .

Damn it, he'd made a decision not to marry her, and he never wavered from his decisions. When had he lost sight of all he'd planned? His first impulse was to leave her. Give her money to see her happy and let her have one or—sod it all—*all* of his homes. The problem with that plan? He was already too attached to her to part from her willingly. Ethan was snared.

He'd hurt her, and she was unwittingly repaying him a thousand fold—just by being herself. Every time he saw her utter lust for delicacies, and every night she woke, cheeks wet from some nightmare, his chest hurt.

The more attached he grew to the lass, the more guilt and strangling frustration he battled. The regret was riding him hard, and having never wrestled with that emotion before, he had no idea what to do with it.

He resented being saddled with that unbearable guilt;

he bloody resented *her* for being everything he could dream of in a wife.

Though he hadn't had a drop of liquor in years, he now found himself lurching to the drink service, pouring a whisky with shaking hands.

Staring into the glass, he muttered, "*Slip.*"

As if he were attempting to drive Maddy away, Ethan hadn't come to her the last two nights, instead spending the time drinking—though he'd repeatedly assured her that he never did.

Maddy certainly had seen pleasanter drinkers. Lying on stoops. In La Marais.

If she and Ethan crossed paths during the day, he'd taken to snapping at her. Indeed, at times she could swear that he begrudged her very presence at Carillon. Occasionally, she'd caught him staring at her from his study window, sometimes frowning, sometimes gazing at her with a disquieting anger.

So each day she climbed up to the widow's walk. When the weather was clear, she could see all the way to the Irish shore. Pondering her situation, she'd stare at the sea for hours, watching the ferries jaunt back and forth to Ireland.

She'd finally admitted to herself that Ethan's behavior had nothing to do with the strain of work. Either he believed she would endure any kind of treatment just to marry him, or he was seeking to drive her away. . . .

That evening she returned at sunset and found him sitting in his study, staring blankly at the whisky in a crystal glass in his palm. Her heart sank when she saw he was well on his way to getting foxed.

Though uninvited, she entered the room, sitting in the chair in front of the desk. "How was your day, Ethan?" When he shrugged, she said, "What did you do?"

"Worked."

"You're drinking," she said.

"You're observant."

Honey! She could be patient. "Have there been any leads on a new steward?" she asked.

"No."

"Can I do anything to help you? I find I have a lot of time on my hands," she added, struggling to keep a rein on her temper.

"No, no' a thing."

"We're supposed to leave in four days."

He finally faced her. "Do you think I doona bloody ken that? As if you'd let me forget it. It's always got to be about Madeleine."

"Already we've been here for—"

"And I'm no' done here yet!"

In as calm a tone as she could manage, she said, "Perhaps you'd accomplish more if you drank less?"

Ethan's expression turned menacing, his scar stark against the tan skin of his face. "*Aingeal*, you doona want to begin this with me, no' tonight."

"Have I done something to you, Ethan? Have I offended you or failed to please you in some way?"

"Aye, it's called intercourse."

Enough! Deuce the honey. "You'll have intercourse as soon as I have matrimony—just as we agreed! It isn't as if I just sprang this on you at the last second."

"No, but then I never expected you to hold out, or I'd never have agreed to something as asinine as that."

"You can be so hateful, Scot. You love to give me reminders that I really shouldn't marry you." And, as she'd begun to suspect, he was doing it purposely, with intent. Maddy knew men.

This one was angling for a way out.

"I'm the best you're going to get"—he raised his glass—"and doona ever forget that."

She gasped, drawing back her head as if slapped. It hurt all the worse because he was . . . right.

"I see. I fear this is all growing wearisome."

He gave a humorless laugh. "Aye, that's what I've been saying—"

"For *me*, Ethan."

Thirty-three

Maddy was finished.

Living across from Bea had taught her that it didn't matter how lovable she was, or how hard she tried to please, some men couldn't see when they had a woman to be treasured. MacCarrick had never hit her, as Bea's man had, but he could still wound.

Last night, she'd stayed awake till nearly dawn, mulling over her options. She'd heard him in the adjoining room, pacing for just as long, it had seemed.

Before she'd gone to sleep, she'd reached a startling conclusion. She didn't agree that MacCarrick was the best she could do.

When she woke, she'd started packing her bags.

Maddy could see now that when she'd accepted MacCarrick's proposition, she'd been cowed, hungry, and afraid of Toumard. Of course the Scot had looked like a godsend in light of those circumstances.

Now she concluded that there was no way she would become his legal chattel. She had other options. At worst, the ring he'd given her would see her through a few years.

When he came downstairs that morning and saw her bags, he said, "You're leaving me?"

"You're observant," she said, repeating his words from

the previous night, astounded to see he was already drunk.

He leaned back against the wall and crossed his arms over his chest. "And how do you think you're going to get anywhere?"

"I was thinking the posting coach. I've been outside so much, I've noted it comes every other day at five on the dot."

His rapidly fading smirk was satisfying. "You little fool. You're going to throw away marriage and wealth because you're *impatient*? I've told you I'm no' done here yet."

She gave him a pitying look. "No, but I am. Ethan, I have too often and for too long been forced into unwelcome situations. Do you think I can't recognize the same trapped feeling in another? You don't want to marry me. You've made that abundantly clear. I'm merely making this easier for you."

"No, you're no'. This is naught but added pressure. An idle threat. Understand that I doona respond well to pressure."

"I'm quite serious."

"You told me you'd stay ten days. I've three days left."

"Don't play games with me, Ethan. You could have married me in this town and then again in your county. You could have done a lot of things differently. All I wanted was to be treated decently by a faithful husband. It would have taken so little to make me love you."

"*Love* me, is it now?" He made a scoffing sound. "So all I would have to do is throw you some scraps of kindness and keep my prick in my pants?"

She didn't bother hiding her disgust at his drunken coarseness.

"Do you think things will be better for you without me?" he demanded. "When you go back to the gutter?"

"Actually, I'm planning to visit Claudia—"

"You mean Quin." He narrowed his eyes. "Well, it's like I said, your precious Quin was ready to offer for you. Especially after I told him I'd plucked your virtue the night of the masquerade."

She gasped. "You told him that?" *Oh, God, how humiliating.* "You utter bastard! You're making this so easy for me. But thank you for reminding me of Quin as an option. I'll be sure to inquire if he's still interested."

Ethan gritted his teeth, staring back at her. "You would," he said, his tone seething. "You'd take him today."

"I'd be a fool not to. He's kind and honorable—and I know that if he promised me marriage, he'd do it!"

So Madeleine was truly leaving him? The idea made his head swim.

When had she gotten under his skin this badly? When had the thought of life without her begun to make him crazed? He felt physically ill picturing her and Quin together. They'd be a perfect bloody match. *Unlike her paired with me.*

This had to end.

She'd won. Whether he married her or not, she'd defeated him.

"If you're going to be too selfish or too impatient to wait for me," Ethan told her, "then what can I do?" He let her see all the fury he was feeling. She blanched.

Bugger this. He knew a fine way to shake his attachment to her, like a fish throwing a lure that pains it.

He'd promised himself that he'd get Madeleine tucked away somewhere, then glut himself on other women, enjoying the return of his appetites. If he could get hard with Madeleine at the drop of a hat at his age, five times a day if he chose, then he was obviously cured.

Why hadn't he thought of this earlier? He'd take his predilections and spend them on a woman of experience, reverting to his old cruel self. Then he could make the break with Madeleine that he'd planned from the beginning. He could go back to work—to the solitary job he was truly suited for.

Decided, he said, "You're so ready to throw me over, I'll respond in kind." He stormed out, leaving her with her chin jutting up, then rode for the village.

When he reached a quayside inn, he strode inside the downstairs tavern, shoulders back, with all the confidence of a man who'd been slaking himself with a woman like Madeleine—a beauty who was longing to marry him. Or she had been. Now she was leaving. Didn't matter. He was done with her anyway. He *had* to be.

He sank down into a booth, noticing that the establishment was filled today. All these poor bastards must be trying to escape their wives. *No' the life for me.*

Let her go. He couldn't keep on like this. The last three nights he'd tried to distance himself, but only ended up pacing his room and drinking because he couldn't bloody sleep without her.

The guilt for her pain was razor sharp inside him.

Take another and forget her. Just common sense . . .

He spotted an attractive, dark-haired barmaid giving him a measuring smile—and she'd seen both sides of his face. She wore a choker like the one Madeleine had that night in Paris, though it didn't look a fraction as good.

But this woman had big breasts, which he'd always

liked. He'd rub his face on them. On the ship, he'd done that with Madeleine's little ones, and she'd gone wild. He had run his shadow-bearded chin over her nipples, abrading her, then suckling her. She'd melted, coming for him before he'd even glanced at her sex.

His ballocks began to ache, and blood pooled in his groin. The woman glanced at his erection and wrongly assumed it was for her. She got breathless, those breasts heaving. No, his cockstand wasn't for her—but did it matter? If he had to fantasize about Maddy to tup this trollop, then so be it.

Break free. The alternative was unimaginable.

Two whiskies later, another wench with pouty lips caught his eye. For some reason, her expression said she liked what she saw.

Three whiskies after that and before he knew what had happened, he was entering a room upstairs with the raven-haired barmaid. He stumbled to close the door behind them, and, surprise—her pouty-lipped friend had decided to join them.

Just like old times. Ethan knew his grin was wicked. A man *couldn't* change his nature.

Maddy sat on her widow's walk, hours ticking by as she waited for the coach. Silently crying, she watched the ferries bandying between the coasts for the last time.

MacCarrick hadn't returned.

What had she expected? Ethan on his knees begging for another chance? Or even politely seeing her on her journey? She angrily swiped at a tear.

She already missed him. Yes, he'd been horrid to her in

the days, but those nights with him, filled with passion and pleasure and tenderness . . . she'd never felt closer to another person in her entire life.

Should I have fought for us more, given him more time?

She shook her head sadly. Maddy well knew that affection couldn't be forced. She couldn't make him miss her. She'd done everything she could think of to make him want her.

And yet still the regret came. *Would I rather stay with him as we've been or live a life without him?*

She swallowed. Maddy had drawn a line with the Scot, and perhaps she oughtn't to have.

Another tear streaked down her face. Especially since she'd gone and fallen completely in love with him.

Thirty-four

The barmaid tried to kiss his lips but Ethan turned away, instead kissing her neck. He brushed against that ribbon choker, just as he'd done with Maddy that first night in Paris—before he'd had any idea what she would grow to mean to him.

The woman didn't taste bad, but she tasted *wrong*. She smelled good, but it wasn't *right*.

Imagine Madeleine's scent. Imagine the taste of her soft skin.

As the barmaid unbuttoned his shirt, her pouty-lipped friend kissed his chest. When the two had his shirt off, they took turns leisurely kissing down to his navel, and he knew what would follow. Madeleine had enjoyed taking him with her mouth, somehow making the act wanton and adoring at the same time.

One of the women began unfastening his belt.

"*. . . taken so little to make me fall in love with you,*" Madeleine had said. All she wanted was a faithful husband who treated her well—and she would fall in love with him.

In love. With *him*?

If she loved him, then she would have to forgive him what he'd done to her in the past.

She would *have* to. Because he hadn't known her then and had never intended to hurt her. But now . . . if he did this . . .

Shouldn't he at least attempt to make her love him before he gave up on everything? Hadn't he learned from her that you fought for something you wanted?

"Stop," he grated. But they didn't, instead attending to his trousers.

Let them . . . Here he could take a woman, two of them, and he *wouldn't?* What the bloody hell was wrong with him? He'd dreamed of this day, when he would finally be a man again. He'd vowed that he would glut himself. Madeleine should have given him what he'd wanted. And she sure as hell shouldn't have selfishly pressured him, harping on marriage. Ethan didn't respond well to pressure—

Madeleine would fall in love with *him.*

Clarity hit him like a lightning strike.

Ah, God, it's Maddy. It's her. It was *only* her for him. It would always be.

"*Stop!*" Ethan roared, plucking their fingers away and shoving himself back. He stumbled, rocked to the core. Maddy was his future embodied, yet he was behaving like before, ten years ago when he'd thought he could have no future. *Weak, drinking, accepting* . . . when, at the same age, she'd been fighting tooth and nail for a better life. He could fight for her; he *could* change, as profoundly as his brother had said.

But Ethan was about to do something so idiotic—so irrevocable—that he would still lose his lass forever. He shuddered.

"What's the matter with you?" the barmaid asked, her tone baffled.

Remembering that night all those years ago, how cruel he'd been to Sylvie—and to those barmaids—and how he'd been punished for it, he said, "Sorry, ladies, but I'm married, and I'm acting the fool." An utter fool. He refastened his belt and buttoned his shirt, wadding up his jacket under his arm.

The second one said, "It's not like married men stop enjoying other women."

"This one will."

They sighed, and the first said, "Your wife's very lucky to have you."

"Other way around," he assured them before striding from the room to stomp down the stairs.

Ethan was a man accustomed to feeling strongly, yet he had never felt *anything* like the growing frenzy that seized him at the thought of Maddy leaving him. Ah, God, he was in a bad way. He wanted the love of one woman, craved it, coveted it. Likely about to lose it.

Tumbling a pair of tavern trollops. Bloody brilliant, Ethan. What the hell were you thinking?

What time was it? *Three thirty*. The coach arrived at five. If he rode hard, he'd make it back to Carillon in time. But if he went back to her empty-handed, with only tired promises, she still might go. He could ride for the village's registrar office to try for a special license, but he would risk missing her.

Unfortunately, he could never predict her behavior. If she left before he could reach her, she might make up her mind never to take him back. Hell, it might be too late anyway, after his own behavior over the last few days—but he had to try.

Deciding quickly, he rode straight for the registrar's.

Doubts about the secrets of his past continued to resurface, but he pushed them away. *Get her*, his mind kept commanding. *Make her yours.*

Ethan would figure out the rest *after* he made sure she didn't leave him today.

He stormed into the registrar's office more frantic than he'd ever been. The village official was understandably terrified of the unshaven, scarred Highlander smelling of whisky and pounding his fist on the counter. Ethan dimly heard the man relating that it would take days for a special license, and himself replying that this was sodding Scotland, the land of marital loopholes—oh, and that he would build the village a grand new church in exchange.

A church—what a fitting penance. Forty-five minutes later, marriage license in hand, he ran from the building, mounting up and riding hell-bent for Carillon. . . .

Ethan's father had once told him that a man would know the woman he was meant to be with because she made him weak. Till he claimed her and she made him strong.

Maddy had only been waiting for him.

His gut tightened when he spotted the posting coach up the hill, nearing Carillon, and he raced even faster. Barely beating it to the drive, he dropped from his horse, his wound aching.

He caught sight of her standing at the end of the drive, her bags at her feet. She looked like a perfect lady, wearing her black kid gloves and her hat with the sheerest black veil falling to her cheeks. But at the same time, she appeared cold as ice. He knew without a doubt that if he'd missed her, she would have left him and never looked back.

He wanted her so much, wanted her for the rest of his

life. And the remarkable thing was that, as of yesterday, she would've accepted a bastard like him. Would she now?

Brows drawn, struggling to catch his breath, he held up the license. "Marry me, lass?"

She tilted her head.

Wee sionnach, wary as ever. And why wouldn't she be? He'd never made the smallest effort to make her feel comfortable or secure. She hadn't been selfish to insist on the marriage—she'd been savvy. "Ten o'clock tomorrow morning. If you'll have me, Maddy, I'll be good tae you," he said with conviction, with *feeling*. Because he meant it. "I've been a bloody fool tae treat you this way."

"Why have you been so cruel?" she asked in an inscrutable tone. "*You* came to Paris for *me*, remember?"

He strode toward her. "And that was the best damned decision I've made in my entire life." He swallowed to see the coach was nearing. "Maddy, I ken I've been acting like a bastard. I said that you could no' do better than me, but that's no' true in any way. I know it more than anybody." He raked his fingers through his hair. "I never lived my life thinking another would share my name. My name and I are a bit . . . tarnished. You'd probably do well to leave me right now—no matter how badly I want you to stay."

She glanced past him to the coach. She didn't seem even to be listening to him. *No, she has to stay.*

When he stood just before her, he said, "Maddy, I doona know if I'll be any good at this, at being a husband, but I *want* tae be. I want tae assume my title again and watch over our lands. But only if you agree tae be my lady. If you can just see your way tae forgive me—"

"You're saying you will give up whatever your dangerous profession is?" she asked, still not facing him.

"If it means I get to keep you, then, aye, gladly."

"Is the marriage license why you were away for so long?"

He flushed uncomfortably. "I had to promise the village a new church to get it," he said, hedging.

"What's changed between this morning and now?"

"I finally saw what was right before me." At last, she met his eyes. "Say you'll marry me."

She was silent for what felt like an eternity before she murmured, "Very well."

He stared down in shock, knees about to buckle with relief. "You mean . . . you will . . . tae me . . . in the morning?"

She nodded. "But don't make me regret it, Ethan."

"You will no'." He clasped her to his chest with shaking hands and buried his face in her hair. *That's the scent I like.* "I was behaving like an imbecile before."

How in the hell had he thought to jeopardize this? He felt as if he'd just dodged a bullet—and having caught several, he didn't feel this lightly.

If she knew where he'd been, it would devastate her. She would gaze up at him, her big blue eyes spilling tears, and he'd tear at his chest, clawing out his bloodied heart in offer to get her to stop.

He squeezed her harder. When the coach pulled to a stop, he waved it away, calling out, "She's stayin'." Once the coach rolled on, Ethan turned back to her with a grin, but she laid her head against his chest as if just savoring the closeness.

"I've missed you, Ethan." Her voice was so sultry that he shuddered with instant lust for her. He hadn't touched or tasted her body for three days, but it felt like a lifetime.

He leaned down to steal a kiss from her, intending only a brief contact. But as ever with her, the kiss turned explosive. Holding her as he took her mouth again and again, he leaned her back over his arm, his free hand gripping her bottom.

When she moaned into his mouth, he somehow drew back, righting them. Shaking his head hard, he yanked his hand from her backside. "Someone will see," he grated. And for once, he cared. He'd not have his wife thought badly of.

"It's market day. Everybody's in town."

So that was why the tavern had been packed. Christ, had anyone seen him? Would it get back to her?

"Have you not missed me?" she asked softly, shyly, her meaning clear.

"You canna imagine, but I can wait until after the wedding. It's what you wanted."

"Can't we . . . be as we were before? During those nights?"

The idea of her yearning as he did was too powerful. "*Anythin'*," he rasped, swooping her up in his arms. "Whatever you like." He kissed her, even as he hastened inside, then up the stairs. He nearly stumbled on the landing when she cupped his face and lapped her little tongue at his mouth.

As soon as he'd kicked the bedroom door closed behind him, they were grasping at each other's clothes between frantic kisses. Once he'd gotten her down to her shift, he shrugged out of his shirt.

She worked on his belt with both hands. "God, I want to . . ." She trailed off, gazing at him with her brows drawn. "Ethan, why do you have lip rouge below your navel?"

Oh, bloody hell.

"In two different shades?"

Bloody, bloody hell.

"I . . . It's no' . . ." And he was so close to telling her

some fantastic lie, but for the first time in his life—when he needed to the most—he couldn't.

Not even when her eyes watered and her bottom lip trembled and she whispered, "*Ethan?*"

The look she gave him before running to her room made him realize his bloodied heart was too black to be offered.

Thirty-five

"I dinna *do* anything!" he bellowed yet again outside Maddy's door.

Maddy had gone from the lowest low to the highest high and back down again. When she'd caught sight of Ethan riding for Carillon, racing the coach, her heart had leapt. Then seeing him in the drive, clutching that license with his brows drawn—she'd been overcome.

But now . . . "Just go away!"

After all the heartaches and tragedies she'd endured, she thought this one hurt the worst. Why did she keep believing in him when he'd never given her any reason to?

"Damn it, I did go to the tavern and get a room. I admit that, but I could no' do it. I told them to stop!"

"So there *were* two?" she cried, suddenly needing to vomit. She'd seen the evidence but had fought against believing he'd just been with not one but two women.

"Wait, wait, now, that sounds worse than it was—"

"You took two women upstairs to a private bedroom—or perhaps it was more than two?"

"But I dinna *do* anything with them."

"Of course not! You stopped their kisses at just below your navel. Most men see reason and make excellent judgments when a woman's mouth is just above their groin. Especially when they're drunk!"

"I could no' do it. For Christ's sake, I'll take you to the tavern and you can ask them." His tone turned bewildered when he said, "You've bloody ruined me for other women."

Though she fought it, for some reason she did believe that he *had* stopped before he'd had sex with *them*. But it didn't matter. "You are not even two weeks into our relationship, and you sound proud of yourself that you weren't unfaithful? What would happen if we were married for years?"

"Do you no' think you're getting ahead of yourself?"

"Oooh, you're amazing! I wish I'd never met you. I'm an idiot! How many times will it take for me to learn that you're a hateful man?"

And now she had to wait another two days for the posting coach.

"Fine. Have it your way."

She lay down, knees to her chest, having no idea how many hours passed, and still she cried. She heard him inside his room, pacing again and again before getting in bed.

How can he sleep through this . . . ?

She heard bitter grumbling in Gaelic, then more pacing.

"Bugger this," he muttered, then directly outside the door, he said, "I canna sleep without you."

"Learn to."

"Even had I done something—which I *dinna*—we're no' even bloody married yet."

Hateful. "And you just ensured we never will be."

* * *

On the second night, Ethan could scarcely believe that he was pacing outside a woman's locked door *again*, asking to come in.

She'd bewitched him. Ach, he missed sleeping with her. And she had cried for hours last night, solely to agonize him, he was sure of it. To torture him for his unthinking words and actions.

She hadn't been able to see, but if one of his comments in their argument had been harsh, he'd cringed behind the door. When he fought, he fought to draw blood, and it was a hard habit to break—even though hurting her now hurt *him*.

He'd wanted to go to her so badly, but the way she'd looked at him before slamming the door in his face had kept him from pushing her.

Yet now . . .

"Enough of this, Maddy. You've punished me enough. I have a right to sleep with you."

"You forfeited any rights when you lusted for another woman. Excuse me, *two* women."

"I dinna lust for them."

"Of course not," she said, her tone dripping sarcasm.

"I was thinking of you, of touching you, the entire time."

"Do you have no shame?" she cried. "You *cretin*!"

"Open the goddamned door."

"*Never.*"

"Open it, or it's comin' down! You've seen me do it before."

"You wouldn't—"

He kicked at the door, almost bowing it in. He reared back to kick again, his leg shooting out . . . *little witch* . . . she'd opened the door—

He went hurtling into the room, skidding on the floor.

Chin up, she brushed her hands off, then stepped around him to saunter out of the room.

"Ah, damn it, lass," he called after her. "I've busted my stitches wide open."

"What?" she cried, hurrying back to him. "Let me see!"

"Ah-ha!" He snared her around the waist, dragging her down with him to his lap. "You still care for me!"

Her jaw dropped. "Unbelievable! You're cruel and twisted—"

"Then you're going to be the wife of a cruel and twisted man."

"The—hell—I—will." She balled her fists, about to pummel his chest.

"It'll hurt like the devil if you do that, but if it will get you to listen to me, then I give you free leave to it."

Lowering her fists, she scrambled to get away, gritting out a sound of frustration when he held her fast. "I'll let you go if you'll just listen to me for five minutes."

"Not a chance," she said, but he ignored her, rising with a hissed inhalation. Taking her elbow, he propelled her to the bed.

"Will it do any good to tell you again that I dinna do anythin'?"

Maddy crossed her arms over her chest as she sat on the edge of the bed. "Even if I believed that, it doesn't erase your intent. You set out with every intention to sleep with another woman—*women*!"

"Aye, I had every intention of sleeping with as many as I could," he admitted, making her gasp. "I'm no' a good man, Maddy." He began pacing. "Everyone who knows me thinks I'm a bastard of the worst sort. Even my brothers do," he said as he passed.

They do? How dare— She shook herself. She agreed with them!

"When I was younger, I went through a new woman each night. If they were married, even better. And if you took all the pleasure over those years and combined it, it would no' be the minutest fraction of what I feel like with you." He glanced over at her to gauge her reaction. "Because I need . . . *more* from you. And a realization like that scared me witless."

"Why?"

He ran his fingers through his hair. "Because what happens if you find out somethin' from my past that you canna abide and you leave me? Where does that leave me? I'll tell you—as good as dead."

Her lips parted.

"You're so beautiful. *Too* beautiful and brilliant. And when you're finally no' afraid and your memories of being hungry and anxious fade, you'll look at me and wonder what in the hell you've done to wed me."

Ethan appeared so . . . tormented that she couldn't speak.

"This is like a sickness I feel for you. Woman, you've got me tied up in knots. I doona know up from down anymore and can think of nothing but you."

He pulled a chair in front of her, then sank down, leaning his elbows on his knees. "If I see something interesting, my first thought is if you would find it so as well. Foods I like, I want you to taste. And all the while I'm wondering what the bloody hell is wrong with me to be like this. It's just . . . no' *right.* I have *never* in my life wanted to put someone else's needs before my own like this."

She shook her head. "But this doesn't explain what you did—or why."

"Maddy, I dinna take a woman for a long time before you. For three years, I was . . . celibate. I was no' myself. And I'd vowed that if I got back to normal, I would glut myself. Then, with you, everything returned, and I thought . . . I thought that *now* having another would . . . Christ, I doona know, *dilute* this thing I feel for you. Make it ebb, but all my actions did was prove to me that I canna ever imagine myself with anyone other than you."

He looked so genuinely confused, so *panicked* even, that she felt her anger easing. The man was falling in love with her.

Finally.

And she was embarrassed to admit it, but she was impressed that he'd stopped in the tavern. Of all the weird, bizarre, licentious scenes she'd witnessed in La Marais—she'd *never* seen a man willfully break away before he'd reached completion. *Still . . .* "How would you feel if the situation was reversed? Two men kissing my body?"

He blanched and his fists clenched. "Murderous."

"What made you stop? With the women?"

"You said you would . . . you would fall in love with me if I was faithful." He looked away and muttered, "I want . . . I think I want you tae."

She raised her fingers to her temples to massage her aching head. "And Quin?"

He scowled. "What about Quin?"

"What could possibly have driven you to tell him we'd been intimate?"

"Oh, that," he said, then explained, "Dinna want him coming for you. I told him you were *mine* and he kept talkin' like there was something tae discuss."

She couldn't even imagine that conversation. "Are you sorry, Ethan?"

"You ken I doona believe in apologies. And in the end, I *was* faithful." He met her gaze as he said, "But, aye, Maddy, I am so sorry tae have hurt you."

He wanted absolution. He wanted . . . *her*. Badly.

Yet, was that enough? She couldn't keep doing this—being tricked into reaching for happiness, then having it snatched from her grasp. "I need to think about all this."

"Aye, of course." He rose, then frowned when she remained seated. "But can you no' think about it back in bed with me?"

She shot him a glare.

"I will no' do anythin'."

"You had two women kissing you just yesterday. Give me a bit of room to breathe, Ethan."

In the early hours of the morning, Ethan heard Maddy cry out, having a nightmare for the first time in several nights.

He ran for her, scooping her up into his arms. "Shh . . . shh, love. It's over." He rubbed his hand over her back, as he knew she liked. "There, lass. It's over." No more awkward pats—he'd gotten good at comforting her

By the time her tears had waned, she was in his lap, in the circle of his arms, her body boneless. Against her hair, he said, "Let me be here whenever you need me. Marry me in the morning."

After a long hesitation, she asked, "But how can I trust you?"

"Just give me one more chance. You will no' regret it."

At last, she gave a shaky nod. "If you vow to me that you'll be faithful, I will."

He cradled her face in his hands to meet her glinting eyes. "Maddy, I swear it. I'll be true to you."

"But, Ethan, I can't have my hopes crushed anymore. I promise you this is it, the last time I'll go through something like this. So please, don't hurt me again."

"I will no', love. I vow it." When he said the vow, he finally *did* mean it—he would do everything in his power to spare her pain.

But he feared no matter what his intentions were now, his past wrongs would prove him a liar. The truth was destructive and would only hurt her more.

Which meant he had to ensure she could never find out.

Thirty-six

Oh, Lord, what am I doing? Maddy thought in the middle of her wedding ceremony. Was she really going to go through with this? If not, she had approximately two minutes to flee before she and Ethan were to repeat their vows.

As much as you've pushed for this, Maddy? Yes, but that had been before the last two days! Now she wasn't as sure about him. . . .

The ceremony was being presided over by the village's registrar—Mr. Barnaby, a kindly older Scot, with a brogue not quite as thick as Ethan's—and everything so far felt dreamlike to her. She dimly heard the man say, "*I have been appointed by the Registrar General to solemnize civil marriages in accordance with the law of Scotland. We are now assembled here in order that I may bind in marriage Ethan Ross MacCarrick and Madeleine Isobel Van Rowen. . . .*"

Thoughts warred in her mind, but she strove to make her expression placid. Ethan stood tensed beside her, watching her like a hawk, probably sensing she was tempted to run.

When she'd awakened this morning, the sorrow that had taken hold of her for the previous two days had been swept away, and the only thing left was pure, unadulterated . . . panic.

But why? Ethan was genuinely sorry for his actions, disaster had been averted, and he'd been so wonderful last night, stroking her hair until she'd fallen asleep. At last, she was going to be like one of those young wives in the boulangerie.

Am I doing something to leave myself vulnerable . . . ?

She wanted to fan herself, to step outside of the close room and catch her breath. Her palms were wet around the small bouquet she clutched, and her corset chafed her. She irritably piped her lips to blow her short, cream-colored veil away from her face. Not only was she panicked, she must be paranoid as well, because she could have sworn that Ethan winced earlier when Barnaby had said her name.

Just before Ethan was to repeat his vows, she sneaked a glance up at him. His shoulders were back, and he appeared both proud to be with her and relieved. Then she saw him swallow hard. He was nervous, too, but here he was standing by her side, ready to pledge his life to her.

Naturally, people became anxious during their wedding ceremony. Everything was as it should be.

As he began to speak his vows, he gazed down at her, and the yearning in his eyes staggered her. His voice was deep and rough, but compelling when he said, "I, Ethan MacCarrick, vow tae love, honor, and respect you, Madeleine Van Rowen. I pledge tae be a faithful, honest, and devoted husband in good times and bad. This is my promise tae you today and for the rest of my life."

Oh, Ethan. And that was when she caught her breath for the first time that morning. A calm suffused her, and she stilled. Maddy had the sudden sense that everything in her life had been leading her to this moment, to this man—a proud, powerful Highlander who gazed at her with fierce, dark eyes and who gentled his touch, just for her.

* * *

Look at her. . . . Ethan thought as she repeated her vows. How could he not do whatever was in his power to call her his own?

Intelligence shone in her bright blue eyes; she raised her chin proudly. Her nervousness this morning had been palpable, but she was still going through with this wedding. *Brave lass, to take a chance on me.*

What man wouldn't lie, steal, or kill to have her?

After their vows had been exchanged, Ethan made a silent promise to himself. He would begin tying up loose ends and covering his tracks immediately—

"Following the binding declaration which you have made before me," the registrar began, "I hereby pronounce that you, Ethan Ross MacCarrick, and you, Madeleine Isobel MacCarrick, are now husband and wife."

Relief. Ethan's hand found hers.

"Scot, we are both unclothed and in bed," Maddy said shortly after they'd arrived back at Carillon. "Is there any particular reason why you're stalling at this juncture?" He'd been kissing her senseless as they'd undressed each other, but then he'd stopped.

He gazed down at her. "I'm not stalling—I'm savoring. It's no' every day a man gets married, and this has been a long time coming."

"Do you think I'll be worth the wait?"

"You *were* the wait. If I dinna have you, I would no' marry. Besides, maybe you should be stalling. After this, there's no getting away from me."

She pressed her palm to his chest. His heart was thundering. "Are you nervous again?"

"Aye," he said with a solemn nod. "Apparently the last time I tried this, I dinna acquit myself so well."

She grinned. "But I'm confident you will now."

He smiled wickedly, leaning down to nip her breast. "Then, Maddy MacCarrick, let's get to consummatin' this marriage."

When she held her arms up to him, coaxing him to her body, he glanced the backs of his fingers down her belly. "*So lovely,*" he said. "Are you nervous as well?"

"Truth?"

"Truth."

"I'm a bit terrified, Ethan."

"I'll go slow. You will no' hurt again."

She rolled her hips. "I hurt now."

"God knows I do, too." He gently cupped her between her legs, groaning when he slipped a finger inside her. "*Aingeal*, you have tae relax."

"I can't," she whispered miserably. "Maybe we *should* wait longer? I think I've changed my mind."

He rested his forehead against hers. "Maddy, you will no' be more ready than you are now. The longer we wait, the worse your misgivings will be. I see that now."

"But you were so awful after the first time. I have this nightmare that once I give in, you'll get that cruel smirk and say hateful things. And then . . ."

"And then?"

"Then you'll leave me."

"Maddy lass, you're stuck with me. You will no' ever get away," he said, then no doubt trying to lighten her mood, he added, "But you best make it good, so there's no doubt."

She gasped, and he pulled her to her side to give her a light rap on her bottom, making her peal with laughter.

* * *

"You're shameless!" she said breathlessly, her eyes excited.

"Aye. But that's what you love about me." *Ach, she dinna deny it.* "Trust me, and I will no' let you down."

After what seemed like an eternity, she nodded and he comprehended that they were truly about to do this—he was about to take his *wife*, for the first time in their married life. By God, he was going to make this so good for her.

She nibbled her lip. "Tell me what you want me to do."

Though he knew the agony he was inviting, he said, "I want you tae be on top." When she frowned, he added, "You can go as slow as you like. Take what you can of me inside you—at your own pace."

He rolled over so she lay atop him, making her nervously murmur, "Ethan?"

Running his hand down her back, he entered one, then two fingers into her sex from behind, groaning when she arched her back down. As he delved again and again, she spread her legs wider over his hips. "That's it."

As he tried to fit a third inside her, she moaned, leaning down to lick his lips.

"I'm going to take my fingers out," he grated. "And you're going tae be needin' something inside you." She whimpered as he removed them. "Just take my shaft"—he grasped her hand and wrapped it around him—"and put it inside you when you're ready."

With his hand on hers, he aimed the head at her entrance, hissing at the wetness he met, gritting his teeth against the pleasure. He ran it up and down her folds, then released her.

Panting, with her eyes heavy-lidded, she continued bringing the swollen tip up and back along her sex. Each time she lowered his cockhead directly to her entrance and they briefly had that tight connection—when he would just barely enter her—he had to fight not to flex his hips up.

When she rubbed him against her clitoris in languid circles, he nearly ejaculated against her there. With a will exceeding anything he'd ever called on before, he didn't thrust. He'd begun sweating from the battle, and her breasts rubbed against his slick chest as she writhed on him.

Torture. Pure and utter. She couldn't know what she was doing to him. "Put it inside, Maddy," he rasped. "I'll make you come hard with it." How much longer could he last till he tossed her to her back and slammed into her, bucking till he came?

Then he realized he could last as long as it took for her to do this, as long as she needed—

She eased the head in.

"*That's it, lass,*" he growled low in his throat, knees falling open as she worked her lithe body on him. So he wouldn't be tempted to press her down, he gripped the headboard behind him. "That's my good wife." He shuddered with pleasure. "Ah, God . . . as deep as you can . . ."

Thirty-seven

Maddy was certain she couldn't take any more of him. But when she saw him visibly struggling to control himself—the lines around his eyes were tight and his jaw was clenched—she wanted to try for him.

"Ethan, I don't know what to do." It was one thing to see others in this position, but another to try it. She felt awkward and unsure.

"Pull up and go down, deeper," he said, his voice husky and breaking.

"Show me how."

"If I touch you, I'm goin' tae lose control." His hands clutched the headboard behind him, the muscles in his arms bulging with strain. His breaths were ragged, his chest rippling with power. "I'm burnin' tae wrench you down my length. . . ." His dark eyes met hers. "Bury it in you so deep . . ."

"You won't. I trust you. Just please show me." Even to herself, she sounded panicked.

"Ah, lass. This is supposed tae be enjoyable," he said in a tone incongruous to his straining body.

She reached for his hands, shocked at how badly they shook when she placed them on her bottom. He groaned and gave a seemingly involuntary buck of his hips. His fingers splayed out, clutching her as he drew her up . . . then back farther down.

Pleasure rocked through her. "Oh! That feels . . . *nice.*"

Once more up and down farther still. She kept expecting pain, but there was none. The stretching sensation was rapturous, a fullness that felt so necessary. He was right—she did need this.

"I'm going tae make you come first if it kills me," he said, his words hoarse. "Work your knees wider open."

When she did, he pressed deeper, but there was no pain—just the opposite. "*Ethan . . . it feels so good inside me,*" she whispered in a wondering tone.

He could only grunt in answer, shuddering beneath her.

Maddy rose up and leaned forward, her hands clutching his shoulders, taking as much of his length as she could.

Her shining hair curled about her face and her brilliant eyes were free of fear—and full of trust. She was so lovely that she awed him.

Catching her gaze, he rasped a vow to her in Gaelic, a promise of self in the old language, binding them together forever. Though she couldn't understand the words, she seemed to grasp the meaning—she cupped his face with her wee hands, leaning down to kiss him tenderly.

When she rose up once more, she said in a throaty voice, "I want more of you, Ethan." She reached behind her, making him hiss a breath as she drew her nails up his inner thighs before cupping his sack. She slid him a satisfied grin, and he knew she'd felt his cock pulsing inside her.

"I want tae give it tae you." He put his knees up behind her, reaching his hands to her exquisite breasts, covering them as he pinned her against his bent legs. Holding her sides, he thumbed her jutting nipples over and over. Once she was helplessly wriggling on his shaft, he dug his heels into the bed and gently bounced her body. She cried out and threw back her head, her hair cascading over his legs.

Forcing himself to slow their explosive joining, he eased her down. As he caressed her clitoris with the pads of two of his fingers, she rocked her hips on him gingerly, as if testing the sensations. When his fingers slid back and forth with her wetness, she began to undulate atop him, her movements growing faster and faster. Moaning, wanting to come, working for it, she rode him with quick snaps of her hips, shocking him until he could barely grate in amazement, "*Ah, you clever lass.*"

Only half his shaft was inside her, and he knew she could take more—*but . . . have to be good . . . better than before . . .*

Yet he didn't know how much longer he could last against this kind of pleasure. "Come for me," he commanded, rubbing her fast.

When she did, the force of her contractions gripped him, instantly robbing him of his seed. He exploded inside her, bathing her womb in heat. Over and over, he pumped into her.

She went boneless on top of him, her heart pounding against his. Even as after-shudders wracked him, he continued to thrust up into her, still hard.

Unwilling to give this up, he turned her to her back, still driving into her body. "Can I take you again?" Somehow the need was building, growing worse than it'd been before.

She gazed up at him not with disgust, not even with mere desire. Somehow he'd gotten a woman like her to fall in love with him. "I'm yours, Ethan . . . anything you want is yours."

The need to take her furiously, to brand her forever, lashed him like a whip. The urges were about to rule him. "Doona want tae hurt you. But . . . I need it . . . I need tae do it hard."

She rolled her hips up to him. "Whatever you need."

Maddy almost took the words back when she saw his eyes darken, burning with lust.

He cupped his hand around her nape and drew her up. "*I'll never let you go,*" he grated, leaning down to take her lips. "*Never* . . . " He was losing control—she could sense it, could feel it. His massive body loomed over her, his muscles tight and slick, from his corded neck all the way to the sharp indentations leading from his waist to his groin.

He pressed one of her knees to her chest, leaning his torso against the back of that leg, wrapping his arm around it, clutching it as he thrust. He placed his other hand low on her belly to thumb her clitoris, making her writhe in bliss.

Whenever he rocked into her, he pushed against her leg, spreading her wide. He seemed to crave the feeling of his chest rubbing against it.

But soon, his rhythm turned furious. Every time she thought he couldn't go deeper, he'd plunge more powerfully, making her cry out in surprise and pleasure.

This was even more than what she'd dreamed it would be like with him. She was captivated by the wild look in his eyes and the feel of his body working against her clutching nails or rippling under her sweeping palms. When he didn't have his firm lips on her neck or breasts or mouth, they were parted with ragged breaths.

This was worth the wait a thousand times over. . . .

Hands clamped to the backs of her knees, he bucked hard between her parted thighs, again and again until her head thrashed on the pillow. She fought the pleasure, wanting this to last forever. But under the steady onslaught of his body, she waged a losing battle.

Just as she realized she was going to climax once more, he bit out, "*Want tae feel you comin' again.*"

When she did, crying his name, a desperate, guttural sound broke from his chest. His eyes met hers as he poured himself hotly inside her. His voice a rasp, he declared, "*Mine.*" And then he collapsed atop her.

Breaths harsh against her neck, arms wrapped around her, he held her too tightly, but he was shaken by what had occurred between them.

I never knew.

As she ran her nails up and down his damp back, she whispered in an awed tone, "Oh, Scot, you've redeemed yourself completely." He clutched her tighter, wondering if he was ever going to be able to release her.

This is what it's all about.

He'd been so ignorant before, scorning what he could never comprehend without giving himself up to it.

Ethan understood that what he'd experienced in the past had been so lacking compared to what Maddy gave him—it was as if he'd been eating all his life without ever having been hungry or ever having tasted a morsel.

Now he starved. And feasted.

And he never wanted to go back.

Thirty-eight

When men like us change, it's profoundly. . . .

Hugh had been right, Ethan thought as he lay in bed, holding Maddy as she slept. Rain poured outside in a black winter's night, but they were warm in their bed in front of a fire.

The peculiar thing was that Ethan didn't feel like he was changing so much as reverting to normal—even though he'd never been considerate or amiable. He just found it easy with her.

When Ethan was with her, he *felt* like a husband. Maybe even . . . maybe even a *good* one.

After their wedding, Maddy had asked him if they could postpone journeying to the Highlands until the spring. She'd told him she liked it at Carillon and wanted to stay for the winter. Easy enough.

For the last two months here, she'd filled his life with excitement, zest. He still didn't understand how those traits hadn't been trampled from her, beaten down by years of hardship, but he was thankful they hadn't. She truly seemed to have shucked off the mantle of La Marais, and rarely had nightmares any longer.

Each night, she slept in his arms, and oftentimes she would stretch out her little body over him and fall asleep *on* him. Which he especially liked because he could hold her in place and enter her so easily.

Whenever he had to leave for an afternoon to work on the estate, she always ran out to greet him when he returned, flying into his arms, hitting his chest hard, her face beaming. "I missed you," she would breathe against his neck as he caught her to him, even if he'd only been gone a few hours.

Last week, he'd said, "Maddy, do you know what it's like, seeing you run to me?"

She'd drawn back and given him a wry half grin. "Do you know what it's like not being able to wait for you to finish the short walk to the door . . . ?"

Ethan was always thought to be bitter and cold—so why did he find himself chasing his wee wife around the house at least once a day as she squealed with laughter?

In fact, their home was filled with laughter. She'd made it inviting. She'd even made friends with all the neighbors. It seemed as if invitations arrived every day.

She was like a bridge for him to others. He figured people assumed he was like her—affable and fun-loving. He had no doubt that when he brought her to his clan, she'd affect how he was viewed there as well.

Maddy especially liked a widow named Agnes Hallee, who lived down the coast with a brood of six mischievous bairns. Maddy enjoyed playing with the children—flying kites, taming and collecting stray pets, outrunning the most ornery peacock—reminding Ethan of how her own childhood had been cut short. . . .

Sometimes he doubted his decision to hide the past from her and was plagued with the need to confess. But she was so damned happy, telling him daily how much. Why ruin this?

Sometimes, he fooled himself, forgetting that all this could end.

When he forgot, he was happier than he'd ever been in his entire life. There'd been another time he'd done this. The week before his father died, his da had promised Ethan he'd take him hunting in the Hebrides for his fourteenth birthday, just two weeks away.

Even after he'd seen his father's body, Ethan had kept forgetting. For days, he'd awakened each morning, bounding out of bed with a grin on his face, because it was one day closer to their trip. Then everything would return in a rush, and he'd be shamed to have forgotten it, to have felt happiness in the wake of such a tragic loss.

Now Ethan stared at the ceiling, squeezing Maddy closer to him. Those were the last times he'd ever been content before now.

But he couldn't imagine any way that she might find out. All the people involved that night were either long gone from England or dead. As an extra precaution, Ethan had fired the land agent at Iveley—who, predictably, wasn't enterprising or particularly hardworking. Then Ethan had instructed his attorney to deed Iveley to Maddy and do whatever he could to obscure the chain of ownership. Only after the new deed was in place had Ethan hired another steward—a young man with limited experience, but who was by all accounts exceptionally dedicated and hardworking.

In any case, no one with any connection to his past knew where he and Maddy were. Few knew at all. Corrine did, but only because Maddy had sent her and Bea money. He'd insisted on that. If Maddy hadn't had Corrine to look out for her in the beginning, she could have . . . died. The two were her family, and he was ready to support them as he would a wife's blood kin.

Now that Madeleine was his, he was determined that he would spoil her so terribly he might begin to make up for all he'd done to her in the past. He bought her delicacies, constantly plying her with food, and every day here she grew even more stunning, gaining flesh in all the right places. She'd beamed with pride once her ring finally fit.

When he allowed himself to think that his wife had been starving in a slum because of him, he took the rage that clawed at him—rage at himself—and suffered it as his penance. Then he would redouble his efforts to make her content.

"You know what I miss?" she'd told him a few weeks ago. "My horse at Iveley. She was so striking with her sorrel coat and expressive eyes. I swear she loved me as much as I did her."

So, naturally, he'd bought Maddy a sorrel mare, because he was like all those other besotted bastards out there, ready to slay dragons for their wives for even a hint of a smile. He took her riding every day.

His new horse, bought from the same stable as hers, was yet another stalwart gelding—which had taken a strong and unwavering dislike to Ethan. As ever, animals either loved him or hated him. Though Maddy had avowed, "I think all animals hate you—except cats." At his expression, she'd hastily added, "but feline approval is important."

At every opportunity, that sodding gelding strove to throw him, buck him, or scrape him from the saddle by slicing against a tree. Which made Maddy howl with laughter so hard, she had to hang onto her horse's mane to keep from falling out of her saddle. She laughed until even he would crack a grin.

Though he feared he was buying Maddy *too* much, he couldn't seem to stop. He could easily afford it, and there were so many things that she'd needed and had been forced to go without. She should own such a collection of clothing and jewels that he would have to wait for her to get ready as she chose among them. If there was one thing Ethan knew husbands did, it was to wait on wives to get ready.

When he'd bought her a pearl choker a couple of weeks earlier, she'd said, "Ethan, this is all a tad . . . overwhelming." Her smile had been wan.

"I thought you wanted a rich husband," he'd said. "This is what rich husbands do."

"I didn't particularly want a man with money to get jewelry and trappings of wealth. I only wanted security and stability. For myself, and, well, for the children I want to have. . . ."

Bairns. *What if I canna give them to her?* he thought yet again, tensing beside her.

Ethan had had that bloody curse hanging over him for so long that he'd begun to worry that he hadn't gotten Madeleine pregnant yet. And Ethan was somewhat annoyed by the fact that Court had been able to accomplish something in three weeks that Ethan hadn't managed in months.

Not that Ethan had ever expected to have bairns before. He hadn't—but for some reason, he'd begun to *feel* that he would with her. Some thought would flash in his mind as though this were a foregone conclusion.

While Maddy still slept, he eased her to her back. Tugging the cover from her, he studied her naked body. He rubbed her flat belly and pictured her big with his child, lush and full, and *looked forward* to it.

Ethan grew hard as rock at that image of her his mind conjured up. It was so primal—so stirring—that he felt possessive to a killing degree and aroused to an undeniable one.

The idea of planting his seed in her, then protecting her, keeping her happy and nurturing her as she grew it . . .

She woke to him pinning her wrists above her, entering her as she gasped. She moaned as he took her harder and harder, until he was plunging into her in a frenzy, *trying*.

Thirty-nine

During her walk down to the beach on a fine spring morning, Maddy was stalked by a black tom kitten.

Ethan had brought him from the village for her. She called him Petit Chat Noir.

After she rolled out her blanket and sat, she ruffled her fingers in the sand until he charged. But he soon grew less interested in *la guerre* and more in *l'amitié*. As Maddy petted his ears, she gazed out at the waves, musing over the last few months as Ethan's wife.

Ethan's transition from rough, secretive, aggressive Highlander to gentle, caring husband had been seamless and effortless.

In Maddy's imaginings. The reality had proved far different.

He was ridiculously overprotective. "You canna walk down to the beach by yourself," he'd decreed. "And absolutely no' into the village."

"Have you forgotten where I grew up?" she'd asked. "I daresay I can handle all that the treacherous seaside village can offer. What do you think I'll have to defend against? Scallops? Seaweed? Shells! Always the damned shells."

"Have your fun, young lass. But I will no' be moved from this. You must bring Sorcha."

He could be moody, sometimes staring off over the sea for what seemed like hours. She would give anything to know what he was thinking about. He was possessive, preferring to have her all to himself. "What do you mean, visitors?" he'd demanded just this morning. "We had some just two weeks ago. Do you no' like spendin' time with *me*?"

And he could be intensely jealous . . . Once, when she and Ethan had spent a weekend in Ireland, an unwitting American tycoon had flirted with her on the ferry trip. She'd consoled herself by musing that the man's bruises would eventually fade. Plus, the Yank would probably never even glance at a Highlander's wife ever again, saving himself another beating.

She'd discovered that Ethan's superstitious nature ran deeper than she'd thought. He believed, for instance, that a clan seer had predicted Ethan and Maddy's union *five hundred years ago. . . .*

And if Maddy didn't know how much income Ethan made, she'd pronounce him a spendthrift. Packages were continually arriving. He'd bought her a horse, diamonds, sapphires, emeralds, and more clothing than she could wear in a lifetime. There was nothing left in the village for him to purchase for her. When she'd casually mentioned that she wanted to restore the orangery, within a week new parts for the furnace and a crop of citrus trees had arrived.

She had to wonder if he was buying her these gifts to make up for how poor she'd been. He couldn't know that every gift reminded her of how much she'd lacked.

Maddy had learned from him that his youngest brother's wife was also rich and even had royal Spanish blood. Maddy had become acutely aware that Ethan's brothers had both married accomplished heiresses, while Ethan had gotten the plucky chit from the slum. Maddy dreaded meeting Ethan's family, and for some reason, she sensed he equally dreaded it.

She'd begun wanting Ethan to see Iveley Hall, her childhood home, so he would recognize that she'd been brought up with great wealth and that her childhood had been idyllic up to a point—he needn't try to give her everything and the moon.

He had an estate he wanted to check on over the summer. Iveley wasn't directly on the way, but it wasn't more than an hour away by rail. She'd decided to write the owners and inquire if they might let her and Ethan have a short tour. Just to see it once more.

Surely Ethan would agree to take her. Yet even as she thought it, she wondered. She'd noticed that for some reason, whenever she mentioned Iveley, he tensed. She didn't think he even realized it, but there continued to be a barely perceptible change in him whenever she spoke of her former home. In fact, the same occurred whenever she mentioned her parents as well.

He claimed that he'd never met her parents or been to Iveley, but sometimes she wondered if he . . . *lied.*

He'd called her mother by her first name on more than one occasion, startling Maddy each time. And once, when Maddy had confided her fear that she would be a bad mother like her own, he'd disagreed so vehemently, she'd been taken aback. "How can you feel so strongly?" she'd asked. "Are you certain you never met her?"

"Aye. It's just clear that she was cruel to you, and since you doona have a cruel bone in your body, you can be nothing like her," he'd answered so smoothly. . . .

But if there were shadows in their marriage, there was a great deal of sunshine as well.

Ethan had told her he considered Corrine and Bea her kin, and he encouraged Maddy to send for them. He'd even offered to hire Corrine as a steward, since he'd seen her work ethic firsthand and still couldn't find anyone here that he trusted. And Bea's job? "A companion?" he'd suggested. "Or, at the rate you're accumulating stray animals from the countryside, maybe a pet caretaker."

Though Maddy had beseeched them to come to England, they were reluctant, citing *de mal en pire*. But she thought she was wearing them down with each letter describing Carillon. In the meantime, he'd suggested that she send an eyebrow-raising amount of money to them, delighting her.

And Ethan laughed more and more each day, regularly demonstrating a droll sense of humor. One morning when she'd been potting in the orangery, he'd strolled in. "What is this?" he'd demanded, his expression perfectly deadpan. "I doona understand the purpose of this exercise." She'd frowned, then glanced down at her kitten, who'd been wide-eyed, affixed by tooth and claw to Ethan's trouser leg. She'd laughed till tears had come. "It's like a burr I canna lose," he'd muttered, walking out with the kitten once more.

Also good . . . his lovemaking was breathtaking and wicked. Yet even his desire for her seemed tinged with the same urgency with which he gave her gifts.

Just this week when they'd gone riding, rain had begun to sprinkle down. He'd led her beneath an oak, beside a gurgling stream, and as the spring mist had lightly fallen, he'd pressed her against the tree, kissing her damp neck.

She'd gasped. "Here, Ethan?"

In answer, he'd slowly lifted her skirts, then ripped the slit of her pantalettes wide, making her tremble with anticipation. When he'd suckled her through her wet blouse, she'd been overwhelmed by sensation. She'd grown lost in the feel of his hot mouth against her nipples and his muscles flexing beneath her palms. The crisp, tantalizing scent of his body had mingled with that of lichen-covered rocks and fragrant heath.

He'd lifted her, his big hand pressing her head firmly to his chest. With his other arm looped around her bottom, he'd held her in place as he'd slid inside her. When she'd moaned, swiftly on the verge, his thrusts had turned hard and furious. As she'd climaxed, he'd pumped inside her, hissing, "*Let this take. . . .*"

She knew he hadn't realized he'd spoken out loud. The desperate need in his words and in his continued actions disquieted her. . . .

It was times like those—when he behaved in inexplicable ways, when she could feel that secrets and barriers and even lies remained between them—that she began to have a growing sense of foreboding.

She told herself that her apprehension arose only because the last time she'd been this content had been directly before her life had been devastated. She'd been so unprepared for the world of La Marais. So afraid. So . . . *useless.*

Maddy had picked herself up, again and again, learning to survive. Reflecting on the past, she didn't know how she'd done it.

De mal en pire. She couldn't help it—she'd begun saving her pin money.

Forty

Ethan located Maddy in one of her favorite places—the orangery, with the black kitten lazing against the warm glass. That little beastie actually liked him, which only further proved Maddy's theory on Ethan and cats.

After leisurely kissing Maddy's neck in greeting, he said, "I've received a missive from my brother."

"Is anything wrong?"

"Doona know." The cryptic message was from Hugh, so it could be about either Network business or family concerns. "Just know it's important. He needs me in London immediately. How much time do you need to get ready?"

"How long would the trip be?"

"No' long. Three or four days, I suspect."

"Then maybe I could just stay here?" she asked. "I know you probably need to hurry."

"Why? Is something wrong?"

"No, no, I'm just a little under the weather," she answered.

He grasped her chin, turning her face side to side. "No doubt from being in this chilly room." Though the glass was sun-warmed, the inside space was cool and damp in the mornings. Yet he couldn't seem to get the furnace to work. He'd wanted to hire a machinist, but Ethan's lass seemed to think he could do anything. So damn if he wasn't crawling under that sputtering boiler at every spare moment.

"Ethan, it's perfectly fine in here—"

"You doona actually expect me to leave you when you're sick?"

"I'm not *sick*," she said. "You have been very demanding lately, keeping me up at all hours of the night. And if you stayed, I'd want you to continue your demanding." She grinned, but she did look tired. "Agnes and her children can come stay with me for a few days. It'll be fun. We'll eat candy and play charades and wreck your house like barbarians sacking a city."

"*Our* house," Ethan corrected. "Best remember you own half of everything you're breaking."

Though he loathed the idea of being separated from her, he knew she wasn't hankering to meet his family. And he couldn't allow her to meet them yet anyway. Hugh might have revealed everything to Jane. Ethan doubted it, but he couldn't risk Maddy's hearing the truth from anyone but him. To ruin what they were enjoying because he couldn't leave her for three days . . . ?

Besides, he needed to meet with Edward Weyland face-to-face—and officially retire.

"Aye, verra well," Ethan agreed. "But only if Agnes and the children stay with you. I'll either return for you or send someone to escort you down within four days."

As soon as Maddy saw Ethan off that morning—with lingering kisses that almost made him miss the train—she and Sorcha began a baking frenzy. Six children meant lots of scones.

Agnes and her brood weren't supposed to arrive before midafternoon, so when Maddy grew overheated, she went upstairs to rest.

Though Maddy already missed Ethan terribly, she was glad she hadn't gone this morning. First of all, the very idea of meeting Ethan's family nauseated her. Second of all, Maddy had questions for Agnes. The widow had six children.

If there was anyone who could help Maddy figure out if she was expecting, it'd be her.

In any case, Maddy was excited about the children coming over. She wanted to make forts for them out of curtains and pillows, forts like they'd never seen.

Sitting at her new escritoire, she collected her pile of recent mail. Yesterday, she'd been too busy to sort through the weekly bunch. She grinned to herself—Ethan had been insatiable.

Flipping through the envelopes, she found invitations, a letter from Corrine, and one from Owena Dekindeeren of the *Blue Riband* coterie. Maddy frowned when she came across a thick missive she didn't recognize. She opened the seal and read the return address. It was from Iveley! She quickly skimmed the lines.

Just two weeks ago, she'd written to inquire about visiting, explaining who she was and her connection to the property. The land agent had responded promptly. He prefaced his note by admitting to being newly hired. He was experiencing some confusion and asked to be pardoned for it, but . . . "*You, Lady Kavanagh, are the owner of Iveley Hall.*"

Yet how . . . ? Maddy's eyes widened. Ethan had bought Iveley for her? "That man!" she said in an exasperated tone, but she was smiling. When was he going to tell her about this?

She could scarcely believe she owned Iveley. And apparently Ethan had at last found a hardworking steward for one of their estates—included in the envelope was a detailed report of improvement after improvement to the property.

Trembling with excitement, she turned to the second page of the note, skimming the lines with growing incomprehension. *Your mysterious inquiry so puzzled me . . . after considerable hours of diligent research . . . discovered your husband had gifted Iveley to you four months ago . . . after having owned the property for nearly ten years . . . assumed directly upon your father's forfeit of the same.*

"This can't be," she whispered, her hand fluttering to her forehead.

How could Ethan not have told her he'd owned her childhood home? And for so long? He had to have made the connection.

Surely it couldn't have been *Ethan* who'd foreclosed on them. Maddy had known Iveley had been seized—how could she ever forget being denied entry into her own home?—but Ethan couldn't have been the one who'd forced them into the streets on the very day of her father's burial.

The idea was too incredible—she could hardly conceive it. She reread the letter, but the content didn't change, no matter how badly she willed it to.

There was no coincidence. Her husband had willfully deceived her about this. Maddy remembered those times when she'd talked about Iveley or her parents and Ethan had grown distant. *Think, Maddy.* Even as she resisted, a nebulous picture began to form from the facts she knew about Ethan.

He'd traveled to Paris for Maddy—though she could have sworn he hadn't even liked her. He'd offered for her, a girl from a slum, instead of someone worthy of his title. And then he'd steadfastly refused to marry her—until she'd threatened to leave. She recalled his unsettling anger toward her earlier and the frenzied way he bought her gifts now.

What if there were deeds in my past? he'd asked. He *had* been trying to make up for something, but not for what she'd thought.

He'd foreclosed on them viciously, leaving them destitute.

But why? He had to have some grudge. Why her family?

She recalled him asking, *How did* Sylvie *die?* Maddy's eyes narrowed. She'd known he'd met her mother! So why would he repeatedly lie about the connection?

What exactly was the connection?

Maddy began to have a sinking feeling in her stomach. Her mother had been ravishing—and faithless. Ethan had been a libertine who'd cuckolded a new husband every night. She remembered him admitting, *"If they were married, then even better."* The two of them had been near in age.

Had Ethan had an affair with her mother? Why else would he lie so persistently?

Maddy had always wanted the key to unlock that night when her life had fallen apart. The questions had driven her mad. Now she felt the answers were there, just within her grasp.

Had her father unexpectedly returned home and caught his much younger wife in bed . . . with Ethan?

Maddy put her hand to her mouth to stifle a shocked cry. At twenty-three and without that scar, Ethan would have been gorgeous. Her aging father, who'd been dearer to Maddy than all the world, would have been devastated to see the wife he adored in bed with a strapping young Highlander.

Granted, Maddy couldn't know for fact that Sylvie and Ethan had . . . that they'd . . .

She shook her head hard. That part could be merely the imaginings of a frantic woman. But Maddy knew without doubt that Ethan had lied to her repeatedly and had sought revenge against her family. She couldn't state with certainty exactly why he'd punished her parents, leaving her as a casualty, but no matter if they'd deserved it or not, Maddy *definitely* hadn't.

It was one thing to be a victim of circumstance and quite another to have a man show up on your doorstep to destroy you. She hadn't deserved to be dragged into this tragedy again.

Considering all that he'd done and deceived her about, she had to wonder if anything was true. Recalling the hasty marriage license—which Ethan had somehow had time to acquire *after* drunkenly plotting the seduction of two barmaids—and the very simple ceremony with the registrar, Maddy realized she might not even be truly married.

Not one of the ladies in the boulangerie after all . . .

Ethan had looked her in the eyes and vowed that if she could just see her way to giving him one more chance, he wouldn't hurt her again.

Lies. He'd broken that vow, among others. *The studied deception.*

She'd been used. She was stunned, feeling so deadened that she was surprised she perceived her heart beating, could actually hear it in the silence of the room.

Maddy remembered Ethan once telling her to leave La Marais behind, not to look back. What had his plan been at the time? And if her friends had come to live with them and depend on them? On *him*? Maybe that was why he'd been so insistent about them coming.

What am I going to do? All she knew was that she wanted *away from him*, to be far away by the time he returned. She rose, and through tears gazed out the window at the windswept sea.

Maddy had called this place a fairy tale, and it had proved just as fantastical. Here, all was illusion. *Peacocks and palm trees; jewels and sunsets over a blue Irish sea?* If it sounds too good to be true . . .

You're a fool.

She'd take the filth and danger of La Marais, hard and real before her, over this, over the lies of her husband, of their life. "Just one more chance," he'd said, even while *knowing* her trust would be in vain. He'd known she would discover his deceit. "What happens if you find out something from my past that you canna abide and you leave me?"

She'd *pleaded* with him not to hurt her again. *How many more times will I endure having my hopes crushed?* How many more times *could* she endure it?

No more. She truly was finished this time.

"I'll never let you go," he'd vowed, and she believed him. Somewhere along the way, he'd fallen in love with her—or as much as possible for a man like him, with the lies between them.

In fact, she sensed that what he felt for her bordered on obsession. If she left, he wouldn't rest until he found her.

But she was Maddy *la Gamine*—she could find her way out of anything. She had the jewelry he'd given her, and all the money she'd wisely begun hiding away.

She'd go back to La Marais. But only to collect her friends.

On their way to somewhere else.

Forty-one

Ethan heard the screams from his Grosvenor town house before he even set eyes on the property.

To his shock, he saw Court and Hugh outside—*not* running to the sound. Court looked as though he was about to murder someone.

Ethan swung down from his horse. "Why the hell haven't you gone up—" Another scream sounded, and Court bellowed in answering pain, punching his fists against the brick wall. Blood was already matted there from previous hits.

"Stop it, Court," Hugh snapped. "She'll no' like that I let you hurt yourself like this."

"How could they send me away?" Court asked, his voice hoarse, his eyes dazed.

"I wonder," Hugh said dryly.

Ethan finally found his voice. "What the hell is going on?"

"They've asked me to keep him downstairs for the present," Hugh said.

"Who?"

"Did you no' get our letters?"

"No letters, just a short telegram to Carillon—"

"I wasn't sure if you still owned that one," Hugh said. "I

sent telegrams to the less likely of your haunts." He narrowed his eyes. "What were you doing there?"

"Spendin' the winter. Now answer me. What is going on here?"

"This is the birth of your niece or nephew," Hugh said proudly. "And the possible loss of your brother's sanity."

"Birth?" Ethan tripped back against his horse. That arse of a horse sidestepped, and he almost fell. "Now?"

Court bit out, "She sent me away. Why would they send me away?"

Hugh responded, "Again, I canna imagine." To Ethan, he said, "Annalía's been in labor for about ten hours now. You're just in time to help me hold Court and keep him out of the way."

"Annalía's *in labor*," Ethan said, stunned. He'd never been anywhere near a birth before.

Court swung his frenzied gaze on Ethan. "Doona even start with me, Ethan. That baby is mine. I *know* her and I *feel* this. Any comment to the contrary, and I'll kill you."

Ethan put his palms up. "I'm no' making any comment about anything."

Court looked confused. "You're no' going to berate me or throw that bloody book at me?"

"No, I just . . . I wish you well."

Now Hugh frowned, too. "Fiona's here," Hugh said to Ethan. "She wants to talk to you."

"She's here? In my house?"

"Aye, she's—"

A scream louder than the rest sounded, and the blood left Court's face. He barreled toward the front door, but Hugh collared him and hauled him back, cursing and swinging. "A hand here, Ethan?"

"Oh, aye. Calm yourself, Court," Ethan said, helping to drag him back outside. "Women do this all the time."

Court grated, "If I hear that bullshite another bloody time . . ."

"This is killing him," Hugh explained. "He never wanted Annalía to have a baby."

"Why no'?" Ethan asked, baffled. That's what men always wanted. Wasn't it? He'd tried to get one on Maddy with a feverish intensity.

"He dinna want to risk her. And he dinna want to share her. If he'd known he could get her with child, he'd have tried no' to."

"They made me leave," Court said again, his tone miserable.

"How about helping me distract him?" Hugh muttered.

"How?" At Hugh's shrug, Ethan said, "Do you have, uh, a name prepared, then?"

Absently, eyes still on the door, Court said as if reciting, "If it's a boy, we have to name him Aleix, after Anna's brother, Aleixandre. Because I put him in jail and stole his house and all that. If it's a lass, we're naming her after Fiona."

Naming his daughter after their mother. *Has everyone lost their bloody minds?*

"Why have the screams stopped?" Court demanded, struggling to wrench free of them.

"I'll go check," Hugh said. "Keep him down here." He crossed to the stairs. A few moments later, he called down, "They're ready for Court."

Court stormed past Ethan and bounded up the stairs. Ethan hurried to follow. Fiona was there at the entrance to

Court's rooms. "You're lucky she's ready this time, Courtland. You have a son. A beautiful boy." She glanced past Court. "Hello, Ethan. Glad the letters got to you in time."

He scowled, uncomfortable with this situation on so many levels. "I dinna get any bloody letters."

"Language, Ethan!" Fiona snapped.

"I have no' spoken to you in a dozen years," Ethan began, tone seething, "and you think you can scold me like that in my own home?"

"Aye," she said easily. "Because I'm still your mother."

Court stormed in and went straight for the bed. When Hugh entered to stand near Jane, Ethan entered as well, struggling to remain outwardly calm. *Jane* was here?

"Jane," Ethan said with a cool nod.

"Ethan," she replied, then added, "excellent work there with Grey. You really slowed him down for me to kill him."

Ethan raised his brows at her nerve. *She's friends with Maddy*, he told himself, biting back a scathing retort.

"*Sìne*," Hugh said warningly, using the Gaelic form of Jane. In turn, she slipped her hand in his and cast him a sunny smile; grave, stony Hugh was obviously helpless not to be charmed by it.

Court dropped to his knees beside the bed, taking Analía's hand. "*Mo chridhe*, vow tae me that you'll never want another. We canna do this, no' ever again."

She gave him a drowsy smile. "I know this was hard on you. Oh, Courtland, what has happened to your hands? You poor thing . . ."

If Court could get a babe on Annalía, why had Ethan failed with Maddy? A quick flare of panic—what if Ethan *had* succeeded? Maddy was smaller than Annalía, who looked like she'd barely gotten through this.

Fiona said, "Courtland, do you no' want to see your son?"

Court scowled up at her, having no interest in the boy. Instead, he put his face against Annalía's neck. Poor bastard couldn't seem to get close enough to her. "Can I pick her up?" Court asked.

Jane said firmly, "No, Court. Not yet. She needs to rest."

After another minute of sneaking her closer to him, Court turned back to them. "I'll be gentle with her."

"No, Court!" Fiona and Jane said at the same time.

Fiona added, "But you can pick up Aleix."

Ethan watched in amazement. Court hadn't even glanced at the babe.

"Since he is no' interested for now"—Fiona brought the infant to Hugh and Ethan—"perhaps you'd like to meet your nephew."

Hugh muttered, "Never touched a baby."

"Never?" Jane asked with a light laugh. Ethan said nothing, though he hadn't either.

Ethan was beyond cynical, yet he took one look at that boy and knew he was a MacCarrick. Felt it down to his bones.

The curse was proven utterly wrong—but even with that shadow dissipating from his life, Ethan still had another. The secret that weighed on him constantly. . . .

"When I sleep," Annalía said then, smiling sleepily up at Court, "you must look out for Aleix for me." When he finally nodded, she dozed off.

Anticipating his panic, Fiona said, "Court, she's been awake and in labor for hours. Let her have some peace and quiet." He began to protest, but she spoke over him. "You want what is best for her. Sleep is what she needs. She's been more worried about you downstairs than for herself. Now, take your brothers and your bairn outside for a bit." When Fiona tried to hand over Aleix, showing Court the correct way to hold a babe, he went wild-eyed with panic, but eventually took his son with an audible swallow. "There, that's perfect," Fiona said. "Now, keep your hand behind his head. . . ."

Five minutes later, when the three brothers were outside the closed door, Hugh scratched his head. "I might be mistaken, but I think they just shooed us out, leaving *us* alone with a baby."

Ethan nodded, about to rail at the wrongness of this, but he saw Court frowning down at his son. "He's a braw lad, Court," Ethan said. "You should be proud."

"It will be no time at all before you're teaching your boy to ride and fish," Hugh added.

The babe was already flailing his tiny fists—definitely a MacCarrick.

"*My boy,*" Court said. "Ach, that sounds odd."

Hugh chuckled. "About as odd as I felt saying 'my wife.'" To Ethan, he said, "When are you going to do something life-changing?"

"Maybe sooner than you think," he answered.

Hugh raised an eyebrow. Court had no reaction, having become completely fascinated with his son.

When the bairn made a movement that approximated grasping Court's finger, Court jerked his head up, his expression astonished. "Did you no' see that?" Turning to amble around the room, Court murmured to himself, "*My lad's bloody brilliant.*"

"I'm told this gets worse as the child ages," Hugh said dryly.

"Indeed."

"So, tell me what's happened in the last few months," Hugh said. "Jane and Claudia both wrote to Madeleine Van Rowen at an address in Paris, but the letters were returned. I thought you might have had something to do with that." Hugh seemed to be bracing himself for Ethan's answer.

"Aye, I did. And she's no longer a Van Rowen."

Grinning widely, Hugh slapped him on the back. "Ach, you doona know how uneasy I've been about this. But now . . . I can only say that I'm proud of you, brother."

Ethan raised his eyebrows. Hugh had never said anything of the sort before. And the approval wasn't *un*pleasant.

"She still accepted you after you explained everything?"

"I dinna quite"—Ethan ran his hand over the back of his neck—"tell her . . . everything. She does no' need to know it," he added defensively.

Hugh's face fell, and he cast him a pitying expression. "Ethan, you best hope you married yourself a forgiving woman."

Forty-two

Sharp pops of gunfire, screams, and the sound of breaking glass.

Maddy sighed. *Ah, home sweet home. . . .*

Perhaps running back to La Marais had been a *bit* precipitous. After half a year away, she simply hadn't recalled it being this bad.

When she'd arrived earlier this morning, she, Corrine, and Bea had adjourned to Maddy's balcony for tea once more. That, at least, was welcome—she'd missed the companionship.

After Maddy explained everything that had happened with Ethan, Corrine promptly demanded, "Well, what did he say when you confronted him?"

"I . . . I was so upset," Maddy answered, flushing under their scrutiny. "And I didn't need to hear his excuses. What I do know as fact is damning enough—"

Corrine looked disappointed in her. "So you didn't even wait to learn his side of the story?"

Maddy stared at her tea cup and mumbled, "No. But he lies all the time anyway. I can't trust a single word out of his mouth."

"I've seen it before," Corrine said sadly. "Sometimes, it's as if people *want* to get back to La Marais."

Bea nodded sagely. "*C'est vrai.*"

"I did *not* want to come back here!" Since returning, Maddy found La Marais harder and filthier than she'd ever remembered. "But I'm tired of being toyed with and deceived. And didn't I just tell you that Ethan might have slept with my own mother?" She felt a wave of nausea at the idea. "I came back for you two. So we could start fresh somewhere else. Maybe open that shop like we always talked about. I have enough money now for all three of us."

"*De mal en pire*, Maddy," Corrine said with a shrug. "My situation here isn't that bad."

"Bea, what about you?" Maddy asked. "Don't you want to be a dress model?"

"Oh, Maddée, can we talk about this later?" Bea said, rubbing her calves with a wince. "My legs and back are aching."

"We can live somewhere without stairs," Maddy said, striving for a cheerful demeanor.

Bea gave her a smile, but she appeared exhausted. "I think I just want to nap for a few hours. Then we'll talk."

"Of course, Bea. Get some sleep," Maddy said, hugging her.

Before she left, Bea peeked back out the window. "I know it's selfish, but no matter what, I am happy to see you, Maddée," she said, then turned toward her apartment.

But Corrine wasn't as pleased to see Maddy back. "I know you've learned the hard way that there are times to stay and fight, and there are times to run. And the difference can be a very fine line." She sighed. "But this time, I think you should have stood your ground with the Scot."

Maddy flushed uncomfortably, deciding this would probably not be the best time to reveal that she was likely carrying the Scot's babe. . . .

The next morning, Maddy rose from her cold bed, struggling to muster the energy to rise and dress.

During the last few months with Ethan, she'd thought she had gotten past the tragedies in her life, believing she'd been adapting well. But discovering what he'd done—and knowing who was specifically to blame—made her reevaluate everything. Reviewing the litany of disappointment and heartbreak in one sitting made her wonder how she'd survived.

How many times could she pick herself up and dust off her skirts?

She'd just finished pinning up her hair when a nearby church's bells began to toll. She frowned and climbed out onto her balcony. Chat Noir deigned to give her a visit, and she picked him up, hugging him close. She already missed her kitten at Carillon.

Suddenly, the cat hissed. "What is it, *chaton*?" With another hiss, he scrambled to get down. "Yes, yes, a minute—"

Scratching down her arms, drawing blood, he leapt away just as tolling began to sound in succession, building a steady crescendo all over the city.

When even the great bells of Notre Dame rang out, Maddy swallowed. There was no Mass right now. She remembered the last time they'd done this, and alarm filled her. She scrambled back inside, then rushed from her apartment. She banged on Corrine's door, then Bea's. No answer came from either.

People on the street would know where they were . . . what was happening. . . . Battling panic, Maddy dashed down the stairs, her breathing loud in the tight stairway.

Down four flights, then five—

The toe of her boot stabbed into something thick. With a cry, she pitched forward, flailing her arms, collapsing onto something solid but soft—something moist.

When her confusion cleared, she realized she'd landed on a body, sprawled dead in the darkness.

A single circular break in the bedroom mirror.

Ethan had known she had left him as soon as he'd seen it, even before he'd been able to question Sorcha. Somehow Maddy had found out the truth, and she'd thrown her ring at the mirror. Yet ever-practical Maddy hadn't left it behind.

The fact that she'd collected it—and every piece of jewelry—disheartened him more than anything. It meant she was preparing to stay away.

All Sorcha had been able to tell him was that Maddy had received some letter and she'd been pale as snow. She'd packed and left in a daze, absently asking Sorcha to take care of her cat until she could send for him.

Remembering Maddy's plan to visit Claudia when he'd refused to marry her, Ethan raced for London like hell was at his heels. Reaching Quin's home at last, Ethan stormed into his study. "Where's Maddy?"

Quin's jaw slackened. "My God, what's happened to you? You look like hell."

"Where is she?" Ethan snapped.

"Just like I predicted," Quin said smugly. "Not knowing up from down anymore. And why should I tell you where she is?"

"Tell me this bloody second." Ethan ran a hand over his face. "She's my wife, and she's . . . left me."

"Maddy married *you*? But she just wrote Claudia and said she was going to Iveley for the rest of the spring. That she owned it now, or something fantastic. Why would she leave you if she actually married you?"

Iveley? Maddy was throwing him a red herring, and he knew why.

She's about to disappear. . . . She'd been gone three days—long enough to sell off everything and book passage anywhere in the world.

"She's no' at Iveley," Ethan said, pinching the bridge of his nose. "She's gone back to Paris."

"You had better hope not," Quin said, shooting to his feet.

Ethan narrowed his eyes. "Why no'?"

"We've just been getting word that there's . . . sickness there."

At Quin's expression, dread settled heavily in the pit of Ethan's stomach. "What kind?"

"MacCarrick, it's . . . cholera."

Forty-three

"Just calm yourself," Quin said. "The early wires say that they've contained it in some of the lower parishes. It might not even touch Madeleine in St. Roch. But I still advise you to hurry, because the city's becoming unstable and there have already been rumors of impending martial law. You remember what happened in the last outbreak?"

Ethan swallowed. Sixteen hundred people had died in a cholera-related riot, shot down by soldiers in a matter of hours. Dead, not even from the disease. No, twenty thousand had fallen from that.

"She's no' in St. Roch," Ethan said, striding out to his horse. "She's likely in La Marais."

Quin was right behind him. "What in the hell is she doing there?"

"Does no' matter—"

"Damn it, Ethan . . . that's the area hardest hit."

Ethan felt like his heart had stopped. "What did you say?"

"There's already been talk of a quarantine for La Marais. I don't understand why she might be in a slum like that, but if she is, you have to get her out. . . ." Quin shook his head hard. "The Network would never officially recommend that you smuggle a subject out of a military quarantine, but you know protocols. You know how to protect others. You could do this safely."

Ethan had been in cholera-ravaged areas many times before. The latest medical texts avowed: *Cleanliness, sobriety, and judicious ventilation defy the pestilence.* In the field, Ethan had learned: *Boil anything that goes in, burn everything that comes out, and splash whisky over anything suspicious.*

"So unofficially," Quin continued quietly, "I'll help you with transport. And you'll get down there and extract her from wherever she might be—regardless of the situation. Do you understand me? Get in and get her out. And don't get caught breaking quarantine." He met Ethan's eyes. "Or you'll both be shot on sight."

Morning crept pale and listless over La Marais.

Yesterday, the streets had been choked with those strong enough to flee. Now the exodus was sparse and slow, as if already defeated.

Maddy sat alone on her building's front steps, with her knees to her chest and her chin resting on them. Her forehead beaded perspiration even in the chill spring air and her body shook. Those damned bells tolled nonstop; regimental drums beat in the distance, reminding them all of the oppressive threat of quarantine.

The stoop was empty of the drunks, most of whom had contracted the disease and swiftly passed on. Two nights ago, one had crawled into the building for help, then died in the stairwell.

The one Maddy had fallen over. She wiped her brow. Now she was infected as well.

Ethan had called her a fox once, but she could find no means to escape this trap. It was too late for her anyway. And too late for Bea. Maddy's tears began anew.

In front of her, not even a hundred yards away, a young man she'd known from the parish market fell to his knees. He gave a strangled scream and clawed at the ground as his body emptied itself of white fluids in a sickening rush. Anyone near him ran shrieking.

The impulse to help him arose in Maddy, but she couldn't aid everyone she knew—all around her the residents were falling as cholera burned through La Marais like a wildfire. At that moment, she heard the unmistakable sound of retching just behind her garret as yet another succumbed.

Across the narrow street, a teary Berthé emerged from her building and sank down on her own stoop. Maddy could tell she had the sickness as well.

When Maddy had arrived back in La Marais this time, she'd been prepared for the sisters to ridicule her for returning. Now their feud seemed so inconsequential.

They met eyes, and Berthé said, "How's Bea?"

"D-died this morning," Maddy choked out, shaking harder.

Berthé nodded gravely. "I am sorry for that, *la gamine*. But Corrine is still well?"

"Yes," she said. "She's resting." Corrine had finally cried herself to sleep after they'd discovered Bea dead in her bed this morning. Maddy shuddered at the memory. "And Odette?" Maddy had heard that Odette was one of the first stricken—and that Berthé had refused to leave her sister behind to save herself.

"Odette will not last the night."

Maddy said, "I'm sorry, too."

Berthé swiped at her tears. A long silence passed between them, then she said, "This was not how it was supposed to end for us, *non*?"

Maddy shook her head, giving her a sad smile through streaming tears. Maddy thought it remarkable how one's wishes and dreams could change so suddenly with the circumstances. Last week, she'd wished she was indeed pregnant and that Ethan would react well to the news.

Now, Maddy wished she could live through cholera just one more time. If not that, then she wished Ethan wouldn't blame himself for her death. No matter what he'd done, he didn't deserve this kind of guilt.

If nothing else, Maddy wished that she wouldn't be burned on the mass pyre. . . .

"At least you once got to see something outside of this slum," Berthé said. "Is Britain as beautiful as they say?"

"It is." Maddy's voice broke as she imagined Carillon. "It truly is."

The murky streets of La Marais were completely deserted when Ethan reached the area late in the night. The only sounds were the constant tolling of church bells, the low drone of nearing drums, and sporadic gunfire. Building doors had been left wide open, belongings dumped on the street.

The people here had fled for their lives. The idea of Maddy alone in all this maddened Ethan.

Even with Quin's connections, Ethan had been forced to wait for a ferry. Rumors were flying out of Paris, and most captains refused to cross the twenty-mile channel to France.

Each hour that Ethan had had to wait had been excruciating. Feeling so powerless, he'd paced, trying not to dwell on cholera's short incubation period—four hours to five days. He'd seen people contract it and die within hours, the speed of deterioration astonishing.

Maddy had been here for at least two days, possibly three. . . .

Then once he'd made France, many of the trains into Paris had been halted. By the time he at last reached her building, Ethan was wracked with fear for her. He sprinted through the open doorway and climbed blindly to the sixth floor, breaking down Maddy's locked door.

He found her room exactly as it had been when they'd left it—except Maddy's bright bed had been stripped completely, the mattress gone.

His mouth went dry.

Bea's door was wide open. When he saw that her bed was stripped as well, sudden sweat beaded all over him. The disease had been here.

He kicked down Corrine's door—her room looked untouched.

Stomping down the stairs, he sprinted into the empty street, having no idea where to find Maddy. Turning in circles, he yelled her name again and again, his voice echoing—

"Are you searching for *la gamine*?" a woman called weakly.

He whirled around as a figure limped toward him from a building across the street. It was the girl from the tavern—the one who'd tripped Maddy. Berthé, he thought her name was.

"Where is she?" he demanded.

"Madeleine fell sick," Berthé said, clutching her sides. Her face was pale as chalk, but for the characteristic dark rings fanning out around her eyes. "She tripped on a dead man in the stairwell. After that, she never had a chance. They took her yesterday when they came for Bea's body. Took her, even with Corrine fighting them."

Ethan's heartbeat thundered, booming in his ears. He couldn't even allow himself to think of what she might be saying. No. This just wasn't possible. "Who took her? Where?" When she bent over and spit up white fluid, he bellowed, "Goddamn it, Berthé! Tell me."

She jerked upright. "The hospital, l'Hotel Dieu. Four blocks down, then north. But she's *fallen*. She'll be on the pyre by now—"

He'd already begun running, pumping his arms, hearing nothing but his breaths.

The hospital entrance was guarded, though only by two soldiers—but then, no one was expected to want in, and no one was expected to be able to exit. Ethan barely slowed to meet the guards head-on. He lunged in between them, swinging punches wildly, knocking them both out.

The inside of the hospital was a den of chaos, with useless smoke and incense oozing thickly throughout. The space teemed with patients; hysterical screams shrilled; huddled figures wept everywhere he turned.

He found a harried nun behind a desk that was filled with scattered papers and bags of tagged personal belongings. "I'm lookin' for my wife," Ethan quickly said. "Madeleine MacCarrick."

"How did you get in?" she asked, eyeing his unshaven, scarred face with suspicion. She had marked circles around her eyes and sweat beading her brow and above her upper lip. *Already infected.* He swung his gaze around—most of the nuns were.

"Special diplomatic dispensation," he somehow thought to say. He would have to get Maddy out of France tonight—or they could be pursued after he'd assaulted the guards and then stolen her from here.

The nun frowned at his answer, but she did drag a weighty, leather-bound ledger across her desk. After scanning some pages, she said, "There's no one here by that name."

"Maddy, then," Ethan snapped, but she still shook her head. "Last name of Van Rowen."

The nun scanned her ledger once more, then gazed up, her face pale. Ethan began to shake.

"Tell me where she is," Ethan demanded, his tone low. When she hesitated, he just stopped himself from reaching across the desk and throttling her.

"I'm sorry, *monsieur*. You're too late."

Forty-four

Ethan swallowed, unable to speak. Finally, he choked out, "She is no' . . . there's been a mistake. . . ."

Over the roaring in his ears, he dimly perceived her saying, "She was given last rites at sunrise and not expected to make it past the morning."

Ethan must have appeared as crazed as he felt, because the woman cowered. "Then she's not . . . ?" Ethan couldn't say the word.

"She's in the *dernière chambre.*" Her gaze flickered in the direction of a darkened back ward. "But, *monsieur,* once they go in—"

Ethan was already loping for the room. Inside, he swung his head back and forth. So many goddamned beds in this squalid, chill room. Children screamed in terror over the deaths of their parents, showing signs of illness themselves. The idea of his Maddy in here alone . . .

No, he couldn't think like that. . . . *Need to focus . . . stay clear, think.*

He began bellowing her name, stopping at beds and drawing sheets back from covered bodies, greeted by one macabre expression after another—sunken faces, glaring dark circles like bruises radiating out from the glazed eyes.

Ethan spied a small figure under a sheet in a corner cot—curled into a tight ball. *Maddy?* They wouldn't cover her face unless . . . So help him God, she couldn't have died, alone here, in that goddamned position.

But she could have; how many blows could she defend against?

As he ran, she grew indistinct until he swiped his sleeve over his face. He kept wiping his eyes, and they kept blurring. At the bed, he swallowed, then drew back the sheet.

He fell to his knees. *"Ah, God, Maddy."* Her lips and face were white but for the shadows around her closed eyes.

She lay motionless. *She can't be . . .*

He buried his face against her neck. *She's warm.* He felt her wrist—and didn't breathe until he found her pulse. "*Aingeal*, wake up." He pulled her to his chest, but her body was limp.

Blood was stark on the sheet and the back of her gown.

Maddy had been oddly sentient since she'd fallen sick. She'd been aware of everything that had happened to her, never finding oblivion in the fever that had wracked her for hour after hour.

She knew Bea had died, and the grief was overwhelming. Again and again, Maddy saw her friend's once beautiful visage frozen in a grimace of pain.

She knew Corrine had fought to keep the soldiers from taking Maddy when she'd grown ill. Recalling Corrine's screams and fierce struggles, Maddy feared Corrine had been injured or arrested.

And Maddy knew that no matter what had happened, she missed Ethan desperately.

As if her thoughts conjured him, she dreamed he was here for her now. After being lucid for so long, Maddy wondered that she now imagined he knelt beside her. In dreams, she felt him rub his unshaven face against her neck, felt startling wetness from his eyes. The backs of his fingers glanced over her forehead.

He felt so real, she squinted open her eyes, but even the dim light hurt. She was hallucinating anyway, because surely Ethan could not be in this dank cholera ward. "*Dream?*" she whispered.

"No, Maddy"— his voice broke—"I'm here with you."

Oh, God, it *was* Ethan, though he looked altered. His face was haggard, his eyes burning with some emotion she'd never seen in him before.

He couldn't truly have followed her into *this* place? Especially when she was already dying? He would have to know better. She gasped in air. "You have . . . to leave—"

"No' without you. I'm takin' you from here tonight."

"Go . . . please. They'll *shoot* you. You can't . . . come here again."

"Understand me," he said in a low, seething tone, "I'm still your husband, and if I can die to save you from this, then that's my goddamned right!"

Definitely not a dream . . . Her rough-around-the-edges Scot was behaving like a hero and still cursing like a sailor. "But, Ethan, I'm dy—"

"You will no' die!" He reached for her, clutching her nape. "You hold on!"

She whispered, "*I think . . . it's too late.*"

He grasped her chin, forcing her to face him. He was pale and staring at her with a crazed expression. "It's no'! Damn you, Maddy MacCarrick, we're goin' tae be together. Believe me." His eyes were wet, his lashes spiking. "Lass, I could no' love you this much for nothing."

A tear slipped down her cheek, and he brushed it away. She felt the smallest tinge of hope.

"Hold on, for me." Two arms slipped beneath her, gingerly lifting. But where did Ethan think he could take her? "Just stay with me, Maddy girl." She felt warmth enveloped in his scent as he wrapped his coat around her. In the cocoon of his arms, the constant screams finally dimmed, the cries dulled.

As Ethan carried her, hastening his long strides, Maddy heard one of the nuns cry, "You cannot take a contagious patient past the perimeter!"

We made it to the perimeter? She squinted her eyes open again and found them at a doorway, so close to being outside in the night—

"You might kill her by moving her!" another said.

But if Ethan thought he could get her free, then Maddy wanted to leave this place. How fervently she wished not to die here—not to be burned on a pile of bodies.

"Step aside," Ethan said. As if in a daze, she saw him draw a pistol and cock it. "I'll kill anyone who gets in my way. And I'll do it gladly."

Then . . . she was kissed by the coolness of the night air.

"We're goin' home, lass," he murmured down to her. "I'm takin' you home."

As soon as Ethan carried her across the threshold of that hell, blackness beckoned and she promptly passed out.

Forty-five

As Ethan ran a damp cloth over Maddy's body, he could hear Fiona speaking in low tones with the doctors in the next room.

Two days had passed since Ethan had brought Madeleine here. Ethan had told Quin to make sure his house in Grosvenor was empty by the time he was due to return, but Fiona had refused to go, browbeating Quin into telling all. Then she'd set about assembling an army of physicians in London for a wife that Ethan had "neglected to mention to her."

Even after two days, and all those doctors working, Maddy was still so pale, as if all the blood had left her body. She tossed in restless sleep, her breathing labored. Tonight she burned with fever again.

"I'm going tae get her well," Ethan had declared to the physicians, but he knew what they'd deemed Maddy's chances.

Yet they simply didn't know *her* as he did. They only saw her size and felt her weak pulse. And after Ethan told them about her possible pregnancy and then of finding blood on the back of her nightgown in the infirmary, they'd informed him that she'd lost the baby and would be further weakened.

Fiona had said, "Doona worry, son, she'll have more bairns once she gets—"

"Do you think I give a damn about that?" he'd snapped.

"But the look on your face when you realized . . . I just thought . . ."

His reaction hadn't been from learning that she'd lost the babe; it had been from knowing she'd lost it in that hellhole.

By herself.

Maddy's body had received his seed and had been ready to give them a babe. But his countless lies had driven her away, straight into danger, putting her in this grueling struggle for life.

When he'd first feared that they'd lost their bairn, his mind had whispered, *It could be the curse once more. . . .*

Yet Ethan knew none of this was about the curse—no matter how easy it would be to assign blame to it. No, *his* actions had precipitated all this, and he fully accepted all the fault.

Hour after hour, Ethan watched over her, staring at each rise and fall of her chest, willing her to keep fighting . . . one more breath in . . . one more breath exhaled. . . .

In between fevered dreams, for what felt like days, she'd heard Ethan speaking to her.

With his voice growing thick, he'd pleaded, "*Maddy lass, doona leave me.*" Other times, he'd threatened her. "You'll never be rid of me," he'd snapped; then, as if he worked to calm his tone, he'd added, "so you'd best . . . you'd best stay with me."

And he'd railed at her, his voice booming so loud the bed had seemed to shake. "*You canna do this—take my god-damned heart and then leave me! You think I will no' follow?*"

She knew he was constantly there, was aware of his movements and comprehended his words, but she couldn't seem to open her heavy eyelids or speak.

At night, he would wrap his body around hers, keeping her warm, whispering against her hair, "You enjoy being contrary. Then prove them all wrong and get better." He'd clutched her hip, then balled his fist there. "Ah, lass, they canna understand how strong you are."

Sometimes she heard other voices, doctors, she thought, and occasionally an older woman with a Scottish accent. The woman spoke now: "Ethan, these physicians are doing their best."

"It's no' good enough!" he roared in answer, then cursed the unseen doctors in some of the vilest language Maddy had ever heard. Directly after he kicked them out of the room, a door slammed, and a cool breeze whistled over her from the impact.

Finally, her eyelids didn't feel too heavy to open. She blinked against the light for several moments. She perceived his form standing near the bed and waited as her vision began to focus.

He raked his fingers through his disheveled hair as a pretty red-haired lady frowned up at him.

"She'll wake soon, Ethan. The fever has broken."

"They said that *yesterday*. And still she has no'."

"If she did right now," the woman said, "you would scare the poor girl to death. You've no' shaved or changed your clothes in days. And you look half-mad."

"You ken I *am* half-mad, well on the verge."

When he began pacing, she said, "You must calm yourself. Your anger with the physicians will no' help your wife"—her gaze flickered over Maddy and away, then returned immediately—"but slamming the door like that just might wake her."

"What do you—?" His shoulders tensed. He rasped, "Are you sayin' she's . . . ?"

"You dinna tell me she has such pretty blue eyes. Look behind you, son."

He whirled around, seeming to loom over the bed. Maddy stared up in shock. His eyes were red and wild, his beard growing. His clothes were wrinkled, his sleeves rolled. He looked as if he wanted to launch himself at her.

The woman said something in Gaelic that made Ethan scowl and his hand shoot up to his *beard*? He froze, and his brows drew together.

How long had he been with her?

Ethan looked at her with such yearning, but he seemed to force himself to back away from her. "You need tae drink," he suddenly said, dashing to a nearby pitcher. When he poured, Maddy could hear the pitcher clanking against the glass.

The woman raised her eyebrows at Ethan, then told Maddy, "I'm Lady Fiona, your mother-in-law, and I'm verra pleased to be meeting you this morning."

When Ethan returned to the bed with a glass of water, Maddy asked, "Where am I?"

He lifted Maddy's head and helped her drink. "You're in London, in our town house." Maddy couldn't seem to drink it fast enough. "Easy, then," he murmured.

When he took the nearly empty glass away, Maddy asked, "C-Corrine?"

"I could no' find her, but I have men searching in Paris," he said. "Maddy, I doona believe she'd been sick."

Maddy closed her eyes with worry, then quickly opened them, afraid to go to sleep again.

He ran his hand over the back of his neck. "But Bea—"

"No," she whispered. "I know."

Lady Fiona said something in Gaelic, then in English added, "Ethan, why don't you go get cleaned up now while I visit with my new daughter-in-law?"

He hesitated, then the two of them seemed to share a look. Before he turned to the door, Ethan gruffly said to Maddy, "Verra glad you're better, lass." As he trudged from the room, she thought she saw him swiping a sleeve over his eyes. *Oh, Ethan.*

Once he'd left, Lady Fiona said, "He's been worried about you, to say the least." She sat on the edge of the bed. "Now, I know you must have many questions. . . ."

"I didn't get anyone sick here, did I?"

"None of us. No' at all. To be on the safe side, I'm staying in this house for a week." She added dryly, "I hope you like cards."

Biting her bottom lip, Maddy said, "I . . . Lady Fiona, I lost the baby, didn't I?"

Fiona brushed Maddy's hair back from her forehead. "Aye, but a slew of doctors all agree you'll be able to have more."

She'd known she'd miscarried, but still, hearing the news made sadness sweep over her, sharp and heavy. "But Ethan's not . . . well?"

"He does no' look it, but he's no' in ill health. I doona think he's slept in a week." She raised her brows as she said, "He loves you quite, well, *fiercely*. I'm just happy you'll be able to be together and start anew."

Maddy's eyes began to grow heavy again. "Lady Fiona, I don't know what you've been told—"

"Lass, I know everything. But understand, he's changed. Speaking no' as his mother but one woman to another . . . when a man like Ethan finally learns to love, it's forever."

"Bloody hell!"

He'd nicked himself again. His hands were shaking so badly, yet Fiona expected him to shave and clean up? Said he'd frightened his own wife with his appearance.

He probably had as he'd battled the nigh overwhelming urge to squeeze her in his arms. Maddy's eyes had been wide in her pale face as she stared up at him.

It had been everything he could do to force himself to leave that room—but earlier his mother had suggested she speak with Maddy alone once she woke. Fiona had told him there was a small chance Maddy might not even have known about the baby.

He clung to that.

When he nicked himself again, he threw the razor down. He rested his hands on the basin and hung his head. *Please, doona let her have known.* With Bea's death and his betrayal and Corrine's disappearance, he didn't know how much more his lass could take. . . .

How long did his mother want with Maddy?

Ethan couldn't stay away any longer. He hastily dressed, then returned. As he strode in, Maddy's eyes were heavy-lidded, as if she was struggling to stay awake.

When he hurried to sit beside her, she weakly lifted her hand to graze her fingertips over a nick on his jaw. He took her small hand in his, kissing her palm, but she'd already closed her eyes. Just as he felt a surge of panic, Fiona said, "She's just sleeping now, Ethan."

"Did she know about the babe?" *Say no. . . .*

"Aye, she did. But she's a strong one, I can tell. She'll heal from all this if you help her."

Maddy might not want his help—or want anything to do with him. "Did she say anythin' about me?" he asked, sounding as desperate as he was. "About what I did?"

"She broached it. But she's in love with you, son. I can tell. You will be able to win her back."

Never again would he feel anger toward Fiona for what she'd said and done in the hours after his father's death. *If Maddy had . . .* He shuddered and squeezed his eyes closed. "I need you tae leave."

Without a word, she hastened from the room.

Just before he lost all control of his emotions.

Forty-six

Over the last five nights, Ethan had silently crept into her room to sleep with her, easing away each morning. Her fierce Highlander craving to sleep with her made her heart soften, but then she grew exasperated.

Every time she'd tried to talk to him about what had happened, he'd shied away, clearly thinking she was not strong enough to handle his confessions after only six days of recovery. But she was healing rapidly now that she'd turned the corner. Today, she'd been able to sit up for a good part of the afternoon to play cards with Lady Fiona, who was scheduled to return to Scotland the next day.

She truly liked Fiona, enjoying that she still scolded Ethan. He grumbled, but Maddy sensed that whatever conflict between them had finally been resolved.

Maddy needed to get something resolved with him as well, settled for good or ill, just so she could begin to make sense of all that had transpired.

That night, she made herself stay awake, waiting for him to steal into the room. He came directly after midnight and quietly undressed. When he slowly pulled back the cover, about to ease in and join her, she said, "Ethan, don't you think it's time we discussed what happened?"

He exhaled. "Aye, I suppose it is." He slung on his trousers without energy, then turned up the bedroom lamp. After placing pillows behind her and helping her sit up in bed, he pulled a chair beside her. "How did you find out?"

"I'd written the land agent at Iveley about visiting the property because I'd wanted you to see where I grew up. But apparently, you had not only been to Iveley Hall—you'd owned it for years. Since my father died."

"Aye. I'd bought up his debts. Including the one against Iveley."

"So you did plot revenge against my family. Care to tell me what it was over?"

"You dinna draw a conclusion?"

"I think . . . I think my father discovered you and my mother in bed together. I think you were the man with her that night at Iveley."

"I *never* touched her!" Ethan said vehemently. "I did go to meet her, but I had misgivings and tried to leave."

Maddy quirked a brow. "Do you make it a habit to go to assignations and then not keep them? Like with the barmaids?"

"I had a strong feeling that I should no' touch Sylvie. I had a realization with the others. Everything's led me to you."

"What happened that night, Ethan?"

He ran a hand over his drawn face. "If I try to acquit myself, I only impugn your parents."

"I have to hear this," she insisted. "I have to finally know what happened."

His brows drew together, and the pain in his eyes staggered her. "Then I'll tell you, though I doona relish it." In his low tone, he described a night of lies and weakness and unimaginable malice.

When he revealed that her mother had accused him of

rape, Maddy was rocked. When he told her Brymer had cut him, Maddy's tears began to fall unchecked.

Ethan had been falsely accused, beaten, and then disfigured—while Maddy had been sleeping soundly not far away.

Her father had allowed it, Brymer had enjoyed it, and her mother had sat back and done nothing, even when she'd known a young man was being tortured in their stables.

"Oh, God," Maddy whispered as the full weight of his revelation sank in. "Ethan, I am so sorry for what they did to you."

"Doona dare apologize for them! This has nothing to do with you. Thinking otherwise was my mistake. And doona pity me—I had my retribution, as you well know. I bought up your father's loans and called them earlier than they would've been," Ethan said, his voice harsh. "And called them at the same time. I'm responsible for your losing your home."

Wait, called them *earlier*? "Would it have happened eventually, or was it all you?" When Ethan clenched his jaw, refusing to answer, and she just stopped herself from sucking in a breath.

Oh, this must be a jest. She'd known there'd been debts, money struggles. She remembered her parents' fights, her mother always wanting more. Maddy probably would have ended up in La Marais without Ethan's interference.

"And your revenge on Brymer? Did you kill him?"

"Aye."

She nodded, glad to hear it. The image of that man stringing up Ethan and eagerly taking a knife to him . . . Maddy shuddered.

"And Tully?" she asked nervously. She remembered he'd always been kind to her.

"I spared him."

She exhaled a relieved breath, and not just for Tully—she was relieved to know Ethan could show mercy when it was warranted. "But what about me? You returned for me only to hurt me further."

"I tried to tell myself it was for revenge but realized early on that there was no way I could willfully hurt you. Take pleasure in knowing that my sinister plan for revenge came right back tae bite me on the arse." He leaned forward, elbows to his knees. "Maddy, I was fallin' for you from the beginning."

"Are we even truly married?"

He raised his brows as if shocked she had doubts about that. "Bloody hell, we are!"

"Was the night of the masquerade part of your plan?"

He shook his head. "I dinna know who you were until the next morning."

A thought struck her, and she narrowed her eyes. "What about Le Daex? Did you have something to do with that?"

Ethan hesitated, then said, "Aye. I dinna want you getting engaged before I could return for you."

"Yet another lie? Any others I should know about? More secrets?"

"There are more secrets. Ten years' worth of bad things I've done. I will no' burden you with the details unless you insist, but know that I ultimately acted toward a greater good. And sometimes . . . sometimes I even did things you might have been proud of."

She'd known he could be heroic if he chose—and that he could also be a scoundrel. She rubbed her temples.

"This has been too much," he said at once, sounding alarmed. "Does your head ache?"

"I'll be fine. I just want to get this over with. Is there anything else?" she asked more faintly, praying there wasn't.

He sighed. "Aye. I can speak French."

"Of course," she muttered in a deadened tone.

"Maddy, I ken that I've wronged you, but do you think you can forgive what I've done tae you? I'm no' saying this minute. But in time?"

"After all these lies, how can I trust what you're saying now? Give me a reason to, Ethan. I *want* to."

He ran his fingers through his hair. "I doona know why you should trust me or forgive me, other than the fact that . . . that I'm in love with you," he said gruffly. "Tell me what tae do tae win you back, and it's done."

It seemed a thousand emotions warred to overwhelm her. She still felt resentment at Ethan's deceit. Shame and disgust for her parents' actions burned in her.

And she was embarrassed by how badly she wished she knew none of this and could just go back to the life they'd made together.

But above all, she felt . . . weary.

"I want to get well, to get strong again before I make any decisions." And one place called to her as no other did. "Take me to Carillon."

Maddy had ached for this place, yearning to return to the life she'd had at Carillon. But even after weeks of healing here, she was far from that existence.

She sat in front of her mirror, combing out her hair for bed, musing over her time here. The tension between her and Ethan had been grueling. He was standoffish. She felt awkward. They didn't seem to know what to do with each other.

Whenever she'd strolled the property, savoring all the new blooms and growth and regaining her strength, she'd felt him watching her, felt his palpable yearning. Once she'd been strong enough to ride her horse, he'd accompanied her, remaining silent beside her. If she'd stopped to gather flowers, he would dash over to help her down from the saddle. Each time, he held her longer as he gazed down at her, his eyes dark with emotion.

And this week, when he'd gotten word that Corrine had been found and was on her way to Carillon, Maddy had been so excited she'd hugged him. He hadn't seemed to be able to let her go, even when she pulled back. Finally he had, but he'd been stiff, looking pained.

It had turned out that Corrine had been knocked unconscious in the frantic struggle for Maddy, then carried away from the city by fleeing friends. But she was perfectly safe now and on her way here. The worry for her had been like a weight pressing on Maddy's chest—and now it was lifted.

With each day that passed, Maddy had formed a clearer picture of how she wanted her future to be. She needed to talk to Ethan about what she'd decided, but he seemed like he'd rather have his teeth pulled. Every time she approached him with a serious demeanor, he got an alarmed look about him and changed the subject, or left the room.

Her infallible Highlander seemed unsure, hesitant, and Maddy was just as much so, having no idea how to proceed with him.

She rose from her dresser with a sigh, then crawled into her large, empty bed, missing him like an ache before she fell asleep.

Sometime in the night, thunder boomed outside, and Maddy shot up in bed, gasping for breath. Tears streamed down her face from one of the worst nightmares she'd ever had.

She'd dreamed she was lost on the coast and couldn't find Ethan anywhere. At every turn, around each craggy bend, she got farther and farther from him, no matter how badly she yearned to find him—

Lightning flashed again. A storm was coming, making her ache turn to apprehension, and she leapt to her feet. Had Ethan not heard her cry out? Each night he slept in the room next to hers.

She ran to his room, but he wasn't there. Searching the manor with growing unease, she finally spied a light coming from the orangery and ran down the stairs and along the covered walk to reach him.

Inside, the loud rumble of the boiler echoed against the glass. She'd known he could fix it! But where was he? Catching her breath, she cried, "*Ethan?*"

The boiler whistled to a stop, and he shot to his feet, dropping tools as he strode for her. "What's happened?" he demanded, grasping her shoulders.

"N-nothing . . ." Now she felt silly for her reaction, like a frightened girl.

"Is a storm coming, then?" He glanced up at the glass ceiling. "I could no' hear it before."

"I . . . I think so. What are you doing here so late?"

"I wanted to surprise you. Get this thing running once and for all." He rubbed his palms down her arms. "Tell me what's troubling you, lass."

She gazed up at him and the words slipped out. "What has happened to us? What are we doing?"

"Truth?" he asked, tenderly brushing his thumb over her cheek.

"Truth," she answered with a firm nod.

He exhaled. "I'm giving you time to come to terms with everything, because I'm . . . I'm bloody dreading that you're going to tell me you want to go."

"Go? Am I going somewhere?"

"Do you no' want to? You have your own estate now. And you said once you got strong again, you'd make a final decision about us."

"Why haven't *you* said anything?"

"I doona want you to go—I *really* doona want you to go—but I dinna want to affect your decision. With everything that's happened—the illness and Bea's death and the babe . . . everyone thinks you must be feeling battered about just now. And I've been told that I occasionally *exert undue pressure* to get my way. I dinna want to push you into a decision you would regret." Catching her eyes, he said, "I'm no' in this for the short cull, *aingeal*."

"What if I've been trying to talk to you because I've decided that I want to give us another chance? That I want to stay here or at Carrickliffe or wherever, just as long as we can start again?"

He looked as if she'd slogged him, and his hands fell from her. "Even after all that I did?"

"Ethan, I admit I still have questions. I still have fears. But I don't believe we have to have everything figured out before I can . . . before I can get my husband back. And I *really* want my husband back."

"You're"—his voice broke lower—"you're keepin' me, then?"

"My life is with you. I just want to get back to it. Mind

you, we still have a lot to muddle through, but I think you're worth the chance."

"*How* can you forgive me? There were times when it dinna seem possible tae me."

"Each day here, things became clearer," she murmured as the rain began to fall, pattering on the glass above them. "To forgive you, I simply recall how you faced hell to save my life. And then I remember how amazing it is when we have good days together." She twined her hands behind his neck and lightly pressed her body against the hard warmth of his, craving this closeness so badly. Their breaths were growing shallow, passion stoking, like the building storm outside. "Don't you think that's enough to start with?"

His big hand cupped her nape in that way that made her melt. "If it means I get you back . . . then, aye, I do." His other trailed to her bottom to gently knead her.

Once the storm began to whip outside, pelting the glass, she strangely was unafraid. For some reason, she didn't feel it was a harbinger of doom this time. She thought it mirrored the intensity of what was growing between them—his dark eyes were promising her a hot, thorough taking, and she knew hers were pleading for it.

He curled his finger under her chin as he rasped, "I'm goin' tae get it right this time, you know."

"I believe that, Scot." She gazed up at him with all the love she felt. "That's why you're still the dark horse I'm betting on."

"Ach, you're lookin' at me like you used tae. A husband could get used tae looks like that."

She smiled, whispering breathlessly, "I wager you're going to have to."

Epilogue

Not to marry, know love, or bind, their fate;
Your line to die for never seed shall take.
Death and torment to those caught in their wake,
Unless each son finds his forechosen mate . . .
For his true lady alone his life and heart can save.

Carrickliffe, Scotland
Easter Sunday, 1865

Ethan MacCarrick was the oldest brother and head of a family that . . . flourished.

He relaxed in the shade of an old oak, surveying the rolling lawn before him. His mother, brothers, and their wives and children were all here, gathered to join him and Maddy for an Easter christening.

Maddy sat on a blanket, laughing with the two older of their three amazing bairns. Three children she'd given him, all with bright blue eyes and black hair.

Their first son, Leith—whose entrance into the world had taken years off Ethan's life, though Maddy hadn't thought it was that bad—was now going on seven. He was larger than most twelve-year-olds and clever, like his mother. Three-year-old Catriona was an imp with delicate features just like Maddy's, who already knew how to manage her da pitiably. And Ethan had their infant son cradled in one of his arms. For some reason, the boy fell asleep better tucked there. They'd named him Niall after one of Ethan's favorite wild cousins, who still harried the Continent with Court's former band of mercenaries.

Ethan had been wary when they'd first had Leith, the infant seeming to take all Maddy's attention away from him. Then his son had begun to cry for *him*. And just like his mother, the lad had looked delighted whenever Ethan entered the room.

None of Ethan's bairns were afraid of his scarred visage, and they knew nothing of their father's dark deeds in the past.

Motherhood agreed with Maddy so damned much, and she was an adoring mother, unlike her own. She'd been able to forgive Sylvie for all that the woman had done to her, but not for what she'd done to Ethan.

When Maddy had confided that to him, Ethan had known she'd accepted him as her new family—the two of them together, ready to defend each other, and their children, to the last breath. . . .

They'd married again here at Carrickliffe in a grand wedding, since Ethan had been so eager to show off the bride he'd somehow managed to win. The festivities had been overrun with Weylands, including Quin—who'd only reminded Ethan about a dozen times that he'd been warned about Maddy. . . .

She caught Ethan staring at her then, and she slid him that grin. It still made his heart speed up, always would. He thought he loved her more than was healthy, but had long resigned himself to it. At night, he held her close, his heart so full that his chest ached.

Ethan knew his brothers and mother had been astounded that he was such a doting husband and father. They could be lost for their families, but Ethan couldn't?

Hugh and Jane had one four-year-old son and were "waiting" awhile for the next. Hugh had unaccountably wanted to name their boy after Ethan—and just as puzzling, Jane had let him. Ethan still scratched his head about that one. The lad was their world, and the three were happiest traveling to far-flung places. They were only in town for Niall's christening.

Court and Annalía had their son Aleix, their daughters little Fiona and toddler Elisabet, and another one on the way. Though Court loved his bairns, he swore each would be the last. Annalía just smiled and started knitting.

Ethan's mother was delighted with all the grandchildren she'd never thought to have and often said she saw a bit of their grandfather Leith in each one. Presently Fiona was waylaid on the lawn by five of them.

Maddy rose from the blanket and strolled up to Ethan. "Is Niall ready for the bassinet?" she asked. "Or should I call in extra help?" Corrine, Maddy's oldest friend, lived on the property and had turned down a position as steward to become their children's nanny. Corrine had proved so deft at her job that other families shamelessly tried to steal her from them.

"He's sound asleep," Ethan said, then added with a chuckle, "He snores like you."

She lightly cuffed him on the chest. "I do *not* snore, Scot." She took the babe, kissing him good night before laying him in the shaded crib beside them. When Ethan opened his arms for her, she settled easily on his lap, gazing out with him. He drew her close, and she sighed. "I love you, Ethan."

He pressed a kiss to her sun-warmed hair, inhaling with pleasure. "How I'm lovin' you too, lass," he said. Then a thought struck him. "Right now, if I could give you anything in the world, what would it be?"

"That's easy. A lifetime of this." She waved her hand over the scene, with their children playing and their entire family strong and happy.

He cupped her face, and her blue eyes went soft as she gazed at him. "Done," he said, kissing her lips tenderly. "I'm going to give you that, Maddy MacCarrick."

And Ethan did.